WESTERN FICTIONEERS PRESENTS:

PEACEMAKER TALES

Western Fictioneers

CONTENTS:

Peacemaker Award for Best Short Story (winners in bold)

*Unfortunately, the rights for this story were not available for our volume- Joyner's other nominated story "Christmas for Evangeline" is here, though, and "Two-Bit Kill" is available in our 99-cent ebook *The Peacemakers, Volume 3.*
**This story was also the winner of the 2011 Spur Award for best short story.

Acknowledgements

"This Old Star" copyright 2010 by Wayne Dundee. First appeared in *Bad Cop ... No Donut* (Padwolf Publishing), and as an ebook single from Western Trail Blazer (2012).

"Catch a Killer by the Toe" copyright 2010 by Pete Peterson. Published by Untreed Reads.

"Left Behind" copyright 2010 by C. K. Crigger. First appeared in *Roundup! Great Stories of the West* (La Frontera Publishing).

"Scourge of the Spoils" copyright 2010 by Matthew P. Mayo. First appeared in *Steampunk'd!* (DAW Books Inc.)

"The Sin of Eli" Copyright © 2011 by Troy D. Smith. Published in *The Traditional West* by Western Fictioneers.

"The Way of the West" Copyright © 2011 by Larry Jay Martin. Published in *The Traditional West* by Western Fictioneers.

"Panhandle Freight" Copyright © 2011 by L. J. Washburn. Published in *The Traditional West* by Western Fictioneers.

Introduction

In 2010, several professional western authors – including Frank Roderus, Robert J. Randisi, James Reasoner, Larry Sweazy, and many others –decided to form a new writers' organization, devoted exclusively to promoting traditional western fiction. We christened our group Western Fictioneers, and decided our first order of business was to sponsor an award that honored the best in our genre each year, which we decided to call the Peacemaker. Recently we decided to do our best to collect the winners and finalists of the short fiction category together in one volume, so readers could have access to them all at once.

We hope you enjoy it, and look for other books by Western Fictioneers. WF extends special thanks to Larry Sweazy, for serving as Awards Administrator for the first three years of the Peacemaker, and to James Reasoner for taking up that baton beginning next year.

Troy D. Smith
President, Western Fictioneers

www.westernfictioneers.com

THIS OLD STAR

By WAYNE D. DUNDEE

It was late in the afternoon when I cut fresh sign from the posse. The cold, rainy drizzle that had been falling on and off all day was turning to flecks of snow as the light started to fade and the air grew steadily cooler. The edge of darkness wasn't far behind, slicing quickly across the land, spurred by the bloated, low-hanging cloud cover that crowded the sky.

Spotting the flicker of a campfire up ahead in a copse of cottonwood trees was a welcome sight.

I reasoned the fire had to be that of the posse, settling in for the night, but I approached with caution all the same.

"Hello the camp!" I called out when I was within earshot.

After an uncertain pause somebody called back, "Come ahead on in … easy-like!"

I swung down out of the saddle and walked in slow, leading my horse. Nearing the circle of campfire light I took note of the half dozen men standing around its shadowy edges. All were watching me and all were poised warily, weapons close at hand. I recognized each of them as good citizens of Flatrock Crossing—the town back to the south where I also hailed from. As I moved further into the light they quickly recognized me in return.

"Jeb?"

"Jeb Stander, is that you?"

"By God, it is … It's ol' Jeb hisself!"

They converged on me then, wide grins, hand claps to the shoulder, everybody suddenly at ease and glad to see me. Only on the face of Ben Tembow did I see a hint of reservation. He was the last to step forward, the sheriff's star on his coat tossing a glint of yellowish silver in the firelight. Ben managed a grin of his own, albeit a somewhat more tentative one than the others, as he said, "I guess you're a sight for sore eyes, Jeb … but what in the world brings you clear out here on a night like this?"

I grinned back at him, back at all of them. "What? You think I was gonna just sit on my duff and leave you boys have all the fun?"

"Fun?" echoed Elmer Dunlop, the newspaper editor. "Riding all over creation, freezing our asses off on what's turning out to be a wild goose chase? You got a mighty peculiar idea of what fun is, Jeb Stander."

Ben turned on him and snapped, "You knew damn well what to expect, Elmer. The weather was already turnin' bad, and I made it clear when you said you wanted to come along that it wasn't gonna be no joy ride. You're the one who insisted it was a story you needed to cover first hand."

"Some story," Elmer grumbled. "Two days now and so far we haven't caught even a whiff of Shake Whitley."

The sheriff glared at him.

I spoke up. "Young Ben's as good a tracker as any around. You know that, Elmer. Rain and mud—and now snow, it looks like we're gonna get … Those are tough odds to buck. And don't forget Shake Whitley's a damned crafty dodger to begin with, that's what's made him so successful at duckin' the law in three states for the past dozen years."

"I appreciate the words, Jeb," Ben said. "But Whitley ain't ducked us yet. Nossir. Leastways I ain't ready to give up … are any of the rest of you boys?"

He got a general muttering of responses signaling everybody was still with him—even Elmer Dunlop—but it was clear that the wet, cold, weary bunch wasn't exactly busting with enthusiasm over the prospect.

I stepped up in front of Ben and locked eyes with him. "Look," I said, "I heard about the trouble back in town—the jailbreak and bank robbery, and how you fellas lit out after Whitley. I didn't come taggin' along to horn in on your show. I ain't the sheriff of Flatrock Crossing no more—you are. So if you want me to step on back out of the way, just say it straight out and I'll understand. On the other hand, if you're open to the notion of me ridin' along as one more deputized citizen then I'd be honored to do so and I figure I could be of some use to you."

Emotion and firelight rippled across Ben's face. "Jeb," he said quietly, "what kind of fool would I be to turn down an offer of help from the likes of you? Of course you're welcome to ride in this posse. And havin' you would make me the honored one."

"Just wanted to make sure how you felt, that's all … I couldn't help thinkin' how you never sent word when you took out on this thing."

"I never sent for you because I didn't want to impose. You already shouldered more than your share of hardship and danger, bein' sheriff for all those years. I figured you didn't owe it to nobody to take on more. What's more, with you livin' in that cabin way out on Wolf Creek nowadays and me needin' to set this posse in motion as quick as possible … well, there wasn't a whole lot of time." Ben grinned again. "You taught that me that. Remember? When there's trouble, you always said, you got to make up your mind and make it quick … So that's what I done."

"Fair enough," I allowed. "And as far as settin' myself up for any hardship or danger that comes of this, that part's my decision and my own doin'."

"Fair enough right back at you." Ben turned and gestured to some of the others. "Here now. A couple of you fellas take Jeb's horse and get him staked over there with the others … That first pot of coffee ought to be cooked by now and then we need to get some grub in our bellies, too."

"So happens," I said, "that in those saddle packs, before you lead off my horse, you'll find some things to help with that. I know how it is when you light out in a hurry on a posse chase. I got extra coffee in there, a side of bacon, a couple spare blankets, and a sack of buttermilk biscuits that Miss Dolly over at the café sent along."

"Now you're talkin'," somebody said. "Hot coffee and a couple of Miss Dolly's buttermilk biscuits—that right there sounds to me like the makin' of a feast!"

"Also, if the sheriff don't object," I added, cutting a sly look over at Ben, "I brung along a couple bottles of a little something to help warm everybody's innards on a mean night like this."

That brought another whoop, even more eager than the news of Miss Dolly's biscuits.

With exaggerated reluctance, Ben said, "Well … long as it's strictly for healthful purposes like keepin' the cold from seepin' clean into our bones and such … I reckon a nip or three before we turn in ought to be allowable."

* * *

The events back in Flatrock Crossing that set all of this into motion started with the arrival in town of the notorious outlaw and bank robber Shake Whitley. Even though he'd been raising hell all through Missouri and Kansas and clear down into parts of Texas for over a decade, he would later admit, after Ben had him behind bars, that he "didn't figure anybody out here in this pissant corner of west Nebraska would ever recognize me." But sharp-eyed Ben Tembow did, and before Whitley had barely cut the trail dust out of his throat with shot of redeye at the Silver Belle saloon, Ben and his deputy Billy Skipper had him under their guns and under arrest.

While waiting for the U.S. marshal out of Deadwood to arrive and haul Whitley away for trial, Ben had determined that the robber's purpose in coming to Flatrock Crossing was to hit the bank there before it transferred over the big payroll it was holding for the railroad crew building a bridge across the South Platte River west of town. Whitley claimed he had a whole gang who would be showing up soon to bust him out and help him still finish the job, but Ben took that for a bluff. Nevertheless, as a precaution, he deputized more men and posted a round-the-clock guard on the jail. Ben took the overnight watch himself. On the second night Whitley was in custody, things went wrong. Somehow the prisoner managed to pick the lock on his cell. He slipped out in the middle of the night, cold-cocked and hog-tied Ben in his bunk, then broke into the bank and blew the vault with dynamite he must have hidden somewhere close by. Went tearing out of town as the handful of citizens who'd been awakened by the explosion were still rubbing sleep out of their eyes and trying to figure out what all the commotion was about.

Ben, cracked skull and all, had formed his posse and ridden in pursuit the next morning at first light. But the rain and intermittent snow had made tracking the fugitive robber all but impossible and now, after two days of being out on the trail, the pursuers were wet and cold and weary and without any clear idea whether or not they'd gained any ground on their quarry.

* * *

After supper, the men were so played out that most of them wasted little time spreading their bedrolls and turning in to get some much needed rest. A light snow had begun falling steadily and moaning gusts of wind blew over the darkened landscape.

Ben and I stood apart from the rest, sipping from tin cups of coffee laced generously with some of the "extra warmth" I had provided.

"You got a plumb tuckered bunch here," I observed.

"Yeah, that's for sure. Clerks and shopkeepers, most of 'em. One stable hand. And one newspaper editor … Not exactly trail-hardened law dogs."

"Fewer and fewer of those kind left around these days. Unfortunately, too many of the trail-hardened ones have rode to the other side of the law." I sighed. "But, with a posse, you take what you're able to pull together and be grateful."

"Yeah, reckon you'd know. You did your share of ridin' out ahead of posses that were made up of pretty much the same mix."

"I usually had you at my side, though."

Ben looked thoughtful. "I got Billy Skipper for a deputy these days. He's a good, earnest kid but is Lord-awful young. He would have added considerable to what I've got here, I guess, but I decided instead to leave him mindin' things back home. Hell, you never know … it could turn out Whitley does have a handful of gang members prowlin' somewhere in the vicinity. Thought it best to leave some protection for the town, just in case."

I nodded. "Good thinkin', I'd say. I saw Billy before I headed out, by the way, and he seems to be lookin' out for things real tight. I don't figure you got any worries there."

"Good to know."

I drank some of my coffee. "Took a minute to look in on Ruth Ann, too."

"Appreciate that." A sidelong look. "She's doin' okay, right?"

"Worried about you. But that's natural enough for a gal in her position. My Clara, when she was alive and I was still sheriffin', she fretted every time I stepped out the door."

"Ruth Ann worries too much."

"Funny. She said the same thing about you … that these days you're worryin' too much."

Ben swiveled his head and looked at me. "She meant about Sally, I take it?"

"That's what's got you so worried, ain't it?"

"How can it not? Our daughter is sick, Jeb. Bad sick. Weak heart, Doc Barnhart says. He also says he ain't good enough to make her well. Says there are doctors in Denver—specialists, he calls them—who know more than he does, know things that would help."

"Denver's a long ways away."

"In more ways than one … in distance, and in money. Even if I got Sally there I could never afford to pay those so-called specialists."

"Ruth Ann said Doc Barnhart thinks there might be a chance Sally's heart could mend itself, get stronger in time."

"I want better for my little girl than 'there might be a chance'."

Things hung quiet between us for a minute or so. Of in the distance a lone coyote yipped mournfully.

I cleared my throat. "I won't say something stupid like 'I understand how you feel'. No person can know the grief or misery inside another. But I do know what I went through watchin' my Clara fade until the cancer finally took her … Times like that test a man, Ben. And there ain't no shame in relyin' on the hand of Providence to reach out and steady you some in order to get through it."

Ben looked at me again. "You're a strong man, Jeb. A stronger one, I fear, than I may be …

But as far as the hand of Providence, you'll pardon me if I say that I ain't seen one damn sign of it reachin' out to help us with Sally's sickness."

* * *

The camp was already stirring when I woke the next morning. This was both surprising and disconcerting to me. I'd always been a light sleeper, alert to things around me, especially out on the trail.

I reckoned that my deeper-than-usual slumber was a sign of getting older and being out of condition for this kind of business. My long ride to catch up with the posse yesterday must have exhausted me more than I'd realized or wanted to admit.

But the good thing about getting up late, I found out, was that somebody else already had the coffee made and the bacon frying. So, having made this discovery, I wasted no time taking advantage of it by retrieving my cup from the night before and pouring myself some of the scalding brew out of the bubbling pot over the fire.

The storm had passed during the night, leaving two inches of fresh snow on the ground. The sky was clear now and a bright, warming sun was edging up above the eastern horizon.

I was taking my first sip of coffee when Ben walked over to me. "Appears we got ourselves a new development this mornin', Jeb."

"What's that? You cut sign of Whitley?"

Ben shook his head. "No such luck." He jabbed a thumb over his shoulder, indicating the other posse members who, I noticed for the first time, were sort of huddled together casting anxious looks our way. "Seems ol' Elmer got the boys to talkin' at some point and now they're tellin' me—"

"You just hold it right there, Ben Tembrow," Elmer, the newspaper man, interrupted. He took two or three steps in our direction. "I'm in favor of this plan, I'll own up to that much, but don't make it sound like I'm the one who somehow spearheaded the whole—"

"Save your breath, Elmer," Ben cut him off. "All that matters is that the lot of you have gassed it over you're of a same mind. That's the way you laid it out to me a minute ago, ain't it?."

"That's true enough. And it's also true that I was the spokesman when we approached you. But that still doesn't mean—"

"To hell with that part of it," I said, taking my own turn at interrupting. "Exactly what is it you're blabbering about? That's what I want to know."

Ben made a gesture. "You're the spokesman, Elmer. Go ahead. Tell Jeb what you and the others have come up with."

Elmer harrumped a couple of times, then took another step forward. "Okay. Here's the thing, Jeb. Since you've shown up and agreed to ride on this chase after Shake Whitley ... well, me and the other men no longer see where it's necessary—or even sensible, really—for the rest of us to stay with it. You and Ben are the professionals, the ones who know how to track and handle gunplay if it comes to that. The other fellows and I were willing to back Ben rather than have him ride out alone. But let's face it, mostly all we amount to is a show of numbers. Now that there's an alternative—namely you, Jeb—we can't help but feel there's no need for us to be here. Plus, we've got families and businesses to think of back in—"

"In case you don't remember, I've got a family back home, too," said Ben.

"Of course you do, Ben. Of course you do. And we're all sympathetic that you've got issues of concern there. But, not to sound uncharitable, you're the one who wears the sheriff's star, Ben. Matters like this are part of your job, part of what you signed on for."

Tom Cutler, the mercantile clerk, spoke up. "Comes to that, if you ask me, Ben has done all a body could be expected to do under these circumstances. He rode out with a busted head, for cryin' out loud, and gave it his all to lead us on chasin' down this damned Whitley. We're way past town juris-diction by now. The U.S. marshal has already been notified and Whitley was on the run from the law long before he ever hit Flatrock Crossing. We made a stab at runnin' him down, tried out best, but the weather and everything else worked against us … I don't see no shame in the whole bunch of us turnin' back and goin' home and lettin' the U.S. marshal take over from here."

Ben shook his head. "Thanks, Tom, but for me there's a whole lot more to it than that. Yeah, maybe I'm out of my jurisdiction by now so technically Shake Whitley don't have to be my concern. But, damn it, I'm the one who's jail he busted out of and then went on to rob the bank of the town I'm supposed to protect … I ain't ready to give up on settin' that straight. Not by a damn sight, I ain't!"

"Seems to me," I said, "that's what it comes down to in a nutshell. I can understand where Ben's comin' from. And, I gotta admit, I can see the point of you other fellas, too." I turned to Ben. "What they're sayin' ain't really unfair or unreasonable. You and me are the ones who know how to track, how to shoot if and when it's called for. If there's any chance of runnin' down Whitley it's as good with just the two of us as it is with the whole bunch. Hell, with this new snow and two days already gone we might come up bust no matter what. I'll stick with it as long you want to, Ben. But let the rest of 'em go on back … and don't hold it against 'em."

* * *

So that's the way it went. Elmer and the others headed back to town, Ben and I stayed on.

We struck north, fanning out and riding in a switchback pattern hoping to cut some sign in the new fallen snow. When I asked Ben what made him think Whitley was headed north, he explained, "Because that's what I'd do in his position. He's too well known down to the south and east. And he can't go west, can't count on gettin' through the mountains this time of year. That leaves north, up into the Dakotas. He's got a sackful of money, things are boomin' up that way, and it's a place he's not well known. With no clear sign otherwise, it makes the most sense that's where he'd head."

I had no argument for his logic.

At noon we stopped for a meal of hot coffee, jerky, and the last of the biscuits Miss Dolly had sent with me. The day was bright and sunny, but still damned cold. And a stiff, cutting wind had kicked up. We hunkered into a pocket of boulders and pine trees to rest and take on some nourishment.

Chewing on a bite of jerky, I said, "Occurs to me you never deputized me, Ben. Reckon that's something we oughta take care of?"

Ben grinned. "Deputize you, Jeb? Is that really necessary? You may be retired, but you're still a lawman through and through. Always have been, always will be. Sworn in or not ain't gonna change that."

"Suppose you're right," I allowed. I fished in my pocket and came up with the tin star I had worn for all the years I'd been the sheriff of Flatrock Crossing. "Wanna see something corny? You let me keep this when I stepped down and you took over. I carry it with me every day. Sorta like a good luck piece. This old star means a lot to me, Ben. Bein' a lawman wasn't all I ever was as a person … but it was a big part. Maybe the best part. I hold it mighty dear."

"Everybody knows that, Jeb. Like I said a minute ago—you're a lawman through and through."

I held the star before me and studied on it for a long minute. Then I swiveled my head and looked at Ben in a way I never had before. "So how much longer you gonna try to carry on with this?" I asked.

Ben blinked. "You heard what I told Tom and Elmer and the others. I'm a long ways from bein' ready to give up. Hell, I can't be exactly sure how long. As long as it takes. As long as Whitley is on the run out there ahead of me."

I shook my head slowly. "That don't wash, Ben. Just like the rest of it don't … the jailbreak … the bank robbery… none of it."

"What are you sayin', Jeb?"

"It's just the two of us here now. That's why I was so willin' to go along with the others turnin' back. I'm hopin' with only me and you there's a way we can talk this out, work it through somehow."

Ben's eyes narrowed. "If you got something to spit out, Jeb, quit chawin' the cud and commence to spittin'."

"Two things bothered me right from the git-go," I said. "First, I couldn't figure out why you didn't send somebody after me to ride in your posse right off. No matter what you say about not wantin' to bother me, it flat don't make sense that you wouldn't ask for my help with somebody as important as Shake Whitley … Second, I couldn't rightly picture how anybody could pick the lock on that cell at the jail."

"Any lock can be picked, Jeb. And, in case you never heard, Shake Whitley has been in and out of a powerful lot of jail cells."

"But nobody picks a lock that solid unless they got the tools to do it. And you're too good—I know because I taught you—to put a prisoner behind bars without makin' sure he's clean of any such tools."

"So I got sloppy one time. I admit that much and I'm miserable damned sorry for it. Why do you think I'm pushin' so hard to run Whitley's ass down, to try and set things straight?"

"Maybe I could've swallowed that much. Wouldn't've went down easy, but maybe … Only then I ran across a couple more things. You know the kind of things I'm talkin' about, Ben. The kind of un-expected, quirky little things a lawbreaker almost always leaves behind to trip hisself up if somebody comes along with either the skill or the luck to spot 'em."

"You're wastin' a lot of time sayin' nothin' so far."

"When I stopped in to see Deputy Skipper," I continued unhurriedly, "he offered me a cup of coffee. Only he'd let the pot run dry settin' on the stove and a hole had burnt through the bottom. He was gonna to go down to the general store to buy a new one when I remembered we had a couple spare pots in that little cubbyhole in the back room. Leastways we did a year or so ago, when I was still sheriffin'. Seemed worth havin' a look before goin' out and buyin' a new one. Trouble was, Billy couldn't find the key to the lock on the cubbyhole … Guess you made sure of that part, didn't you? … But what you didn't think of—and I never did either, not until just then—was that I still had my extra key from the old days. So I put it to work on the lock, then leaned in to rummage for one of those spare pots … Reckon I don't need to tell you what caught my attention instead."

"You're too damned helpful for your own good, Jeb."

"I snatched out one of the pots and locked the cubbyhole back up before Deputy Skipper saw anything. I went ahead and had a cup of coffee with him but all the while my head was reelin' from what I'd seen. I chewed up a dozen, maybe a hundred different possible explanations for how the bank money could have ended up there … but it kept comin' back to only one that held up. You put it there, Ben."

He nodded. "Yeah. I did."

"And Whitley? The jailbreak? You staged it all?"

Ben kept nodding. His gaze was aimed somewhere away from me and there was a faraway look in his eyes. "Whitley's deep under the ice of Wolf Creek now, not too far from your cabin as a matter of fact. Got a bullet hole in his head and a couple melon-sized rocks stuffed in his shirt to keep him down."

"So you did for him, then robbed the bank yourself. Blew the safe, hustled back to the jail to hide the money, then staged the rest of it by clubbin' yourself in the head and droppin' to the floor to wait till somebody came runnin' to find you."

"You got it all figured. I confiscated a half dozen sticks of dynamite off some drunk construction worker who was wavin' 'em around in the Silver Belle one night a couple weeks ago. Was meanin' to get 'em back to the construction foreman out on the railroad bridge but hadn't got around to it yet. Turned out they came in real handy for the safe."

My coffee had grown cold. I flung what was left in my cup off into the snow. I said, "Got a lot of things boilin' in my gut I'd like to say to you right now, Ben. But I guess none of 'em really matter. Reckon you already told yourself most of 'em ... But you went ahead and did what you did, anyway."

Now his eyes found me and I could see torture and desperation in them. "Don't you see, Jeb? I did it for Sally—for the money to take her to Denver. I got to get her the best care possible. She's my baby girl. I can't just let her stand by and ... "

"And you can't do what you did, either. Not and get away with it."

"Once I had Whitley behind bars and he spilled to me what he was plannin'," Ben went on as if he hadn't heard me, "how he was gonna hit the bank and take the fat payroll that was waitin' there to be plucked ... That's when it came to me, all in a rush. How I could be the one to pluck that money and use it to get Sally the proper care to fix her poor little heart. Blame it all on Whitley. And then, after I ran out this phony chase, I figured I'd go back and resign out of shame for lettin' Whitley escape. Then me and Ruth Ann and Sally would pull up stakes and go off … go off and head for Denver as soon as we was clear."

"There had to have been other ways, Ben. Damn it, I've got a little nest egg put away. It woulda been yours for the askin' if you'd only spoke up. And there are other people in town, good people who appreciate all the years of service you've given Flatrock Crossing. I'm sure enough of 'em woulda chipped in, just like me, to get Sally to Denver."

"And leave me beholdin', indebted to all those people for the rest of my life? I got too much pride for that, Jeb Stander, just like you'd have in the same position."

"Maybe. But I'd also have too much pride—in myself and for the star pinned on my shirt—to turn to murder and bank robbin'."

"To hell with you and that lousy tin star you think so highly of!"

"You're right, I do think a great deal of this old star, like I already told you. And I think a great deal of you, too, Ben … It's for those two reasons I can't let you get away with this."

"I won't go back in irons, Jeb, if that's what you're thinkin'. I won't add humiliation and shame and prison time on top of already not being able to take care of my child. That can't happen."

"There are other ways. I pondered long and hard on the ride out here to find you … I reasoned that a desperado like Shake Whitley has got to have rewards out on him."

"I'm a lawman. I can't claim rewards."

"But I'm not a lawman. Not any more. I ain't even deputized. We do it this way … We fish Whitley's body out of the creek where you sunk him, reclaim the bank money out of the cubbyhole and turn everything over, sayin' we caught up with Whitley and had to kill him in a shootout but still saved the money. I'll claim the rewards on Whitley and hand the pay-off over to you for Sally. Your slate is wiped clean and nobody is the wiser except you and me."

"I killed Whitley in cold blood, Jeb."

I gritted my teeth. "I can live with believin' he was overdue for killin'."

"You'd do that for me?"

"I offered it, didn't I?"

Ben passed the back of one hand across his mouth. "I don't know … How sure can we be of those rewards? How long will it take for them to be paid?"

"It's the best offer you're gonna get, Ben. It's all I got. I'm bendin' as far as I can."

His eyes hardened. "Do you know how much of my adult life I've been in your shadow, Jeb? All the years I was your deputy and now, even a year and more since you stepped down, I can still feel it hoverin' over me. I can see it in folks eyes every time there's trouble in town. They watch what I do, listen to what I say, but all the while they're wishin' you was still there handlin' things."

"That's crazy talk, Ben. The folks in Flatrock Crossing think just fine of you."

"And now you make me the offer you just made. The big, grand gesture." Ben sneered. "You think that ain't gonna lay the weight of your shadow even heavier on me, Jeb?"

"It's all up to you, Ben. Like I said, it's the best offer you're gonna get."

"What makes you so sure I need a stinkin' offer from you? What if I tell you to shove it and go ahead with my plan the way I already had it laid out?"

I shook my head. "I can't let you do that."

"And you think you're good enough to stop me?"

"If I have to."

We both stood up, slow. Ben brushed the coat flap back away from the gun holstered at his hip. I did the same.

"I didn't want it to come to this, Ben."

He made no reply.

We stood facing one another for what seemed like a long time. The fire crackled under the coffee pot. The pine trees creaked under gusts of wind.

And then two gunshots rang out, momentarily shattering all other sounds around us.

* * *

It took some doing to first find the spot on Wolf Creek where Ben had sunk Shake Whitley's body and then to get it hauled out of the icy water. I finally managed it, though. Took the frozen carcass back to my cabin where I stripped it down, thawed it out some, dried the clothes then redressed it. While I was doing that I kept Ben in a cold enough place to keep him from starting to spoil. Then I tied both bodies belly-down across the back of Ben's horse and rode with them back to Flatrock Crossing. I stopped by the jail long enough to report in to Deputy Billy Skipper and to send him to break the sad news to Ruth Ann. While he was doing that I covertly sneaked the bank money out of the cubbyhole and into my saddles bags. By then the rest of the townsfolk were converging and I was ready to tell my tale to them.

I related how Ben and I had finally cornered Shake Whitley and how he'd put up a fierce fight, mortally wounding brave Sheriff Tembrow before I got lucky with a bullet of my own that cut down the outlaw a second too late. I turned over the bank money and told everybody to never forget how lucky they'd been to have had a man like Ben Tembow packing a star for their town.

The reward for Shake Whitley was paid to me in short order and I used it to make sure Ruth Ann got Sally to those specialists in Denver. From the letters they write it sounds like Sally is doing well and the doctors are confident she will lead a long and healthy life.

The townsfolk tried to get me to go back to sheriffing, but I turned them down. Billy Skipper is growing into the job right nicely.

I keep mostly to myself these days, out at my cabin on Wolf Creek. I fish and hunt and fuss over a little garden in the warm months. When they're in bloom I take fresh flowers every couple weeks to put on my Clara's grave in the town cemetery. While I'm there I'll usually pause for a moment beside Ben Tembrow's grave. But for him I leave no flowers.

I still carry the old sheriff's star in my pocket.

For luck, I tell myself.

But when I take it out sometimes and ponder on it, it no longer seems to shine quite as bright as it once did.

END

LEFT BEHIND
By
C.K.CRIGGER

We was lost. I knew it, Ma knew it, shoot, even my little sister Faith knew it. And Pa? Pa blustered.

"We'll make camp alongside this river." Pa pointed through the pouring rain at the swollen stream. One of many tumbling through these towering North Idaho mountains, it ran fast and loud. One thing sure, the river'd get where it was going faster than we would, 'cause not only was we lost, we didn't know where we was headed.

"It's too high to ford anyways," Pa told ma. "I'll park the wagon yonder under them trees and start a fire. You and the young'uns can get warm, Rosemarie, and everyone'll feel better."

Shoot, I knew who'd be starting the damn fire and it wasn't Pa.

Ma, too worn out to talk, nodded and bent over my little brother Andy, trying to keep him out of the wet. Pa reined our team of mixed-blood Percherons into a cluster of cedars.

See, Andy was sick. Had been for a couple days now, keeping us awake at night with his coughing, and worrying ma with a fever she couldn't bring down. Ma was sick, too, but her problem was different than Andy's. Ma's belly was pooching out that way it did just before a new brother or sister arrived. Since Andy, who was six years old, none of them babies had lasted longer than a month or two. Ma cried something fierce when they passed, but Pa always said, "Don't you take on so, Rosemarie. We'll just start us another."

So then we'd have a burying and I'd put a little cross over the grave with a name and a date carved on it, which seemed to ease Ma. They always named the boys William, and the girls Mary.

One by one, we'd leave those little crosses and the graves they guarded behind when Pa took a notion to move on. Shoot, Pa always took a notion to move on. And Ma would look back with her face sad. I sure hoped this time would work out different.

"Grady Edenfield, I'm talkin' to you."

At the tone of Pa's voice I snapped out of my woolgathering and said, "Yessir," without the least idea of what he wanted. When he sounded like that, it meant he was nursing a big thirst, no surprise considering the weather and Andy's being poorly and Ma's condition. He always got itchy when Ma was about to pop or when his traveling plans got interrupted. Pa got itchy a lot.

I caught Ma mouthing, "Wood," proving me right about the fire. There was plenty of dead limbs laying on the ground under the cedars, kept dry by the drooping branches. I had a good fire going in no time, and Faith helped me throw a tarp over some bushes to make a shelter to keep the rain off. Ma settled Andy under it and got a pot of water boiling so's to brew him a potion.

Didn't work, though. He kept right on coughing, and I saw Ma wiping little sprickles of blood off his mouth. His skin had turned awful pale. Shoot. I knew what that meant. I turned away so Ma wouldn't see me scrubbing tears, and saw Pa saddling Fore, one of the Percherons.

Faith had seen him too. "Where you going, Pa?" she asked.

This dragged Ma's attention from Andy. "Mark? What…?"

Pa settled his floppy old hat tighter on his head. "I'm going back to that town we passed yesterday. I'm going to get a doc out here for Andy."

Ma's lips tightened. "That was a pretty small town, Mark. There may not be a doctor there."

"Then I'll go on until I find one." Pa snapped the reins, making Fore shake his big old head.

Ma snugged the blankets up around Andy's neck. "That could take days. I'm…" she made a funny gesture. "I don't have days. Send Grady. He can do it."

Shoot, yes, I could do it. I'd've liked something warm to eat first, but I saw how worried Ma was so I walked over and tried to take the reins.

He jerked them out of my reach and said, "He'd be too slow, or he'd get lost and never find the town."

"Shoot," I said, "we're lost already, but I can backtrack as good as anybody. I'll do it, Pa."

He cuffed me alongside the head. "Don't backtalk me, boy. Rosemarie, get me some of that leftover cornbread and bacon to eat while I ride. Hurry it up. The sooner I'm gone, the sooner I'll be back."

Ma stared at him. "You can't just leave us like this, Mark. You haven't even set up camp properly. I'm going to need your help."

"I'll go, " I said again. "I'll hurry, Ma." This time I got hold of the reins and started clambering up on Fore—a mighty stretch of my foot to the stirrup, I can tell you—when Pa grabbed me by the belt and flung me off onto the ground.

"Oomph!" I was glad it was muddy or it'd've hurt worse.

"Mark!" Ma was crying a little now, not too loud because Pa didn't like it.

He pointed at Faith. "You, child. Bring me that cornbread."

Seeing me all full of mud and with my ear swelling, my sister, her eyes big, hastened to obey.

Ma stood up like she was lifting a house, her face white as paper. "The baby is coming."

"Women's business," he told her. "You don't need me. You've been through it plenty of times, and the girl is old enough to help."

Pa swung up on the horse and glowered down at us until Faith ran over and handed a packet of food to him.

"Expect me when you see me. I'll be back when I've found a doctor for the boy." With that, he kicked the horse into a ponderous gallop back the way we'd come. What had the name of that town been? St. Maries? Or had that been the one before?

Faith squished her toe around in the mud. "Is Pa going to buy whiskey, Ma?"

Ma sighed, sank down beside Andy as if her bones ached something fierce, and dabbed his forehead with the wet cloth. "I expect so." Her head drooped, hiding her face.

Shoot. There wasn't no "expect" to it.

* * *

Andy died in the night. We was all, Faith and Ma and me, awake to see him go. Faith thought she'd see the Lord our Savior come take Andy's soul up to heaven, but I told her it was too dark.

Ma, her head bowed, was folding Andy's hands over his chest when all the sudden she reared back with a shrill yell, dang near scaring Faith and me into falling into the fire. Faith screeched, too, their noise scaring poor old Aft, our other horse that I'd picketed just beyond the firelight's reach.

Ma stifled her cry and gasped, "I'm having the baby."

Now my sister, being only eight years old, didn't rightly know what that entailed. Ma had a habit of dropping her babies at night, so Faith always missed the big event. But I knew what was going on, having seen a few critters birthed in my time. Faith was gonna have to grow up quick, because it didn't look like Pa would be back. Her and I would have to see Ma through.

I remembered what the women had done last time. "Set some water to boiling, Faith," I said. "And look for those flour sacks Ma's been saving up. I reckon those are to wrap the baby in."

Ma, clamping her mouth on another pain, nodded approval.

That rainy night seemed like it was going to last forever, what with Andy passing and Ma hurting so she couldn't even talk. But dawn came at last, and with it a breeze that blew the clouds away. Blew away the new baby's life, too, without it ever having drawn a real breath. Faith, despite everything, managed at the last minute to sleep through the birthing. Wisht I could've.

"Boy or girl?" Ma eyes was closed, like maybe she'd have less to forget if she never looked at the body.

"Another William." I wrapped the poor little mite in one of the flour sacks and placed him beside Andy. Two brothers in one night. I figured that must be some kind of record.

We sat around most of the day waiting for Pa. When she wasn't sleeping, Ma had spells of crying, so Faith cried, too. I just did what had to be done, which was stake Aft in a nice patch of meadow grass I found, gather more firewood, and cook up some beans for supper. While I was doing those chores, I was thinking on where we could bury my brothers. Tomorrow they'd have to be planted whether Pa was back or not.

So that's why I ambled to the top of a little knoll overlooking the river. With the water going down, the river was as pretty a stream as you'd care to see. The knoll was a good place to put the boys, I thought, well beyond the high water line, and with a good view.

I'd drug a shovel along with me and started in digging the grave. When I figured it was big enough, and deep enough—shoot, Andy and William together didn't amount to much—I stuck the shovel in the pile of dirt and looked around while the sweat dried on my face.

That's when I spotted a log cabin nestled on some rising ground a couple hundred yards east of the ford. We'd missed seeing it through the rain , but I sure was glad to see it now. Whoever lived there was bound to help Ma.

When I ran over to the cabin, though, I found the place abandoned and no help to be had. The cabin was in good shape, or would be once somebody cut new leather hinges for the door. The two rooms was empty as a walnut shell except for a note stuck up on a bent nail.

Ain't no gold in this crick, it said. You want this place, yer welcome to it. I'm moving on. It was signed Jackson Parth. The note reminded me of Pa.

I told Ma about the cabin, but she said as how we'd better stay at the ford so's Pa could find us. Happened he didn't make it by nightfall, nor by noon the next day when it came on to rain again.

"We've got to bury the boys," Ma said.

Faith, her eyes big, looked over at the shelter where the boys was covered with a blanket. "What about Pa?"

"I don't think we better wait on Pa," I said. To tell the truth, my brothers was getting a little ripe.

Ma took a shaky breath. "You're right, Grady. We can't wait for Mark. Help me up."

She and Faith had been sleeping in the wagon while I slept under it, which ain't so bad in warm weather, but gets damn uncomfortable on wet ground.

Ma seemed light as thistledown as I pulled her up, and I wondered if she was strong enough to attend the burying. Howsomeever, she insisted on carrying little William while I toted Andy, and with Faith trailing along, we all got to the hole I'd dug. We lay the boys in and I covered them up. We didn't have much of a ceremony. Ma said a prayer, we all cried, and that was that. Me and Andy'd had some good times and I was sorry as I could be they was over.

Afterward, I pointed out the cabin and Ma insisted we go over for a look-see. Faith ran ahead, but I stuck with Ma who was still walking slow. She kept twisting her head this way 'n that. Admiring the countryside, I reckoned, same as I had done. Just so happened the sun had come out, warming us up and making the river sparkle like jewels.

I could tell she liked the cabin. She read Parth's note three or four times before folding it and putting it in her pocket. A little smile crossed her face. "Mr. Parth may have come up empty, children, but it looks to me like we've struck gold."

"What do you mean, Ma?" Faith asked.

"I mean we've got a ready-made home here, Faith. Your brother is right. This is a fine, strong cabin. We can fix it up a little and be snug as bugs."

"Until Pa comes for us," Faith said.

"Hmm," said Ma.

I made Ma stay in the cabin seeing as she was too weak to be walking all over creation, and Faith and I went and loaded anything we'd unloaded back into the wagon. Then I hitched up Aft, which was kind of awkward with a harness meant for two though we got to the cabin just fine. We spent the rest of the day moving stuff inside. Hoping we wasn't making a mistake and just making more work for ourselves, I fixed the door hinges, swept out the dirt and mouse droppings, and we was set. Shoot, it felt just like home.

In fact, that night as Ma rested in her rocking chair in front of the fire I'd built on the hearth, we decided we didn't want to leave. None of us did. It was like we made a pact.

Ma got strong again pretty quick when she wasn't worn out from being constantly on the move, caring for sick young'uns, or working on another baby. Faith pitched in and we managed the work. Shoot, I was twelve years old, a man, or would be onct my voice changed, and I set out to do a man's work.

I repaired the pole corral behind the cabin so we didn't have to hobble Aft anymore. I chopped enough wood to last a month, stacking it under the house eaves where it'd keep dry. Shoot, I even built a sorry looking table and a bench for us to sit on. Faith brung in early blooming flowers she found, and Ma...well, Ma visited the boys' graves up on the knoll every day.

As for Pa, there was no sign he was ever coming back for us.

I'd been hunting the day our first visitor stopped by. We was glad to see him, too, since we'd been living here better'n a month all by our lonesome.

From halfway up the mountain, I'd seen the man crossing the river at the ford. About then a nice three-point buck hopped in front of me and I flung up my grandpa's old 30.06 and shot it. I was right gleeful, too, since this would be the first fresh meat we'd had in a while, except for prairie chickens and rabbits. Shoot, I'd druther have venison any old day.

Anyways, when I'd lugged a deer hindquarter down the mountain to the cabin—thinking I'd have Aft pack the rest of the carcass home before dark—I found a feller sitting in our kitchen drinking coffee out of Ma's best cup.

"This is Mr. Juris, Grady," Ma said. "He heard your gunshot and stopped to investigate. Then he saw our smoke and thought he'd better say howdy."

"Looks like you had good hunting, Grady," he said.

I nodded and shook the hand he offered. "Have you seen my Pa?" I asked.

"Sorry. Your mother asked that, too. Like I told her, I'm just passing through." His nose twitched as Faith pulled the Dutch oven from the fire and the scent of prairie chicken stew and dumplings wafted out.

"You'll eat with us, Mr. Juris?" Ma poured the man more coffee.

He glanced around, which made me examine our surroundings with new eyes. The contents of our wagon was set around, but it didn't do much to fill up the space. We weren't using the second room. Ma and Faith slept on a narrow bed in the corner, and I slept on a pallet in front of the fire. We felt more comfortable if we stayed together.

"Are you sure I wouldn't be putting your family out, Mrs. Edenfield?" he asked gently. Guess he could see we didn't have much in the way of supplies.

Ma's shoulders stiffened. "My son does well by us, with his hunting. Tomorrow we'll feast on venison."

Mr. Juris smiled. "Yes, ma'am, I can see that."

So Mr. Juris ate supper with us, put his horse in the corral, and helped me pack the rest of the deer out before dark. He camped in our dooryard, joining us for venison steak and flapjacks at breakfast, and when he left, we found a dollar on the table for our trouble.

Two days later another traveler stopped by. He, too, ate a meal with us, and when he traveled on, left a dollar on the table. The next night there was another, and the day after that, a man and his wife. They took our spare room and paid three dollars.

We was getting rich, or so I figured until Ma, with a worried look on her face, drew me aside. "Grady, " she said, "do you think you could hitch Aft to the wagon?"

"What's wrong, Ma?" I had visions of her being sick again.

"We need to go into that town and buy supplies. We're almost out of flour and sugar, and the coffee is the same as gone. We've had too many visitors."

"Yeah, but those folks all paid. We got us some cash."

"Yes." She had a strange look on her face. "We would've been destitute without them since your father took all our money. We might've been starving by now."

"Not with me and my rifle," I said, standing proud.

She drew me to her in a hug. "Yes. At least he left that behind."

No need to remind her the rifle hadn't been Pa's anyways. It'd belonged to Ma's Pa, and he'd willed it to me. But then I figured she hadn't actually forgot. She was being sarcastic.

With the top off the empty wagon, after a little rerigging it wasn't too much for Aft on his own, so the next morning I took off alone. There'd been another feller arriving cold and hungry during the night, and now Ma didn't want to leave the place empty, or let Faith stay by herself.

That was fine with me, because I planned on asking a few questions around town. The first was at the store, 'cause buying supplies was the most important chore on my list. Shoot, sure didn't take long to spend six dollars, I can tell you, but I managed to wrangle a handful of lemon drops for Faith along with the staples.

Turned out the storekeeper hadn't seen Pa, but he told me there was a doctor in town, so that's where I went next.

"Sorry," the doc said. "Four weeks ago, you say?" He shrugged. "Your father didn't come here."

When I told him about Andy, and Ma losing the baby, he shook his head. "Sounds like your brother had pneumonia, and your ma...well, son, sometimes babies just aren't meant to be."

Shoot, seemed like all of Ma's weren't meant to be.

My next stop was the livery stable, figuring the hostler was the one to have seen Pa and Fore. "Sure I remember," he bellowed. Guess he was deaf. "I got five dollars for helping sell that big old horse to one of the loggers hereabouts. One of his team got crippled by a runaway log and they had to shoot it."

Made me sick, Fore being in danger. Damn, Pa, anyhow.

"And my Pa?" I persisted. "Where did he go."

"Hell, I don't know. I sold him a saddle horse and away he went. Somebody'd told him there was a silver strike in the Coeur d'Alenes and he didn't want to miss out."

"Was he drunk?"

The feller got a crafty kind of look on his face. "Well, now, I sure couldn't say about that. I didn't ask, and he didn't tell."

Shoot!

"You want to sell that horse you got there?" he asked. "I could give you a good price."

I'll just bet he would. Skin me alive is what he'd try to do. "Nope," I said.

I made the rounds of the three drinking establishments, and learned Pa had been at all of them. Not that anybody knew his name. What they remembered was the fight he got in and that he'd broke a man's arm. Mining strike, my eye. Pa had run from an angry crowd, and nobody knew which way he'd gone.

Shoot, I guess I knew which way he hadn't. But here was a curious thing. When I got back home and told Ma, she shrugged like she didn't even care.

* * *

The garden was up and growing, my last trip into town I'd finagled some laying chickens, and by mid-summer, we was running a regular hotel. Ma had a few dollars set aside, and it seemed we was doing better than ever in my memory.

Every day Ma walked to the knoll and visited my brother's graves, but she didn't seem near as sad as she used to. And then early one morning a feller by name of Kemper Bacon visited our cabin.

Turns out Kemper was the logger that bought Fore from Pa, and now he was looking to buy Aft.

"He ain't for sale." I glared at the man standing in front of Ma and me with his hat in his hand. He was a big feller with scarred arms, a couple of missing fingers, and a craggy face darkened by sun and wind. "I heard your other horse got killed. I ain't letting Aft go get hit by no runaway log."

"And I ain't planning on letting another good horse get killed," Kemper shot back. "Fired the sonsabitch—sorry, ma'am—that caused the accident."

That was something.

"Truly, Mr. Bacon," Ma said, "we can't let the horse go. We need him."

"You don't need a horse that heavy for a garden and some haying." Kemper cast a knowing eye over the meadow. "These big horses eat more'n an elephant. Are you folks prepared to see this one through the winter?"

Ma chewed on her lower lip. "We'll manage."

He left, but returned a week later. This time he had Fore hitched to a wagon alongside a bay mare two hands shorter than him. Kemper caught my disparaging stare.

"Kind of funny looking together, ain't they? Maddy is lazy, too. Lets poor old Fore do all the work."

Faith squinted up at Kemper. "That isn't fair."

"No, it isn't, but until I find another horse as big as Fore, I reckon he'll have to put up with it."

"Mr. Bacon," Ma said, wiping her hands on a towel she'd grabbed up when he interrupted her bread-making, "I know what you're trying to do. But really, we're fond of Aft. We were fond of Fore, too, and it breaks our hearts to part with either of them. My father trained them, you see, and he's gone now. It seems disloyal to him."

Kemper scowled. "Then why the hell—begging your pardon, ma'am, little missy—did your husband sell this one?"

Ma looked down at the ground and Kemper, sensing that was a road he didn't want to travel, tried another tack. "It's a shame to break up a good team."

"Yes," I said, "and they're full brothers. It ain't right to break up brothers, either."

Kemper kind of settled into the ground and when he spoke, his voice was gentle. "Guess that's the point I'm trying to make."

My face got hot as fire. Shoot, that Kemper Bacon was a twisty bugger. Ma held firm, though, and during the next week, I stepped up my efforts by scything more grass from the meadow and bringing it in to dry for winter hay.

Then it was a Sunday and as was becoming a habit, Kemper showed up driving a buckboard with the horse Maddy and her twin hitched to it. Shoot, did I ever envy him that buckboard. I was tired of using a peeled down prairie schooner every time I needed to go to town.

He'd hit at dinner time, so he sat down at our rickety table to eat with us and the guest staying in our spare room. Afterward, he had another proposition.

"What I'll do," he said, a hopeful look on his face as he swallowed the last of his coffee, "is trade the team I'm driving today, along with the buckboard, for Aft."

I could see Ma was thinking it over.

"And," Kemper added, "I'll bring in my crew and we'll log out that hill above the meadow. It'll give you a sunnier spot for the garden and hay field. I'll take expenses and you can have the profit. Logs are going high, right now. They need timbers in the mines."

Ma looked at me. I sure hated to let Aft go, but Kemper's deal was a good one. Before either Ma or I could say anything, he sweetened the pot.

"I'll add another room onto your hotel, and build a barn and woodshed."

Ma's eyes widened and she took a deep breath.

"I can't do more than that," Kemper said.

"No," Ma said. "I know you can't."

Kemper started getting that hang-dog expression, until she said, "And you won't have to. I'll take your deal, Mr. Bacon. I just ask that you treat both those animals right."

Which, naturally, he promised to do.

To tell the truth, the bay mares were easier for me to handle than the Percherons. Oh, not because Fore and Aft were ornery. They was just too big for a boy.

Like Kemper had promised, the barn got built, the room added on, and he came to stay in the extra room while they was logging the hillside. Paid his dollar a day, too, regular as could be. He was good to my sister. He was awful nice to my ma, and shoot, he even tolerated me.

Then, on the very day I saw Kemper steal a little kiss from Ma, everything changed.

It was evening. Kemper and two of his crew, Mr. Juris, who'd spread the word about Ma's cooking, and a married couple passing through, was sitting at our supper table. Faith was serving pie made from huckleberries she and Ma had picked up on the mountain. We was all laughing when Pa strode in like he owned the place. He was duded up with high-heeled boots and a leather vest; a six-shooter hung at his hip. He looked like an outlaw and he stunk of whiskey.

Our laughter died. Ma stood up, her chair falling over behind her. "Mark!"

"Hello, Rosemarie," he said.

"Where have you been all these months, Mark?"

Pa's eyebrow arched up like it always did when he was looking to belittle her. "Away. I see you're entertaining. With all these men here, I hope you've been making money, because I need a stake."

I guess it was an insult, because Ma turned dead white. "Men? What are you insinuating?"

"Yeah," said Kemper. "What are you insinuating."

Pa set his hand on the pistol butt. "Mind your own business, mister. I'm talking to my wife."

I could see he disremembered Kemper, even though he'd sold him our horse. I could also see he didn't scare Kemper none.

In a voice soft as kitten fur, Kemper said, "My friends are my business, Mr. Edenfield, and I ain't in the habit of letting people I care about down."

Sounded to me like Kemper could insinuate as good as anybody.

Ma broke in, her words tumbling over themselves. "After you abandoned us, Mark, Grady found this house. Mr. Juris has been kind enough to recommend my cooking, and Mr. Bacon, his men, and these people," she nodded at the married couple, "are paying for their supper."

Pa's hard gaze roamed the room. "How did you get money to start?"

"The cabin was here. Our friends helped make it better. I'm running a hotel, Mark. A small hotel."

She didn't say who'd helped, or that she'd filed homestead papers on the land yesterday, and that Pa's name was not on them.

Pa, he just acted like our hard work meant nothing. "Pack up, Rosemarie," he said. "We're moving on."

Everybody went still. Ma's hand went to cover her heart. "Aren't you even going to ask how Andy is, Mark? Or our new baby?"

He shrugged. "I suppose the new one died, as usual. And the other boy? Well, he always was puny." He turned to me, "Boy, get packed. And hurry it up. I ain't got time to waste."

Which meant he probably had somebody on his heels and they was mad.

Ma looked at me and Faith before letting her gaze drift to Kemp. "No," she said.

Pa got a bug-eyed look. "What did you say?"

"I said no. This family isn't moving again. I'm staying here, Mark, with my live children and my dead babies and I'm giving them a home. You can keep on traveling the rest of your life. I don't care anymore."

He slapped her so hard she fell, and he knocked me to my knees when I tackled him. Last, he tried to fight Kemper Bacon, a bad idea. When Pa woke up, he climbed atop his horse and rode off toward town.

"A man who'll abuse his wife and children don't deserve them," Kemper said.

That was the last time we seen Pa. About six months later we heard he'd been killed in a brawl somewhere in Colorado. It was a long way from home.

Shoot. I guess Pa was lost then, too.

The End

SCOURGE OF THE SPOILS

by MATTHEW P. MAYO

Tico squatted in riverbank mud the color of an old miner's skin. His coarse brown hair hung from under his hat like ends of frayed rope, and the water he scooped in the bowl of his hands leaked slowly through his thick fingers. He cut his eyes upstream, then back to the girl. Finally he drank, swallowed, made the noise that men the world over make after they've finished a needed drink, like pressure released from a worn valve.

"Shall we continue, then?" asked the girl from a horse behind him.

Tico remained squatting in the mud, his suede boots darkening as the water leached upward. "No."

The young woman said nothing, but straightened in the saddle and gritted her teeth.

Tico drank more, filled his canteen, then squelched back through the mud to where his horse, Colonel Saunderston the Third, had finished drinking. Tico checked the four glass tubes that served as reservoir level indicators, one in each of the horse's legs, the graduated numbers long since worn away. Satisfied with the water levels, he gathered the sopping reins from where they hung in the water, sluicing the excess through his fingers, then he mounted.

The young woman forced a smile and nodded toward Colonel. "I've been meaning to ask—is that a special model? I don't recall seeing any quite—"

"Modified mount, same as that one." He nodded toward her horse.

Under the grime and welted ropes of brazing from years of repairs, Constance Gatterling saw something of the beast it once was. "The original creature must have been a beauty."

Tico stared at her as if she were speaking a foreign language. "Been a long time since it was a real horse."

"Surely you're curious."

"Gets me from here to there and back." More of the stare, then he said, "You talk too much. Let the bay drink full, then catch up with me." He heeled Colonel into a lope.

"Catch up? What? Hey!" Constance looked at the receding back of the stained buckskin shirt, an ancient holstered pistol bouncing on the man's hip with each clanking gallop. "Hey, Tico! I'm paying you to get me to the West Edge, not leave me here!" But the horse decided for her and plunged into the river up to its knees, the cool grey water sizzling and becoming steam vapor where it touched the hot metal of its legs and sipping muzzle.

"Damn you horse, no! Tico is getting further away with each second you waste in this disgusting runnel of stinking liquid!" The flurry of words, which would have impressed her friends back home in East City, sounded childish out here in the Spoils.

The reins, looped in her hands, slipped free and slid into the water. She grabbed after them, bending

46

low, the saddle leather creaking with her weight, her stirruped left boot inches from the river surface. As she reached out, her fingertips trembling, clawing at the dangling rein, she noted with despair that the frilled edge of her tailored shirt's cuff, jutting from beneath the blue crushed velvet sleeve, was now grimed from constant wear. Still she strained a little further … then slipped from the saddle, a quick cry and her splash the only sounds until she rose spluttering and gasping from the rank, swirling river.

* * *

It was the clanking, and more than that, an overriding grinding screech of steel on steel that pulled Constance from her bankside nap—her pounding heart seemed to fill her throat. The sounds, from the East, grew louder, but still she saw no sign of anything interrupting the flat, stark land.

She had not intended to fall asleep, but figured Tico would ride back, at least for his other mount, if not for her. She'd stripped off her smelly, wet garments and arranged them on the twisted branches of the stunted trees lining the river. Perhaps Tico was only scouting ahead, and left her here because he knew this spot was relatively safe from the people of the Spoils. Constance chose to believe this, and so had waited for her hired guide's return. After all, she reasoned, she was his employer.

The grinding noise increased by the second. And then she noticed something else was wrong—the horse, what Tico had called "the bay," was gone. How could that happen? Horses, even modified mounts, didn't just vanish, did they? But it was full of water, so it could well walk off for miles, perhaps days, in any direction. She saw no tracks, even though on both sides of the river, the solid-seeming earth gave way to softer sandy soil as the land stretched away from the river. Constance held up a hand against the dimming light and stared southward, then West, toward the far bank.

The clanking grew louder from behind her, now joined with a grinding screech as though sand were being pressed between spinning metals.

Constance turned in time to see emerging from the sand the nose of what looked like a pre-war steam-power locomotivator drive upward from beneath the ground, churning and chewing raw earth—rocks, clods of dried, powdery dirt bigger than a man's head collapsed into clouds of powder, boulders cracked like rifle shots.

It dragged itself free from its earthen tunnel, a collapsing ridge of sand, its forward set of great steel mandibles gnashing the last rocks, bouncing in its maw like unpopped corn kernels in a cast-iron pan. She was surprised to see the rest of the machine was not black steel, but instead an old-time elixir wagon, wood, from the looks of it, like she'd seen pulled behind horses in pictorials in history tomes. She knew such transports still existed, but back East they long ago had been replaced with soft-tracked conveyances topped with polished chrome travel compartments.

The grinding, squealing sounds lessened, and great jets of steam drove at the ground from between the spoked wheels, raising swirling clouds of dust. A smell like melting metal curled its way into her nose and she fought down a sneeze.

A third of the way back, where steel met wood, a thick plank door with black strapping squawked outward and a stout little man in a long, plaid coat with once-sculpted tails, a style the likes of which Constance hadn't seen except in books, nearly fell out, surrounded by belching clouds of smoke.

He swung on the door, the hinges screaming for lubrication, and coughed as if soon he would be overcome. He stopped abruptly, pulled in a deep breath, then spat a great quantity of something that splattered in the dust, before hopping down and slapping his coat sleeves. He strode forward from out of the last of the steam, and stood still, smoke rising from a dented black bowler hat.

The little man reached up and pulled at massive goggles that came free from his face with audible pops. He lowered them to his neck, but his eyes were still covered with what looked like smaller goggles in thick brass frames. The lenses, of a dark hue, perhaps black, were surrounded with dials that looked to be for focusing. He reached up with practiced, albeit greasy, fingertips and adjusted one.

Then he just stood there smiling, his doughy, sweat-pocked face bubbling through a sparse beard, ginger eyebrows, and thick side whiskers. His coat continued to smoke, as if he himself were a source of heat.

"Good day to you, sir." She pointed at him. "You appear to be on fire."

His eyes never left her, though he slapped at himself a few times more. In a voice that rattled like gravel in a cup, he said, "It gets a bit … hot in there." He spat again, then slowly stepped closer. Everything

49

about him seemed of another time, as if he'd been apart somehow from normal society and fashion. He stared at her.

"Is there a problem?" she said, a hand still visoring her eyes.

"Oh, no, no ma'am. That is to say, I'm not put out in the least by your state of … undress, as it were."

Constance barked an oath she reserved for more private affairs and felt her face heat even as she turned away, groping for the stiff garments draped on the shrubs. "I'm … I'm so sorry to …"

She pulled on her clothes fast, noting the sad, wrinkled state her expensive fashions were now in. Blue velvet, silk luxlace, and camphor cotton had perhaps not been the best choices for traveling across the Spoils. At least they were drier than she expected. She continued picking and plucking her clothes from the brittle arms of the bushes, all the while keeping her brocade satchel close by, nudging it from bush to bush as she dressed.

"Why, sir, surely you must have a sense of decorum, propriety? Avert your eyes."

"I think not."

She heard the smile in his voice.

"It's been far too long since I've seen such an exquisite female form and I'll not look away. No indeed, I shan't do it."

She half-turned toward him as she finished buttoning her second blouse. "Then you, sir, are a rogue."

"Mm-hmm. Among many other things, I can assure you."

"Who are you?" she finally said when she had covered enough of herself to feel bold again.

"Who am I?" The portly man spluttered, stepped aside as if to let a lady pass him on a crowded streetside, and waved an arm at his wagon. "Can you not read, my dear?"

Constance leaned to her right as she continued to button and smooth her shirt. She saw faded writing on the side of the caravan through the dissipating steam and smoke. She shook her head as if disagreeing. "I can't make it out yet."

The man sighed, let his arms drop. He looked at his belly. "Ocularius." He looked up at her. "My name. It's Doctor Ocularius." His ample eyebrows seemed to rise higher with each syllable. "And you are …?"

Constance froze in the act of primping the once-stiff collar of her inner coat. "I am Constance Gatterling. But wait … you said you are Doctor Ocularius?"

The man smiled and pulled the massive goggles away from his neck, stretching his chin. "Why, yes. Are you unimpressed?"

"No, it's just that … well, I didn't expect you to use your own name."

"Ah, so you have heard of me. Why should I not use my name? I know I'm here, they know I'm here. What good would it do to try to deceive anyone?"

"Pardon me, doctor, but isn't that what you're best at?"

"Deceit? No, dear lady, that's but a sideline. An admittedly practical, and occasionally profitable one, but nonetheless a sideline to my primary distraction."

"Which is…."

"Ha—I like you already. Come, let's resume this conversation over a blue flame and a decanter of refined mint wine."

She raised her eyebrows.

"Yes, dear lady, you don't think Doctor Ocularius travels the wastelands of the Spoils without the refinements of clean fire and fine libation, do you?" He smiled and disappeared inside the wagon.

In faded yellow paint arched across the side of the wagon, she read his name and the words, 'Traveling Tinctures, Tonics, and Bifurcated, Multi-Purpose Nostrums for the Betterment of the Eyes, Ears, Nose, Throat, and Sundry Other Parts…. '

"So, Doctor, what do you call this contraption?"

"Contraption!" He peeked his head out the door. "You cut me to the core, dear girl! Why, this 'contraption,' as you call it, is more than a mere conveyance. It is more than a converted burrowing miner, more than a superior collection of hydraulic, steam, and forever-gear technology." He hopped down, green bottle in hand. "It is more than a home, it is more than a workshop, it is, indeed, to a man once said to have promise—considering the limitations forced on me due to my unfortunate and unearned yet imposed exile—this beautiful brute," he patted the cooled black steel of the silent mandible, "is the incubator of my brilliance."

"Well your incubator sounded to me like it's on its last legs."

He pursed his lips, his brow puckering as he dragged an ancient gasbox from its rack underneath the wagon and rummaged in a vest pocket until he

produced a small box of scratchers. Within seconds a
warm, blue-flame fire hissed on the ground at their feet.

He stared at the flame. "Well, it is true she isn't
suited to much more than sand travel these days—this
river-valley rock nearly killed her, but this is where I
found you."

"Why Doctor, I am flattered.... "

"Think nothing of it, dear girl. Thoughtful is my
middle name."

They were quiet a moment, dark rose around
them, and Constance pulled her satchel close. She
thought she saw the doctor watch her, though with his
eyewear, it was difficult to tell just where he was
looking. "Tell me about those peculiar spectacles,
Doctor."

"Ah, you have a gift for stroking the peacock's
feathers, my dear!" He smiled, sipped his wine,
smacked his lips, and said, "In a nutshell, these odd
eyepieces enable me to not be seen better."

She snorted, covered her mouth with a hand, and
said, "Please, continue."

He sighed. "The technology is something I've
spent my life developing. It's far more advanced than
anything those dolts back East have come up with, I can
assure you."

She regarded the pudgy man for a moment, then
shook her head, smiling. "I think you're a talespinner, is
what I think."

"Believe what you need to," said the Doc,
finishing his wine. "I do." He winked and slapped his
knee. "So, just what brought you out here?"

"Simple. I am a spirited young woman with a
certain proclivity for the hard sciences who has just

spent her formative years in the clutches of well-intentioned but fusty instructors, and I am desperate to do something tremendous with my life. Before I become one of those fusty instructors myself."

"And so…. " prompted Doc, pouring more wine into their goblets.

"And so," said Constance, crossing her boots "I aim to become the first person—a woman, no less—to cross from East to West. At least since the Long War ended, that is."

"But no one's—"

"That's why I'm doing it. If someone had, then I wouldn't be here."

"No, I suppose not. But that still doesn't explain how you came to be alone at this spot." The blue flames of the gasbox reflected in the small, dark lenses of his glasses.

"I hired a tracker who came recommended … in a roundabout way. And then he abandoned me here, at the river."

Doctor snorted. "Let me guess. His name was Tico?"

She sat up straight. "How did you know?"

"And you paid him half up front?"

She nodded. "How do you know…. "

"Everybody knows of Tico. He's no guide. He's more like … a sort of an anti-bounty hunter."

"How's that?"

"He loses people."

Constance nodded but couldn't think of a reply. She felt an urge to stretch her legs. It had been a long day. She stood—and a strange dizziness pulled at her from all sides. Then she fell prone by the gasbox. She tried to rise and could not figure out how to do it. Doctor Ocularius stared at her, not quite smiling, not moving to help her.

"What's wrong, my dear?"

"The wine—what did you do?"

He spread his arms wide. "The wine, the night air, the gas, the Spoils, me—something isn't agreeing with you." He laughed then, an abrasive chuckle built into a head-thrown-back guffaw that rocked his slab of a belly.

He rose from his seat and with a grunt, snatched the loop handles of her satchel and dragged it back to where he was sitting.

"Why?"

As he untwisted the clasp, the bag parted like the mouth of a fish. "I know Tico. And I know he always gets half up front for taking people across. I figure the other half has to be here somewhere. I didn't see it on your person earlier." He winked at her over the hissing gasbox.

Another short laugh erupted from him and trailed into the darkening, still night. The last thing Constance saw before her eyes closed was Doc rummaging in her satchel, smiling and humming as he held up various articles and marveled at them in the blue light.

* * *

"Hey."

Constance opened her eyes, shut them. She felt like mud. Aching mud. Her neck was as stiff as wood and it throbbed.

"Hey."

Something nudged her leg. "What…." She squinted her eyes open. The sun was up. A dark shape hovered over her and she raised a hand to visor her eyes. Someone in a wide-brim hat. The hat turned, looked up toward the sky, then back down. In that moment, something had glinted beneath the brim—glasses? The shape shifted, blocked out the sun, and she didn't have to squint so hard. A faint image of Doctor Ocularius filled her mind for a moment.

"Who—" She coughed. Her voice was dry, full of holes. She tried it again as she sat up. "Who are you?"

"Nope, that's my question."

"What?"

The man in the hat sighed. "I'm Rollicker, Sheriff of the Spoils." He sent a rope of thick brown liquid to the ground, dragged the back of one hand across his mouth, then smoothed his ample moustaches. He squinted at her through finely wrought spectacles, small lavender lenses set in brass frames.

"Are you sickly?" she said, standing and stretching her back.

"What? No, not that I'm aware of…. "

"That … stuff you just spit up…. "

"Chaw, missy. That's all."

"That was intentional?"

His jaws chewed slowly, then he pursed his lips and sluiced another stream just a few inches from her boots. "Yep."

She looked at him fully for the first time. He was a tall, thin man and wore a sweat-stained shirt of rough cloth the color of sand. His trousers were of a darker, stronger material, tucked into tall boots. His hat was a stained affair, massive in height and width, and a dull brown leather vest ended just above a holstered pistol that seemed crude and of old-time construction, certainly older than the one Tico had worn.

She wondered if these men carried their ancient guns as an affectation, in the way the wives of Societeers back home carried their clockwork pets, yipping, purring, growling knots of gears wrapped in fur and feathers, as a way to show they'd not lost touch with their urban forebears, what they liked to call their "instinctual selves."

"You must be parched," he said as he untied thongs that held a leather-wrapped bottle to a saddle horn. He handed it to her.

"Is that a real horse?" She nodded toward the beast behind him, the same deep brown color as his spittle.

Rollicker snorted a laugh, "As opposed to what? One of those modified contraptions you're used to? By god, if those dandified clothes didn't give you away, your reaction to seeing a live, kickin' horse surely does."

She uncorked the top of the bottle, sniffed it, and did her best to keep from gagging as she swigged. "It's just that in the civilized East we have modern conveyances of all manner that are far tidier and less cruel."

He shook his head, half smiling, then said, "Tell me, missy, if it's so grand in the East, what are you doing out here alone into the Spoils?"

She turned her back on him. "Constance Gatterling. That's my name."

He gave her a nod.

"Thank you for finding me."

"Dumb luck on my part—and yours. I'm headed back to town anyway. So, what are you doing out here?"

She said nothing. Despite the morning's dry heat, a shiver worked up her back. "It's so bleak."

"Didn't used to be—used to be beautiful prairies, rich with wildlife, birds, grasses taller than a man's head."

"What happened?"

"Long story." He mounted the horse and gathered the reins, then offered a hand down to her.

She backed up and said, "Hmm, that vile doctor told me to be wary of you people of the Spoils.... "

So fast she had no time to react, the sheriff leaned further and snatched her shirtfront, balling her four layers in a grimy, calloused fist. "You saw Doc?" He shook her once. Her head wobbled in a nod. "Doc Ocularius?"

She nodded again.

Rollicker released her and said, "Take me to him and I won't leave you out here." They stared at each other a moment. His jaw muscles working hard, his eyes glinting behind the lavender lenses. Then he freed his left boot from the stirrup and extended his arm again. After a moment, she mounted up behind him and he guided the horse north.

Most of an hour passed, and she found that if she turned her head to one side and breathed, she could lessen the blended stink of horse, unwashed man, and raw Spoils air. Finally she said, "What do you hate Doctor Ocularius for?"

He answered quickly, as if he were waiting for Constance to ask. "You name it—theft, murder, trickery. Years ago, when the damnable Long War was still on, the dust from the blue stone you all so desperately need back East was making everyone who mined it go blind. Some genius decided that would be bad for business, so they sent Doc Ocularius out here to help us all keep our sight, since he seemed to be the greatest thing since wind-up lightning. But they didn't figure on him bein' a greedy little weasel. He's been playing the middle against both ends ever since, keeps everybody blind, so to speak—us and the powers that be back East, while he drains off profits for himself."

"So you're out to get him."

"Pure and straight. All I need is one clear shot at his mangy hide.... "

"But why? Didn't he save everyone's sight? And that in turn kept the mineworks open, correct?"

"You know, for a little bit of a thing, you sure talk a lot."

"You're not the first to tell me that."

"Might be you wanna listen to others once in a while instead of flapping your gums."

"For better or worse, it's my curiosity that got me here."

"Yeah, smack dab in the Spoils. If this is the plan you had for yourself, I'm not so sure your gears are lining up quite right." He tapped his forehead and grinned.

"Well, aren't you going to tell me?"

He sighed. "Tell you what?"

"Why you haven't ... eradicated the Doctor."

He was silent for a few paces, then in a lowered voice said, "I can't find him."

Behind him, she smiled. "Well, that doesn't seem

so difficult. I found him in short order."

To her surprise, he nodded and kept riding. After a few minutes of silence, he spit again and said, "He fixed me up, same as the rest. Only he did a little something different with my eyes. I suppose you noticed these here spectacles."

She nodded. "They're not the most masculine looking things, I'll grant you. But at least you can see."

"Yep, I can see. But not everything."

She waited for more, but he grew silent again. After a few quiet minutes, Constance said, "What is that stench?"

The sheriff sat up straight, tilted his head back, and pulled in a deep draught of air. "Aaahh." He half-turned to her and said, "That, little missy, is the smell of fashion, and music, and theatres, and cinematographs, and cyclerigibles and all manner of modern advance that you so enjoy in the East." The he turned fully toward her, his leather saddle creaking. "That, little missy, is the smell of Rankton."

"I should say.... "

He laughed wide-mouthed then, and she saw for the first time the blackened nubs of his teeth. "Capitol city of Abandonia.... "

"How very wistful. Tell me, is it as forlorn as it smells?"

"No, Lord no … it's worse."

"If it's so bad, then why don't you leave, Sheriff Rollicker?"

"You know, for a smarty-type, you're none too bright. There ain't no leaving the Spoils, girl. Once you're in, you're in. The only folks ever end up here are those born into it, those sent here because they have no choice," he spit, looked her right in the eye, and said, "and fools."

* * *

As the horse walked slowly into the little town, the whole of which seemed backed up to a blunted rise of blue-grey rock, everywhere she looked Constance saw remnants of what seemed a thriving mining past. Great steel-and-wood conveyors, their canvas belts tattered and hanging, jutted at the base of a sprawling mass of shale that leaked between buildings and dissipated in the street. Brass tubes and mammoth rusted gears poked between leaning planks of wind-chewed boards the color of thick smoke. Valves and smokestacks atop steel skeletons on steel wheels, shot through with rust and holes, lay dragged and forgotten in the middle of the street, the rotted carcasses of the machinery of promise.

Signs on some of the collapsed, gaunt buildings told of once-lively trade: Abandonia General Mercantile; Flo's Pleasure Palace; The Blue Dream Bar, and at the end of the street, faded black letters on a leaning sign close by a gaping hole in the rock mound read: J.S. Kalibrator's Blue Stone and Gasworks. To her surprise, Constance saw smoke lifting up and out the top of the entrance rough-cut into the rock, and several men straggled in and out, carrying arc rods and flatpicks.

"We'll get you cleaned up at the jail house, then set to work finding Doc. Strikes me he's never too far off."

"No need."

"Now see here, missy.... "

She sighed. "Keep your big hat on, Sheriff Rollicker. He's here."

"What … in town? How do you know?" He looked left and right, his glasses glinting.

"Sheriff—he's right over there." She jutted her chin toward The Hard Shine Saloon. "See, there's his wagon."

Rollicker followed her pointing hand, looked right at the wagon, then to the left and right of it, shaking his head.

She opened her eyes wide and stared at him as if he were a dumb child. "You know, the one that reads: 'Doctor Ocularius and his Traveling Tinctures, Tonics, and Bifurcated Nostrums for the Betterment of the Eyes, Ears, Nose, Throat, and—"

"Girl, I don't see a damn thing but Horace Gorton's broke-down mule and a drunk floozie sleepin' off a toot by that post out front. What are you playin' at?"

She stared at Rollicker. "You're not kidding me, are you sheriff?"

With his little finger he pushed the glasses up the bridge of his nose and smoothed his moustaches. She guessed he was fighting the urge to shout at her again.

Then she understood and her mouth dropped open as she stared at him. He looked away. "So that's what you meant when you said you can't see everything. Of course! Last night I laughed at the Doctor when he said his glasses helped him to not be seen. It must have been the wine that made me so very ignorant. Those spectacles of his would make—"

"Girl, you're doin' it again. Chattering away like old Judge Bulger when he gets a few snorts in him—"

"Sorry.… "

But the sheriff was squinting harder now at the mule. "Doc Ocularius, huh? Right here under my very nose! Hell, I'm callin' him out right now."

"What? Wait, what does that mean?"

"Means I'm aiming to get the Doc out here, settle his hash once and for all, right here in the street."

"But how will you see him?"

"I won't," he smiled and spat at their feet. "But you will."

"What?"

"Yep, just muckle onto him when he tries to climb aboard his wagon there. I'll see you and I'll pepper whatever it is you're grabbin' onto."

"I'll not do it."

"You will … and I'll tell you why." He smiled wide. "I'm the only one here who knows how to get you back East to your fine, cushy life. All this here could be but a bad memory and a hell of a story to tell your little friends when you sit around a fancy dining table some night back in East City."

She smiled. "I'll just find Tico. He'd take me back to the border." She looked around as if expecting to see him waiting for her.

"Sure, just wave a coin in the air. He'll find you."

Her smiled faded as the sheriff forced his moustaches into a big frown. "What? No money? Oh that's right, Doc Ocularius took your traveling cash. And if I'm not mistaken, he's in the Hard Shine right now, transforming it into little glasses full of libation for him and all his new friends." As if on cue, a round of laughter bubbled out the batwing doors.

She bit the inside of her mouth. Of course she wanted out of the Spoils, but she also wanted the Doctor's glasses. If she could get those, her future would be set—no dry academic career for her. She could travel, see Europaia, the Far Orient. The world would be hers….

"All right. I'll do it. But first I need a sip of that foul water."

"Attagirl." He handed her the leather-covered bottle. "Now here's what we'll do…. "

* * *

In her mind Constance replayed her plan, meager though it was, as she crossed the street to the wagon, swinging the leather-wrapped bottle by its strap handle. Up close and even in such grey light as Rankton received, the doctor's old burrowing mine machine was nothing more than a bent, haggard relic—wood and steel, grimy, worn out, and faded. Like everything in this place.

If this withered, bled corpse of a country had a face, she thought, then it was certainly this toothless crone of a town. What had the sign at the end of Main Street said? 'Rankton, Jewel of Abandonia'? Jewel indeed. Get me those glasses and a ride out of here and I'll not so much as give it a second thought for the rest of my days.

"Well, little lady! Imagine my surprise at seeing you here."

Constance froze, then turned and looked up, and there stood Doctor Ocularius on the boardwalk, leaning against a faded wood post. The drunk floozie continued to snore, propped at the base of the next post, wearing nothing but one holey brown sock, a tattered underdress, and two black eyes beneath small brass spectacles with green lenses.

Doc's head wobbled enough to tell Constance he was inebriated. He held her satchel by the handles, almost bouncing it against his knees. A short, thin man and an even smaller woman, both wearing clothing so begrimed she didn't know where skin ended and fabric began, walked right by the doctor, close enough that they nearly brushed his arm—and they paid him no heed. And both wore green-lens eyewear in brass frames.

She waited for them to pass, then Constance strode to him and swung the water vessel hard by the thong handle and caught the doctor just above his left ear. His dented black hat pinwheeled upward, then dropped to the street. He grunted and sagged to a sitting position on the edge of the boardwalk, his back to the post.

She rummaged in the satchel. "My, but you made a mess of my things, Doctor. Shame on you."

Doctor Ocularius sat weaving and shaking his head.

She pulled a white shirt from the bag, held it up, sighed, and tore at a hem with her teeth, ripping it in two. With one half she tied his hands together behind the post.

His struggles were weak. "What are you doing? Oh, my head…. "

She lashed his feet together with the other half-shirt. "It occurred to me, Doctor, that the bounty on you I would imagine is rather substantial. Not to mention

65

what I can do with those glasses of yours." She smiled and depressed a small button on a polished copper device she'd retrieved from her bag. It was palm-sized and when the click sounded, it split in two, and she pulled the halves apart. Between them stretched a thin, limp thread. "Why go all the way to the West Edge—if it's even possible—when you represent all I've been searching for."

The doctor swallowed. "What ... what is that, my dear?"

"I believe I hinted that I was a recent graduate of the Academy? I fear I may have neglected to mention some of the Chancellor's last words to us all: 'Bring me the head of Doctor Ocularius and your future is secure!' Funny thing at the time. We all laughed. But now I know exactly what he meant."

She pulled tight the device in her hands and the thin wire glowed a vivid blue. "Yes, this little notion heats water, helps with manicures, oh, and did I mention that it's also useful in ... slicing? You see, it cauterizes as it cuts. Makes rather a neat job of it, really."

The doctor swallowed audibly, straightened against the post. "You think you're the only one to come after me? Every time a new class graduates, it seems at least one fresh face intends to make a quick name for himself by capturing me."

She raised the wire up and held it at neck level. "Now, I'll need my money ... and those glasses."

She lowered the device and with the back of one hand patted the worn black fabric of his vest. Then, still watching his dark lenses, she reached in a pocket and pulled out a wad of wrinkled circular paper bills. Coins, green with tarnish, spilled to the dirt at his feet.

"And the glasses," she said.

"N-no, no, I can't! They are part of me, you see. Attached directly to me, to my skull, in my eye sockets. They can't be removed…. "

"Masterful, Doctor. But I will have them, one way or another—" She pushed the wire closer to his neck, so close that the hairs of his shaggy whiskers smoked and curled. A sound like steam hissing from a touchy valve rose from his mouth.

"I can't let you do that, missy!"

Behind her she heard the sheriff's voice, ragged like wind through shredded metal.

She turned her head. "Why ever not, sheriff? You're going to do the same thing…. "

He didn't respond, but lurched into the street, his pistol drawn and aimed at her, though it wagged in time with his unsteady gait. His hat was gone and she was shocked to see the split purple welt and spatter of blood that covered the side of Rollicker's face, an unfortunate by-product of hitting him with the water bottle. He'd dropped as if shot, but she hadn't thought to take his pistol.

"Yes, but I'm a lawman and you're doing it for the wrong reasons."

She snorted. "Sheriff, my reasons are as valid as yours. Perhaps more so, considering I have a future—a brilliant career ahead of me as potentially one of the greater minds of my generation. While you are, well, here. A comparison can hardly be drawn, sheriff."

"Badmouth me and Rankton all you want, girly." Rollicker's voice was right behind her now. "I've heard it all before. I got to go through you to get to him, fine by me. You're both burrs under my saddle anyway. One shot, two burrs gone." She heard the throaty click of the ancient gun's mechanism, felt the barrel of his pistol grazing her ruined blue velvet coat.

Constance's lips drew tight across her straight, white teeth. She stared at the doctor's unblinking lenses, the fine, beautiful precision work of the thick brass mechanisms surrounding them. And she also smelled the foul, bitter stink of his boozy breath. She wanted nothing more than a long bath in clean water— and she knew there was only one way to get back to that life. With a slight grunt and a strained smile, she pushed the wire forward.

* * *

From the sagging balcony of the Hotel Abandonia across the street, Tico saw the sheriff's knuckle whiten, and he knew that trigger was but a baby's breath away from opening the ball....

"In for a penny," Tico mumbled. He took one step sideways, eyeing the scene in the street below, his boot heel clunking soft on the rotting wood, his spur singing like the whisper of a far-off breeze. Then he shot the sheriff in the back.

It all played out as he expected: The sheriff lurched forward, squeezed his pistol's trigger, the girl's pretty blue jacket burst apart, she pitched forward with her hotwire tool straight into Doc's throat ... *ssup*! Clean as you please, the old goat's head burned free from his body, teetered for a second on the stump, like a coin dropped on a bartop, then it flopped to the ground.

Tico led his horse from the shadows across the street and stood looking down at the unfortunate trio. Doc, he was sagged against the post, belly-blasted and headless, and the other two, their last was bubbling up, soaking into the dust. The sheriff's trigger finger kept curling into the dirt, reaching for the thing that was no longer there.

The girl whimpered something, her mouth moving like a clockwork toy nearly wound down.

"You talk too much, girl," said Tico, looking at her.

He rolled a quirley, patted his vest for a scratcher. "Aw hell." Then he saw the girl's gadget still gripped in her hands, the blue wire arcing small sparks against the dirt. He stepped on her hand and lifted it free, fiddled with it a moment, and worked it back up to a full glow, hot enough to light his cigarette.

Tico heard a scuffing sound, looked up at the dozen or so drawn faces of the diggers trying not to look at him, the dark green lenses of their spectacles not quite hiding their fear. They advanced, hoping, he knew, for a chance at something of value. He stared until they turned and dragged themselves back inside the Hard Shine to whimper about this day for years to come. From her post, the drunk floozie snorted in her sleep.

Tico snatched up Doc's head by its greasy knot of hair, stared into its taught, shocked face, and worked a grimy couple of fingers on one of the dials surrounding a lens.

"Well, that's one way to get ahead." He blew smoke in the dead man's face, then dropped the head into the satchel. He plucked the wad of cash from the girl's hand and stuffed it into his vest pocket.

Then Tico looped the handles of the satchel over his saddle horn, climbed atop the waiting Colonel Saunderston the Third, and spurred the clanking horse East, toward the sunrise.

END

CATCH A KILLER BY THE TOE
By PETE PETERSON

1

Deputy Rome Warfield reached for the blackened coffee pot atop the cast-iron stove. "Ouch." He jerked back his hand from the hot handle, reached into his hip pocket for his kerchief and poured his tin cup full of the simmering liquid. He raised the pot toward Marshal Sam Catlin, seated behind the desk. Sam shook his head in refusal, so Rome set the pot back on the fire and walked toward the desk, sipping carefully from the cup in his hand.

"Anything different about this last killing, Sam?"

Catlin leaned back in his chair, clasping his hands behind his head as he plopped his boots on the corner of the desk.

"Nope. Same as the other three. Caleb Tinker, a hard-working miner trying to make a living off a small claim. Worked alone, never bothered nobody. Shot once at close range, like he recognized his killer and had no reason to fear him."

Rome shook his head sadly. He had witnessed his share of violence and death, usually resulting from hot tempers, warm women and raw whiskey in one combination or another. But these coldly calculated murders for a few meager dollars in nuggets and dust were different, and far more tragic to his mind.

This most recent killing had hit Rome harder than any other for one reason--Janet Tinker. Unlike the other victims, who had no kin or had left their loved ones in safer climes, Caleb Tinker had come to Fairplay with his daughter. Now she stood alone, grief-stricken and stranded. Rome had been the one called upon to inform her of her father's death, and he had felt woefully inadequate in his attempts to comfort her. Following a man's trail, facing a renegade's gun or living off the wild country, Rome Warfield was as good as most, but faced with a beautiful woman's troubled tears, he was helpless as a newborn pup.

Sam studied the hangdog expression on his young deputy's face. He knew that Rome had special feelings for the murdered man's daughter. "How's Janet taking it," he asked.

Rome shrugged. "Asked when we were going to catch her daddy's killer. I had to tell her that we have no notions who could have done it. She just turned and walked off."

Sam nodded his head. "Sure beats me. There's generally a bootprint to go on, some yahoo spending more than he should, a drunken slip of the tongue...something. But I haven't been able to turn up a damn thing. We'll both ride out there tomorrow after church. Maybe you can spot something I missed."

Rome knocked down the last swig of coffee, set the cup on the edge of the desk and walked to reach his coat off a hook on the front wall near the door. He checked the loads in his Russian .44, returned it to the leather holster riding low on his hip, then slipped into his coat.

"Time for rounds, I reckon," Rome said in an enduring Texas drawl. He was a tall, easy moving young man, with sandy hair and keen brown eyes. "You going to be around this evening?"

"Not for long. I've missed supper three nights

running, now. If I don't spend the evening at home with the missus, I'm apt to be bunking with you."

"Then head for the house, Marshal. I've heard you snore."

Rome left grinning.

It was Saturday, and the main street of Fairplay was clogged with traffic at this time of evening. Merchants closing up shop and headed for home, freight and ore wagons making their final runs of the day, early arrivals looking to make a long and lively night of it in the saloons. A plump crimson sun was just settling behind the jagged peaks of the Continental Divide, and already the air was filled with tinny piano music and the first awkward sounds of gritty laughter filtering into the street through batwing doors.

Rome was new at this law business, a deputy for only six months now. He had been riding the shotgun seat on the big ore wagons out of the Climax diggings when a half dozen hard-eyed highwaymen, bristling with hardware, stormed from the rocks at the top of a grade and opened fire on the train of three mule-drawn wagons. When the gunsmoke had cleared from the scene and the echoes of gunfire had stilled in the surrounding forest, Rome Warfield stood alone in the road, his shotgun and sidearm empty. Three of the bandits were dead. Another lay wounded, and two had crept off into the trees. The very day the story reached Fairplay, Marshal Catlin, needing a deputy, rode to Climax, sought young Warfield out and offered him the badge.

Rome had always imagined that being a law dog would be an exciting, romantic, action-packed way of life, but he was discovering that it was more a matter of serving as combination night watchman, paper shuffler and nursemaid to drunks, even in a frontier town as unruly and unkempt as Fairplay. The only occasion he'd had to draw his gun was to bend the barrel over the head of a cantankerous Cousin Jack who was trying to throttle the bartender for pouring too light. He still had not decided if he was cut out to wear a badge.

Not that Rome sought gunplay. Far from it. The shootout with the gunmen who waylaid the ore wagons was the first and only time he had been forced to kill a man. After it was over, he had rushed stumbling into the brush at the side of the trail and lost his breakfast, sickened by the senselessness and the waste of it. He was not anxious to repeat the experience.

As he patrolled the plank walkways, he thought of the girl, Janet. He had been taken with her from his first glance, captivated by her large green eyes, her pert little button of a nose, sprinkled with freckles. He liked the way she allowed her blond hair to cascade over her shoulders, and the way her nose crinkled when she laughed. Most folks might not see her as beautiful, but to Rome she was the loveliest creature he had ever encountered.

It wasn't as if they were keeping company, though. Rome was shy, and so, he supposed, was Janet. He had made no overtures to her, though he thought she knew his feelings. His only contact with Janet Tinker was when she waited on his table in the restaurant at the Paragon Hotel, or when they chanced to pass on the street. She always seemed pleased to see him, always favored him with a bright and cheerful smile. And Rome Warfield had hopes. Had hopes, anyway, until Caleb Tinker was murdered. Now any chance at a blossoming relationship seemed doomed. Janet would probably leave Fairplay and return to wherever the Tinkers had called home before gold fever lured her father West.

Raucous laughter jerked Rome from his reverie. Three of the town toughs were hovering over a beggar on the walk in front of the Tenstrike Saloon, mocking and badgering the poor cripple. Rome rushed forward.

"You boys find it so amusing to be without the use of your limbs, may be I can break a few bones for you."

The trio straightened as one, spreading across the walk. One stepped forward, grinning.

"Aw, Deputy, we was just funning him. No harm done, and no concern of the law."

"I'm making it my business. You fellows get on along, or I'll take you in for questioning."

"Questionin' about what? We ain't done nothing."

"There's been some killing and thieving going on hereabouts. I know you hombres, all of you. Dutch Cabiness, Rusty Bonner, Andy Pruitt. You always got plenty to spend on rotgut and female company, but I never heard of any of you turnin' a tap where work is concerned. Makes me wonder where you get your money."

"We ain't done nothing," Rusty told him, "and it's none of your affair how we come by our money. You got no call to bedevil us."

They peeled off one by one and sauntered into the saloon, eyes narrowed, lips stuck out like chastened children.

"Thank you, Deputy Warfield."

Rome looked down into the upturned face of the

beggar, Martin Tandy. He would have been a small and frail man, even if his body had consisted of more than a torso, but that part of him where his legs should have been was encased in a sort of sack, resting on a small, square wooden platform on wheels. His upper body was covered by a faded plaid shirt and a threadbare coat that dragged the ground on either side of the platform. He wore no hat.

"This is probably not the best place for you to park, Mister Tandy. It's liable to get rough here tonight."

"Deputy, this is where I make most of what folks give me. The miners and prospectors that frequent the saloons become munificent, it seems, in direct proportion to the amount of whiskey they have consumed. I'll take in more tonight than I have all week," he said, smiling.

"Yeah, well, whatever. But you watch out for those three hardcases I just pulled off you. Drink just makes a mean man meaner."

Rome tipped his hat and proceeded down the boardwalk, wondering what '*munificent*' meant.

Coming to the Golden Egg, the mining camp's most notorious dance hall and gambling establishment, Rome found his way blocked by a stunning satin-and-feather-adorned figure.

"Still harassing the innocent, huh, Warfield?" Jessie Colette said, her eyes flashing with malevolence.

Jessie was a sporting lady, called by many who knew her, "the most beautiful female between the Mississippi and the Continental Divide". Rome did not know if that were true, but he reckoned her to be one of the hardest. The woman controlled the ventures of the commercially available hostesses working the saloons and dance halls of Fairplay and Climax--a gold mine that put most of the diggings in the region to shame.

"What do you know about innocence, Jessie?"

She smiled, slowly licking her full, red lips, turned and entered the swinging doors of the saloon.

It irked Rome that he had been forced to release Jessie from jail the previous week. He had arrested her, kicking and clawing, after she walked halfway around an amorous miner, the blade of her knife in his ample girth. The altercation had been sparked by a dispute over money owed for services rendered. The miner was sewn up, he sobered up and left town on a fleet-footed mule, neglecting to file charges.

Cabiness, Pruitt and Bonner were frequent companions of Jessie Colette, and Rome figured the three of them had talked with her victim, convincing him that his wounds would heal faster in a milder climate. Whatever the circumstance, the charges against Jessie were dismissed, and she reigned again on the mean streets of Fairplay.

As Rome neared the Paragon Hotel, he wondered if Janet was working at her job of waiting tables. He peered between the shade and the painted lower section of the restaurant window. She was there, her pencil poised over the order pad in her hand as she waited for the four men at the table to decide which of the items on the bill of fare to order. But the smile had gone from her lips, and her eyes were red-rimmed and swollen. Rome let the urge to go to her pass. He would not know what to say.

He crossed the street, starting up the other side. Suddenly, from in front of the Tenstrike, came a frantic, high-pitched cry for help. He peered through the gathering dusk to see several murky forms struggling at the edge of the walk. Vaulting over a hitch rail into the churned earth, Rome rushed catty-cornered across the street toward the disturbance, dodging riders and wagons and drays.

Cabiness, Bonner and Pruitt had the beggar, Tandy, poised at the top of a ramp that sloped into the busy street. As Rome opened his mouth to shout, the trio of ruffians launched the wheel-borne beggar down the ramp.

When the wheels on Tandy's platform struck the soft earth at the base of the ramp, he was hurled through the air and into the street, landing with jarring impact in the dirt directly in front of the pounding, clod-throwing hooves of a charging team of horses pulling a loaded wagon.

Rome made a dive for the sprawled, abbreviated form of the beggar, snatching him from danger as the team and wagon rumbled past. He sat in the dirt, Tandy in his lap, catching his breath, fighting to calm the quivering that had turned his muscles to mush.

Sweeping Tandy up in his arms, Rome carried him back to the Tenstrike entrance and deposited him on the boardwalk. He walked to the ramp and retrieved the splintered platform, placing it at Tandy's side. Then he turned toward the three snickering hulks standing in the door of the saloon.

"Outside. All of you."

"What's wrong, Deputy?" Pruitt said, walking to face him, "Can't some folks take a joke, it seems."

A fist, come screaming out of nowhere, knocked the smirk from Pruitt's lips and dropped him to the decking. As Cabiness clawed for his gun, the barrel of Rome's .44 slammed into the side of his head, sending him on top of Pruitt as he was clambering to his feet. Bonner backed away.

"All right, all of you, listen up." Rome's back was up, and his attitude would brook no sass. "Cabiness, you and Pruitt get to your feet. I want you to pick up Mister Tandy, real gentle, and you carry him to his house around back. I'll follow you. Bonner, take that cart down to the blacksmith shop and you fix it or have it fixed, then deliver it back to Tandy. After that, meet me and your two running mates, here, back at the jail. All three of you are going to be the town's guests tonight."

2

Church services in the mining camp of Fairplay, in the new Territory of Colorado, were held in an open, abandoned farrier's shed. The property had come available when the smithy had been stricken with gold fever, taking to the heights with pan and pickax. Seating was catch-as-catch-can, of halved logs, upended crates or counterpanes spread on the wood-chip floor, all arranged in a semi-circular pattern. As there was no regular preacher in the tiny community, members of the congregation alternated in the holding of the service. Marshal Catlin's pretty wife, Ruth, stood before the meager gathering, leading the final hymn.

Rome Warfield waited a respectable distance from the open shed, holding the reins of two saddled horses, the Marshal's big sorrel and his own zebra dun. The singing done, the worshipers began to scatter toward errands of their own.

Rome's heart jumped as Janet Tinker, clothed in black and wearing a heavy veil, passed a half dozen feet from his position. He tugged at the brim of his hat in salute. She looked at him and nodded. She did not smile. She did not stop to talk.

The Marshal and his Deputy rode from town along the east bank of the infant middle fork of the South Platte River, its origin high in the peaks to the north, behind and above Fairplay. The lawmen were bound for Tinker's placer claim, up Red Hill Creek from where it joined the river.

It was a thrilling thing for Rome to ride these mountain trails. The transplanted Texan had loved the high country from the day he rode in--felt at home here, as he never had on the dry, rolling plain of West Texas. Primroses, buttercups, wild iris and columbine brightened the open parks. Great towering trees, the spruce, pine, fir and white-trunked aspen, filled the steep slopes with splendor. Jagged purple peaks, many over 14,000 feet, thrust their mighty snow-draped shoulders into the clouds and beyond. Rome wasn't a church-going man, but he figured if there had been a Garden of Eden, it must have been located somewhere near this place.

The claim was as Sam had last seen it. A lean-to shelter set back in the trees a few yards from the swift-flowing creek. A pick, a shovel and a gold pan lay on the ground in front of the lean-to. An empty whiskey bottle. A water keg. Rumpled blankets in the shelter. A small rocker sluice sat beside the stream, another shovel leaned against it.

They tethered their horses in trees outside the

camp and approached on foot, so as not to disturb any trace of intrusion. A deer had crossed the open area on its way to the stream and there were raccoons' prints along the sandy banks, but they saw no human tracks aside from Sam's own, from his previous visit, and those of Caleb Tinker himself.

"The body was layin' right there on the bank," the Marshal said, pointing. "Half in the water. I figure he was workin' his rocker when the killer came up on him.

"He had scratched something in the sand, like a stick figure of a man. Ol' Tinker couldn't read or write, so he may have been trying to leave a clue to his killer, the only way he could. But he died before he finished the bottom half of it. The drawing is washed away, looks like. I couldn't make head nor tails of it, anyhow."

"You check the other side of the creek?"

"Yep," Sam replied, "no tracks there, either."

Rome was circling the spot, eyes to the ground.

"He's bound to have left some sign, Sam. He didn't just fly in and out of here."

"Must have brushed his tracks out. See here how the sand is scuffed up?"

Rome was bending over the rocker. "Come here, Sam. Look at this.

"Somebody has scraped the sediment out from behind these riffles to get at any gold that was there, leaving finger trails. See how thin they are, almost like they were left by a woman's hand. If I recall, Caleb had big hands, and stout fingers."

"He did," Sam said in agreement, "but you don't think a woman could have killed him, do you?"

Rome shrugged. "One of the whores from the saloons, maybe. Might be worth checking."

"That could explain how they got so close without alarming him." Sam bent quickly to the ground on the stream side of the rocker. "Hey, look at this. What is that? A moccasin print?"

Rome rushed to bend over Sam's pointing finger. "Doesn't look like any moccasin I ever saw. More like a stockinged foot, or a slipper of some kind. And look here." Rome placed his boot beside the faint track. "See how small that is? Barely half as big as mine."

Rome rubbed at a deep scratch on his left forearm. It was just starting to scab over, and it itched.

"What did you do to your arm?"

"Not sure," Rome said, furrowing his brow, "I noticed it after that incident last evening. Must have done it when I snatched that beggar out of the street."

"Best let Ruth put something on it when we get back to town."

Rome shrugged his shoulders and rolled down his sleeve.

They toured the camp, but found nothing more. They turned and walked back toward their horses.

"Well," Sam said, lifting his hat and scratching his head, "we know more now than we did when we rode up here, but I don't know what good it will do us.

"Does rule out those three you jailed last night, though. They're all big galoots. You let them go yet?"

"Yes. Turned them loose at first light, so I wouldn't have to feed them breakfast."

The marshal and his deputy swung into their saddles and headed back downslope, more confused than when they had arrived.

As Sam and Rome rode from town on their exploratory junket to the camp of the murdered miner,

Cabiness, Bonner and Pruitt sat in huddled conversation at a table with Jessie Colette, in a dark and musty corner of the Golden Egg Saloon. The buckets of beer they had consumed since their release from jail had not softened the glowering expressions on the men's whiskered faces.

"I'd like to teach that smart-pants deputy a lesson he'd never forget," Pruitt said. "I don't take that from no man, badge or no."

"You'll wind back up in jail, or worse, you take out after Warfield," Bonner warned. "He's a real catamount with a gun."

"That may be," Jessie interjected sweetly, "but that damn cripple wouldn't be a problem, would he?"

Pruitt, Bonner and Cabiness whipped their heads toward the queen of the gold fields as smiles crept onto all their faces.

"Yeah."

"Yeah.

"Right."

* * *

As Catlin and Warfield neared town, Ruth Catlin came rushing out to meet them.

"Sam, hurry, there's been shooting, down behind the Tenstrike."

They spurred their horses down the street and around the corner of the saloon. A circle of men were standing in front of the shack of Martin Tandy, the beggar. Sam elbowed his way through, Rome right behind him.

Rusty Bonner lay face down in the open doorway

of the shack, half in, half out. There was a bullet hole in his back, and he was obviously dead.

"Anyone see what happened here?" Sam asked the gathering of curious onlookers. "Anybody been in there?"

The men looked at one another, shaking their heads.

"Just heard the shots…three of them. Came running to see what was going on."

Sam and Rome pulled their guns and walked to the shack.

"Who's in there?" Rome shouted through the open door.

"You can come in Deputy. It's me, Tandy."

Each nodded his readiness and they burst through the door, Rome first, flattening themselves against the wall as they scanned the dim interior of the one room shanty.

"Good gawdamighty!"

The spindly beggar was perched on a cot against a wall, his lower torso encased in burlap sacking, his back leaned against the window frame. A small caliber, five-shot revolver lay on the blanket before him. Martin Tandy was spooning beans into his mouth from the tin plate in his hand.

The blood-splattered body of Andy Pruitt lay on the floor at the foot of the cot, half his face blown away. Dutch Cabiness was dead, too, slumped in a sitting position against the far wall.

"What the hell went on here?" the Marshal said.

Tandy set the plate on the cot beside the gun. "They were going to throw me in the river, Marshal. Watch me bob up and down like a fishing cork, they said."

"You did this?" Rome asked. "You shot and killed all three of these men?" He was stunned.

"I did. It was them or me."

"Where'd you get the gun."

"Had it a while. Got it from a miner that was giving up and going back East. He gave it to me. There's men in these parts would rob even a beggar."

Sam walked to the door of the cabin.

"Hey. Some of you men out there…come in here and haul these bodies down to the carpenter shop. Tell Mister Goodspeed to take however much money he needs for building the coffins off the bodies, then bring what's left, along with their effects, to me at the jail. Come on, now, move. Let's get it done."

As the Marshal's draftees carried away the detritus of the shootout in the shanty, Rome looked around the room. It was neatly kept, if dusty, with canned and sack goods lined in ordered rows on shelves on the wall. He examined the dusty rough-plank flooring, noting the scuffed footprints. A small stove in one corner, a dented coffee pot atop it, a washstand and basin, the cot on which Tandy was sitting, a chipped and stained honeypot and a bureau that doubled as kitchen cabinet completed the scant furnishings. There was a rear entrance.

Rome opened the back door and stepped out onto a low ramp. A path, rutted by the wheels of Tandy's platform, led to an outhouse twenty yards away. Rome walked to the privy, looked inside, then returned to the shack, eyes down, examining the path as he walked.

After asking if there was anything they could do for Martin Tandy, and receiving a "no, thank you", Sam and Rome retrieved their horses and rode to the jail.

"That beats all I ever seen," Sam admitted. "Don't you know those three hoodlums were surprised?"

"He's a good shot, Tandy is," Rome observed. "Three shots, three men dead."

"Well, I don't suppose the man has been crippled all his life. May be he was a soldier, or a hunter. Close quarters, too."

"Still and all, there's something strange about the whole thing."

"What?" asked Sam.

"That's just it, Sam, I'm not sure what I've seen that bothers me. I'm going to have to think on it. When I know what it is, I'll tell you."

* * *

Ruth Catlin asked Rome to eat Sunday dinner with her and Sam, and he gladly accepted. It was not often he had the opportunity to pull his chair up to a home-cooked meal.

After polishing off double portions of fried rabbit, fresh baked bread with honey, mashed potatoes and gravy and three slices of mock apple pie, Rome excused himself. He headed back to the jail to catch a nap before evening rounds.

As he neared the Tenstrike Saloon, he saw that Martin Tandy had taken his position by the door, comfortably ensconced on his newly refurbished platform.

"Evening, Deputy Warfield," the little beggar said brightly.

Rome returned the greeting with a tug at his hat

brim and walked on. Suddenly he felt very cold.

3

As it was in every boom town and mining camp, the population of Fairplay was unstable at best, ranging from several hundred to several thousand souls, one day to the next. The seekers of gold and silver were inveterate rainbow chasers, and rumors of a new bonanza could send men rushing over the next misty mountain in fevered search of El Dorado.

A new breed of hardcase had begun to sift into Fairplay——deserters and draft dodgers from the Civil War. Most came without funds, skills or any other means of support, and the lawmen knew that men of their cut rode with trouble for a partner. Marshal Catlin was even now petitioning the town fathers for funds to hire additional deputies, whenever the need should arise.

In this summer of 1861, the early months of the terrible war between northern and southern states, that war's hateful, divisive poison had yet to spread to the gold and silver mining fields of the Colorado Territory. Rome feared, however, that the madness would eventually encompass the whole Western frontier. Rome Warfield knew little of the reasons for the conflict or the politics that had spawned it. Something to do with states' rights and the institution of slavery, he thought. Though his home state of Texas had seceded from the Union earlier in the year, to align itself with the Southern cause, Rome knew no one, personally, who kept slaves, and he could not conceive of anyone wanting to *own* another person. Nor could he imagine himself facing old friends and neighbors over the sights of a gun. He was glad that, at least for now, he was removed from the insanity. There was enough of that going on around Fairplay.

Reaching his hat, Rome left the office and walked hesitantly toward the restaurant at the Paragon. He was going to see Janet Tinker. He did not know what he would say, or what he could do, to be of comfort to her, but he knew he must make the effort.

She sat at a table in the corner of the dining room, folding napkins. She looked up as he approached.

Hat in hand, Rome asked, "Okay if I sit down?"

Janet nodded. "Have you caught the man who killed my father?"

Rome pulled out a chair and settled himself next to her.

"No ma'am, not yet. I just wanted you to know...I mean, I just wondered if there was anything you needed? Anything I can do?"

He paused, his eyes cast downward, fingering the brim of his hat.

"I should have come sooner. I didn't know what to say. I felt helpless, and...I guess I didn't want you to think of me that way. I'm sorry."

Janet placed a hand on his arm. "I'm sure I will need your support, Rome, and I thank you for your concern. Will you stand with me...at the funeral?"

"Of course."

Her eyes filled with tears and they fell silent.

Three men entered the double doors from the hotel lobby. They looked around and selected a table near the front window. Janet watched them seat themselves, squeezed Rome's arm and whispered, "I'd better go."

The pressure on his forearm irritated the healing scratch that was there. He winced, then jumped to his feet, the light of revelation in his eyes.

"That's it!"

"What?" Janet asked, startled by his sudden action.

Rome grasped her by the shoulders.

"I know who killed your daddy."

* * *

Rome Warfield rode from town, bound again for the claim of Caleb Tinker. He had not disclosed to Janet or to Marshal Catlin who it was he suspected of the killings. He had told them only that he had a theory, and that he needed to return to the scene of the murder.

Janet wanted to ride with him, but he refused her request, feeling the need to weigh the evidence with no distractions. He had reached an astounding conclusion as to who had murdered four innocent miners in cold blood, and he felt an urgency to bring the killer to justice. Who knew when that killer might strike again?

He forded the river, starting his horse upslope on the rocky trail flanking the crystal cascades of Red Hill Creek. Once free from the crush of the tacky town of Fairplay——with its swarming fortune seekers, ruffians, gamblers and prostitutes, its cacophony of jangling trace chains, tinny piano music, yelping dogs, hammers and saws—tension began to leave him. He fell again under the spell of the pristine wilderness he had come to hold dear. His spirit was replenished by its beauty, and his senses became attuned to the world around him.

Rome did not allow his caution to be dulled by his relish for the country through which he made his way. He was constantly alert to the sights, sounds and movements about him as he rode the forest trail. This state of vigilance was a carefully honed habit of long standing, a practice that had held him in good stead on the Comanche-infested plains of West Texas.

As he cleared the trees and rode into the clearing of the camp on Tinker's placer claim, he was startled to see two strangers bent over the rocker sluice, completely involved in working the sands of the creek. Claim jumpers!

"You gents are trespassing," Rome announced.

The two men jumped in alarm at the sound of his voice. The smaller one slipped and fell, righted himself, then went scrambling toward a rifle leaned against a tree.

"Don't try it."

Warfield's voice was calm, but it halted the claim jumper with the effect of a shouted command. He slumped to the ground and lay there, watching the horseman with round eyes. The other man walked forward, his arms spread wide.

"Mister, we figure these here to be deserted diggin's. Look around you. Ain't been nobody here for days."

"You figure wrong, friend. I'm Deputy Marshal Warfield of Fairplay," he said, flashing the metal on his vest. "This is a filed claim. Man that was working it was murdered. It belongs to his daughter now."

Rome dismounted. He kept his eye on the pair of interlopers as he walked to the rocker. It was blind luck, maybe, but with all their stomping and splashing, they had not disturbed the small footprint he had come to examine. With a satisfied grunt, he turned and retraced the path to his standing horse.

"No harm done, I reckon," Rome told them. "You men move on along, leaving things as you found them, and you'll have no trouble with me."

He bent to retrieve the reins, put his hand to the pommel of his saddle and raised a booted foot to the stirrup. A rustling in the brush behind him spun him around—too late. The barrel of a pistol extending from the heavy foliage spouted orange flame and a thick cloud of gunsmoke.

As Rome Warfield fell wounded, the echo of the shot resounded through the tall, dark trunks of the surrounding trees, repeating itself in his head as blackness engulfed him.

* * *

Rome awoke with a throbbing headache and a searing thirst. His eyelids felt as if they were weighted down with horseshoes. He recognized the fresh smell of line-dried sheets.

"I think he's coming around."

It was the voice of a young woman, sounding as if it were coming from a deep well. Rome forced open his eyes.

Slowly she came into focus. Janet Tinker was bending over him, a frown of concern clouding her face. Rome squinted, making out the figures of Marshal Catlin and his wife, Ruth, behind Janet at the foot of the bed. He was in a bedroom of the Catlin home, then.

"Water." His voice was weak and raspy.

Ruth Catlin reached a milkglass pitcher from a washstand near a curtained window and poured a glass half full of water. She walked to him, placed her palm at the back of his head and helped him to drink.

"More?"

He shook his head. "How'd I get here?"

Sam swung a chair around to the side of the bed near Rome's pillow and straddled it. He put a calloused, gentle hand on his young deputy's shoulder.

"You sure you're up to talkin' about this now? It'll wait."

"I'm sure. How bad was I hit?" Rome pushed himself up on his elbows, propping his back against the heavy headboard.

"Bad enough you been out more than five hours. But you were lucky. The slug entered on the right side of your head and skittered across that granite skull of yours under the scalp, lodging just beneath the skin on the left rear. We plucked it right out.

"Did you see who shot you?"

Rome shook his head and put his fingers to his eyes.

"Naw. He was in heavy brush. How did I get back down here?"

"Across your saddle. Two men hauled you in. They thought you might be dead...you know how scalp wounds will bleed.

"Anyhow, after I told them you weren't bad hurt, they figured they better tell it to me straight. Said how you'd braced them on Tinker's claim and was set to run them off when somebody opened fire from the bushes. By the time they recovered from the surprise and got to their guns, whoever did the shootin' was long gone."

The Marshal paused to fill and light his pipe. Janet moved in and dabbed at Rome's brow with a cool, damp cloth.

"I didn't arrest them," Sam said. "Figured they wouldn't have bothered bringing you home if they weren't square. Names are Abner Peck and Jebidiah Hale. They were broke, so I said they could sleep in an empty cell in the jail until you came around. Told them to stay in town in case you wanted to talk to them."

"Just to tell them 'thank you'," Rome said. "You got that slug?"

Sam reached in his pocket and came out with a small, misshapen lump of lead. He handed it to Rome.

"I thought so," Rome said, turning the slug in his fingers, weighing it. "Hand me my pants."

"Oh, Rome," Janet said, "you can't get up yet. You're hurt."

"Got to. I don't want it on my conscience if the killer should strike again."

"You mean that you found what you went up there for?" Janet asked. "Can you tell us now who killed my father?"

"Yes. Now I can tell you."

4

"I'll go with you, Rome...but I'm not at all sure you are right about this. It's too far-fetched."

"I know it sounds crazy, Sam. That's why it took so long to figure it. All the evidence, all the clues, were commonplace, everyday things. That's why I took no note of them. Come on, I'll show you."

Rome gingerly placed his hat over the thick bandage on his scalp and the lawmen started off down the street to arrest the killer of Caleb Tinker and three others.

* * *

Jessie Colette slipped a .41 caliber two-shot Remington derringer into a pocket in the folds of her skirt and made her way down the side stairs from her quarters above the Golden Egg. She kept close to the deepening shadows as she made her way along the backs of buildings toward the shanty behind the Tenstrike.

Jessie had not been close to Cabiness, Pruitt and Bonner. She had not even particularly liked the crude and devious trio. But they had been allies, and their deaths at the hands of that hideous, insignificant little beggar chafed at her distorted sense of justice.

It was Jessie's intention to go to Tandy's shanty, shoot the little cripple and return to her rooms above the saloon, no one the wiser. The law would not suspect her. She was not that involved in the matter, as far as they knew, and she was a woman. Her simple plan was thwarted, however, when she looked through the window of the darkened shack and found nothing. The beggar was nowhere to be seen.

Jessie turned away with a shrug and headed back to the Golden Egg, her motives strangely satisfied, simply by the effort she had made. She would feel no need to make another attempt on the cripple's life.

As she disappeared into the shadows, Tandy's face

appeared in the window of the shack. He was smiling.

* * *

Sam held the lantern high as Rome rapped at the front door of Martin Tandy's shack. The beggar had not been at his station in front of the Tenstrike, and the lack of response to the knock at the door indicated he was not at home, either. Rome tried the latch. The door swung open under his hand. They entered the dark interior.

Marshal Catlin set the lantern on the cracked and peeling bureau, looking around as the light crept into the corners. A heavy leather contraption atop the unmade cot caught his eye.

"What's that thing?"

"I don't know, Sam. Looks like some special kind of harness, or truss. Douse that lamp and let's wait here a while. Maybe he'll come back."

They waited in the dark, time dragging. Rome could hear Sam's fingers drumming on the bureau top as he peered out the window.

"Quiet now," Rome whispered, "someone's coming."

The latch was lifted and a figure appeared in the open doorway. Marshal Catlin fired the lamp, illuminating the shack.

Martin Tandy was struggling to bring a heavy carpetbag up the ramp and into the house. The glare of the lantern whirled him around and he stood there——on two good legs.

"I was afraid you were going to figure me out," the beggar said, looking at Rome. "How did you know?"

Rome rolled up the left sleeve of his shirt, exposing the long scratch.

"You ought to cut your toenails," Rome said.

Tandy's hand crept to the back of his waist.

"Don't try it, little man." The Russian .44 in Rome's fist accentuated his warning.

Sam walked to the beggar, pulled the pistol from the back of his waistband and told him to hold out his hands. Then he manacled his wrists.

"What's in your valise, here, mister cripple?" the Marshal asked, opening the carpetbag. He let out a long, low whistle.

The bag was filled with greenback dollars in fat bundles tied with string, sacks of gold eagles, pouches of nuggets and dust.

"Seems I've seen that case before," Rome said, "when I arrested Jessie Colette in her quarters." He looked into the cold eyes of the crippled beggar of Fairplay. "Is she dead?"

Tandy smiled. "I doubt she would have allowed me to take it otherwise."

They sat Tandy on the cot while they questioned him. The homicidal beggar talked freely, knowing he was caught red-handed.

He explained that he had been a performer in a traveling circus of which he had been part owner. A fire in a small Missouri town had destroyed the tent and most of the rolling stock, and the show was bankrupt.

Tandy had billed himself as the world's greatest contortionist, a human pretzel. In his pose as a cripple and a beggar, he simply drew his spindly legs up his sides and strapped them in position, knees in his armpits, legs pointed downward with toes to the ground. That was the function of the harness that Sam had wondered about. He was wearing slippers on his feet, of the type acrobats and aerialists wear, which explained the strange footprint the lawmen had seen at Tinker's diggings.

His motive for the murders, of course, was money. Tandy wanted to rebuild his circus, and felt that the gold fields would be easy pickings for a clever thief with a perfect disguise.

"Almost perfect," Rome reminded him.

"Show me what tipped you, Rome," the Marshal said.

Rome pointed to the wall. "See those shelves?"

Sam looked puzzled. "Yeah. Nothing unusual. Just a shelf full of canned goods and such."

"Right. Nothing unusual, and there should have been. No way a man with no legs could reach those foodstuffs, or use that cabinet top, either. There's no stool or chair or ladders around to boost him up.

"And look at this floor. Dusty, and tracked up, like any ordinary cabin that isn't swept regular. But a man with no feet doesn't leave tracks.

"I found tracks on the path out back, too. Clearer ones, same as the one we found at the scene of the crime. There were wheel ruts from his platform. He used it in the daytime when he could be seen, but if he needed to use the privy at night, he just trotted right on out there."

Rome turned to look at Tandy.

"We were seeing normal, everyday signs of living in a setting that should have been abnormal. It didn't register with me until Janet squeezed my arm, and I figured out what had made that scratch——toenails, on a man that had no feet.

"I realized then, too, what that stick figure meant that old Caleb had scratched in the sand. He finished his drawing, leaving the legs off on purpose to point the way here."

Sam took Tandy by the arm, leading him toward the door.

"I'll put this yahoo behind bars. Rome, you better go on down to the Golden Egg and see to Jessie Colette's remains."

"You'll never keep me in a cell," Tandy shouted over his shoulder as the Marshal shoved him through the door.

"You won't be there long, killer," Rome told him, "and even you can't squirm out of a noose."

* * *

Jessie Colette had a daughter in a school back east, in St. Louis, so Rome saw to it that her effects and her fortune were sent to the girl, minus any trappings that might have revealed the woman's occupation.

After she and Rome had visited with Abner Peck and Jebidiah Hale, and had decided that the would-be claim jumpers were good men down on their luck, Janet offered them the opportunity to work her father's claim on equal shares, a three-way split. They eagerly accepted. Rome offered his help, too. He would grubstake the penniless pair as a payment of gratitude for bringing him down the mountain.

Two of the murdered miners, besides Caleb, had kin. Tandy's stash was divided four ways, with the estate of each victim receiving a share. The town of Fairplay claimed the portion of the one man who had no heirs.

* * *

Rome stood at the fresh grave site of Caleb Tinker, his arm around the dead man's daughter. Marshal Catlin, Peck and Hale were in attendance as well. Abel Goodspeed read a passage from the tattered Bible under his nose. Ruth Catlin sang a hymn, a favorite of the deceased, according to Janet. The grave was closed.

Rome turned Janet downhill toward town with a gentle pressure on her arm. She looked into his eyes.

"If I'm to stay here, Rome, I'll need a friend."

He put a strong arm around her shoulders.

"You've got a friend."

THE END

THE SIN OF ELI

By TROY D. SMITH

Robert Darnell had always tried to be a good father. When his only son, Spence, was a child, Darnell had thought he was succeeding at that task. The boy's mother had died in childbirth, and Darnell had been father and mother alike to him. It had been hard, in some ways, but it had been easy in others. Little Spence had his mother Lorene's soft blue eyes and dark hair, and held his chin like her when he laughed. Lorene had been the love and light of Darnell's life. When Lorene's spirit fled to heaven, that love and light was transferred to the son she had given him with her last push of life.

He had doted on the boy. It was easy to do, and hard to avoid. Spence was so much the image of his mother —perhaps he, too, would be as fragile as her. What if the warmth of his smile, like that of his mother's, should blow away one day like dry leaves, leaving nothing behind except the sound of the wind? Robert Darnell could hear that wind every time he looked on his son's face. The pride and joy he felt was tinged by a sadness at the knowledge that the Lord was a Taker as well as a Giver. The pride and the joy and the sadness and the loss mixed so completely together that they all became the same thing, a bittersweet amalgamation which, if forced to put a name to it, Robert Darnell could only call love. At those moments, his heart swelled so great that he felt it would burst, but it never did.

As the years went by, however, Darnell was crowded in by the growing suspicion that he was not a good father after all. Good fathers produce good sons, and any claim to the word "good" seemed to wash out of Spence Darnell with each passing summer. It started when he was small, dominating his classmates and taking whatever he wanted with no regard to rights or propers.

Sometimes Darnell would thrash the boy with a strap, the way all fathers he knew did, but they were half-hearted and infrequent efforts. Darnell could not hold such a strap in his hand without remembering his own pa—a stern, implacable man—and how much, as a boy, he had hated the old man. He could not bear the thought of his own son hating him—of Lorene's sky blue eyes looking at him with tearful reproach—and so his hand wavered, when he raised it at all.

By the time Spence Darnell was seventeen, everyone in the valley knew him as a holy terror. No one was surprised when he shot down an unarmed man in the midst of a robbery—no one except Robert Darnell. The boy had come to him, pale-faced and desperate, begging for money and a fresh horse.

"I have to leave, Pa, or they'll hang me, sure."

"Where to, son?"

"Anywhere."

"When will you come back?"

The boy's face shined wet with tears.

"I can't never come back, Pa. Please, I have to hurry."

Robert Darnell had handed over all his money with numb fingers. He wanted to speak, but his throat constricted and no words could escape. *How can I live without you, boy?* he wanted to say. *Who will I be, if I'm all alone?*

"I'll send word soon as I can, Pa, I promise."

Spence embraced him, if only for a moment. Darnell channeled all his strength into his arms, all his life, pumping it like his heart was a bellows—and then his son was gone. His only son, and all that remained of the sweet woman he had loved. It was like Lorene's ghost withdrew her hand from Darnell's brow and followed behind their son, not even leaving the broken man the comfort of her haunting. He sank to his knees in the dirt and watched Spence ride away.

He was still on his knees when the posse arrived half-an-hour later. They did not even bother asking which direction the boy had gone, for Darnell's anguished face still stared after him, giving them their cue.

"I'm real sorry, Mister Darnell," the sheriff said, and several of his companions mumbled as well. He could feel their pity wash over him—and, beneath that, their contempt.

Robert Darnell was a God fearing man, and he knew that their contempt was deserved. He had sinned. He was like David of old, who refused to visit the full punishment on his son Absalom when he had murdered his own brother. The old king had even tried to spare the youth from harm when he plunged Israel into civil war—and when the rebel was killed in battle, David grieved beyond all comfort.

Oh Absalom, Absalom, my son, my son. Would that I could die for thee, my son.

Even more, Darnell realized as he sat in the dirt, he was like the high priest Eli. That old man's sons were cruel and wicked, stealing from God and abusing their power. Eli lectured them, but did not give them the

punishment they deserved—and so shared in their guilt.
Finally God took action Himself and struck them dead.
When Eli got word, his grief was so powerful that he
fell from his seat and broke his neck.

Some could argue that Eli's swift demise was a
blessing, in a way, for he did not long survive the sons
he loved. But it was not a blessing. A single moment of
knowing your child is dead while you live on—a single
such moment was more profound a torture than all the
fires of hell.

Robert Darnell was spared such a knowledge that
day. Spence avoided the posse, and reached safety. That
had been five years ago. In those five years, Spence
Darnell managed to smuggle two letters home—they
were short, and vague, but the old man treasured them.
Beyond that, the only news of his son came in the
reports of the crimes he had committed.

Until today.

Today the sheriff had arrived with a telegram.
Spence Darnell, the notorious outlaw, had been
captured, tried, and was sentenced to hang in three days
in Wichita.

"I wish we'd have got word on this sooner," the
sheriff said. "You could've had plenty of time to get
there. If you was of a mind to. As it is, there ain't no
train or stage due soon enough."

"I'll get there," Darnell said. "It'll be a hard ride,
but I'll get there. I have to see my son."

The sheriff sighed. "I hope you make it in time."

Darnell did not respond. The sheriff no longer
existed to him. He was walking to the stable to saddle
his horse. The sheriff mounted his own animal and rode
sadly away.

Darnell left his little ranch less than twenty minutes after the sheriff had arrived. He rode his chestnut mare, leading his blue roan—all the horseflesh he owned—with the aim of switching back and forth as each grew tired. Three days' rations were in the saddlebags—there would be no time for hunting. Darnell's Winchester was in the rifle scabbard, and his old Army Colt—well-oiled, caps set—was on his hip.

He rode until it was too dark to see, and made a dry camp. He stared into the darkness for hours, and slept very little. There was a time, not long before, that he would have spent the time in prayer—but God had not made camp with him, he could feel it. God had no approval for what Robert Darnell planned to do—the rancher had cast his lot, once and for all, with his own flesh and blood over his God. This ride would be a journey to Hell. It was a hard choice, at first—not the choosing between God and Spence, but the deciding on whether to go to Heaven to be with his beloved Lorene or to follow their child to the devil. He knew she would understand his sacrifice. She would have the angels for company—Spence would be alone in perdition when he finally got there. Paradise would be no comfort, knowing his son was in the flames of damnation. The trail Robert Darnell rode now would surely take him there, as well.

On the second day he passed a young family on the road. Their wagon wheel had given out on them—the husband had been thrown from his seat and suffered a broken arm. He was gamely trying to fix his wheel with one arm, face white with pain, while his wife swayed back and forth with a screaming infant.

"Thank God you come by, mister," the young

man said—then his mouth slowly fell open in shock as Darnell rode past him without a word.

"For God's sake, we need help!" the injured man cried out.

For God's sake. Any other day Darnell would have stopped to help, but there was no time. It was no longer God's sake that drove him on. Still, his face burned with shame. He half-turned in the saddle.

"I'm real sorry," he told them. "If I pass anybody, I'll send 'em back. But I can't stop." He almost added that he would pray for them—but he knew that, to them, it would seem like adding insult to injury. Besides, his prayers at this point might do a body more harm than good. He rode on, therefore, the injured man's impassioned curses following behind him.

That night he took the time to build a fire and cook up some bacon to go with his cold corn dodgers. It was almost done when his hobbled horses whinnied. Darnell was on his haunches, gloved hand on the handle of the skillet he was just about to draw out of the fire—his head jerked up at once, eyes alert. There'd been no Indian trouble in those parts for years, but it was still not beyond the realm of possibility.

It was no Indian voice that called out to him, though.

"Howdy, friend. That sure smells mighty good."

Two men rode near Darnell's camp and dismounted. They stepped out of the shadows—they were unshaven and trailworn.

"Mind if we warm up by your fire for a little spell, mister?"

"I don't mind," Darnell said. "Y'all can eat this bacon, if you want, I'll make more." He knew this would mean going hungry later, but he could not be inhospitable—especially after leaving the stranded family behind him earlier. That had been in the afternoon, though, and he could not afford to burn any daylight to help them. He was done riding for the night now, and could afford to be a good host.

"If you boys are headed north," he said, "there's a young family up the trail with a broke wagon wheel. Unless somebody else has come along to help 'em, I reckon they're in a bad way. Maybe you can help 'em out, if you come across 'em. I ain't got no plates or nothin', you might want to find somethin' to set this bacon on, it's hot as the dickens."

"Why, that's mighty kind of you, mister," the taller of the two said. He was apparently the leader, he seemed to do all the talking. "Offerin' to share your supper with a couple of total strangers, and worryin' about some poor travelers at the same time. That's plumb Christian."

"I try."

The other man spoke for the first time. "Seems like I remember the Lord said, if somebody was to ask you for your coat, give him your cloak as well."

"I recall that."

"Well," Number Two continued, "it don't seem Christian, you havin' them two fine horses, and you just a useless old man."

Darnell's eyes narrowed. "What are you gettin' at."

The leader's hand dropped to his pistol. In a flash, Darnell tossed the pan of sizzling bacon grease at the leader's face with his left hand, while drawing his own pistol with his right. The leader screamed in agony—his gun had cleared leather, but he dropped it to clasp both hands to his burned face. His partner went for his own gun, but only after a moment of shocked hesitation. Darnell put two bullets into him, and the man's gun flew away as he spun and fell.

The leader was on his knees, feeling in the dirt for his lost weapon. Darnell put a bullet in his forehead, and he dropped like a wet sack.

Darnell stood silent, almost in shock himself, as the smoke curled from the barrel of his Colt. He had never killed a man—not even in the war, that he knew of—and was rather amazed that it had happened so quickly.

The second bandit moaned weakly. Darnell walked over to him. The man managed to roll over onto his back.

"You're—you're just a damned old farmer," he gasped. "We've shot our way through posses. This is crazy." He coughed, and frothy blood bubbled from his mouth.

"Holy God," the man said. "You've kilt me."

"When's the last time you seen your pa, boy."

"What?"

"Your pa. How long since you've seen your pa."

"Hell, I don't know."

"I reckon he loves you, son, even if you're a piece of shit."

"My pa's a ignorant old farmer like you, and a mean son of a bitch. I don't give a damn what he thinks, or you neither."

He coughed again, and moaned in pain. His fingers scratched the dirt as his arm swept up and down, trying desperately to find his own weapon, just as his partner had.

"I'll tell you the same thing I told that family back yonder," Darnell said. "I'm truly sorry, but I ain't got time to fool with you."

He shot the outlaw in the head, and cooked up some more bacon.

* * *

He was almost too late.

The whole town, it seemed, was gathered around the scaffold—and maybe folks from several towns close by. The preacher stood up there, Bible in hand, and a fat middle-aged man whose badge glinted in the afternoon sun.

There was only one other figure on the scaffold. A sack had been pulled over his head, and the noose was fitted around his neck. Robert Darnell did not need to see a face to recognize his only son. He dropped the lead rope of the chestnut which trailed behind him and spurred the flanks of the roan. He galloped straight into the gathered crowd. People scrambled out of his way to avoid being trampled—and trample them he would have. He reined in near the base of the structure and hopped out of the saddle. Two rangy men with rifles, deputies, stepped toward him.

"Spence!" he yelled up. "I'm here, Spence!"

"Pa!" the outlaw called back, his voice muffled by the sack. "Is that you, Pa?"

"It's me! I'm with you, son! I'm with you."

The sheriff looked flustered.

"I reckon it's Providence you made it here in time, mister," the sheriff said. "But we can't delay this none."

It was in that moment, while the deputies' eyes were on their speaking boss, that Robert Darnell put his desperate plan into action. The Army Colt seemed to leap into his hand, just as it had with the horse thieves—Darnell had never known, or even dreamed, that he was especially fast with a gun. He shot down both of the deputies in almost the same instant. Men shouted all around him, and women screamed. Darnell looked all around, desperate, scanning the crowd for more deputies. Hoping for them.

"Nobody expected this crazy old man to show up to rescue Spence Darnell from the gallows," folks said afterward. "That was a bold plan."

But they were mistaken. Such was not Robert Darnell's plan, and never had been. His first goal had been merely to lay eyes on his beloved son, to hear his voice one more time in this world. As for the rest of his plan—he had expected far more resistance, and a far better prepared constabulary. Like the horse thieves, they had not expected such deadly and efficient action from the frail-looking rancher. He had killed the two men almost before he himself had realized it, and before he realized there were no more deputies in sight.

Once he started shooting, Robert Darnell expected to be cut down by a hail of bullets. In fact, he had planned on it. His goal was two-fold—to see his living son, and never to spend a single instant knowing that son was dead. One such instant would be worse than an eternity in Hell—and he was willing to trade that eternity for avoiding the instant.

But no bullets came.

The sheriff, rather than drawing his own gun,

stepped toward the lever which would open eternity beneath Spence's feet. Robert Darnell emptied his revolver rapidly into the lawman's large gut—the sheriff had reached the lever, though, and as he fell it went down with him. Spence dropped, then bounced at the end of the rope with a horrible snap.

"No!"

The snap signified not only the breaking of Spence Darnell's neck, but of his father's heart and soul. He sank to his knees in the dust—they were too weak to support the weight that was upon him. Rough hands grabbed at him and threw him to the ground. He was smothered by the weight of bodies. The townspeople had found their courage when Darnell ran out of bullets.

In the back of his mind he was dimly aware that he would be locked away until such time as a noose would be fitted for him. His own body would take the drop, and dance though it might, the soul would be ripped from it and continue its plummet straight into Hell, and to his son.

But it did not matter. He had not been spared. All the soothing flames of Hell could not strip away the awful pain of knowing that his son was dead before him. Like Eli, he could not escape God's punishment for his sin—not even by fleeing to the devil.

The bodies of his attackers bore ever harder upon him, until he could scarcely breathe.

My son.

My son. Would that I could die for thee, my son. My son.

END

PLANTIN' SEASON

by JOHNNY BOGGS

Far as we could tell, the two dead men had nothin' in common, not at first, no how. Strangers they was, to us and themselves, when they sat down inside Jess Leach's bucket of blood and commenced playin' poker. If they introduced themselves, Jess never heard 'em, and he didn't ask nothin' hisself because Jess is a polite sort of fellow. So forty minutes and too much forty-rod later, them two strangers pulled out their six-shooters and blasted one another to Kingdom Come.

Now, truth be told, things like that happened with some frequency on Willow Creek each spring, when folks started comin' back to the mountains to work their claims. Most miners and townfolk knowed better than to winter in this country, no sir. They'd head south, spend their earnin's, then come back when the snow began meltin' to make their piles again. You see, miners, and the parasites that follow 'em, tend to be like rattlers. When they come out of hibernation, their tempers are short-fused and hard.

Jess called it Plantin' Season, and, come every spring, we planted many a man up on the ridge overlookin' our town of canvas tents and rawhide log affairs like Jess Leach's saloon.

The spring I tell about, however, proved to be a mite different only 'cause, like I done said, Jess Leach is a polite fellow, and a man of his word, unlike most beer-jerkers who work gold towns. Which brings me to the two dead strangers at Jess's Mayflower Saloon. The shootin' didn't last long. Seldom do. The fellow with the handlebar mustache, he expired immediately, but the other gent, the one in the black broadcloth and high-topped boots with pretty crescent moon inlays, he lasted a few moments, chokin' on his blood and the thick white smoke that clouded the insides of Jess's place the way it always done durin' Plantin' Season.

"I'm kilt," the man told Jess. "Don't bury me in some unknown grave."

Problem was, he joined the fellow with that well-groomed mustache before he could tell Jess exactly what his name was, so there they lay amongst the sawdust and blood, with Jess just a-squattin' there and scratchin' his beard when I come upon the scene after hearin' the shots and enterin' the Mayflower to investigate.

First thing I done was hold a coroner's inquest, not that we had a coroner or nothin', but we was tryin' to be as legal as we could in the Territory. I brung in six good citizens for my jury, had Doc Towner examine the two dead men, which we placed up on Jess's two billiard tables -- shipped all the way from St. Louis by way of Santa Fe -- and then got down to business.

The only witness to the shootin' in question was Jess, and he told Doc, me and the jury that he really hadn't seen nothin', busy as he was behind the bar waterin' down the latest batch of whiskey, when he heard the first gunshot. Then a misfire. Then several more shots. When the ruction ceased, he took a cautious peek over the top of his bar and seen that the two men had shot each other down.

Next, Doc Towner identified the two pistols found on the floor, a Starr revolver with four shots fired and one failed percussion cap, and a Navy Colt with two rounds spent. The Starr allegedly belonged to the man with the fancy mustache, and, accordin' to Doc's testimony, rounds had struck the gent with the nice boots twice in the chest while another ball must have taken off the man's left index finger. That victim had placed two rounds in the throat of the man sportin' the tonsorial masterpiece.

"Some shootin'," Clay Bakker, one of my jurors, commented.

"Scratch shot," Ben Tiedeman argued.

"Have you ever seen either of the men in question?" I asked.

"No," Jess said. "Don't recognize 'em from last fall or nothin'. They was strangers."

"How about you, Doc?"

"Can't say I've seen either man before. Probably both of them came in to set up a game."

I told Doc I couldn't allow such testimony as it was speculation, and instructed the jurors to ignore what Doc Towner had just said.

"I never listen to that old goat no how," Ben Tiedeman commented, and I had to threaten Ben with contempt of court before askin' Ben and Clay and Zeke Newton, Baz Salazar, Mountain Gallagher and Placer Bill, my jurors, to file by Jess's billiard tables and see if they had ever seen either of the late arrivals to Willow Creek.

None of 'em had.

Thus I made my rulin', which I would send on down to the Capital, that on Tuesday the 13th inst., two men, unknown in these parts, rode into the Willow Creek minin' camp and entered the Mayflower Saloon at approximately the same time, and approximately forty minutes after their arrival, for reasons unknown, with pistols then and there loaded and charged with gunpowder and leaden balls did then and there put said pistols in their hands and then and there unlawfully feloniously and of their malice aforethought did shoot off and discharge at one another into their own bodies aforesaid leaden balls out of aforesaid revolvers by force of the aforesaid gunpowder and fall onto the floor of the aforesaid Mayflower Saloon, owned by Mr. Jess Leach, in the aforesaid settlement on Willow Creek in this Territory, and thusly then and there expire of mortal wounds inflicted upon themselves.

"That's all settled," I said, and asked Jess to pour us all a drink that we would bill to the Capital. We'd plant the two boys, and also invoice the Capital for our services, divide up their money and wares, and be done with the matter.

"Well, there's one other thing." Jess went and told me about the fellow with the fancy boots and his wish to have his handle on his marker.

"He didn't tell you his name?" I asked.

"No. He just died."

Now, me, I was a mite thirsty, but Placer Bill began claimin' that a man should be remembered and it really weren't fittin' to have some crooked cross over one for all of eternity without a name or nothin' on it to remember him by. And I told Placer Bill that it really didn't matter because if he rode up to the cemetery he would be hard-pressed to find the names of anyone that we planted last Plantin' Season 'cause winters and the like is hard on graves.

Which worked Zeke Newton into a snit 'cause he had burnt the names of the dead, at least the names we knowed, onto the crosses and pine plank markers with his runnin' iron. "If somebody wants to be remembered, let him buy hisself a marble monument and have it shipped up from Santa Fe," Zeke said.

"No one's blamin' you, Zeke," I said, and told my herd to get itself in line, that all we had to do was learn the name of the man with the handsome mustache.

"No," Jess said, "he didn't say nothin'. It was this fellow here who wanted to be remembered."

Thusly, I began to go through the man's broadcloth coat, but while I was findin' not much of nothin' except a box of Lucifers, pipe tobacco and L.I. Cohen playin' cards, Baz Salazar said we should not forget the man with the mustache, neither, that he had a right to be remembered at least till next Plantin' Season. I muttered an oath, my throat awful parched, but Doc Towner agreed and then and there searched for some identification on the other expired stranger.

Still, all Doc turned up was a Barlow knife, plug tobacco and yet another box of L.I. Cohen cards.

"See," Doc said all haughtily. "I told you they were both here to gamble. Why else would they have extra decks of cards?"

Well, I was some frustrated because I recollected that durin' the Plantin' Season of '70, we come across a stranger who got caught in a flash flood but at least he had a letter that had been posted to him from his sister in Bowlin' Green, Kentucky, as the writin' on the letter wasn't too washed out and faded, so we knowed his name even if Zeke Newton didn't burn it on his cross with a runnin' iron as the drowned man had not made no such dyin' request.

Upon Clay Bakker's suggestion -- "Let's check their horses!" -- we all piled outside. One horse was a bay gelding, the other a buckskin mare, but we turned up no form of names, even when we unsaddled the two mounts and looked to see if per chance a name might have been carved on the underside of their saddles.

Nothin'.

By jacks, the horses didn't even carry brands none of us had ever recognized before.

"Well," I said. "Let's have ourselves a whiskey and think on this matter."

Thusly, at last, I slaked my thirst, and we leaned against the bar and studied on our predicament.

"Maybe we should call one man Mister Starr and the other man Mister Navy," Ben Tiedeman allowed as he fingered the revolvers that had belonged to the recently deceased strangers in question.

"No," Jess said. "That ain't right."

"I wonder," Baz Salazar said, "how come they killed each other."

"Maybe it was over a woman," said Mountain Gallagher.

"Maybe one was on the dodge," Zeke Newton guessed.

"No, then how come they would sit down to play poker together if one was a-chasin' tuther?" said Clay Bakker.

"Who plays two-handed poker anyhow?" asked Placer Bill.

"Gamblers!" Doc Towner shouted. "I tell you they were gamblers."

About that time I finally noticed that durin' all that shootin', the table where they was playin' that final game of cards had remained undisturbed. One chair had been overturned, and Clay Bakker had borrowed the other so he could sit down while he was servin' on my jury, but even the money remained in the pot, exceptin' the gold piece I had procured while nobody was lookin'.

Curious, I ambled over to that table again, and looked at the deck, the top card, a jack of diamonds, splattered with blood. I counted and examined the money in the pot, yellowbacks and greenbacks and some coin, but nothin' that could identify either Fancy Boots or Fancy Mustache. And then I studied the cards, the hand each man held at the time of his demise.

Suddenly, I laughed, and announced I had learnt the names of both men and we could proceed with the plantin' at the cemetery atop the ridge. Everyone got all excited, except Zeke Newton, who frowned when I told him I had no need of his runnin' iron for this plantin'. Instead, I fetched tacks and a ball-peen hammer from the shed next to Jess's waterin' hole as we hauled off the two men to their final restin' place.

Not only that, I now knowed why they had shot each other so I could change my official report, even if I wasn't quite sure which stranger had really been the cause of it all. Mayhap both of 'em.

Jess Leach, he got all upset upon learnin' what I was up to, but I told him I was the closest thing to a judge and there wasn't much point to argue on the matter no longer as Fancy Boots and Fancy Mustache would get ripe if we kept dickerin' over picayune matters.

Baz Salazar nailed a couple of crosses while Clay Bakker, Ben Tiedeman, Placer Bill and Mountain Gallagher dug the graves. We wrapped Fancy Mustache in his sugans and tossed him into the pit, and covered Fancy Boots in his saddle blanket and dropped him next door.

Doc Towner thought I was right on the mark, but Jess Leach said I wasn't so blasted funny. On Fancy Boots's cross, I took out hammer and tacks and fastened to his grave marker his poker hand:

Ace of hearts
Ace of clubs
Ace of spades
King of clubs
King of diamonds
On Fancy Mustache's grave, I nailed up:
Ace of clubs
Ace of spades
Ace of diamonds
King of spades
King of hearts

Jess didn't speak to me for a month, but then he accepted how I had fulfilled the dyin' stranger's request as best we could. Fancy Boots was remembered, and so, for that matter, was Fancy Mustache. By grab, folks at Willow Creek come up to the cemetery just to look at them two graves and laugh at how they both most likely was cheatin' at cards and killed each other. For certain sure, them two was the tourist attraction that Plantin' Season, I mean to tell you.

Naturally, it didn't last. A raven must have made off with Fancy Mustache's ace of spades, and a late blue norther blowed in come May and took down every single king except Fancy Boots's diamond. In mid-October, I headed south, and by the time I rode back north next April, not only had all the cards disappeared, but so had the crosses Baz Salazar had fixed -- just like I had done told Placer Bill -- blowed down by the wind and washed away with the snowmelt, I reckon.

That made Jess Leach a mite sad, but he cheered up real soon because it was Plantin' Season again, and that was the year we lynched Ben Tiedeman, and ol' Ben's tombstone became the popular tourist attraction in Willow Creek as Zeke Newton had burned on that piece of warped pine with his runnin' iron.

Here Lies
Ben Tiedeman
Hanged By Mistake

Some kid, we think it was Little Jimmy Roripaugh, later wrote underneath that, "The joke's on us."

Jess Leach didn't find that funny, neither, but he's gettin' over it this Plantin' Season, which is when I take pencil in hand in the Mayflower Saloon to record these recollections.

You see, I reckon this'll be the last Plantin' Season at Willow Creek 'cause the claims have all played out and there ain't hardly a body comin' here this year, exceptin' cowmen, while most miners and merchants be optin' for the diggin's up in Summit County. Won't nobody remember the two card cheaters, not even Ben Tiedeman, a few months from now, but we'll have ourselves one more fine Plantin' Season the way I hear some cowmen talk inside Jess Leach's bucket of blood.

If I was a bettin' man, I'd lay good money down that we'll be plantin' Zeke Newton 'fore long. That fellow is a mite too handy with a runnin' iron.

END

BLACKWELL'S RUN
By Troy D. Smith

Dakota Territory, 1864

Max Blackwell's heart was pumping furiously, reminding the cavalry sergeant that he was still alive—and of what a sweet treasure life itself could be. He ran, though each tortured breath felt like he was drawing live coals into his lungs. His feet were raw and bloody. The sun had blistered his naked body, and sweat flowed iron his black beard like rain. Still he ran.

Behind him he heard the ragged gasps of Byrd and Siemanski—Blackwell knew that the privates were as bad off as himself. Occasionally he heard Byrd's footsteps pause. Blackwell knew that the young man was looking over his shoulder, trying to spot the Sioux.

It was a futile effort, and wasted time which was better spent running. Blackwell knew that the renegades were back there. They would show themselves when they were ready, and not before. Siemanski whimpered. Once Blackwell would have sneered at the youth's fear, but no more. The sergeant had seen the atrocities that their pursuers were capable of—seen them over and over again during the past several days—and it was all he could do not to whimper himself.

It was hard to believe that all Blackwell's troubles were ultimately due to one arrogant lieutenant. For the thousandth time, the pompous face of Joe Jacobs rose before the sergeant's eyes like a heat mirage. Blackwell laughed aloud at the irony of the whole thing. His comrades must have taken the laugh as a sign of slipping sanity. Perhaps they were right.

It was on these same grassy plains that Company G had suffered its crucible two years earlier. It was supposed to have been a routine patrol—the beginning of the fresh-faced lieutenant's first command. Jacobs had not been content with a routine patrol; where was the glory in that?

Lieutenant Jacobs had a very influential father. The elder Jacobs had foreseen the war brewing between the states, and did not wish the sole heir of his business to be slain by some ignorant Southerner. Young Joe's beloved godfather just happened to be Colonel B.F. Skelly, commandant of Fort Bryce; it was a simple matter to ship young Lieutenant Jacobs out West to the Great Plains, where the hostiles had been quiet for several years.

Lieutenant Jacobs was not completely pleased with the arrangement. Like most young men—perhaps more than most—he hungered for adventure and accolades. Neither was to be found at a post like Fort Bryce. Jacobs made that fact known to his subordinate

Blackwell. He made it known immediately, repeatedly, and to the point of irritation.

Blackwell could understand the lad's frustration, to a point, although Blackwell's own thirty-odd years had taught him a few lessons about glory. The troubles which had escalated into conflict back East, however, were causing the sergeant some anxiety. Blackwell's youngest brother had joined the Union infantry, while his other brother was now a Confederate cavalryman in Tennessee. A third brother was a peace officer in Colorado, and was sitting the war out.

The forces which were doing the fighting were made up of volunteers. The regular army, which numbered only a few thousand, had remained for the most part at its frontier postings, at least in the beginning. That was fine with Blackwell. He would rather fight Indians than his own countrymen.

Jacobs made it clear that it was not all right with him. None of the troopers in Company C had any idea just how desperate their new officer was for glory until that first—and only—patrol.

Jacobs had insisted that the little group go deeper and deeper into hostile territory. The toughened veterans of the company began to murmur. They looked to Max Blackwell to handle the situation.

"Beggin' the lieutenant's pardon," Blackwell had said to the young man, "but this is a patrol. We ain't supposed to leave our own territory."

Jacobs brushed an imagined speck of dust from his prized deerskin jacket. He had bought the garment in St.Louis because he wanted to look like a Westerner; it was the only breach of regulations he had ever allowed himself, before that day.

"I am perfectly aware of the meaning of the word 'patrol', sergeant."

Blackwell nodded, but still stared hard at the young man riding beside him. Jacobs flinched a little at the scrutiny, and a little of his aloof composure faded.

"Is there something else, sergeant?"

"Yes, as a matter of fact there is, sir. At this rate we're going to wind up surrounded by Indians. They're going to be stirred up like a bunch of yellowjackets, lookin' for somebody to sting."

Jacobs chuckled. "The entire Sioux nation is no match for a handful of good American soldiers. Once we've bloodied a few of them, the savages will run before us like whipped dogs."

Blackwell had sighed then. This one was worse than he had expected. "There've been quite a few men to talk that way," he said. "They had short, very unpleasant lives."

The lieutenant nodded in deference to Blackwell's point. "I have heard the stories, sergeant. But it will not turn out that way for me, I assure you."

Blackwell scowled openly. "Exactly what is it that makes you so different, sir?"

Jacobs looked around, as if conspiring, and nudged his own horse nearer to the sergeant's. He beckoned Blackwell to bend closer.

"I had a dream," Jacobs whispered.

"What kind of dream?" Blackwell said uncertainly.

Jacobs looked down—the sergeant believed that the youth was blushing. "I was sweeping through the plains on a black charger," the lieutenant said. His words were halting at first, but then they rushed out like a dam had burst in his mind. "My hat was blown off, and the wind whipped through my hair. The fringes on my jacket danced like flames. The savages bowed before me in submission, conquered, and the troopers…"

Jacobs cut his sentence short, embarrassed.

"What about the troopers, lieutenant?"

Jacobs looked up, his face neutral. "The troopers bowed down before me, too—groveling like dogs."

Blackwell had found the young officer irritating before, but from that moment he regarded Jacobs as not just arrogant, but perhaps demented as well. There was a strange look in the youth's eyes as he recounted the dream, as if his brain smoldered from some long-dampened fire. Like an obstructed flue, he showed signs of buckling.

"We all have strange dreams from time to time," Blackwell said, unconsciously drawing away. "This land brings 'em out in us, for some reason. There ain't nothin' to 'em—no need to let 'em upset us. There's enough real-life dangers around to do that."

"Oh no," the lieutenant said sincerely. "I'm not worried, not at all. Excited, I suppose—I have an odd feeling in my spirit. It is a conviction. I believe that I have received a vision from Providence; I am destined for glory. I have always suspected it, but now I have a sign as proof." He reached over and placed a hand on the sergeant's shoulder. The hand's grip was more powerful than Blackwell would have imagined—he was forced to suppress a shudder.

"We are all of us destined for glory," Jacobs had said then, almost whispering.

Then the lieutenant spurred his chestnut mare forward, anxious to intercept his destiny. Blackwell was left alone with his thoughts—they were disconnected and confused. In all his years on the Plains he had never been confronted with such a problem. Blackwell had known many brash officers. He had also known some fools; but this was his first experience with a true madman as a commander.

They made camp that night in fretful silence. Each rustle of the wind through the grass was mistaken by someone as an approaching Indian. The men stole furtive glances at Jacobs—they were baleful glances, full of anger. The lieutenant was oblivious to them.

Privates Ledbetter and Shyer, a pair of leathery veterans, sat beside Max Blackwell.

"Did you talk to him?" Shyer whispered. "What is he up to?"

Blackwell shook his head and stared sorrowfully at the lieutenant, who sat a few yards away. Jacobs noticed the attention. He smiled and nodded to his subordinate.

"He's crazy," Blackwell whispered.

"You can say that again," Ledbetter agreed. "I ain't never met no dern fool crazy enough to go traipsin' through the Sioux nation with no twenty men before."

"No, you don't understand," the sergeant said. "I don't mean he's stupid. I mean he's flat out *crazy* -a lunatic."

The privates stared at him, puzzled. "I don't foller ya, Sarge," Ledbetter said.

Blackwell leaned toward them. "He's doin' all this on account of a dream. He believes that God is tellin' him to take on the whole tribe at once." Blackwell related the lieutenant's vision.

Shyer showed his appreciation of their dangerous position by releasing a low whistle. Ledbetter unleashed a string of expletives.

"With somebody like that takin' the lead," Shyer said, "we don't have a chance in the world of ever gettin' back alive. How'd could a fella as moony as him ever get a commission?"

Blackwell shrugged. "His daddy bought him one, I reckon."

Ledbetter was less concerned with military propriety than with his own pride. "I sure as heck ain't gravelin' before that jackass," he said.

"Groveling," Blackwell corrected him. He was ignored.

"I might have to take orders from these green dudes," Ledbetter continued, "but I don't have to bow and scrape to 'em."

Ledbetter and Shyer wandered oft to bed down. They harbored no illusions about finding sleep easily. Jacobs walked past Blackwell; he smiled at the sergeant.

"The dawn will bring glory," he said. Then he lay down, and soon was submerged in a welcome dream. Blackwell was able to sleep eventually, but was tormented all night by the gruesome images conjured up in his own disordered mind.

As it turned out, Jacobs' words to Blackwell that night were indeed prophetic. Within minutes after the sun's rising, the camp was besieged by furious Sioux warriors. Arrows filled the sky like flocks of blackbirds, and the morning was filled with gunfire and the screams of the dying on both sides.

Blackwell was on one knee, firing his revolver at the painted faces. Gunsmoke swirled around before the sergeant—the Indians seemed to float out of it like the specters of his own nightmares.

Jacobs laughed like a schoolboy whose team was winning a tug-of-war. Waving his saber and firing his own pistol, he waded into the enemy as if he were welcoming them. The lieutenant fought with a savage fury such as Blackwell had never seen before, unless it was a few of the exceptional Indians he had encountered.

The bloody episode was over in less than half an hour. The Indians retreated, carrying their dead; the cavalrymen remained, less than half their original number. Jacobs and Blackwell were unharmed, as were Ledbetter, Shyer, and Brown. Troopers Franz and Trusty had minor wounds. Two others, Vaughan and Dial, were too badly hurt to ride. Some of the horses had been scattered.

"You've had your taste of glory, Lieutenant," Blackwell said. He had wanted his words to sound bitter, but he did not have the energy.

"I don't understand," Jacobs said. "It wasn't supposed to be..." His voice trailed off.

Blackwell waved his arm at the eleven dead soldiers who lay in the reddened grass. "These men are stretched out before you, all right," he said. "But they're not groveling. They're dead."

Jacobs nodded. "We need to get moving."

"Wait just a minute!" Ledbetter said. "Them two fellers can't be moved yet!"

"Then leave them, soldier. They'll die soon anyway. We have to pursue those hostiles."

"Pursue 'em?" Brown said, his eyes widened. "Chase 'em back to their village—by ourselves?"

"That's right," Jacobs said. The glint had returned to his eye.

"What we need to do," Shyer said, "is rig up a couple of travois to drag these hurt boys home."

"You can forget about Vaughan," Blackwell said. "He's dead."

The sergeant was kneeling beside the two casualties. At Blackwell's words, Dial started making a funny noise deep in his throat. A tomahawk had opened the lad's chest up like a crab shell, and a pink froth bubbled from his lips. In his fear, Dial's eyes bulged out so far that his face resembled a fleshless skull, and he spit up little pieces of lung.

Jacobs stared at the boy. "We'll wait here, then, until he dies."

Dial whimpered.

Blackwell stood up. "We'd best saddle up and beat a path back to Fort Bryce, Lieutenant. Those Sioux rode off to round up their cousins. They'll be back with 'em soon, and if we're still here they'll run over us like locusts."

"Good," Jacobs said, smiling. "Perhaps this little setback is God's will, after all."

Ledbetter motioned to Blackwell. "Say Sarge," the man said,"hadn't we ought to scout around a little?"

Blackwell nodded. "That'd be the wise thing to do." He walked to his horse. "Excuse me, Lieutenant." The words burned in his throat.

The two veterans rode out about fifty yards, eyes sweeping through the grass. Both men knew that a Sioux warrior bent on destruction did not need much of a hiding place.

Ledbetter sighed. "We're gonna have to kill that ignorant fool, Max, you know that."

Blackwell shook his head. "That's mutiny. I don't want my hair decorating some tipi, but I don't want to get involved with any mutiny either."

"I think the others will go along."

Blackwell laughed. "The United Stated Army is not a democracy, Ledbetter. You must have us confused with the United States of America."

Tears of rage welled up in Ledbetter's eyes. "You seen how he talked about poor Dial, right in front of him! He don't care a whit what happens to any of us, so long as he can chase after that crazy vision of his! And if you want to get all military, just remember that he's disobeying direct orders his own self, just by leadin' us out here."

"I'll have to think about it," BLackwell said, which was a lie. There was no need to think. The sergeant knew the answer, and all his training rebelled at it.

"All right, Max," Ledbetter said. "You think about it. But while you're thinkin', you're liable to be pickin' arrers out of your backside. Just remember that."

They rode back to the others. Jacobs stood over Dial, watching like a carrion bird. The grass all around the boy was red, whereas the soldier's face was white as chalk.

"He's gone now," Jacobs said. "Let's mount up."

Blackwell did not look at the young trooper's body. He turned his back on the bloody scene, patting his chestnut mare as she nuzzled him. She was used to gun-fire, but the nearness of the blood had upset her. They comforted one another in silence.

The company was very fortunate, Blackwell knew, that all of the horses had not been scattered. The sergeant looked over the little herd once again to make absolutely sure there would be enough mounts for them all. Ten chestnuts remained—Jacobs had insisted on matching horses for his command.

The lieutenant had climbed into his saddle. He straightened his fringed jacket and nodded. "We're losing ground," he said.

"We ain't just leavin', are we?" said Franz. "All these men still need to be buried."

"Let the dead bury their dead, and follow me."

Franz's finger tightened on his arm wound. "I ain't leavin' my friends for the buzzards to pick at. Sir."

There was a loud click—it was so unexpected that it took Blackwell a moment to recognize where it had originated. Lieutenant Jacobs had drawn his revolver, pointed it at Trooper Franz, and cocked it.

"I grow weary of all this insubordination," he said in a cold tone. "None of you are indispensable. You'll all do as I say when I say it, or I will blow your brains out. Now come on."

Jacobs trotted away, and the men stared at him uncertainly. Then they followed, each one ashamed of his inaction.

Company C—the third of it which remained—rode in silence for several hours. The only noise other than the horses came from Lieutenant Jacobs; he whistled sternly as they drew closer to the enemy.

"Won't be long now, lads," he said. "We'll strike a blow for white men everywhere."

Ledbetter cast a vicious glance at Blackwell, shaking his head. Blackwell understood the implied message: act soon, or we will rebel against you as well. Max Blackwell breathed deeply. He had made his decision.

"Hold up, Lieutenant," he said, inwardly cursing himself. "Look at those tracks." Blackwell pointed at the grass.

"What tracks?" Jacobs said. "I don't see anything."

"Look closer." Blackwell dismounted and knelt in the grass. Jacobs hopped to the ground.

"They've cut to the south," the sergeant said. "They may be trying to flank us." Blackwell glanced up, meeting the approving eyes of Ledbetter and Shyer.

Jacobs stared over his subordinate's shoulder. Blackwell moved back, and when the lieutenant leaned over Blackwell jerked the man's pistol out of its holster. He pointed it at Jacobs.

"So," the lieutenant said, smiling. "Brutus has shown his colors at last."

"You have to be stopped," Blackwell said. "I can't let you kill these other men too."

"If I am not mistaken, Sergeant, the only people who have killed any U.S. soldiers here are the filthy savages. That will have changed, of course, if you kill me."

"Put your hands up, sir," Blackwell warned. He did not want the man reaching for his saber.

"You can not stop God's will, Sergeant. Like Lucifer, you can only succeed in delaying it. And then you will be cast into hell."

The other soldiers were also on the ground now, clustered behind their sergeant. Ledbetter aimed his carbine at Jacobs.

"If we're cast into hell, you lunatic," he snarled, "you'll be there waitin' for us."

"Put that gun down," Blackwell said.

Ledbetter whirled on him. "Are you crazy too, Sergeant? Or do you just want the privilege for yourself?"

Ledbetter had jammed the weapon into Blackwell's face; he could smell the gun's oil. "We're not going to murder anybody," Blackwell said. "Much as they might deserve it, we don't have the right."

"The right?" Shyer said. "This idiot Jacobs is the commandant's lapdog! He'll get a slap on the wrist and we'll get hanged for forcin' him to come back."

"What do you think will happen if they ever find out you murdered him?"

"Who would tell them, Sarge?" Franz said. "You? You'd swing just as high as us."

"We're not going to commit murder," Blackwell repeated.

Ledbetter's desperate face sneered at him over the gun barrel. "Don't make us kill you too, Max."

Blackwell did not move. Jacobs laughed. "Well, Sergeant, it looks like our little mob doesn't care for your way of doing things, either."

"Shut up, Jacobs," Shyer said. "We're talkin' to a man."

"I have another idea," Blackwell said, still looking at Ledbetter without acknowledging the carbine. "A compromise."

"Go on," Ledbetter said. "It'd better be good, though."

"Let's leave him here."

Ledbetter laughed. "What good would that do?"

"Leave him here alone," Blackwell continued. "No horse, no weapons—set him adrift, like they did with the old tyrannical sea captains."

Ledbetter shook his head, unconvinced. Brown, however, was smiling.

"It's perfect," Brown said. "If we head for Fort Bryce now, we might make it if we're lucky. There's no way a man on foot—in the middle of Indian territory—could do the same. That way we wouldn't be killing him, the Indians would."

Shyer had begun to brighten to the idea as well. "It's what he wanted, anyway. The lieutenant wants Indians, hell, let's give 'em to him."

Ledbetter lowered the gun. Blackwell exhaled softly, hoping no one noticed. Images of Bess and two-year-old Max Junior still floated before his eyes, as well as the foggy image of the second child which was on its way. He had not thought about his family during the

Indian attack—there was not enough time—but the cold gun barrel had been a more immediate threat.

"You're smarter than I thought, Max," Ledbetter said. "This way everybody is happy. Even the Indians." The private laughed.

Jacobs blanched a little at Ledbetter's remark. The lieutenant had reason to be afraid, Blackwell knew. It would be a kinder act to kill the man now than to let the Indians have him. Unfortunately for them both, Blackwell was not able to do that.

"Give me that pig-sticker, boy," Trooper Trusty said as he took the lieutenant's saber. He then slapped his commander. "We'll take that fancy jacket, too." Jacobs peeled off his coat and handed it over, the private's red hand-print on his face.

Trusty held the jacket, grinning as he felt the soft material. He turned around—out of the corner of his eye he saw a fist approaching. He was flat on the ground before he realized that his attacker had been Blackwell.

"That's for striking an officer," he said, scooping up the jacket and tossing it to its owner.

Jacobs let the coat fall, making no effort to catch it. "I don't want anything that you scum have touched."

"We'd better be gettin' out of here, Max," Ledbetter said as he climbed onto his horse. "Them Sioux could be back any minute."

Blackwell stared sadly at his commander. Jacobs was defiant.

"You heard your friend," Jacobs said. "Go! But you can't outrun the wrath of God. You will all burn in hell, but before you do you will bow to me!"

The lieutenant stumbled forward, yelling at his men as they rode away. He raised a fist at then.

"My vision has spoken—mortal men can't change that! It will come true, you'll see! I'll be back!"

Blackwell winced at the madman's shouts. He could almost feel the hatred being hurled at his back.

"I am Chosen! Chosen for glory, you jackals—I will see you all beg!"

Jacobs alternated between angry shouts and laughter. Blackwell ignored all of it, his mind focused on reaching the safety of the fort.

Colonel Skelly had raised a lot of difficult questions, but the six survivors of Company C had managed to provide answers. Other patrols were sent out to retrieve the bodies for burial. All of the casualties were accounted for except Lieutenant Joe Jacobs— nothing was found of him except his prized jacket. It was believed that when the young officer was separated from his command—how or why the men did not profess to know—he had found himself pursued by Indians. He must have cast away the garment in his flight, Colonel Skelly decided. It was odd that the braves did not take it, but then Indians are an odd lot anyway. The fringed jacket was buried in Lieutenant Jacobs' stead, with full honors. Much speculation was made around the fort about what manner of grisly death the young man might have suffered.

Sergeant Blackwell was sometimes awakened by nightmares in which the mad officer was being flayed alive by Indians. His terrified eyes stared at Blackwell in accusation.

Even the dreams subsided in time, however, and life returned to normal. Blackwell's second son was born—Billy—and Company C was reinforced. The new Lieutenant was green and foolish at times, but a great improvement over Jacobs. Private Brown was mustered out and returned home to Indiana. Franz was killed in an accident; he was killed by a raw recruit who had never even touched a gun before, let alone tried to clean one. Ledbetter was made a corporal again—the old veteran had been a corporal three times and a sergeant twice. His vile temper had always kept him from holding any responsibility for long.

Company C continued to patrol the plains around Fort Bryce; in fact, their patrols became more frequent as the months went by. The Indian tribes were taking advantage of the undermanned forts and the fact that many of the able-bodied locals had gone back East to fight in the white man's war, leaving homes and herds with less protection.

The company found itself attacked by renegades more than three times its number. The new lieutenant had disregarded the advice of his enlisted men—as new lieutenants are wont to do—and they had all paid the price for it.

The renegades were well-armed, and smothered the troopers with their numbers. One warrior had run up behind Blackwell while another wrestled with him, and had delivered a powerful blow to the sergeant's head. The grass had spun up to meet him, fading from green to black, and his last thought was a sincere hope that the Indian's blow was a fatal one. Immediately fatal.

Blackwell was disappointed. He was vaguely aware of being slung over a large black horse, arms and legs bound, and he knew nothing else until he finally awoke.

When Blackwell raised his aching head, it was to behold a horrific vision. He was in an Indian encampment, naked, and tied to an upright pole. A large fire was burning not far away—its heat assailed him.

He was not alone. There were also five other naked, bound white men. Blackwell immediately recognized Shyer, Ledbetter, and Trusty. The other two were green recruits, named Byrd and Siemanski.

Around two dozen men stood around them; most were Indians, but Max had been on the Plains long enough to recognize that they were not all Sioux. Cheyenne, Arapaho, Crow, even Utes from the distant mountains—all had representatives in the small band, even though some of those tribes were enemies to one another. About a third of the renegades were not Indians at all, though some wore paint and feathers. There was a Mexican and two Negroes, and half-a-dozen or so white men. Blackwell had heard stories of such renegades down along the border, where they were called *comancheros*, but had never encountered such a mélange of raiders on the plains. One of the white men was given a wide berth by all the others—they seemed to fear him. The renegade stood before the captives. His face was covered with greasy paint, and his hair was long and braided.

"I am Vision-man," he said in perfect English, smiling with his mouth and not his eyes. "But I am known by other names."

"Vision-man" shoved his face to within a few inches of Blackwell's. A slow, sickening feeling spread through the sergeant's gut as he realized who his captor was.

"Jacobs," he said hoarsely.

"You recognize me. How touching." Jacobs pulled away, then threw back his head and laughed. "Private Shyer! Private Ledbetter—no, it's corporal now, isn't it?" Ledbetter stared at Jacobs fiercely, and spat at him.

"Excellent," Jacobs said. "You haven't lost your spirit. That should keep things interesting." The renegade walked over to Trusty and slapped him with his open hand. Trusty snorted an obscenity.

"Did that hurt, private? Soon you will be praying that I do nothing more than strike you."

Blackwell could not help shivering at Jacobs' words. The rough wood irritated his naked skin; he tried not to think about what other irritations might be in his future.

"We didn't expect to see you again, not after two years," Blackwell said. "I'm glad you made it." Despite their predicament his words were sincere.

"Oh, it was close going there for awhile," Jacobs said, and then he added in an exaggerated whisper, "They let me go, though—they thought I was crazy."

"The savages are smarter than I thought," said Ledbetter.

Jacobs chuckled. "Spout off while you can, jackal. The Oglala respected me—even feared me a little. A few of them spoke English and I told them of my vision. I have had others since. Nothing impresses them more than a mystic—a vision man. The Oglala would not take me in, but as you can see I've gained followers. Men like me, who are not bound by their worldly affiliations but by their visions.

"Behold, this dreamer cometh! That's what Joseph's brothers said, just before they sold him into slavery. I bet they never dreamed that one day he'd have the power of life and death over them."

Jacobs paced around the fire, and its glare flickered serenely upon his painted face. "As you can see, sergeant, my vision has come true. Both you and the savages are submitted to me—why, I even have a black charger. And now, gentlemen, the time has come for a little revenge. It's sad that our friends Brown and Franz aren't here to share this moment with us, but we'll just have to make do."

The next several hours were filled with more horror than Blackwell could over have dreamed possible in a world crafted by a loving God. The sergeant was not touched, and neither were the two recruits, but Ledbetter, Shyer, and Trusty were tortured without mercy. Jacobs insisted on doing almost all of the torturing, occasionally taking a break for a drink of water. The victims screamed like souls in hell, and even the recruits joined in a few times.

With every creative action Jacobs made with a knife blade or a live coal, he stared at Blackwell and grinned. The sergeant prayed that the three men would die soon, but then he realized what that would mean for him. He cursed himself for what he was thinking, but could not help it—he started praying they would live longer.

The unfortunate soldiers were finally killed. They were gone to their greater reward, Blackwell knew— whatever sins the men had committed in life, they had more than paid for them.

The three remaining prisoners were left standing, undisturbed, all night. When dawn came, Jacobs and his cronies were there.

"Now, Sergeant Blackwell," Jacobs said. "There is only us. I owe you a debt of blood for your sins against me, but in an odd way I also owe you my life. You convinced your cohorts not to kill me, but to 'set me adrift' instead. It is only fair that I now extend to you the same courtesy."

Blackwell stared at the wild man, not understanding. Indians came forward and cut the men's bonds at a gesture from Jacobs. The sergeant stumbled forward—weakened, hungry, and with circulation slowly returning to his limbs.

"You are free to go, at least for now," Jacobs said. "We will hunt you down, but at least you'll have some chance. To be sporting, we will give you something of a head start." He pointed at Byrd and Siemanski. "I give you these dogs as a favor. Now run—if you're lucky, you may gain a swift death."

They had run. They were still running now, though nearly exhausted. Blackwell could feel their pursuers' presence just a short distance behind them, and could almost hear Jacobs' grating laughter.

He felt bad for Byrd and Siemanski. They had done nothing to deserve this. Blackwell wished the same thing could be said for himself. He knew that he was reaping what he had sowed. He had mutinied against his commander and left him for dead, a serious breach of his own personal code, to say nothing of military law. At the same time, by sparing Jacobs' life, he had helped create the demon which now pursued them. He was doubly responsible. He strained his mind trying to figure out a way to undo the things he had done, at least to an extent.

He thought of a way. It was a good plan, although not so good for him—but it was the only choice he could live with.

The refugees topped a small rise. The grass was deeper there. "Hold on a moment," he said. The other two stopped—very reluctantly—and tried to catch their breath.

"If you make it back," Blackwell said, "tell my family that I love them. I'm going to stay behind and try to buy you the time to escape."

"But sergeant—" Byrd began.

"No time for arguments! Go!"

They loped away. Blackwell stretched himself out full-length in the grass. He would be concealed, at least for a moment, when the enemy came over the rise.

Blackwell had a feeling that was almost joy when he saw that—as he had hoped—Jacobs was in the lead of the group which suddenly appeared beside him. Blackwell launched himself through the air at his former commander. His momentum knocked Jacobs from his mount, and for a moment the two of them lay tangled together in the grass. The other renegades drew close to them; Jacobs pulled free from the sergeant and motioned at his men to back away. Blackwell had pulled Jacobs' knife from its sheath and waved it warily at him. The mad "vision-man" gestured to one of his men, an Indian, and the subordinate tossed a tomahawk to his leader.

"Don't touch him," Jacobs said. "Don't touch him, any of you. I'll finish him myself."

The two men circled one another cautiously, their weapons at the ready. "If you aim to finish me, you son of a bitch," Blackwell said, "you're gonna need all the help you can get."

Jacobs chuckled coldly at his opponent. "I need no assistance, sergeant. I've seen this in a vision, after all, and I know how it turns out."

Jacobs lunged, swift as a serpent, and his tomahawk hissed through the air, barely missing the sergeant's face. Blackwell rocked back on the balls of his feet, immediately catching his balance and swiping his own blade at his enemy. The knife's tip cut a thin swath across Jacobs' belly, barely breaking the skin.

"Touché!" Jacobs called, and laughed.

They continued circling, gauging one another, lashing out and missing. The renegades pulled back, giving them room, and the two combatants danced slowly in the open ring which their audience created.

Jacobs feinted to the left, and when Blackwell lunged the renegade stamped his boot on the sergeant's bare foot. Blackwell roared in pain—in the moment his guard was down, Jacobs' tomahawk swung. The naked cavalryman managed to twist away and avoid being disemboweled, but the heavy blade struck him in the side. Pain exploded behind his eyes and he crumpled to the ground. He knew that he suffered a broken rib, at minimum, but that seemed a minor concern under the circumstances.

"Goodbye, Sergeant," Jacobs said, and raised the tomahawk high into the air.

In that moment, Max Blackwell had visions of his own. Visions of his wife and his children, and the life which had stretched before him just a few days before and was now about to be snatched away. It was not hatred of his enemy that spurred him, it was the primal rage to live that ignited inside Blackwell and shot his body upward like a rocket. He was on his feet in an instant, driving the knife deep into Jacobs' abdomen. Blackwell's free hand clenched his enemy's weapon hand in a steel grip, while his right drove the knife ever deeper, twisting as it jabbed upward into the madman's heart.

"No!" Jacobs gasped. "My visions! This can't—" Jacobs choked on his words, and they became a gurgle. His eyes, bulging, stared intensely into Blackwell's.

"The only visions left for you," the sergeant whispered hoarsely, "are visions of hell."

Blackwell stared into those eyes until the light faded completely from them, then lat Jacobs fall to the ground like a wet sack. He scooped the tomahawk from his hand and, grasping both weapons firmly, turned to face the other renegades.

They stared at him in silence for several moments.

"Well?" Blackwell demanded. "What the hell are you waiting on?"

They still did not move. One of the black men spoke.

"Vision-man said don't touch you."

Slowly, one by one, the renegades turned to go.

"Ain't you gonna take him with you?" Blackwell said. "I thought he was your leader."

One of the white renegades answered. "Don't reckon his magic can help us anymore," the man said. "Sure didn't help him none."

One of the Indians, a Crow, pointed at Blackwell. "Strong medicine," he said. Then they all rode away, leaving Jacobs' black mount loose nearby.

Long before they disappeared from sight, Blackwell collapsed to the ground beside the vision-man's body. The horse would do him no good, he didn't have the energy to mount it. He wished he really did have some strong medicine.

Blackwell was not sure how long he lay on the grass before the troopers arrived. Byrd and Siemanski had run into a patrol that had come looking for them. They had expected to find Blackwell's dead body, and were not far wrong. A detail took the wounded sergeant and the dead renegade back to the fort while the rest of the company rode on in search of the raiders.

Colonel Skelly recognized the dead man at once, despite the corpse's unmilitary appearance. Blackwell, once recovered enough to talk, felt compelled to confess his role in the mutiny—but the colonel cut him off, and forbade him to say more on the matter.

"Jacobs was killed by Sioux Indians two years ago," Skelly said, "while leading a heroic action. More recently, your patrol was attacked by hostile renegades. That's how it's been written up, and that's how it's going to be. There's no need for Jacobs' father, or the press, to think any different."

"It weighs on my conscience," Blackwell said.

"Let it." The colonel's visage relaxed into a friendly smile, and he patted the injured cavalryman's shoulder. "Before you know it you'll be back on your feet, back in the saddle, and back in action."

Max Blackwell was, in fact, back in the saddle soon.

His dreams, however, were never the same. For the rest of his life his nights were haunted by dark visions, evil laughter, flames and the screams of his comrades. Years later, Billy Blackwell asked his father why he woke screaming so often. Max Blackwell shook his head sadly and spoke in a soft voice.

"I reckon I'm a vision-man."

Confused, Billy asked the same question of his mother.

"Your father was a soldier," she told him.

END

PANHANDLE FREIGHT

By L.J. WASHBURN

"Close the damn door!" the station agent yelled at Lucas Hallam. "You're lettin' all the warm air out!"

And all the cold air in, Hallam thought as he shoved the depot's front door closed behind him. People sometimes said there was nothing between the Canadian River and the North Pole except a barbed wire fence, and on a night like tonight, when a blue norther swept down over the plains, it sure felt like that old saying was right.

Hallam was a big, rugged man in a sheepskin coat, with his hat pulled down tight on his head so the wind wouldn't blow it off. He tugged his gloves from his hands and stuck them in a coat pocket as he crossed the spacious waiting room toward the ticket window.

"I hope you ain't here to buy a ticket," the agent said from the other side of the counter. "No passenger trains comin' through tonight, only a freight that's due in about an hour."

"No, I don't need a ticket," Hallam told the man, who looked like he wanted to just close up and go home for the night. "I'm here because of that freight."

He unbuttoned the coat and slipped a hand inside it.

The agent dropped a hand below the counter.

"You'd better not be reachin' for a gun, mister," he warned. "I got a .45 here, and I know how to use it."

Hallam grunted and shook his head.

"Take it easy," he told the man. Moving

155

deliberately so as not to spook the trigger-happy agent, he brought out a leather folder and opened it so the man could see the badge and identification papers inside. "I'm a Pinkerton agent, working for the railroad."

The man relaxed and blew out his breath.

"Well, why didn't you say so?" he demanded irritably.

"Thought I just did," Hallam said as he put away the folder. "I'm here about that freight. Rode all the way from Lubbock in the teeth of that gale to get here in time."

He was half frozen to prove it, too.

The station agent shook his head in confusion. "What about that freight?"

Hallam rubbed his hands together and blew on them.

"Somebody's going to hold it up when it gets here."

That just confused the agent even more.

"How do you know that . . . and who'd bother holding up a freight train, anyway?"

"The telegram I got from my bosses back in Chicago didn't explain that. It just said they'd gotten a tip that Seth Brackett was gonna stop the freight here and take something off of it."

"Brackett!" the agent repeated. "Why, he's raised hell all over this part of the country! He must've held up half a dozen express cars."

"And killed a dozen messengers and guards," Hallam said with a bleak nod. "Nobody knows how he gets on board, and he never leaves any witnesses. That's why we don't know what he looks like. Wouldn't even know his name if he didn't leave those

156

notes braggin' about what he's done."

"And you say he's comin' here?" The agent's voice quavered a little.

"So I'm told," Hallam said. "My job's to stop him."

"How are you gonna do that when you don't know what he looks like?"

"That makes it a challenge, all right," Hallam said.

The station door swung open again, letting cold air swirl through the waiting room. The agent's head jerked in that direction. His eyes widened.

"Blast it, don't act like that!" Hallam said quietly. "We don't want Brackett to know we're waitin' for him. A killer like that, best to take him by surprise."

The agent swallowed and nodded.

"Yeah. Sorry, Mister . . . what was your name again."

"Hallam."

The man who had just come into the depot pushed the door closed behind him, appearing to struggle a little against the wind as he did so. He had a large box wrapped with paper and tied with twine hanging from one hand and wore city duds. He looked to Hallam like a drummer of some sort, middle-aged, with fair hair under a derby and a long, hangdog face.

"Evening," the man said as he came over to the window. He nodded friendly-like to Hallam and the agent. "Colder than a witch's tit out there . . . although I have no personal experience on exactly how cold that is, never having made the close acquaintance of a witch. Bitches are a different story." He paused, then asked Hallam, "Were you conducting business here, friend? I don't want to interrupt."

Hallam shook his head and said, "Nope, just passing the time of day with my amigo here."

The man lifted the package. "In that case . . ."

Hallam moved aside so the man could set the bundle on the counter. "Sure, go ahead."

"I need to ship this," the man said. "There's a train coming through tonight, isn't there?"

The agent nodded and said, "Yeah, but this ain't a scheduled stop on tonight's run. I'd have to lower the signal."

"But you can do that, can't you?" the man insisted. "The sooner this package gets back to St. Louis, the better."

Hallam had heard a faint clank from inside the package when the man set it on the counter. He gestured toward it and asked, "What is it?"

"I'm not sure what business that is of yours." The man shrugged. "But it's no secret. I travel in kitchen appliances, and that's some defective merchandise I've accumulated from the past few shipments my company has sent me. I need to return it so it won't count against my balance sheets."

"Don't seem like that's urgent enough for the train to make a special stop," the agent said. "There's a regular freight comin' through tomorrow. It can go out then."

"I'd just as soon not wait." A sheepish smile appeared on the man's face. "My account's not in the best shape. I need the credit for these returns as soon as I can get it." He lowered his voice to a conspiratorial tone. "I'm willing to pay a mite extra."

"Thought you were havin' money trouble," the

agent said.

"You've got to spend money to make money, as the old saying goes."

"All right. No extra charge," the agent grumbled. "Lemme weigh this and figure it up."

The transaction took a few minutes. Hallam stood off to the side in apparent disinterest as it went on. The drummer paid the charges as if it hurt him physically to hand over the bills, and then the agent said, "I'll take care of it from here, mister. You can go on back to the hotel."

There was no need to mention which hotel. In a settlement of this size, there was only one.

The drummer shook his head dubiously. "I think I'll wait here until the train comes in, just to be sure that the package goes out all right."

"I told you I'd take care of it," the agent said, not bothering to hide his irritation. He seemed to have forgotten his earlier nervousness. Doing business had settled him down.

"I'll just sit over there," the drummer said, waving a hand toward the empty benches where passengers waited for their trains. He walked over, took a seat, picked up a two-week-old copy of the Fort Worth Star-Telegram that somebody had left there, and started leafing through it.

The agent leaned forward through the ticket window and cut his eyes toward the drummer as he whispered, "That's a mighty thin story. You think he's — "

Hallam lifted a hand to stop the man before he mentioned Seth Brackett's name.

"He could be tellin' the truth," Hallam said. "I'll

keep an eye on him."

The agent looked pretty doubtful, but he nodded.

The minute hand on the big clock on the wall ticked over with an audible sound every sixty seconds. Each one of those minutes seemed to take at least five times that long as Hallam, the station agent, and the traveling salesman waited for the train.

So it seemed like quite a while but really wasn't when the door opened again. The cold wind brought two people in this time, a man and a woman. He wore work clothes and a battered old hat, and the woman was bundled up not only in a thick coat but also a blanket. She walked delicately, like there was something wrong with her. The man helped her over to one of the benches. The drummer watched them curiously as the woman sat down.

The man hurried over to the window and asked, "Has the train come through already?" He was somewhere between thirty and forty. The lines of strain and hard work on his face made it hard to be sure of his age.

The agent shook his head. "No, it's not due for a little while yet. What do you need, mister?"

"I have to get my wife to Lubbock tonight."

The agent shook his head and said, "You're outta luck, mister. No passenger trains tonight, just a freight."

"But it's headed that way, isn't it? They could take us in the caboose, couldn't they?" the man insisted. "It's an emergency."

"What sort of emergency?"

The man turned to look toward the woman who sat huddled in the blanket on the bench.

"My wife's going to have a baby."

"Why, Doc Spurgeon here in town can handle that. He's delivered plenty of babies."

"Not like this one. There's something wrong. The doc said I need to get Sara Beth to the hospital in Lubbock as soon as possible. If I don't . . ." The man's face, tanned and seamed by working outside, turned pale. "If I don't, could be neither her nor the baby will make it."

"Well, if that don't beat all. I dunno. The railroad's got rules . . ."

Hallam said, "I'll bet the conductor would be willin' to make an exception to the rules in a case like this."

The agent's fingers rasped over the beard stubble on his chin as he frowned in thought. "I reckon since I got to stop the train anyway, I could at least ask the conductor."

The man reached through the window to grab the agent's hand and pump it. "Thanks, mister, thanks so much! This means the world to me."

"Why don't you go sit with your wife?" the agent suggested. "You'll know when the train gets here."

The man nodded and hurried over to the benches. He sat down beside the woman and put an arm around her shoulders.

"I don't believe it for a second," the agent told Hallam. "Why, the way she's bundled up, there ain't no way of tellin' for sure if she's even in the family way!"

"I never heard anything about the fella we're lookin' for havin' a female accomplice," Hallam said.

"Yeah, but we can't be sure that he don't!"

Hallam nodded. "I guess that's true."

The agent ran his fingers through his thinning

brown hair and said, "Lord, who knew the place would get so busy, tonight of all nights! Ain't that always the way!"

They resumed their wait. The drummer rattled the newspaper, the man and the woman talked quietly with each other, the blue norther howled outside, and the clock on the wall continued its ticking. Hallam had warmed up enough now in the heat that came from a pot-bellied stove in a corner of the waiting room that he took off the sheepskin coat and draped it over the back of the nearest bench.

When the door opened again a while later, the agent muttered, "Lord have mercy! Now what?"

The man who came in on the cold air was tall and lean and dressed mostly in black, from his Stetson to his frock coat to his high-topped boots. The only bits of color about him were the diamond stickpin he wore in his fancy cravat and the ivory grips on the handles of the twin Colts he wore belted around his hips.

The agent swallowed hard and bit back a moan.

"That's gotta be him," he said in an urgent whisper to Hallam. "Look at him! You can tell he's an outlaw!"

"Or a gambler," Hallam said. "Looks more like that to me."

"Get ready! He's comin' this way!"

The stranger walked up to the window and asked, "Has tonight's freight arrived?"

The agent pointed a shaking finger at the board where the schedule was chalked and managed to say, "Not yet. Soon, I reckon."

The man smiled. "You look like you could use some nerve tonic, friend. I have a package coming in on

162

the train."

"A package . . . comin' in?"

"That's right. It's being shipped special to me from New York. Will the train stop, or will someone just toss the package onto the platform as it goes past?"

"Oh, the train's stoppin' tonight," the agent said. "Freight or not, it's stoppin'. Which reminds me, I got to go lower the signal."

He came out of the door next to the ticket window shrugging into a coat.

"Why don't you come with me, amigo?" he said to Hallam. "It's a cold, dark night for a man to be out all by his lonesome."

"Sure," Hallam said. He reached for his sheepskin coat.

They went out through the door that led to the platform. The building blocked some of the wind's force, but the way it was whipping around, the bone-chilling cold it carried penetrated the men's coats anyway.

"Which one do you think it is?" the agent asked as he went over to the lever that raised and lowered the signal beam on a post next to the platform. "One of 'em's got to be Seth Brackett."

"Seems that way," Hallam agreed with a nod. He hadn't put his gloves back on, but he had his hands stuck in the coat pockets to keep them out of the wind.

The agent shoved the lever over and lowered the beam. A new-fangled electric light glowed redly on it. The engineer would see it far enough back along the track to bring the train to a stop as it rolled up to the station.

"Tell you what," the agent said. He pulled his coat

back to reveal the butt of a pistol stuck behind his belt. "Let's go back in there and throw down on the whole bunch of 'em. We'll herd 'em into the storeroom and lock 'em up until the train's come and gone."

"What about that pregnant woman?" Hallam asked.

"Oh, yeah." The agent frowned in thought. "I guess if she can prove that she's really pregnant, we'll let her and her husband stay out so they can get on the train. But we'll lock up the other two."

"If we do that, they're liable to file a lawsuit against the railroad. Your bosses won't like that, and mine won't either." Hallam added wryly, "And I doubt that the lady will want to show you her belly to prove she's with child."

"Then what are we supposed to do?" the agent asked in exasperation. "Just wait?"

Hallam glanced at the signal. "It shouldn't be much longer."

The agent sighed and led the way back inside. The man in black had taken a seat on one of the benches, too.

"Gettin' damned crowded in here," the agent muttered.

The man who looked like a farmer told the woman, "Don't worry, honey. I'm sure the train will be here soon."

"I hope so, Henry," she said in a voice tight with strain. "I sure hope so."

Hallam took off his coat and wandered over toward them. He lifted a finger to his hat brim, nodded, and said, "Ma'am." Then he turned to the man and asked, "You have a place somewhere around here, mister?"

"Yeah," the man said with a nod. "Fifty acres about five miles west of town. It's a nice little farm. Won't mean much, though, if . . ."

He stopped, obviously unwilling to go on with that thought.

The woman squeezed his hand and said, "It'll be all right, Henry. I'm sure it will."

Hallam touched his hat brim again and said, "Best of luck to you, ma'am."

He moved over and sat down next to the drummer.

"Cold night out there, isn't it?"

The man nodded and said, "Cold as a . . . Wait a minute. We did that before, didn't we?"

"I reckon we did," Hallam said with a grin. Since most drummers were talkative sorts, he primed the pump. "You like bein' a salesman?"

"Oh, I used to. I enjoyed the traveling, even though these trains aren't the most comfortable conveyances in the world. And to be honest with you, the necessity of being away from the little woman back in Dallas most of the time didn't particularly bother me, either." The drummer shrugged. "But the miles are starting to pile up, and so are the years. It's getting harder and harder to make a living, too. Merchants buy from the bigger outfits now, and hell, you can't sell to individuals anymore. Everybody's got a Sears Roebuck catalog or a Monkey Wards catalog, and they just send off for what they want. Time for men like me to pack it in."

"That's a shame," Hallam said.

"What about you? What line of work are you in?

165

You look like a cowboy, if you don't mind my saying so."

Hallam nodded. "I've done some cowboying in my time." He didn't say anything else. Manhunting was his line these days, and he didn't figure that business would ever dry up. There would always be outlaws.

The man in black was sitting close enough to eavesdrop on the conversation. He leaned toward them and said, "Pardon the interruption, but you look like a gunfighter to me."

"Me?" Hallam said in apparent wonderment.

As a matter of fact, when he was younger . . . when he was tracking down the men responsible for his father's death and for a few wild years after that . . . he'd been getting a reputation as a fast gun. It would have been easy enough for him to wind up like John Wesley Hardin or one of the other infamous pistoleers.

But then he'd pinned on the silver star-in-a-circle of the Texas Rangers and gone down that road instead, a road that had now led him to the Pinkertons. He shook his head and told the man in black, "No, I'm no gunfighter."

"You have the look about you," the man insisted. "I know it well. I've made a study of shootists."

"Is that so?"

"Indeed. They're my bread and butter, you see."

Hallam didn't see at all. But before he could say that, the man in black went on, "I'll show you, when the train gets here."

The station agent had gone back into his office. He was at the ticket window, close enough to hear what the man in black said. The agent cleared his throat and tried to catch Hallam's eye. Hallam saw him but pretended not to.

When Hallam first heard the locomotive's whistle a few minutes later, he thought it was that blue norther keening and shrieking. Then the sound came again and he recognized it for what it was. He put his hands on his knees, pushed himself to his feet with a faint protest from muscles starting to grow stiffer with age, and said, "Train's comin'."

The other three men stood up. The woman remained seated on the bench. Her husband told her, "You just stay there and rest until we find out for sure they'll let us on this train."

"All right," she said. She sounded tired and weak.

The train's rumble reached into the station. The agent came out of his office and headed for the platform. The drummer, the farmer, and the man in black followed him. Hallam brought up the rear, keeping a close eye on the three men in case one of them them tried anything.

It occurred to him that the woman could easily have a sawed-off shotgun or a hogleg under that blanket, and the skin on the back of his neck crawled at the thought that she was behind him.

But when he glanced over his shoulder, she hadn't budged, and she looked as weary and miserable as ever. Hallam was convinced she didn't have anything to do with that train-robbing Seth Brackett.

With a squeal of brakes and a hiss of steam billowing from the engine into the frigid air, the train came to a stop with the caboose alongside the platform. The conductor, wrapping himself in a blue greatcoat, hopped down to the platform and demanded of the station agent, "Why's the signal down, Grady?"

"Got a shipment goin' out," the agent said, hefting the box the drummer had brought in. "And you're supposed to have a special shipment for this fella here." He jerked his head toward the man in black.

"What's your name?" the conductor asked.

"Boothe, with an 'e'," the man said. "John B. Boothe."

"Yeah, sure," the conductor said. "I forgot about that. It's in the caboose. I'll fetch it for you."

Before the conductor could turn around, the farmer stepped forward and raised his voice to be heard over the wind.

"Mister, I've got to get to Lubbock tonight!" he said. "My wife's fixin' to have a baby, and she's in a bad way. The local doc says she needs to get to the hospital. Can you take us in the caboose?"

The conductor frowned at the agent. "Is this true, Grady?"

"All I know is what he's told me," the agent answered. "Far as I know it's the truth."

The conductor frowned. "The line has rules against carrying passengers on freight trains. However, in the case of a medical emergency, I have some leeway. Is your wife here? I've got a schedule to keep, you know."

"She's right inside," the farmer said eagerly. "I'll go get her."

"Fine. We'll have you to Lubbock in an hour or so." The conductor took the drummer's bundle from the station agent, then turned to the man in black. "I'll get your package."

He climbed back into the caboose while the farmer hurried into the station to fetch his wife. The couple came back, the man holding an arm protectively around his wife's shoulders again. The conductor met them at the steps and helped the woman up into the warmth of the caboose. Once they had disappeared inside, the conductor came over to the man in black and handed him a cardboard box tied with twine, much like the one the drummer was shipping back to St. Louis only smaller.

"Here you go, Mr. Boothe."

"Thank you very much, sir."

"Grady, we're pulling out in five minutes. You got anything else for us?"

The agent glanced at Hallam, then said, "Not a thing. I'm gonna lock up and go home."

"It's a good night for it," the conductor agreed.

While the conductor returned to the caboose, the man in black took out a penknife, cut the twine, and opened the box enough to reach inside it. Hallam watched him closely in case it was a trick. The only thing the man took out of the box, though, was a thin, yellow-backed book.

"For you, sir," he said as he extended the book toward Hallam. "A complimentary copy of my latest masterpiece."

Hallam took the book and read the title aloud. "'The Brazos Kid vs. the Blacksnake Gang'." He looked up. "You're a writer?"

The man in black nodded. "John B. Boothe, sir, at your service. Just as it says there." He pointed to the author's name on the garish yellow cover. "This is my first effort for Beadle & Adams. I'm justifiably proud."

Hallam chuckled. "Well, good for you, I reckon. I wouldn't want to sit down and make up a lot of words, but I guess if it's what you want to do . . ."

Boothe tucked the box under his arm. "I hope you enjoy it," he said. He turned to leave the platform. The drummer was already gone. Hallam had noticed him walking away, head bent against the wind, as soon as the package he was shipping was on board the train.

That left Hallam and the station agent alone on the platform.

"I don't understand," the agent said. "You got that tip – "

Hallam shrugged. "Tips are wrong sometimes. So long."

"Good night! And no offense, Mr. Pinkerton man, but I hope I never see you again."

Hallam laughed. He walked back through the waiting room and out the front door to where his horse was tied. He felt bad about leaving the animal out in the weather for the past hour. But the horse would be in a warm stall at the livery barn soon enough.

Not quite yet, though, Hallam thought. Not quite yet.

He swung up into the saddle and rode toward the hotel. When he looked back over his shoulder, he saw the lamps in the station go out. The agent was done for the night.

The engineer pulled the whistle cord, sending another shriek through the night. The train lurched ahead, then smoothed out as it began to roll faster.

Hallam sent his horse galloping down an alley.

He swung back toward the railroad tracks, angling toward the steel rails. The train was picking up speed. He urged his mount on, knowing that lives depended on him intercepting it.

He'd had a pretty good idea what he was going to find here tonight, but he had been willing to be proven wrong. Everything had worked out pretty much the way he thought it would, though.

The horse was big and strong and had a good burst. It drew even with the caboose. Hallam reached over, grabbed the railing around the rear platform, and left the saddle. He swung onto the platform and drew his gun as he carefully tried the doorknob with his left hand. Locked.

Of course it was. Seth Brackett didn't want to be disturbed while he was at his work.

Hallam leaned back, raised his right leg, and drove his boot heel against the door with all his considerable strength and weight behind it. The door crashed open, and Hallam went through it in a rush.

Taken by surprise, the station agent whirled toward him. The gun in the man's hand spouted noise and flame. Hallam felt as much as heard the bullet rip past his ear. His long-barreled Colt .45 roared. The slug tore through the agent's right shoulder, rending flesh and shattering bone. The impact threw the man back against the conductor's desk.

But he was too stubborn to quit. He reached across his body, grabbed the gun from the hand that no longer worked, and started to raise it.

"Drop it, Brackett!" Hallam shouted.

The outlaw ignored him. Hallam couldn't wait any longer. The conductor, along with the farmer and his pregnant wife, were huddled on the other side of the caboose, wide-eyed and terrified. With every second that went by, their lives were at risk from a stray bullet.

Hallam triggered twice more, driving both slugs

into Brackett's chest. This time Brackett dropped the gun as he rocked back. He started to slide down the front of the desk, then lost his balance and pitched forward on his face.

"My God!" the conductor exclaimed. "He was going to kill us! Phil Grady was going to kill us all!"

"He's not Phil Grady," Hallam said. "Or maybe he is, I don't know. But he's Seth Brackett, the train robber, that's for damned sure. He locked up the station, slipped onto the caboose platform, and waited until the train was movin' to bust in here and get the drop on you. I reckon he's got a horse stashed up the line four or five miles. All he had to do was kill the three of you, take what he wanted, drop off the train where he could pick up the horse, and ride back to town. Then he could go to bed and act just as shocked as everybody else tomorrow when the news came about there bein' three dead folks in this car when the train got to Lubbock. He's done it half a dozen times before. What I want to know is what he was after."

The conductor pulled out a bandanna, wiped sweat from his face, and said, "There's a special shipment of money in the safe. Upwards of fifty thousand dollars in cash from a bank in Denver bound for one of those big Panhandle ranchers. The bank made special arrangements with the railroad to ship it like this. They're sending another package with half a dozen guards, but it's just a dummy. Nobody on this train even knows about it except me. I didn't think anybody knew about it!"

"Somebody did," Hallam said. "Brackett, or Grady, had a partner somewhere along the line tipping him off. But somebody tipped off the Pinkertons, too, because I work for them and they knew something was gonna happen on this train tonight." Hallam's eyes narrowed in thought. "Brackett thought he was mighty smart, workin' out this scheme. Maybe he sent that warning to the agency, just to rub our noses in it, like he did with those notes he left after the other robberies. He seemed to be taking a lot of pleasure in his play-actin' tonight."

"Well, you're a better detective than I am, mister, because I never would have figured that out," the conductor said. "But I reckon that's why you work for the Pinks and I don't. Now what? Are you gonna try to find Grady's partner?"

Hallam shook his head. "Somebody else can do that. I'm ridin' on to Lubbock with you so this lady can get to where she needs to go, and then schedule or no schedule, this train's backin' up until I find my horse. I'm sure as hell not leavin' him out all night with a blue norther blowin'!"

END

THE WAY OF THE WEST

By LARRY JAY MARTIN

"Aye, Mr. Hogart, I hear you perfectly well, and I understand you, but I still think it's about as good an idea as ticklin' a mule's heel to cure your toothache." Big John Newcomber spat a stream of tobacco juice in the dust to punctuate his point.

"Come on inside and let's gnaw a cup of coffee," Hogart said, trying his best to sound like the men who worked for him.

The owner of the recently renamed Bar H, Harold L. Hogart, reared back in his chair, stuffed his fat banker's cigar in his mouth, and narrowed his eyes. He wasn't a banker, but he was the next thing to it; he was an investor. And he had invested in the Bar H a year ago after old man Wells lost it to the Merchant's and Farmer's Bank – but then, old man Wells wasn't the only one to lose a ranch in 1886. All hoped this year would be a lot better.

The two men took a seat at the plank table that served the bunkhouse. And Hogart did his best to sound the empire builder. "You and I have gotten along fine so far, Newcomber, I hope to continue the relationship . . . But you've got to abide by my wishes, and his mother and I wish to have our son accompany you on this drive."

"I've already got a half dozen whelps green as gourds, Mr. Hogart – "

"Then another won't matter much. Wilbur will be ready and waiting at sun up. He's eighteen, older than

175

some of your hands, and perfectly capable. We want him to have this experience before he leaves for college in the East."

So it was settled. John Newcomber had his back up over the whole affair, but he said nothing knowing from long experience as a segundo, foreman, that it was hard to put a foot in a shut mouth, and besides, it's usually your own throat you slice with a sharp tongue – and he wasn't about to walk away from a good job when even a poor one was nigh impossible to find. Still and all if he could change the man's mind, he'd give it a go, but he knew that trying to make a point when Hogart thought otherwise was like trying to measure water with a sieve. He'd end up all wet with nothing to show for it. Hogart was slick as calf slobber, but he was the boss.

Ah Choo, the cook, who was nicknamed Sneezy for obvious reasons, filled the two men's coffee cups, but was thinking of his honorable ancestors as he did so – which he had a tendency to do when he had to face unpleasant tasks. He was the bunkhouse cook at the Bar H, not the main house cook. That was Mrs. O'Malior's job. The two of them spatted like a pair of cats whose tails had been tied together before they were tossed over a clothesline. And this afternoon, Sneezy had to go to the main house to round out his chuck for the month-long trip ahead. He did not look forward to the afternoon's chore, nor to having John Newcomber, who he had to be as close to for the next month as a tick in a lamb's tail, start on a long drive with a burr already festerin' under his saddle.

Mr. Hogart finished the varnish Sneezy called coffee, acted as if he enjoyed it, then rose and extended his hand to Newcomber. "You know how important this trip is to the Bar H, John. These cattle have to be in Mojave by the 16th of September in order to fulfill the contract with Harley Brothers Packing. A day late and those robber barons will want to renegotiate, and the price I have now will just barely cover this year's costs. Be there on time."

"God willin' and the creek don't rise...and some tenderfoot don't stampede the stock, we'll make it. Dry year or no." He couldn't help put the dig in to the boss's withers like a cocklebur, but it rolled off Hogart like rain off an oiled slicker, not that there'd been enough rain this year to test the theory.

Hogart left the bunkhouse, and John Newcomber stood at a window staring out through the dirty glass, shaking his head. "This is gonna be like startin' a long trip with a sore backed horse and hole in yer boot sole," he mumbled, more to himself than to Sneezy.

"Pardon, Mr. Maycom'er?" the little cook asked.

"Nothin', Sneezy. Pack a lot o' lineament and bandages, an' a Bible if you own one. I got a bad feelin' about this go."

"Yes, sir, Mr. Maycom'er, sir. Renament and ban'ages and the Christian book, snap snap."

Morning dawned fresh and breezy, with the Sierras at the ranch's back and the Whites, also the better part of 14,000 feet above sea level, between it and the rising sun – it took a while before the sun touched the Owen's Valley bottom with its warmth. It was the better part of two hundred fifty miles down the valley and across a piece of the Mojave Desert to reach the rail station at Mojave, and to be comfortable they'd have to average ten miles a day to keep the schedule.

Ten miles should be easy, all things being equal. But John Newcomber had driven stock long enough to know that all things never stayed equal for long.

Sneezy had rung the chuck bell at 3:30 A.M., a half hour earlier than usual, so he could feed the men the last of the eggs and milk they'd see for a good while, and still get a jump on the herd. He wanted to stay ahead of them if he could, at least on this first day – for he'd be eating dust the rest of the drive. And the four-up of mules he had pulling the chuckwagon would keep ahead of the herd, given no major trouble.

True to his father's word, just as Sneezy whipped up the chuckwagon team to get a jump on the drovers, Wilbur Hogart pranced up on one of the Hogarts' blooded thoroughbreds, a dun colored horse with fine long bones that stood sixteen hands. It was a pleasurable animal to look at, but . . . Wilbur carried a quirt and wore a fine new Palo Alto fawn colored hat, twill pants, a starched city shirt, and English riding boots. On his hip gleamed a new Smith and Wesson chrome plated .38 in a polished black holster. The bedroll he had tied behind the saddle couldn't have carried more that one blanket and one change of clothes. John Newcomber stood cinching up his sorrel quarter horse as Wilbur's animal proudly single-stepped over to the hitching rail.

"John," the young man said, "I'm ready – "

"You'll call me Mr. Newcomber while you're working for me," the Bar H segundo said quietly, his voice matching the cold-granite of his chiseled face – but Wilbur heard him clearly enough. The young man's eyes and nostrils flared a little, but he said nothing in reply. "Understood?" Newcomber asked, unsatisfied with the boy's silence, his own voice a trifle louder.

"As you wish, Mr. Newcomber," the boy replied, stressing the mister in a manner that rang of sarcasm. John left it at that, knowing it would be a long trip and that time and the trail would work out most of Wilbur Hogart's kinks. Hard work had a way of doing that to a man, or breaking him, if he wasn't much of one to start with. John really had no way of knowing if Wilbur Hogart had any sand, but time and the trail would tell.

"Dad said I was to ride point," Wilbur added, rubbing salt in the spot Harold H. Hogart had already galled on John's back.

"You'll ride drag, like all new hands do, Mr. Hogart." John Newcomber swung up in the saddle, forking the sorrel and waiting for him to kick up his heels with the first saddle pressure of the morning – he didn't, but John knew the sorrel was saving it for later. He took the time to switch his attention and give Wilbur a hard look.

The boy glared at him. "Dad said – "

"Wilbur, let's get something straight right up front. Your daddy's not going on this trip, and if I hear you say one more time, 'daddy said,' I'll not take kindly to it and I might lose my temper. I've got a deep well of temper, Wilbur, and I can lose it every hour of every day and not run out. It's been tested. That's the kind of trip this might be, Wilbur, if you say 'daddy said' ever agin'."

"But – "

"There ain't no butts about it, Wilbur."

"Yes, sir," Wilbur said, to his credit, and reined the tall dun colored horse away.

Sally Fishbine had ridden for the Bar H for

fourteen years, the first thirteen when it was the Lazy Loop, and the last one under John Newcomber. He reined his bandy legged gray over beside John and paced him out to what they called the creek pasture, where the eight hundred fifty seven head, by yesterday's count, of Hereford mix – with Mexican Brahma – were gathered. The rest of the hands, a dozen of them, were holding the cattle and getting their minds right for the drive.

"Salvatore," John said quietly as they gigged the horses toward the creek pasture, "is the weather a'gonna hold."

"Bones say it is," he said, stretching. About that time John's sorrel decided he was awake enough to shake loose, and began a bone-jarring humpbacked dance. "Step lively!" John shouted, giving the big horse his spurs and whipping him across the ears with the rein tails at the same time. The sorrel settled, and John knew from long experience that that was it for the rest of the day.

"I swear, you two are like an old married couple . . . got to have yer spat or you can't get the blood to pumpin'," Sally said, rolling a smoke with one hand as his own mount plodded along.

"Both of us got to show how young we still are," John said, reaching forward and patting the big horse on the neck. "If'n I didn't pop 'is ears ever' mornin', he'd think I didn't care for 'im."

They picked the pace up to a cantor, with Wilbur Hogart keeping a respectful twenty paces behind. Wilbur had learned to ride English, in Oakland at the Hogarts' breeding ranch, across the bay from their home in San Francisco, and he could sit a saddle with the best of them by the time he was sixteen, and rode jumpers, but it was different from western riding – considerably different in that you handed the horse to a groom when finished for the day, and you finished for the day whenever you tired of the animal and the exercise. Still, he knew he was equal to anything the country and John Newcomber could throw at him – at least he was quite sure he was.

They crested a rise and looked down into creek canyon, and a thousand bald faced and mixed breed cattle lowed and grazed while a dozen cowhands waited the chance to earn their dollar a day and found.

Stub Jefferson had ridden in the year before, and John Newcomber had hired him on without so much as a second glance. His rig, and the way the black cowboy sat the saddle and kept his own council was enough of a resume for John.

Sergio and Hector Sanchez, a pair of young brothers up from San Diego were hired on just for the drive. John knew nothing about them, other than they rode fine stock and carried the woven leather reatas of the vaquero, and theirs were well tallowed and stretched to seventy feet with the weight of many a cow.

Old Tuck Holland had been working cattle on the east side of the Sierra for as long as John could remember. He had tales both older and taller than the Sierras and would tell 'em until they chopped ice in Death Valley, if you'd listen. His age was indeterminable but he had to be on the shady side of seventy. He looked so puny he'd have to lean against a post to spit to keep from blowing himself down; but he was tough as wang leather, had a face carved and etched like a peach pit by sun, sand, and wind, and spent most of his time looking back to see if the younger hands were keepin' up. And they were struggling along wondering why he made it all look so plum easy.

Colorado, which was the only name he gave and consequently was the only name used for him, was red-headed befittin' his name, bow legged enough that a pig could charge twixt his knees while he was clickin' his heels, and loud; but he pulled his own weight. He too had been hired on just for the duration of the drive.

Pudgy Dickerson was the last of the hands hired on, and John had to bail him out of the Bishop jail in order to do so, but he needed a hand and the rest of the able bodied men in the valley had run off to another silver strike in the high country – another whiff of bull dung as far as John Newcomber was concerned. But particularly when times were tough men seemed to jump at the chance for easy money. It normally turned out to be grit and grime and beans and backache, but still they chased the will o' the wisp.

The remuda man was Enrico Torres, as good a man with horses as John had ever seen. He pushed three dozen head of rank half-broke stock so the cowhands could trade off a couple of times a day. It was hard country between the north end of the Owens Valley and Mojave. Some spots of good grass and sweet water, but more than enough hard-as-the-hubs-of-hell ancient lava flows and flash floods, cactus and snakes, and heat if the weather decided it wanted to run late, or snow if it ran early. And it usually decided to do one or the other – and sometimes both – when a herd was being shoved to market. It was hard on horses and men, and hard as hell on a good attitude..

They pushed the herd out, jittery, but then all of them were when a drive began and before they settled into the routine. The men found their positions, all unassigned except for Stub Jefferson, the black cowhand who was riding point, and the Sanchez brothers, who were assigned drag with Wilbur Hogart and quickly took up positions flanking and staying out of the dust. The Sanchez boys had ridden enough drag to know they could stay out of the most of it on the flanks, and still do their job. So they gave Wilbur the position of honor . . . or so they told him . . . dead center trailing the herd.

John Newcomber floated from position to position, judging the men he didn't know, watching the herd, eyeballing the weather, and worrying – that was his job.

They hadn't gone three miles before Wilbur Hogart let his horse drift over close enough to Hector Sanchez so he could call out to him. "I'm Wil Hogart," he called.

Hector looked over and nodded, and touched the brim of his sweat soiled sombrero.

"What's a fella to do about the privy?" he shouted again.

Hector looked at him, a little confused.

"I need to pee," Wilbur said.

"Sí," Hector repeated, "the señor needs to pee.'" He reined over closer to the fancy looking gringo, who didn't look quite so fancy now that he was covered with a half-inch of dust. "Well, señor, you ride sidesaddle to accomplish that task."

"Sidesaddle?" Wilbur questioned. "You're funnin'

me, *amigo*. I meant do you take the drag while I drop out, or just what?"

"Senor Newcomber will be very angry if you stop to water the sagebrush, señor. It is the tried and trusted sidesaddle method – "

"Fill in for me, señor," Wilbur said, and reined away to find a bush, which was no problem as the country was chaparral covered.

"Sidesaddle," Hector said to himself, then laughed aloud. He couldn't wait to tell his brother.

"Sidesaddle," Wilbur repeated to himself, pleased that he had not fallen for the obvious prank of the other rider. He knew he would be the butt of many attempts, but was wise to them.

He dismounted and unbuttoned his trousers and began to relieve himself, just as the grass under his attacking stream came alive in the most terrible buzzing and thrashing Wilbur had ever heard. He stumbled back and pawed at the Smith and Wesson when he realized it was a four foot rattler he had the misfortune to awaken from his repose in the sun.

Wilbur emptied the six shooter, managing to scare the snake into retreating even faster than he already was, but not managing to kill it.

Still, Wilbur was satisfied with himself – until he heard the men begin to yell, and felt the vibration of four thousand hooves begin to beat in rhythmic stampede.

"My God," Wilbur said aloud to himself. "Did I . . . ?"

He raced for the thoroughbred, mounted, and rode after the advancing wave of cattle and men, and into a wall of dust as he had never seen.

The cattle ran for three miles, then the heat and the sun dissuaded them and they slowed, and finally, no longer hearing the explosions that had set them off, stilled and grazed.

John Newcomber sent Stub and Sally back along the flanks to pick up any strays, and checked with each of his men to make sure they were present and accounted for.

Wilbur Hogart, who sat at the rear of the herd, catching his breath as the thoroughbred stood and hung his head sucking in wind, was the last man he approached.

"You managed to keep from getting ground up," Newcomber greeted him.

"Yes, sir."

"Let me see that firearm," Newcomber said, his face turning to granite.

"It was a snake, Mr. Newco – "

"You shot at some poor ol' snake who was trying his best to get the hell out of the way!"

"He was only a couple of feet away, makin' a terrible noise."

"Give me that weapon."

"Dad said – "

"What did I tell you about that 'dad said'?" Newcomber snapped.

Wilbur looked red faced, but quieted and reached down and slipped the Smith and Wesson out of its holster and handed it over. Newcomber slipped it into his saddlebag. He eyed the boy up and down shaking his head. "Don't make any more trouble, Wilbur. You just cost the Bar H about a thousand dollars in lost weight. At a dollar and a half a day, not that you're worth that, it'd take you some time to pay it back should Mr. Hogart want his due."

"A thousand dollars?"

"A thousand dollars . . . that is if we get all the steers back."

John reined the sorrel away.

Wilbur sat chewing on that for a while, when Stub and Sally approached, pushing a half dozen head that had strayed during the stampede. They reined over next to him as the strays rejoined the herd, kicking up their heels like a reunion of old friends.

"You the jefe's pup?" Sally asked.

Wil gigged his horse over and extended his hand. "I'm Wil Hogart." Sally shook with him, but Stub just touched his hat brim, and Wil said "Howdy."

"Did the boss tell you about Oscar?" Sally asked.

"Oscar?" Wilbur said.

"Oscar, the new hand with the six kids and the crippled wife."

"He didn't say – "

"Oscar got stomped under," Sally said, keeping a straight face. Stub eyed him but, as always, kept his own council.

"Stomped under?" Wilbur asked.

"Ain't enough of 'im left to bury," Sally said, shaking his head sadly.

"You mean – "

"Oscar's cold as a mother-in-law's kiss, boy." Sally looked as if he was about to break into tears.

"It's all my fault," Wilbur said, his face fallen.

"Don't know about that," Sally said. "It's the Lord's place to judge reckless behavior . . . the kind what causes the good to die young. Yer misbegotten ways will be laid out a'fore St. Peter soon enough. You may not even survive this drive. Many won't. Maybe you'll meet Oscar in heaven and can explain to him why you got him stomped into salsa. Well, it's nice to make yer acquaintance." He reined away. Both he and Stub were doing their best not to break into uproarious laughter, and in doing so, their shoulders quaked. Wilbur thought they were both in the throes of grief.

"Aren't we going to bury him?" Wilbur called after them.

Stub turned back, wiping the tears of laughter from his eyes. "He's already stomped so deep he'll take root and sprout." He turned away, and the shoulders shook again.

Wilbur Hogart had never felt so terrible. What kind of a man was John Newcomber to worry about running off a thousand dollars worth of fat, and not even mention a man who had been stomped to death?

The word traveled quickly among the men, and all stayed away from Wilbur for the rest of the afternoon – knowing they would break into laughter if they rode up beside the dejected boy, and give it away. Wilbur clomped along behind the herd, his eyes and ears filled with dust, his mind filled with remorse.

They caught up with where Sneezy had made camp, an agreed spot ten miles from the home place on the edge of Bar H property and on the bank of a fair cold creek, lined with willows, a couple of spreading sycamores, and a few Jeffery pines.

Wilbur was the last to the camp, and the men parted from a group as he rode in – Wilbur presumed it was because he was approaching, and that they didn't want to have anything to do with the man who'd caused

Oscar's death. Not that he knew who Oscar was. He'd only met a couple of the men, and Oscar had not been one of them.

Wilbur dropped the saddle from the thoroughbred and turned him out with the remuda, then walked straight over to John Newcomber.

"They told me about Oscar," he said, his weight shifting from foot to foot. "I want to go back and pick up his body. A Christian – "

John Newcomber gave him a dubious look and started to say something, but was interrupted.

Sally stood nearby and offered quickly, "Oscar wanted the coyotes and other critters to have him, boy." Sally removed his hat and placed it across his heart, "It was his last wish. He always was a kind soul to the little critters. And it's the way of the west. We'll say a few words about him after we bean up."

Wilbur was still unsatisfied, but didn't know what to say. It was a custom he'd never heard off, but little would surprise him with what he knew of cattle drives and drovers.

"The coyotes?" he finally managed to mumble in amazement. His gaze wandered from man to man, but none would meet his and none offered to disagree with what he thought was a pagan practice.

"Oscar was a religious soul, but he was the outdoors type...thought these here mountains was his...what do ya call them fancy churches... his cathedral. He wanted to be spread all over these mountains," Sally added. "Nothing like a band of the Lord's scavengers to spread a body about. Crows and buzzards and such fly for miles doing their business and the coyotes and skunks and wolves'll deposit him in all the places he loved – not in exactly the way I'd personally favor it, but he'll get spread. Ashes to ashes, dirt to dirt, dung to dung, so to speak."

Wilbur thought he was going to be sick to his stomach. All the men turned away, and some were obviously overtaken with grief. They held hands to face and shook, or turned away. He walked away from the camp and into a clump of river willows and found a rock by the creek and sat, watching the water tumble by, wondering what would happen to "Oscar's" six starving children. He sat there until he heard Sneezy bang the bottom of an iron skillet, and hurried to get his beans – grief and remorse was one thing, hunger was another.

The men ate in relative silence. Once in a while, one would mention one or another of Oscar's children, or his crippled wife.

The men cleaned up the biscuits, bacon, and beans, and hauled their tins to Sneezy. Darkness was creeping over the camp, and chill setting in. The drive would take them from 5,500 feet elevation on the slopes of the Sierra that rose to 14,000 feet behind them, down to less than 2,000 feet at the railroad corrals at the town of Mojave.

"Time for the ceremony," Sally said. "Gather round, boys."

All the men gathered in a circle, standing, drinking their coffee, gnawin' chaw, smoking roll-your-owns. "Now, what do you remember about Oscar?" Sally said. "You start, Stub."

Stub removed his hat and scratched his woolly head. "Well, I ain't much on reminiscence, so to speak, but I might remember something, given as how Oscar was such a fine fella." He took a long draw on the tin cup then began. "You know that ol' Oscar used to run the Rocking W down near San Berdo. He was countin' cattle there for a buyer from San Francisco, and knew the W didn't have enough cattle to meet the contract, so ol' Oscar set his countin' chute up again' a small hill. The buyer set up on the top rail and went to markin' off the stock. Ol' Oscar had the boys drive those heifers and steers round and round that hill till the buyer counted what he needed, then drove the herd off to the yards. The W got paid for nigh 500 hundred head...twice. Oscar saved the Rocking W, which the bank was sure to grab."

The boys laughed at that, but Wilbur found it to be downright dishonest. He smiled tightly.

"How 'bout you, Tuck," Sally encouraged the old cowhand.

"Well, Oscar was a tough ol' bird." Tuck scratched his wrinkled chin and its stubble of a day's growth of beard. "One time the foreman of the Three Rivers Ranch bet him a season's pay that he couldn't make love to an Indian squaw, kill a grizzly bear, and drink a fifth of whisky in one day...and the foreman knew where the bear's den was and knew an ol' squaw who was a mite friendly to all the Three River's hands, were they to bring her a bag o' beans or sugar. Well, Oscar took that bet, but the thing was, he drank the fifth a' rye first, then . . . a little confused with the fire water an' all . . . he shot the ol' squaw dead as a stone. The hard part was holdin' that griz down . . . but he did an' that's why some bears here a'bout is such sons a' bitches."

The boys laughed and slapped their thighs.

Wilbur began to get a little suspicious.

"How about you, Colorado?" Sally asked the pock-faced redheaded cowhand. He sat away from the others, sharpening a ten inch knife on an Arkansas whet stone.

"I never much cared about tellin' tales," he said, and spit a mouthful of tobacco juice, then went back to his work on the blade.

"You, Pudgy," Sally asked the man John Newcomber had bailed out of the Bishop jail to join the drive.

"Nobody," Pudgy began, "could ever find his way home, good as old Oscar. One time over at the Whisky Holler saloon in Virginia City, old Oscar went up to the bar with a bunch of hands he'd just finished a drive with, and they got to drinkin' and drinkin'. A couple of the boys, realizing how drunk ol' Oscar was, went out to his nag and turned the saddle around – they didn't want him riding into trouble. Oscar, hanging onto that poor ol' nags tail, rode clean to Sacramento before he sobered up and realized he was facing backward. He never could find his way to Sacramento after that, unless he reversed his saddle. But he was always real good at knowin' where he'd been."

By this time Wilbur was red in the face.

"We need to cheer up," Hector Sanchez said, after he quit holding his sides from laughing. "A little friendly competition. Who's the newest hombre to sign on?" Hector asked.

"Must be ol' snake killer," Sally said, putting an arm around Wilbur's shoulders. "You get to go first."

"Wait a minute," Wilbur said. "Did any of you fellas even know this Oscar fella? In fact, was there even any Oscar at all?"

"I've knowed a few Oscars in my day," Sally said. "How about you, Stub."

"Cain't say as how I ever knowed an Oscar."

All the men broke into laughter, slapping their thighs. Wilbur reddened again, and he felt the heat on the back of his neck. He didn't know whether to get angry and stomp away or offer to fight, so he just stood and got a silly grin on his face.

"Ain't you proud you didn't cause nobody to get hurt with that fool stunt?" Sally said, more serious than not.

Tuck cut in before Wilbur could answer. "Give the boy a chance to show he's as good as the rest a' ya," old Tuck looked serious. "Ya'll been funnin' him enough."

Hector stepped over in front of Wilbur. "Can you swing an ax, Señor Hogart?"

"I imagine."

"Good, then we have the notch cutting contest."

"Notch cutting?"

"Sure, every drive has the notch cuttin' contest."

John Newcomber walked away shaking his head, but was unseen by Wilbur who was anxious to redeem himself for being stupid enough to be taken in with the stomped rider story.

"Notch cutting," Hector said. "You go first, so the rest of us know what we have to beat."

Sneezy had already fetched the double bladed ax out of the chuckwagon and offered it to Hector. "Come on, over here," he led Wilbur to a fallen log, two foot in diameter.

"This is a good log for notch cutting," Hector said,

and the other men agreed with him. He lined Wilbur up in front of the log. "Get your distance, *amigo*," he suggested, and Hector adjusted his distance from the log.

"Now, here is the rub, *amigo*." Hector stepped behind Wilbur and encircled his head with his red checkered bandanna.

"Hold on, now," Wilbur tried to protest.

"This is how it is done, *amigo*. Blindfolded. You can do it."

Wilbur allowed himself to have the blindfold put on.

"Wait until I give the signal," Hector said. "Your hat, *amigo*," he said, and removed Wilbur's new fawn colored, now dusty, wide brimmed hat. "You will do better without the hat."

"One, two, three, go," Hector called and, and the men yelled their encouragement.

Wilbur with vigor born of embarrassment and a desire to show these men he was equal to any of them, swung the ax five times before Hector yelled for him to stop. "Time is up, *amigo*."

Wilbur reached up and removed the blindfold, anxious to see how much of a notch he'd cut. And he'd cut three fine ones . . . in his hat. His new Palo Alto lay in front of the log, its crown split, its brim with two wide splits.

"*Carumba*," Hector said, a sorrowful look on his face, "you have cut the notch right where I put your *sombrero* for safe keeping."

The men roared with laughter.

"You win the contest, Wilber," Tuck said. "The prize is a free millinery re-design. That's now what's known as an Owens Valley special."

Wilbur's mother had bought him that hat, just for this trip. The anger began to crawl up Wilbur's backbone, and to the men's surprise, he cast the ax aside and went after Hector Sanchez with his fists. Hector was quick as a snake, and back peddled as Wilbur took four or five healthy swings, then charged in low and tackled him and drove him to his back. He got astride him and pinned him down. Wilbur was red in the face and spitin' mad, but he couldn't move.

"Hey, *amigo*, you can't take a joke?" Hector asked.

"Let me up and I'll show you."

"I think I hold you here a while until the pot she don't boil so much," Hector said.

"Let him up," John Newcomber said, crossing the clearing from where he'd been leaning against a log, taking it all in. "And Mr. Hogart, you will find your bedroll and a place to bed down. The fun is over."

"You might think it's fun."

"I notched my hat, as did most every man here. It'll pass and you'll see the humor in it."

"The hell I will."

Hector unloaded off of him, and Wilbur regained his feet, spun on his heel and stomped away.

"Remember the Alamo," he said under his breath, but no one heard.

He found a spot away from the others for his bedroll, and ignored the feigned compliments to his hat the next morning as the men ate beans and cornbread by the dawning light. He turned in his tin and got a handful of jerky and hard biscuits for his noon meal, and was the first to saddle up for the day's work.

The wrangler, Enrico Torres, cut out a new horse for him – ignoring Wilbur's suggestions that he ride his own thoroughbred with a terse, "Horse has to last the trip, and you will get a new *cabillo* at least twice a day, sometimes thrice, from here on."

The ragged looking buckskin selected by Torres stood and allowed the curry comb then the saddle and bridle, but went into a stiff legged bounce as soon as Wilbur forked him. As much as the boy fought to control the animal, he turned and bounced right through the middle of Sneezy's camp, kicking fire, and ash, and dust in every direction. The Chinese cook scattered for cover, cursing in Oriental jabber, then sailed a pot lid after the boy and high-jumping horse as they moved on into the chaparral.

But to the surprise of all who watched in amusement, Wilbur stuck in the saddle.

He tipped his hat after he got control of the animal, yelled, "Sorry, Sneezy," then gigged away the snorting horse, keeping the animal's chin pulled to its chest, to take up his position riding drag.

"Not bad for a stall-fed tenderfoot," Enrico said to Sally and Stub, who were currying their animals nearby. "His ridin' ability is a bit better than his sense of humor."

"Spent his first day admiring his shadow, cause there was no mirror handy," Stub said, "I thought at first he might be studyin' to be a half-wit, but I believe he might just end this trip knowin' dung from wild honey. He's game enough, and has more sand than I figgered."

"I dunno," Sally offered. "He seems to me he's taken too much of a liking to thick tablecloths and thin soup, but we'll see . . . we will see. My bones is goin' to achin', weather's a' comin'."

Before noon, the sky turned from deep bright blue to flat pewter and the temperature plunged forty degrees. The wind whipped down out of the Sierra, and men pulled coats from rolls behind their saddles.

Wilbur Hogart had a coat, but a light one that served as little more than a windbreaker, and the gloves he pulled from his saddlebag were kid leather – not working gloves, nor warm. Before long, he was cold to the bone, hunkered over like a ninety year old man, and shivering in the saddle. To add injury to insult, the hole in the crown of his hat leaked water, and his head was soaked.

Hector Sanchez had kept his distance and the two young men had no more than exchanged glances.

By mid-morning, flakes of snow began to drift. Both Enrico and Hector Sanchez had pulled heavy *serapes* from the rolls at the back of their saddles, and their wide *sombreros* kept the snow from their shoulders. A steer began to fade back from a position between Hector and Wilbur, and both men moved to haze it back into the herd.

As they did so, Hector spoke for the first time that day. "You do not have a heavy coat?"

"I'm not cold," Wilbur managed through teeth gritted to keep them from chattering.

"I see that, *amigo*," Hector said, and smiled and reined away.

"Greaser," Wilbur said under his breath, and pulled the light jacket closer as he moved back to his position. At least the dust had stopped.

After a moment, Hector again moved closer and

yelled to Wilbur. "I must leave for a *momentito*. Cover the flank."

Wilbur said nothing, even though he heard. He watched the Mexican gig his horse and lope away, then laughed to himself. If the herd did fade and stray on Hector's side, Hector would get a dressing down from Newcomber. He ignored the herd on Hector's flank and tended only those cattle directly ahead of him.

But as fate and the cold would have it, the herd did not stray but rather bunched closer, and Hector soon returned. He drifted over to Wilbur and tossed him a bundle. "It was Oscar's *serape*." He laughed and slapped his thighs. "He needs it no longer so he left it to me. It is not because I am generous, *amigo*. If you continue to knock your teeth together like the castinets, you will cause another stampede. And more work for us all."

Wilbur held the wool *serape* in his hands and stared at the young Mexican, saying nothing.

"Ayee! You stick your *cabaso*...your head through the slit, tenderfeets."

"Though the slit," Wilbur repeated. And without hesitation, learned the use of the *serape*. The same one he had seen Hector use as a blanket the night before.

"*Sí, amigo*," Hector said, and spun his horse to return to his position.

"*Gracias, amigo*," Wilbur called after him.

"*Da nada*, Wil," Hector said, and gave the spurs to his horse. "You have mastered the serape, a difficult task. Tomorrow, if the weather is better, I will teach you the use of the *reata*...it should be nothing for a man who can chop a notch as you can."

"Tomorrow, if the weather is better," Wil called

after him, and wondered what new trick Hector had up his sleeve and he knew that if Hector was fresh out, the others weren't. He wondered if he could borrow a needle and thread from Sneezy to sew up his hat – if Sneezy wasn't still wanting to sail pot lids at him for riding thorugh the middle of camp.

But he was sure Sneezy had long forgotten the incident.

The wind picked up again. But he didn't care. He was warm, for the first time that day.

He removed his hat, eyed it skeptically, and began to chuckle.

END

THE DEATH OF DELGADO

By ROD MILLER

I came face to face with my future the day Christian Delgado rode onto our ranch. At least I hoped—dreamed—I had.

Delgado was a cowboy.

Oh, there were plenty of cowboys in our part of the country. But Delgado was a different sort. Flashy isn't the right word, but there was a certain amount of sparkle to the man and his trappings. He was some strange crossbreed of what nowadays we'd call Californio, buckaroo, and vaquero. Heavy-roweled Mexican spurs, high-topped boots with tall, underslung heels, short chaps that covered his lower legs with nothing but leather fringe, wool vest up top.

His saddle was especially eye-catching. Unlike the plain and practical kacks around our place, his slickfork was silver mounted with conchos, buckles, and bands; his other tack and horse jewelry likewise festooned.

As I said, I was enthralled the minute I saw him. He filled the dreamy eyes of this eleven-year-old Idaho ranch kid with a near-perfect vision of what a cowboy ought to look like.

Mind you, he wasn't anything outside of ordinary from a physical standpoint. He wasn't tall, maybe seven inches above five feet, hung on an average frame that was neither slender nor stocky. Not particularly handsome, I'd say, but neither was he hard to look at. His face, save for a sharp-trimmed mustache, was so

199

clean-shaven it always looked as if he'd just now toweled off the last flecks of lather. He was, I suppose, in his twenty-third or -fourth year that summer.

Even though Christian Delgado had never seen the south side of the Rio Grande, he was, to folks hereabouts, a Mexican. (Some called him a greaser, but never within his hearing.) But he claimed descent direct from the Spaniards of old, and offered deep green eyes and the pale skin on the inside of his forearms as proof of his genealogy. And, to this fascinated boy, he did carry himself with the elegance of a conquistador, a caballero, a Don. There's no doubt he was the kind of man folks paid attention to—the focus of attention in most every crowd, with the quiet confidence of one accustomed to that attention.

He showed up in the Curlew Valley because he heard that Dad had horses that needed rode. He'd heard right.

Dad and Uncle Evan had a sizeable ranch and raised a good many horses for sale. Nothing fancy, mind you, just good solid cow horses and some heavier stock for driving. We also put up a considerable amount of winter feed cut from hay meadows, and ran cattle on range that required the beef to graze at a fast walk just to get to enough grass to work up a cud of a size worth chewing.

And so Delgado went to work. Most of the time he spent horseback, either tending the cow herd or breaking horses. His means of training was simple: a good horse is the result of a lot of wet saddle blankets. When he wasn't sweating the edge off green-broke colts on long trails up and down the hills and canyons of our rocky, brush-covered country, you'd find him starting even greener colts in the round pen. He'd sometimes have half a dozen tied up outside waiting their turn.

Every chance that summer, you'd find me hanging by my elbows from the top rail, eyeing his every move. On a lucky day, I'd ride beside him through the brush, doing my best to handle one of his graduating students like a real hand—like Delgado— would. While abroad on the range we'd see to the cattle; doctoring any that needed it and drifting them back toward home if they wandered too far. Lucky days, for sure, for a kid with cowboy dreams.

But I wasn't all that lucky all that often that summer.

Dad, you see, was digging a well up in the corner of the south pasture. Water was scarce in Curlew Valley, and the stream through that end of our place, while wet enough in springtime, flowed only shallow dust by late summer. A reliable water supply was always to be desired, and always to be realized when chance presented itself. So when Dad watched a forked willow stick in the hands of an itinerant water witch take a nosedive, he dedicated his summer to digging a well.

Digging a well in those days and in that place wasn't a complicated job—you just grabbed the handle of a shovel and put the business end of it to work. The only thing you needed to worry about, Dad always said, was to fill up the back half of the shovel—the front half would take care of itself, he said.

He also told me that when you stood in the deep bottom of the long hole the well was becoming, you could look up at the narrow opening and see stars shining in the middle of the brightest day.

But all I could see those long days helping out at the well was lost opportunities—squandered time, wasted time, time I wanted to be with Delgado.

Instead, I spent my time daydreaming about what I was missing. Now and then, in answer to Dad's call echoing up the hole, I'd pull the well rope off the stake it was anchored to and knot it to the clevis on the singletree, then kiss ol' Socks into a shuffling walk, watching the rope feed its way through the squeaky hand-carved wooden block lashed to the top of the cedar pole tripod over the hole. When the heavy bucket cleared the hole I'd whoa-up Socks, swing the laden tub over to solid ground and call the horse back to slack the rope until the bucket landed. Ol' Socks didn't even need a jerk line to control, just voice commands.

Bucket settled, I'd walk over to the horse, unhook the rope out of the clevis, walk back and two-hand-heft-and-grunt the bucket over to the pile and dump out the hole it held. Hand-over-hand all along the length of the rope, I'd lower the bucket back down the well, careful not to let it fall too fast for Dad to grab before it beaned him, then take another hitch to the anchor stake. As Dad commenced putting more of the hole in the bucket, I'd bring Socks around and back him up close to the hole so we'd be ready to haul up the next load.

Mostly, the big bucket would be heaped with dirt and rocks, but for a few days now it had been showing more and wetter mud so Dad was feeling like the bottom of the well couldn't be far off.

A couple of times a day, besides the trip up for dinner and the one at the end of the day, Dad would ride the bucket up for a rest and some fresh air.

Sometimes the air down there would get pretty thick, he said, and that meant more trips up the hole and longer stretches in daylight before going back down.

From time to time he would fashion a bundle of grass hay about the size of the hole, tie it to the rope, and plunger it up and down the well to force the heavy air out. A trick he learned, he said, from an old Cousin Jack miner who lived in town.

Dad sensed my fascination with Christian Delgado, and knew I saw in the young man the realization of my cowboy yearnings. And, of a normal summer, he would not have objected to my making of myself a full-time apprentice to the horseman. But he needed my help at the well, what with Uncle Evan and the hired hands busy with haying from dark to dark those long hot days. And he often enough made me to realize he appreciated my help, and promised there'd be a time for cowboying.

Truth be told, Dad wished he could be out cowboying too, for he was a man who loved horses and cattle. I knew, too, that he admired the touch Delgado had with horses. Not as much as I admired him, maybe, but even through eyes wrinkled with experience Dad saw something beyond the ordinary in that cowboy's ways.

The day Delgado died dawned like any other.

He haltered and tied that day's mounts to the rail outside the round corral.

Uncle Evan and the hay hands hitched up a team and hayrack and rolled out for the meadow.

And Dad and I and ol' Socks shuffled slow toward the hole in the far corner of the south pasture.

"It's getting pretty boggy down there, son," he

203

said.

"How much deeper you gonna have to go," I asked through a wide yawn as I fisted some of the sleep out of my eyes.

"Can't say. The mud makes for a messier job, but the water does cool it down some."

The past day or two he'd been coming out of the hole muddy above his knees, and he'd said the bottom got softer with every shovelful he hefted out of it. We were threading a good sixty feet of rope down the hole by then.

"I hope, in another day or three, to have to tread water down there. Then I'll know it's a good well. If it draws water enough in the dead of summer, it ought to serve year round. And, near as I can tell after straining the mud through my teeth, it's going to be good, sweet water."

Being a kid, and lacking proper appreciation for such things, I answered with another yawn.

We soon settled into the day's routine, and it did not appear anything would be along to break it. As usual, a breeze kicked up as the day warmed then grew gusty and dusty as the air got hotter. A dust devil whipped up out on the flat and I watched tumbleweeds spin around and around and up and up and eventually peel off to roll back to earth.

"Up!" Dad hollered from down the hole, but his call didn't register.

"Up!" he said again, louder, jolting me back into the present.

I worked the rope off the stake, knotted it through the clevis, and kissed Socks into motion. Unlike me, he'd paid attention to Dad's call and was ready to lean into the harness. By now, the both of us could practically do the job in our sleep and I was soon back on the powder box I used for a seat with barely any recollection of having left it.

This time it was the wind that woke me from my daydreams—heavy, hot gusts peppering me with dirt and debris. I squinted over my shoulder to see that dust devil right there and bearing down on us. With arms wrapped around the top of my head, I fell to my knees and made myself small.

Through the blow I could hear, barely, rattling harness and ol' Socks snorting and blowing. I peeked past a bent elbow in time to see the horse sidestep then shy backward, haunches down and head up as he tried to back away from the swirling wind.

It was gone in an instant, but by then Socks was caving off the raw rim of the well, raining dirt and pebbles down the hole. Upset all the more, he kept snorting and shuffling until his hind legs slipped and he rolled onto his back and into the shaft.

He couldn't fall far—he wedged tight against the sides no more than six or eight feet down, all the while thrashing and screaming. He skidded another few feet and settled there.

"Dad?" I squawked with what little voice I could find. Socks blocked the echo I was used to hearing in the hole, and I thought maybe he blocked my voice as well. Beyond the horse there was nothing to see but darkness. The falling dirt must have broken Dad's coal oil lantern or knocked it into the slop.

"Dad?" again, louder this time.

I didn't even realize I'd been holding my breath until it rushed out with relief when I heard Dad's reply.

"Honey?" he yelled. "What happened up there?"

"Socks fell in the well!"

"I see that. Think you can help him out?"

Our yelling upset the horse again, and his scratching and thrashing sent another rain of dirt and stones rattling down on Dad.

"I don't think so," I said. "He's too far down. And he's upside down."

"Damn!" I heard Dad say—the first foul word I'd ever heard out of his mouth, the hearing of which shocked me almost as much as the mess we were in.

"We'd best be quiet so's not to spook him any worse than he is," he said. "Check the rope, see that it's tied off tight."

I hustled over to the stake and took another double half hitch around it just to make sure.

"Is it all right?"

"I think so."

"Now, son, you just sit tight." I heard him working the shovel as he chinked a ledge in the shaft where he set the bucket to get it out of the way. "What I'm going to do is try to climb out of here. Think there's room for me to squeeze past ol' Socks if I can get up there?"

"Maybe," I said. "I don't think so."

The horse took another fit and in the squirming and straining slipped another foot or two. The block lashed to the tripod started to sway and rattle, the rope jerking rhythmically as Dad pulled himself steadily upward. Dirt and rocks splashing in the bottom said he was using his feet to help claw his way out of the well.

The rope stopped jerking from time to time as he wedged himself against the sides to rest. Soon, the pulse of his grasping hands would travel up the rope again and before long I could hear his breathing, and the strain in it.

Then the horse must have sensed Dad's presence beneath him, and not known what to make of it. In a renewed bout of heaving and clawing, twisting and straining, ol' Socks came loose of a sudden and slid down the well scraping rocks, dirt, and Dad off the sides and taking it all down with him. They bottomed out with a thick splash and heavy thud that reverberated all the way to the surface. A few more pebbles and dirt clods trickled down, falling into silence along with the fading echo.

I wasn't there to hear the quiet.

After crossing the pasture at a dead run, I stumbled to a stop, the rails of the round corral the only thing keeping me from tumbling all the way down.

Delgado had seen me coming and waited quietly across the fence atop one of the colts, which shied and scrambled backward when I hit the fence. When the colt stopped, Delgado flexed his hips and kissed his lips to urge it forward, finally touching it with the spurs. A soft haul on the hackamore reins stopped the colt's sudden lunge and Delgado settled down into the saddle as I struggled for breath.

"It's, it's Daddy," I said. "He's down. The well. Socks fell in. On top. Of him."

The corral gate was already swinging open. Delgado had dismounted in an instant as soon as he and the colt were on my side of the fence. Without a word, he grabbed me by the waist and swung me aboard the skittish colt.

"You hurry. Tell Evan to bring the team and his

men to the well. They are unloading. Tell him to bring the derrick cable. Hurry. I will go to your father."

That horse was only half under my control, if that, on the run to the hay yard. Once or twice he kicked up his heels and tried to bog his head, but by sawing on the reins I was able to prevent a come-apart or complete runaway.

He didn't want to stop when we tore out of the hay meadow and into the stackyard. I cranked his head to one side until it was practically in my lap and he finally came around in a circle and stopped as Uncle Evan and the three workers looked on.

Before the story was half told, Uncle Evan had scrambled down off the stack of loose hay, chopped the derrick cable in two with a hay knife and was pulling it screaming through the pulleys on the derrick. The hay hands lit into the load like windmills, forking it off every side of the wagon. They kept at it even as Uncle Evan heaved heavy coils of derrick cable over the rack on the front of the wagon then climbed up, hooked a leg over and whipped up the team with the lines.

As the haywagon clattered and bounced out of the stackyard, I tapped my heels to the colt's sides and hoped he'd do something other than go to pitching. He snorted some and flung his head around, but another soft kick in the belly convinced him to line out and walk. Once he settled in, I urged him into a long trot and figured to let it go at that.

Delgado was just clearing the lip of the well when I rode up. Any hope I had for Dad washed away in the tears streaming down his muddy face.

He'd stopped only long enough to grab a lantern from the milking stall and an ax and shovel from the tool shed. By the time Uncle Evan had arrived, Delgado was already at the bottom of the well, having slid down the rope with the lit lantern in his teeth. But all he could find to do was pull the bucket out of the mess, tie it to the rope, and ask Evan to haul him up—which he did, by hand, with help from the three men on his hay crew.

The cowboy stepped out of the bucket as it reached the surface and plopped down on my box.

"I cannot find him," he said as he absent-mindedly scratched with a fingernail at the mud that covered his chaps, then unbuckled and peeled them off. "The hole is full of nothing but broken horse and mud. I felt around as much as I could. Nothing." He unbuttoned and pulled of his vest then tugged his shirt over his head.

Delgado unsheathed his knife and went to whittling on the ax handle. It seemed a poor choice of activities in the circumstances. I said "What—"

"There is no room to work the ax in the hole," he said, cutting off my question. Although his voice was quiet, anger, frustration maybe, was as evident as if he had shouted. "It is too tight."

Still unsure what he was doing, I thought it best to keep my peace.

Snapping off the handle, he shaved the raw edge to smooth the splinters as best he could. To Uncle Evan, he said, "I guess we won't be needing that cable. There is no way we'll lift that horse out of there without caving in the sides. He will have to come up in the bucket. Lower me down, then get your team ready. It will be too much lifting to do by hand."

Evan and at least one of his hay hands were years older than Delgado. It didn't occur to me at the time, but I have since wondered why it was the younger man giving orders in that tense situation, and why the others complied without question or comment.

It did not dawn on me, either, what Delgado was doing down there until the first bucket came up. Blood sloshed over the sides as Uncle Evan swung it away from the well. The horse's head hung over the rim, muzzle stained scarlet and nostrils dripping gore.

I hit my knees as that red mess splashed to the ground and I heaved up what was left of breakfast and kept heaving until there was nothing left to come up and then I heaved some more. And even after that, the sound of Delgado and his ax at work down the well would set me to gagging all over again.

One front quarter, then another, came out of the hole in poorly butchered pieces. Then Delgado came up. Blood-spattered and gasping, he sat flat to the ground and sucked in air.

"Anything?" Evan asked.

"No. Nothing."

Uncle Evan asked no more questions, simply stared vacantly at the hired man on the ground.

"You're spent. I'll go down," he finally said.

"No. There is no room. I can hardly get any leverage myself, and I am smaller than you. I will finish the job."

He said the lantern kept flickering out from lack of air, so he gave up trying to keep it burning and did his awful work in the dark. Worst of all, worse than the dark, worse than the heat, worse than the mud, he told us, was the stink. Even in the open air the stench of blood and torn flesh was overpowering when the wind swirled it your direction. It got worse when broken

210

entrails and smashed organs topped the pile.

Finally, the second hind leg, broken at an odd angle, plopped out of the bucket and onto the pile dripping mud and blood and that was the end of ol' Socks.

Standing with hands grasping spread knees, Uncle Evan bent over the lip of the well awaiting word from Delgado. From time to time he would hear him sloshing around down there, or the occasional splash.

Finally, "I have found a hand."

Later, "I have freed as much of him as I can, but he is stuck fast. You will have to send down the cable."

From the hay wagon, Uncle Evan fetched a steel pulley and short length of chain and hooked it to the tripod next to the wooden block through which the well rope was threaded. As he tested the strength of his work, his men stretched the kinks out of the cable. He threaded it through the pulley, quickly clamped a clevis to the end, and shoved the wire rope down the shaft an arm's length at a time.

It seemed an eternity until Delgado asked to be lifted up in the bucket. He stepped out, cut the well rope from the bail, then pulled the end through the block and tossed it out of the way so it would not tangle with the cable.

"I don't know. He is stuck pretty tight. I got a loop around him but I don't know," he told Evan as they watched the hands hitch the cable to the doubletree harnessed to the team. "I never could feel his feet. Too deep."

As the slack slowly came out of the cable he said, "I hope he doesn't come up like that horse."

Uncle Evan took over the team, and with his easy

hands at the lines they leaned slowly into the load.

Nothing.

He urged the horses on—tugs creaked, singletrees cracked. The cable hummed, the pulley trembled. The heavy cedar posts in the tripod groaned and their thick bottoms pushed up ridges in the dirt as they tried to spread wider, threatening collapse.

The team grunted and strained and leaned harder into their collars as Uncle Evan, in desperation, slapped one horse then the other on the rump with the lines. Slowly, almost imperceptibly, they moved ahead. Half the length of a hoof. Another. And then, with a release felt deep in the belly of every one of us, the team was walking free.

The pulley from the hay derrick squealed as it slowly rotated. Uncle Evan handed the lines to another of the men as the team's distance from the hole increased and he quickly followed the cable back to the well to stand beside me and Delgado.

Dad came up belt buckle first. Uncle Evan collapsed in a heap when he saw his broken brother, bent double, backwards, swinging slowly from the derrick cable.

I stared, uncomprehending. I guess my day's ration of distress was long since used up, to be replaced by shock and resignation.

Like I had done so many times, Delgado swung the load away from the hole as the team backed slack into the cable and settled it to solid ground. He pulled the pin out of the clevis and cast it aside and carefully, gently, gathered Dad's limp body in his arms and carried him to the hay wagon. Then he turned for the house and walked away.

* * *

Delgado did not die that day.

At least not like Dad was dead.

But the spirit was gone out of him as surely as if it had been his body we pulled out of that temporary grave at the bottom of the well.

In a way, I guess it was.

He didn't stop at the bunkhouse any longer than it took to stuff his few belongings into his war bag. I don't know what he wore on his feet when he left our place. His soggy high-topped boots with the blood-and-mud-encrusted Mexican spurs still strapped to them were left standing outside the door, abandoned to the well as surely as Dad's were; his sucked off in the muck in the bottom of that hole where, I suppose, they still are.

So far as I know, ol' Socks was the last horse Delgado ever touched.

For years, he stayed around these parts setting his hand to a variety of jobs—sacking wheat at the feed and seed, clerking at a grocery store, tending bar, that sort of thing. Last I heard, he was somewhere off in Wyoming pushing folks around in wheelchairs in a convalescent hospital.

I led that green-broke colt he'd mounted me on that day back to the yard and pulled off Delgado's silver-mounted saddle and hauled it inside the tack shed. It has been there ever since, hanging from a rafter on a rawhide tether.

AUTHOR'S NOTE: Although the people and

particulars in "The Death of Delgado" are imagined, the incident at the center of the story is real, as told in "The Land is Free," a September/October 1961 *True West* magazine article by Colen Sweeten as told to Colen Sweeten, Jr. My thanks and appreciation go to Colen Sweeten III for the use of the story, and to his father and grandfather for telling it.

END

STAY OF EXECUTION

By Lucia St. Clair Robson

Prospectors working the far-flung subterranean tentacles of the Comstock Lode cursed the blue-gray mud that clung to their shovels and clogged their rockers. They cursed it until an assay done in neighboring California proved the "blasted blue stuff" to be silver, and worth $2,000 a ton.

The two Californians who ran the assay sneaked out of town in the dead of night, but not before they shared the information with a few trusted friends. Those friends told their friends. Within days, thousands of friends of friends of friends had packed up and set out for the western part of Utah Territory called the Washoe. The next mob to arrive were easterners who had churned into motion a decade too late to strike California gold. Whether they came from out of the sunrise or the sunset, every man-jack dreamed of finding a silver lining for his personal cloud.

In a hullabaloo of hammers and whip-saws, the metropolis of Salt Lick sprouted from the high desert's hardpan like a cluster of malnourished ticks on a mangy dog's duff. Both ends of the town's rutted main thoroughfare frayed out into a sprawling suburb of wagons, tents, lean-tos, dug-outs, and huts resembling trash heaps.

The discovery of silver also attracted drummers and drifters, sutlers, duffers, gamblers, bunco men, thimbleriggers, and peddlers of poisonous whiskey called Devil's Broth. A troupe of hurdy-gurdy girls charged miners four bits a dance, and a bevy of congenial strumpets set up shop in a row of cribs called The Line. They all settled on Salt Lick thick as black flies on cow pies. Whiskey flowed like snow-melt down a mountain sluice, and the town gained a reputation as a haphazard shebang of sin and scurrility.

Make no mistake, Salt Lick did have a sheriff, Eliphalet Bangert. Banger for short. Some said Banger was the best sheriff that money could buy. He usually could be found at the bar of his cousin's saloon, O'Shea's, where the dented tin star pinned to his suspender strap was all that distinguished him from the other elbow-benders.

The few who thought about it at all gave odds of a hundred to one on civilization being forever a no-show in Salt Lick.

Those odds changed on a sweltery Sunday twilight in August when the weekly stage coach rattled to a halt in front of Salt Lick's mercantile. Stage company hirelings used ropes to lower a trunk the size of a chicken coop from the coach's roof to the ground. A hail of valises and carpet bags followed.

The foothill of baggage hinted that the owner was of the female persuasion, but the stack of drum-shaped hat boxes supplied the tell. The mercantile's front porch loungers snapped to attention as if someone had electrified the pegleg slab-lumber benches beneath the shiny seats of their corduroys. They set aside their whittling, adjusted their sagging suspenders, and spat out their chaws.

Their hopes were confirmed when the stage driver hustled around to lower the steps with more than his usual enthusiasm. The door swung open. The driver wiped his hand on his shirt before he held it out to help his sole passenger descend.

To the audible intake of breath from the sweat-drenched porch roosters, a cool breeze wafted out in a flurry of velvet flounces. Her dress was the dark blue of a midnight sky. The velvet's nap had a subtle shimmer like moonlight behind a dark cloud. The dress matched her eyes in hue and moon shine.

She laid a hand, pale and graceful as a lily, on the driver's forearm. With her other hand she lifted her skirts out of the way of her black satin shoes. The porch roosters leaned forward, hoping for a show of lisle-clad ankle and maybe even a glimpse of calf.

She didn't disappoint.

She paused in the doorway, as if about to make an entrance onto a stage of a different sort. The lilac-dyed

egret plumes in her wide-brimmed straw hat swayed
when she bestowed a nod on the men.

"Good evening, gentlemen." Her voice registered
in the tenor range with a huskiness full of promise. "My
name is Casandra, but folks call me Miss Cassie.

She smiled into the flurry of "Pleased to meet
you, ma'am" from the porch. She held one satin toe
above the top step, as if to give them time to admire the
scenery. And such scenery. One fogey announced to his
bench-mates that Miss Cassie was the Pacific Ocean,
the mighty Mississippi, Niagara Falls, and the marbled
Halls of Congress combined.

A gentle swell of milk-white bosoms crested the
lace levee of her bodice. She had bounteous hips and a
waist that a man's two hands could span with thumbs
overlapping. More awesome was an item the mercantile
crowd couldn't see, but were trying their best to
imagine. Beneath the velvet dress, crinolines, and
camisette, Miss Cassie wore a silk corset with weft-
float patterning, silk laces, pewter eyelets, and whip-
thin stays of springy Sheffield-cast steel.

With hoop skirts lifted to clear the dusty ruts of
the street, Miss Cassie sashayed over to engage in
negotiations with the driver of a grocery wagon. The
roosters left the porch to gather in the street, but not to
eavesdrop. Miners were adept at assessing the lay of the
land, and these fellows knew the driver would be
unable to say "No, Ma'am" to Miss Cassie. Well before

he nodded agreement to her request, half of them were tossing sacks of flour and sugar and crates of bacon, molasses, and coffee off the tailgate The other half replaced them with her trunk and bags.

Miss Cassie settled onto the wagon's passenger seat. The freighter gave one of the hirelings two bits to watch his heap of goods, then set a bumpy course toward the other end of town. The men figured he was taking his passenger to Miss Hattie's Gentlemen's Club, the centerpiece of The Line. As they sauntered off down the wooden sidewalks in the wagon's dusty wake, each was estimating how much an hour of Miss Cassie's undivided attention might cost. The wagon stopped short of Hattie's though, and Miss Cassie alit at the Baltimore House.

The Baltimore was the largest den of iniquity in Salt Lick. Reasons to go there were easy to come by for those with jingle in their jeans. The steaks arrived hot and tender enough to cut with a dull pocket knife. The cigars burned pure Orinoco, the whiskey didn't contain enough water to notice, and the newspapers on display were less than a month old. What's more, only a few of the Baltimore's hurdy-gurdy girls had mustaches, and the floormen briskly escorted egregious sharpers out the front door.

The Baltimore also served as theater, opera house, dance hall, billiard parlor, courtroom, wedding chapel, fraternal lodge, post office, and hospital. On rare occasions a circuit rider would hold Sunday revival meetings there. A Come-to-Jesus sermon always attracted an enthusiastic crowd, but salvation rarely survived past Monday's cock-crow.

Eight rooms on the second floor accommodated travelers. A large handbill pasted onto the outside wall advertised "Spring beds in clean sheets with no fleas, $1 a night. Hot Water Baths, $2. Listening to Lodgers' Tales of Woe, $3."

The Baltimore encompassed almost an eighth of an acre. Tables lined both sides of the long main hall, with a wide aisle down the center where the floormen patrolled, on the look-out for cards that were sanded or stripped or lurking in sleeves. The house featured no-limit games and separate rooms for faro, brag, ecarté, and poker. It hummed day and night with conversation, the snap of pasteboard cards, and the clink of bottles. Piano music played to a crisp counterpoint of cue sticks striking billiard balls.

As Cassie stood in the doorway she put a hand in the pocket sewn into the side seam of her skirt. The feel of the advertisement torn from the St. Louis Intelligenser reassured her. It announced a position for a singer at the Baltimore House in Salt Lick, Utah Territory.

Her entrance created a swell of silence that rolled out toward the four corners of the smokey hall. Men left their tables in the back rooms to gather in the doorways and see what the hush was about.

The piano player didn't generate much revenue for the house so he and his battered instrument occupied the farthest corner. Only the dented crown of his plug hat was visible above the upright. The driver of the grocery wagon had told Cassie that his name was Schulz.

Being heard and not seen suited Schulz just fine so long as the barkeep sent him drinks, and at the end of the night more than a shot-level of coins had collected in the whiskey glass on top of his piano. He was the last to notice Cassie's arrival, but when he did the notes of a new ditty called "Lorena" trickled to a halt.

Miss Cassie strode across the dance floor and down the aisle between the tables. Heads swiveled, hypnotized by the sway of her hips below the fulcrum of her tiny waist. In Schulz's far corner the gray tobacco smoke hung lower overhead like a mackinaw blanket. Her passing set it to dancing, reflecting swirls of golden light cast from the whale oil lamps mounted along the walls.

She leaned over and murmured something to Schulz. He nodded and started the intro to the song again. With one hand resting on the upright Cassie sang.

The years creep slowly by, Lorena,
The snow is on the ground again.

The sun's low down the sky, Lorena,

The frost gleams where the flow'rs have been.

Her voice had operatic power and range infused with the resonant warmth of a mother's lullabye. More than a few men wiped their eyes, and their noses too, on their sleeves. Cassie took song requests for the next few hours. Halfway through the evening Schulz fetched a much taller glass from the bar to hold the overflow of coins, nuggets, and poker chits.

Behind the bar, a clock sat on a shelf beneath the life-sized painting of a naked Venus smirking from behind a large scallop shell. As the clock's hands crept toward midnight Cassie sat on the piano bench to rest her feet. The bartender approached along the room's perimeter.

He wore black trousers and waistcoat and a white linen shirt. He was the color of ebony himself so he blended with the shadows. When the song ended he leaned over and spoke just loudly enough for Cassie to hear him above the clapping, whistling, and thunder of boots stomping.

"You must be weary, Miss Cassandra."

Cassie wasn't surprised that he knew her real name. A good barkeep made it his business to know about everyone who walked through the door.

"If you would like to retire for the night, the porter will escort you to room eight upstairs. Your bags are there and a maid will deliver a repast. Breakfast is served from five of a morning, but the kitchen will send it up if you prefer."

She started to show him the advertisement from the Intelligenser, then thought better of it. Allowing her arrival to seem like a stroke of Fate could work to her advantage.

"Then I am hired? And I might stay here?"

"Yes, ma'am." His bow was courtly. "The boss has been looking for a chanteuse."

The muscles around his eyes and mouth twitched at the word "boss." Cassie wasn't sure if it was the ghost of a smile or the flicker of lamplight and shadow across the calm, dark surface of his face.

She wanted to ask who the boss was, where he was, and what he expected of her, but experience had taught her not to push her luck. It also had taught her to recognize an ally and a valuable one. She added a curtsy to her smile, but one so slight only the barkeep could see it. Anything more might have endangered him, and her.

"And what is your name?"

"Prince Rivers, ma'am. But folks call me Riv."

Of course they do, Cassie thought.

Calling a son of Africa Prince or Mr. Rivers would stick in the craws of even the lowliest of Salt Lick's much paler denizens. Especially a son of Africa who wore a starched collar, spoke with impeccable diction, and used words like "repast" and "chanteuse."

After bidding her admirers goodnight, Cassie followed the aged porter, Jonesy, upstairs. The room was comfortable and clean, but she didn't stay there. If she was going to be employed at the Baltimore, she wanted to see how it operated. She sat on the stair landing and peered, unnoticed, through the balusters until the clock struck three and Riv announced closing time. Or at least as much of a closing time as even happened at the Baltimore.

The dealers from the back rooms ponied up the whack, the house's percentage of the winnings, and delivered it to Riv. Then they caught their second wind and went back to work. The tyros in the main hall put away their cards, their dice, their chips, and their billiard cues and filed out the front door. Their docility didn't surprise Cassie even though Riv was at least fifty years old, not much bigger than a minute, and as best Cassie could tell, was not wearing a side arm.

* * *

The next morning two young maids knocked on Room Eight's door. They announced that they would help Cassie don her corset each morning. Number eight, they said, was the only room with an iron bedstead sturdy enough to hold steady during a lacing. Riv must have had that in mind when he gave her this room. And he must have known that one maid would not suffice for the task of cinching Miss Cassanda into her unmentionable.

The maids stood, awed into silence, before the ladder-backed chair where the hour-glass-shaped cage of silk sat. The twenty-eight flexible steel stays fit inside their narrow casings like fingers into gloves. They created the garment's graceful curves and held it as stiffly erect as a dowager at a debutante cotillion.

When Cassie went downstairs the piano had already been moved up front, next to the dance floor. Many of last night's customers had resumed their card play. Fifteen or twenty miners, eager to start another eighteen-hour-day of back straining labor, were wolfing down fried steak, fried eggs, fried potatoes and fried bread. A boy of about twelve was sweeping out the manure-laced mud tracked in on boot soles. Jonesy the porter lay curled up on a billard table and snoring like a jug band. His false teeth rested on a saucer near his head.

Riv was polishing the 35-foot-long mahogany bar when she approached. "Good morning, Miss Cassandra. What will you have for breakfast?"

"I'll eat in the kitchen later, thank you, Riv."

"This is for you, ma'am." Riv handed her a small sack. "From Schulz."

Cassie turned to one side and tested its heft before she slipped it down the front of her bodice. She shook her shoulders to settle the poke more comfortably.

225

"What's the whack?" she asked.

"Ten percent."

Cassie could tell by the sack's weight that it held about half of what had collected in the large glass on the piano, minus the house's cut, the whack.

"Is Mr. Schulz agreeable with this arrangement?"

"Yes, Ma'am." There was no mistaking Riv's grin this time. "After dividing with you he still went home with two regular nights' get." He leaned slightly forward as if to impart a secret. "And I never heard him play so well before either."

He set six of the small tin pails called growlers on the bar and ladled warm beer into them from a keg. He nodded toward the boy sweeping the last of the dried mud out the door.

"The lad's name is Scully, but everyone calls him Growler. If you want anything fetched or delivered, he's your man. He also shines shoes and can recite the Declaration of Independence."

The boy turned red and mumbled "Pleased ta meetcha, ma'am" as he stowed the broom in a corner. Holding the pails by their wire handles, three in each hand, he hustled out the door without spilling a drop.

Cassie was hungry, but her first task was to make herself indispensible. She went into the kitchen to befriend Biscuits, the cook, whose barrel-belly was his best advertisement. He was as parsimonious with words as he was with salt, but she charmed him so thoroughly she was able to wheedle some empty flour sacks.

She tore them into useful sizes, rinsed them out, and draped them over bushes outside the kitchen door. The arid wind dried them about the same time Cassie finished reading the future written in the lines of Biscuit's palm. For the rest of the day he would turn his hand over now and then and stare at the calluses as if he expected them to talk to him.

Cassie discarded the filthy bar towels, stiff with sweat, sputum, tobacco juice, puke, and booze, and hung the new ones on the pegs. She folded some of the other cloths and stacked them next to the glasses and the pepperbox pistol on the shelf under the bar. Finally she dusted everything that didn't move out of the way, except for Jonesy. As she walked past his bunk on the billiard table Riv called out to her.

"Miss Cassandra, would you take a gander at Mr. Jones's false teeth?"

"Why?"

He beckoned and she went back to the bar to hear the story.

"He forgets to check them before he puts them in of a morning. Maybe the leftover food between the teeth attracts squatters."

"Squatters?"

"Ants made a nest there. The stinging kind. The queen moved in and the rest followed with the larvae.

Once, a scorpion delivered scads of little ones and Jones didn't notice. The scorpion stung him and his mouth and gullet swelled up so bad he had to subsist on beer for a week."

On her way out to explore Salt Lick's amenities that afternoon, Cassie saw the large placard that Riv had posted on the outside wall. "Miss Cassandra, World Renowned CHANTREUSE, will present SOIREES MUSICALES nightly." So it was no surprise the Baltimore was more crowded than usual that evening.

Cassie divided her time between singing at the piano and circulating with smiles and small talk among the less serious gamers in the main room. She mustered the Baltimore's waiters to make sure glasses were filled, worn decks of cards were replaced, broken glass swept up immediately, and spitoons emptied before they overflowed.

On the third day Riv sent the two porters and the floormen out to scour the town for more chairs. The fourth night, Banger, the sheriff, ghosted in around eleven o'clock and leaned, glowering, against the wall by the door. He must have seen a lot of O'Shea's regulars in the crowd because the glower turned meat-axish. After fifteen minutes he left as silently as he had entered. Riv wore a worried look as he watched Banger go.

On the fifth night men lined up three deep at the Baltimore's bar and dancers bumped elbows. Cassie was halfway through "Woodman Spare that Tree" when she sensed a sea change in her audience. The hurdy-gurdy girls and their ad hoc swains slowed their pace, then stopped altogether, but Cassie sang on to the end.

Old tree! the storm still brave! And woodman, leave the spot:

While I've a hand to save, thy axe shall harm it not.

Schulz, as unaware of the world as usual, finished with a flourish of trills and glissandos. Then he glanced up and noticed that all heads were turned toward the colossus standing in front of the bar. Cassie had already locked looks with that six foot and three inches of broad-shouldered, narrow-waisted swank.

Some of those there that night insisted that sparks flew when Cassie and Lud first set eyes on each other. The less romantic held that the fireworks happened when a bat flew into the candelabra in pursuit of a plump moth. Only the urchin named Growler knew the real story. Oblivious to the drama, he chose that moment to light a squib from a candle and toss it up onto an overhead beam.

Cassie guessed that the Boss had finally made an appearance. Riv had politely declined to gossip about the Boss, but Cassie had heard a few facts and a lot of fiction about him. He said his name was Plantagenet Calvert. He hailed from England and he claimed to be a relative of Lord Baltimore himself, which was how he'd acquired the moniker Lud.

Rumor was that he owned the Baltimore House, but for a year and a half he'd left the everyday affairs of the place to Riv. People said he had built a shack on the upper reaches of the Carson River basin and spent his days working his claim there. As for his nights, that's when the rumors turned fanciful bordering on scandalous. Ladies from The Line, some said, had beaten a path to his door.

His mane of russet-colored hair brushed the top of his collar. More curls peeped from the open neck of his starched linen shirt. He had rolled his sleeves up, revealing a bumper crop of red-gold hair on his muscular forearms. He sported mustachios and muttonchops enough to establish two grand ducheys. The thought of how all those whiskers would tickle a person's bare skin caught Cassie off guard. Her cheeks heated to a pink glow and her heart beat fast as a flutter wheel.

She expected him to come over and introduce himself like the gent he claimed to be. Instead, he put on his Wellington top hat, adjusted it forward to a jaunty angle, and left. Cassie turned on her heel and marched upstairs without looking back.

The next morning Growler and two of his fellow urchins accepted her offer to teach them to read. The four of them were sitting at a table in Cassie's favorite retreat, the Library, when Lud filled the doorway. The boys replaced their books on the shelf and thanked Cassie for the lesson. Lud moved aside to let them pass.

And so it began.

Neither of them was the sort to do anything by halves. They fell into love the way the unwary plummeted down mine shafts. If they shared the bed in Number Eight they were discreet about it, but describing their romance as fractious understated the case. They took their spats to the Library so often the regulars called it the Growlery.

Their differences over spitoons became known as the War of the Cuspidors. Cassie wanted one for every table so players wouldn't be tempted to attempt long shots from wherever they sat. She insisted that the spittons be emptied three times a day, and that men be encouraged to improve their aim enough to hit them, preferably on the inside.

Lud argued that puddles of tobacco juice were good enough for both Houses of Congress, and they would do for the Baltimore too. Hounding the gamers about their erratic aim would embarrass and upset them, he said. And when customers were embarrassed and upset, the daily whack diminished.

But the cuspidor conflict was a williwaw in a thundermug compared to what happened when the renowned Adah Isaacs Menken passed through on her way to San Francisco. Lud invited her to perform at the

Baltimore. The prospect of "The Great Menken" gracing Salt Lick for a matinee of Shakespearean readings put the hobnail-and-denim set in a fester. The rumor that Miss Menken occasionally disrobed on stage did nothing to diminish their enthusiasm.

As luck, or fate, would have it, one of the hurdy-gurdy girls had contracted a persistent cough. Cassie mounted her mare that day and rode off with a growler of chicken soup and two bottles of brandy mixed with a generous amount of laudanum. Laudanum was good, after all, for just about any ailment. Mothers spoon-fed it to colicky babies. It would ease the patient's cough and help her sleep.

When Cassie returned, the other hurdy-gurdies couldn't wait to tell her that the Boss was entertaining Miss Menken at a private dinner in an upstairs room at Miss Hattie's on The Line. When he returned, a little tipsy, at ten o'clock Cassie was waiting. Smiling and full of questions about the performance she collected the second bottle of brandy and went upstairs arm-in-arm with him. Their laughter lingered in the air.

Early the next morning, Cassie came downstairs carrying Lud's clothes and boots and the empty brandy bottle. She told Riv she was taking the duds to the Chinaman's laundry.

"The boots too?"

"They want repairing."

She didn't fool him. "Miss Cassandra, what have you gone and done?"

She only smiled over her shoulder at him. She had just cleared the door when a stentorian roar came from upstairs.

Lud loomed on the landing. His entire skull -- cheeks, chin, and jowls included -- had been shaved bald as a billard ball. He descended the stairs in a blue cloud of oaths, imprecations, and a creative inventory of obscenities. The blanket draped around him exposed enough to show that more than his head had been shaved. Neck, chest, arms, legs, hands, feet, all were hairless. It took no great imagination to assume that the barbering did not stop at his extremities.

Folks said he looked like Samson after Delilah finished with him. The comparison was apt. Most agreed afterward that his hairless humiliation was what gave that little whiffet of a sheriff the courage to act. And the consequences of Banger's new-found pot-valor were Biblical. Maybe if Cassie had returned to the Baltimore that day none of it would have happened. But she didn't. And it did.

After spending the afternoon drinking in his cousin's near-empty saloon, Banger's resentment came to a boil. About sundown he reeled into the Baltimore with his two Colt Dragoons drawn. People bolted for the back rooms or dove under tables.

"We don't cotton to uppity darkies and snooty furriners here." Banger waved one barrel at Riv and the other at Lud whose clothes had been retrieved from the wash house.

"Now, sheriff." Lud held up a placating hand. "You don't want anyone to get hurt. Let's discuss this outside."

"We're discussing it here. Or would you rather let your whore settle it for you?"

With no whiskers to hide it, Riv saw the blood rise from Lud's neck and spread to his cheeks, leaving a pale line along the band of tensed jaw muscle. Riv slid one hand slowly down toward the pepperbox, but Banger saw the movement. Riv ducked below the bar as Banger shot wildly in his direction. One bullet shattered the clock on the self. Another hit the painted Venus between her slightly crossed eyes.

Someone reached up from under a table nearest Lud and handed him a single-shot derringer. Lud dodged Banger's third bullet and fired before he could pull the trigger again. Banger dropped, quivered like a dog dreaming of squirrels on the run, then went limp. The town mortician crawled out from under a table. He bent over Banger and declared him dead as mutton.

The mortician and several of the more respected of Salt Lick's citizens threw the body across the back of a horse and led it down the street to O'Shea's. Their intention was to explain to the sheriff's cousin that Lud had fired in self-defense. No one expected much trouble about it.

Riv gathered the pieces of the clock. Growler mopped up the blood. Cards and billiards started where they left off. Lud retired to the Library to stare blankly at an opened book while he pondered how to win Cassie back.

It took Timothy O'Shea about an hour to round up fifteen or twenty of the lower ilk and stalk into the Baltimore. O'Shea wore his cousin's star pinned on his shirt. He and his posse comitatus took Lud away at gunpoint.

Riv sent Growler in search of Cassie. The boy found her having tea with Miss Hattie amid the fainting couches, silken cushions, and tasseled damask draperies in the madame's apartment.

Cassie arrived at the Baltimore out of breath and with Growler close behind her. "Where is he, Riv?"

"In the jailhouse, Miss Cassandra."

"But they'll let him go tomorrow, of course. It was self defense. No judge will convict him."

"The circuit judge isn't due for a week." For once, Riv avoided looking her in the eye. "They won't wait for him."

"Why not?"

Growler piped up. "They'll try him by lynch's law."

"They can't. They won't." But Cassie could see from Riv's look that he believed they could and they would.

"O'Shea won't do anything more tonight," Riv said. "He'll wait until dark tomorrow to hold his lynch party".

"How do you know that?"

Riv looked at her with a sadness so intense it brought a sting of tears to Cassie's eyes.

"My people know about lynchings."

"Where's the nearest gunsmith?"

"Now, Miss Cassandra, who are you planning to shoot?"

"No one."

Riv consulted his pocket watch. "The gunsmith will be asleep."

"I know where there's a good one, ma'am," said Growler. "He won't turn you away."

"I'll get the night clerk." Riv was too much the diplomat to tell Growler he was not man enough to protect Miss Cassandra on the dark streets of Salt Lick. "We'll go in the buggy."

Cassie went upstairs. She returned wearing her travel cloak and carrying a long, narrow package wrapped in sacking.

Growler was right about the gunsmith. Yawning, he opened the door with a Paterson Colt loaded, cocked, and pointed at them, but he listened to Cassie's story. He took them to his workshop and lit the lamps. When Cassie unrolled the sacking and told him what she wanted, Riv laughed out loud, the first time she had heard him do it.

As they drove toward home, Cassie asked, "How early do you suppose they'll allow a visitor at the jailhouse, Riv?"

"Around seven when a flunky from O'Shea's brings the morning meal and the noon and the evening's too. He empties the soil bucket, then the rest of the day everything's locked up tight. Sheriff Banger spent most of his time at O'Shea's, and you can bet his cousin won't be around the jail either. He's got a saloon to oversee and a lynching to organize. All those torches take time to make."

"I can help, Miss Cassie." Growler was eager for adventure. "Tell me when to meet you and I'll pasture the horses out back.

Riv gave Cassie a stern look. "You're not thinking of involving a child in an escape from jail, are you?"

"You said I could count on Growler for deliveries." Cassie's smile was a sorrowful one. "And if anyone needs delivering, it's Lud."

* * *

Riv was right about Timothy O'Shea and his merry band of miscreants. A lynching required preparation. O'Shea served his cheapest whiskey until the fifteen members of his posse reached the hollering stage of inebriation. They were all hard drinkers so that took until after dark. And then there was a rope to test, a tall mule to find, and those torches to distribute and ignite. The mob set out all a-bristle with guns, knives, clubs, shovels, picks, and alcohol-induced righteous indignation.

As they marched, shouting, through town with torches raised high, folks came out onto the sidewalks to watch them pass. The crowd from the Baltimore House, Riv in front with Growler close behind, stepped down into the street and followed quietly. As they passed the Gentlemen's Club Miss Hattie joined Riv.

O'Shea unlocked the front door of the jail and led his men inside. They squeezed through the small office and into the hallway behind it. The light from their torches threw bar-shaped shadows across the dirt floor of the cell. Moonlight flooded through the large, ragged opening high up in the wooden wall where a small window with an iron grate had been. On the floor in the middle of that moonlight was a piece of sacking. Atop it lay ten slender steel saw blades tied in a bundle with a silk cord. They obviously had had hard use. The men stood around them, speculating about their original purpose and origin.

O'Shea went out onto the front steps and held up the bundle so the gathered townspeople could see it.

"We'll hunt down whoever has this sort of equipment, and try him as an accomplice."

Miss Hattie approached for a closer look, threw her head back, and laughed.

"Land sakes, O'Shea, those are corset busks filed into saw teeth. The cord that binds them is the lacing."

O'Shea dropped the steel stays like a handful of live coals, and laughter spread through the crowd. O'Shea's men were primed for confrontation, but not humiliation. They doused their torches in a horse trough and slunk off down the shadowy side of the street.

Cassie and Lud, meanwhile, were riding along a moonlit trail headed west, with San Francisco as their destination. Cassie wore a long split skirt and sat a-straddle. Lud had on a rakish slouch hat that covered his shaved head, though he often reached up to scratch under it. As the hair grew back all over his body, he scratched a lot.

They rode so close together that their legs brushed against each other. A mule loaded with belongings followed on a lead. Lud's saddlebags were tightly packed with bars of silver.

Lud looked over at her. "Doney girl, I swear I did not betray you."

"I know. Miss Hattie told me the three of you talked about the theater all evening."

After a comfortable silence Cassie asked, "What about the Baltimore?

"What about it?"

"Well, you are the owner."

"No, I'm not."

Cassie turned to stare at him. "Then who is?"

"Prince."

"What Prince?"

"Prince Rivers. Riv. He's the building. I was only the façade. He thought the enterprise would go more smoothly that way, him being a colored chap and all."

"Will he be alright?"

"Yes. He's established now. People know him. They trust him. They like him."

"Then that notice in the Intelligenser about a chanteuse…?"

"Riv's idea." He grinned at her. Without all those whiskers he looked boyish, roguish, and killingly winsome. "Ain't Destiny grand?"

As his horse ambled along Lud began to sing. His rich baritone echoed back from the stony bluffs around them.

Doney girl, dear Doney girl, what makes you treat me so?

Caused me to wear that ball and chain, and now my ankle's sore.

I'm going to build a scaffold on some mountain high

So I can see my Doney girl as she goes riding by.

* * *

The next morning, when the two maids came to change the bedding in Room Eight, they found the corset sitting slumped forward on its chair. It was missing a silk lacing cord and ten front stays.

END

ADELINE

by WAYNE D. DUNDEE

AUTHOR'S NOTE: *This story is based on historical fact. The Orphan Train program operated in the United States for nearly eight decades, starting in the early 1850s and ending in 1929. Abandoned, vagrant children were taken from the cold, dirty, dangerous streets of eastern cities like New York and Boston and transported to foster homes in rural Western states. In all, over a quarter-million children were relocated in this manner. Like so often happens, the original intent was good, but the execution came with flaws and unintended consequences. Regulation improved in later years, but during the 1870s and 1880s, the turbulent times following the Civil War, the operation ran under its loosest control. Many children went to farming/ranching families where they were treated as little more than slaves or indentured servants; others, like the title character of this story, were destined for even worse fates ... WD*

"It's what you do, ain't it? Bring back people for money?"

"Bring back people who got wanted papers on 'em, yeah ... But not just any old 'people'."
"This ain't any old person. This is the sweetest little girl you ever saw. Tiny as a tick, with big, innocent, trusting eyes, and—"

"Is she a criminal? A wanted fugitive?" Rawson interrupted.

"Of course not. I told you, she's just a little girl. It's what's about to happen to her that's criminal … As far as that goes, so is what's *already* happened to her."

"You said she came through on the Orphan Train, right?"

"Uh-huh."

"I thought that was supposed to be a good thing— Getting those abandoned kids out of the overcrowded orphanages and filth of the big cities back east and delivering 'em out here to folks in smaller towns or on farms and ranches ready to welcome 'em into their own families."

"It might *sound* like a good thing," Miss Maybelle responded, frowning. "It was probably meant to be, and I'm sure it seemed all fine and uplifting to whoever thought it up and the politicians they got to sponsor it. Hell, when I first heard about I thought it sounded kinda good and noble, too. But once you see how it actually gets conducted, the way those kids are treated … No, there's a lot about it that ain't good and noble. Not by a damn sight. It's downright degrading and humiliating, is what it is. And that's not even the worst part, for sure not in the case of this little girl I'm talking about."

Clete Rawson leaned back in his cushiony chair and drew thoughtfully on the fine cigar Miss Maybelle had provided once he'd been ushered into her private quarters. The latter were quite handsomely appointed, especially for a no place little town like Hesterville on the far edge of western Nebraska. Miss Maybelle herself was quite handsomely appointed, too, with her piled high hair, glittering jewelry, and a form-fitting dress that showed an intriguing flash of leg and a daring amount of cleavage.

She remained among the most requested in her house of "soiled doves", despite her maturity in years and the fact she herself had long since stopped entertaining clients. This didn't prevent her from being on hand each evening to greet and mingle with the guests, however, and to do so while always dressed enticingly—either as an example for her girls to emulate, an added stimulant for the men, or simply to satisfy her own vanity. Perhaps all three. The only thing Rawson knew for sure was that whenever he stopped by Miss Maybelle's place during the times he passed through Hesterville, he looked forward to drinking in the sight of her as part of his visit, even though he knew it would be one of the other girls he'd be going upstairs with. So tonight, when summoned to join the renowned madam in private, he'd been equal parts surprised, puzzled, and excited by the invitation.

"I went down to the station when the Orphan Train stopped here two days ago," Miss Maybelle continued. "Curiosity, I guess—like most of the others who showed up. Except for those actually looking to adopt one of the children, that is. Seeing how they went about making their selections was where the whole thing started to go sour for me."

"What do you mean?"

"It was like they were examining livestock they might be interested in buying, that's what I mean." Miss Maybelle's nostrils flared indignantly. "For starters, they had the children parade out onto this platform that had been set up. The kids all did their best to manage smiles, some of them pirouetted in little circles—like they obviously were trained and encouraged to do. A couple of them even did dance steps and sang some song refrains … Then, if that wasn't humiliating enough, the people who'd signed up as being interested in adoption took turns getting up on the platform for a closer look. They poked and prodded. Made the kids open their mouths so they could check their teeth. Felt their muscles … Made me half sick, just watching."

"I saw some slave tradin' once, down South before the war," Rawson recalled. "Don't sound too much different from that."

"Exactly. Eight children were adopted that day. I'd like to think at least a couple of them went to homes where they'll be welcomed into a family and loved like a kid oughta be. But it was clear that some of the others, for sure the older ones who were selected for their size and strength, are going to end up little more than an extra pair of hard working hands on the ranches they went to … And then there was Adeline, the little girl I mentioned. And Hiram Fortner, the man who adopted her."

"How old is this girl?"

"Can't be more than eight or nine."

"You said before she was small. Tiny. Don't sound like a child who was picked for hard labor."

Miss Maybelle shook her head. "No, that would almost be a kindness. What Hiram Fortner picked Adeline for is a whole lot worse than hard labor."

"Sounds like there's more to tell on this Fortner fella."

Miss Maybelle's face clouded. "Hiram Fortner is the lowest form of vermin you can ever imagine."

"In the bounty huntin' business," Rawson replied, "I've encountered just about every kind of vermin there is. Ain't much left I need to use my imagination on."

"The thing about Hiram Fortner," Miss Maybelle argued, "is that he likes little girls. And I don't mean he likes them in a good way … I mean in a way that ain't normal or healthy. A way that's sick."

She paused, letting her words sink in. Watched the grim expression settle over Rawson's face.

"I don't make a habit of talking about the peculiarities of the men who come to visit my gals. If I wanted to, believe me there's plenty to tell. But obviously that wouldn't be smart for business. Only, in the case of Hiram Fortner, I'm willing to make an exception."

"Think I'm already beginnin' to get the picture," Rawson said.

"He comes round every couple months or so," Miss Maybelle went on. "Always asks for my youngest gal. Always picks the slimmest, most girlish one out of the lineup. When he gets her up to the room he has her put her hair in pigtails, dress in the closest thing she has to little-girl clothes. Insists she call him 'Daddy' the whole time, even when they're—"

"I said I got the picture."

"I wanted to make sure."

"So when he heard about this Orphan Train, Fortner saw it as a way to hand-pick his very own little girl—a real one, instead of pretend—to satisfy his sick desires. That what you're tellin' me?"

"If you saw the way he looked at Adeline up there on that platform. The way he stroked her hair, her shoulder." Miss Maybelle shuddered. "To anyone else looking on—anyone who didn't know about his peculiar tastes in the sex department—it might look like any loving parent affectionately touching their child. But I knew better. I saw it for what it truly was."

"Don't this sick bastard have a woman of his own?"

Miss Maybelle nodded. "That's the excuse for adopting a little girl. Fortner's wife never healed right after a bad fall on the ice last winter. She has a lot of trouble getting around, even for simple house-hold chores. They never had children of their own, so a daughter in the home would be able to help Mrs. Fortner and sort of look after her while Hiram works the ranch."

"Is the wife in on what *else* their new daughter will be expected to do?"

"No way of knowing for sure. But not likely, would be my guess. At least not at this point. Elsie Fortner is one of those browbeat, worn-down-looking women who never lifts her face in public and always walks a step behind her husband. Hiram bosses her like a work mule and seldom has an un-harsh word for her. Leastways that's how it was *before* her accident. She don't make it into town with him much any more these days … No reason to expect it's any different, though."

Rawson's grim expression grew grimmer. "In other words, anything Fortner does in his own home—even if comes to makin' visits to little Adeline's bedroom at night—ain't gonna get spoken out against by his wife."

"I'm afraid not. That's why the only chance for the little girl is to get her out of there as soon as possible. That's why I'm offering to pay you—a bounty, if you will, just like you're used to collecting—to ride out there and bring her back."

"What about the sheriff? Or a federal marshal? Ain't what we're talkin' about *illegal*, for Chrissakes? Shouldn't they be the ones to handle something like this?"

"Based on what? What proof do I have? Only the events I claim took place in a bawdyhouse, and what I feel and know in my gut. Hiram Fortner might not be the biggest rancher around, but he's got a decent-sized spread and he's never caused anybody any trouble. It'd be his word against a bunch of whores, and that's if the law would go far enough to even question him."

"If I was to ride out there and snatch the girl— kidnap her, in other words—*that* for damn sure would be illegal. Be no question about it."

"It might be illegal. But it would be the right thing. No question about that, either."

Rawson scowled. "If I was to bring Adeline back, what would you do with her? You surely ain't plannin' on keepin' her and raisin' her here, are you?"

Miss Maybelle smiled faintly, pleased that the bounty hunter was clearly considering her proposal. "Of course not. Don't be ridiculous," she said. "But it so happens I've stayed in contact with one of my gals who left the business a couple years back. She ran off with a ranch hand who'd fallen in love with her and they moved across the border into Wyoming and got married. The kind of thing that's supposed to happen only in storybooks, except sometimes it actually does in real life, too. Anyway, they've got their own spread now and, slowly but surely, they're making a go of it. The only thing is, they've found they can't have kids of their own. They'd welcome little Adeline like a gift from Heaven and I know Marilyn—that's the name of the gal who used to work for me—would be a wonderful mother."

"Sounds like you've got it all figured out," said Rawson, rubbing his jaw.

Miss Maybelle regarded him. "Why do you think I care so much about this little girl I barely laid eyes on, Rawson?"

"Been wonderin' that."

"Yeah, I've wondered on it some myself." One corner of her mouth lifted wryly. "The thing is, there's nothing much in this old life that's more pure and innocent than childhood. At least, that's the way it *should* be. I'm not making excuses, mind you, but in my years working this trade I've met way too many gals who started down this path because their childhood was robbed from them. Either by abandonment or physical abuse … or, maybe worst of all, the kind of treatment that's in store for little Adeline. I'm not saying she's guaranteed to end up a whore. And I'm not even saying that's the worst thing she could be. But however she turns out, her innocence will have been robbed from her and it will have been done in the worst way possible— by somebody pretending to be a parent, a person she ought to've been able to trust above all others. Any way you slice it, that's a hell of a cruel blow for a little kid to try and make it past."

Rawson didn't say anything right away. When he did: "What's to prevent Fortner from comin' after the girl? And, even if we manage to get her away and keep her away, what's to stop him from waitin' for the next train and 'adopting' another little girl?"

"If you work it right, Fortner will have no idea who took her," Miss Maybelle answered. "Maybe he'll think she just ran away. Wouldn't be the first time one of these Orphan Train children did that. As far as him getting his hands on another girl … well, we can only fight one battle at a time. We can't do any-thing about the future, Rawson, but we can damn sure do something about the here and now—if, that is, you're willing to sign on for what I'm proposing."

* * *

Rawson rode out to Fortner's place the following day. The ranch lay more than a dozen miles from town, over rugged country, so it was late in the afternoon when he arrived.

He approached cautiously, wanting neither his presence nor his interest to be known. In a hilltop stand of cottonwoods, he found a well-concealed position with a clear view of the house and outbuildings. Using his spyglass, he was able to closely and leisurely monitor the activities around the house as he mentally put the final touches on how he was going to go about getting the girl out of there.

As evening was settling in, he got his first look at Adeline when she appeared on the front porch and tossed a pan of table scraps out onto the ground. A flock of scrawny chickens and two pot-bellied shoats came scurrying to make short work of whatever had been in the pan. Adeline paused to watch them for a moment, her mouth curving into a wide smile before she turned and went back inside.

She was indeed a lovely child. Big, luminous

eyes, rosy cheeks, golden hair dangling in loose ringlets. Watching her, Rawson's gut knotted like a clenched fist at the thought of what lay in store for this frail innocent if Hiram Fortner had his way.

The bounty hunter swore under his breath. He was damned if he was going to let that happen.

He'd gotten plenty of looks at Fortner, too, as the man busied himself with chores around the property before calling it a day and going inside for supper. Stocky build, average height, with bristly mutton chop sideburns and a weary yet purposeful stride. Outwardly just another hard-working rancher, a common enough type to these parts … except this one harbored a dark evil on the inside.

The way he'd work it, Rawson had decided, would be to wait until well after full dark, close to midnight. Then, when everyone was sleeping their soundest, he would steal into the house and simply take the girl. He'd long ago learned the art of stealth from an old Indian fighter and it had served him well more than once in the bounty hunting business. In his saddlebags, he even carried a pair of whisper-quiet moccasins he could slip on when the need arose.

The biggest risk would be that of alarming Adeline and having her cry out. He'd have to deal with that if it became necessary, but for the girl's sake it was something he hoped to avoid. In addition to startling the child, any outburst resulting in a confrontation with Fortner was almost certain to turn violent and, as a result, could have an even more traumatizing affect. The whole idea was to spare Adeline exposure to things that would strip away more layers of her childhood innocence. Still, worst case, even if an alarm somehow *was* raised, Rawson's main objective remained to rescue her from this place and he would do whatever it took to succeed in that. He'd solved problems in the past with bullets and, if given no choice and that's what it came down to tonight, he would again. On a strictly personal level, he couldn't deny he'd get a measure of satisfaction from pumping a couple slugs into the likes of Fortner.

In the meantime, now that he'd seen the layout of the place and had a plan fixed in his mind, all he could do was wait. The old Indian fighter had taught him patience, too. But that didn't mean while he was waiting he couldn't make himself reasonably comfortable. The early spring day had warmed nicely but now, with the sun gone and no cloud cover to retain any of the afternoon's heat, the night was quickly growing chill.

Rawson withdrew a quarter mile and found a shallow gully where he could build a small, unseen fire to warm himself and cook some coffee. It was there he waited. A thin slice of moon rose and the cloudless, now-darkened sky became sprinkled with glittering stars. That was good, it would provide illumination for making his approach on the house. In case of pursuit, however, it could work against him —but Rawson didn't plan on allowing any pursuit.

He drank coffee. Smoked another of the fine cigars Miss Maybelle had given him. Waited.

The problem with holding off like this was the nagging question that kept creeping through Rawson's mind—the question of what Adeline might be going through in the meantime. He had no idea how someone like Fortner would proceed with his vile plans. Would he would immediately brutalize and abuse the girl? Or would he work up to it more slowly, like some sort of sick seduction?

Adeline had been at the ranch for two nights now. If Fortner meant to force his way with her, then it might already be too late. If otherwise—which, needless to say, was Rawson's fervent hope—then another few hours shouldn't be crucial. He reminded himself that when he'd seen Adeline on the porch earlier she hadn't shown any signs of being misused or troubled in a way you might expect if the actual molestation had begun. He recalled her big smile when she paused to watch the pigs and chickens go after the scraps she'd thrown to them.

He told himself that was a good sign … and hoped to hell he was right.

When it was finally time, Rawson kicked out his fire then mounted up and rode back toward the Fortner ranch.

* * *

From the same stand of cottonwood trees as before, Rawson again paused to gaze down on the layout below. The starlight cast everything in a bluish silver glow that revealed details almost as clearly as in the daytime.

Everything was quiet. No lights were burning. No signs of movement or activity anywhere in or around the house. He heaved a sigh of relief that his earlier reconnaissance had determined the premises was free of any damned dog for him to worry about.

Dismounting, Rawson sat down on the grass and exchanged his boots for the moccasins he'd pulled from his saddlebags. Then, after stuffing his dusty boots into the same leather pouch the mocs had come out of, he took his horse's reins in hand and led the way slowly down the slope.

About fifty feet from the main house, he tied the animal to a rough-bark corral rail. The horse's nostrils flared at the scent of the other horses in the corral and some of them stirred and snorted in response. "Easy, boy," Rawson soothed. He wanted the big gelding close by when he made his exit from the house but couldn't afford for it to cause a disturbance.

Once the animals seemed settled down, he turned and started toward the house. As he walked, he reached down to slip the hammer thong from the Colt riding on his hip and lifted the gun a couple inches to make sure it rested loose in its holster.

A moment later, the first gunshot blasted apart the silence of the night!

Rawson immediately threw himself to the ground and scrambled for the cover of a piled-stone well housing. A second shot rang out and, from the corner of his eye, Rawson caught the flash of gunfire through the darkened windows of the house.

He squirmed in tight behind the piled stones, Colt now clenched tightly in his fist. Everything had gone quiet again, except for the chugging of his breath and the hammering of his heart. After several tense seconds, Rawson came to the realization that neither of those shots had been aimed in his direction. He removed his hat and slowly peered around the edge of the well housing. The front door was still shut and the glass in the front windows was intact, unshattered. Everything inside remained dark ... but no, peering closer he could now see a faint glow way back toward the rear. Where the bedrooms most likely were located.

Adeline!

Rawson gathered his feet under him and rose to a crouch. He continued to watch the house intently. The glow—a softly burning lantern, he'd decided— remained steady but motionless. Sucking in a deep breath and holding it, Rawson shoved away from the well and, staying in a half-crouch, covered the remaining distance to the house at a hard run. Leapt onto the porch, plastered himself against the outside wall just to the right of the door.

More tense seconds, but no more gunshots. Silence again, interrupted only by his heavy breathing. Cautiously leaning to peek around the edge of the nearest window, Rawson got a closer look at the lantern glow but there appeared to be no change in either its location or brightness. Leaning back the other way, he thumbed the door latch and gave a hard push.

The door swung inward, creaking faintly on its hinges, and a wedge of silver-blue starlight bathed the interior. Rawson could see a tidy kitchen area off to the right, a simple but comfortable-looking parlor area off to the left. Straight back, where the shadows converged again beyond the spill of starlight, there was a short hallway with the faintly pulsing lantern glow emanating from a corner at its far end.

Rawson stepped quickly through the doorway and cut immediately into the dense shadows on the kitchen side, mindful not to silhouette himself against the window. He stood frozen there for several beats, Colt held at the ready, willing himself to keep his breathing under control.

Nothing but stillness and silence all around him.

Sticking to the shadows, Rawson began moving toward the hallway and the lantern glow. His moccasin-covered feet glided ghostlike across the wood plank floor.

He'd taken his first step into the hallway before he was able to make out the bulky shape lying on the floor at the opposite end. After another step he was able to determine that the bulky shape was the head and shoulders of a man, the rest of his body extending through an open doorway into the room where the lantern was burning. It wasn't hard to guess that the man must be Hiram Fortner, and the milkweed-like tufts of mutton chop sideburns caught in the lantern glow was enough to confirm it.

Rawson covered the rest of the hallway quickly and then, stepping over Fortner's prone body, went through the doorway with his Colt raised and ready.

He found himself in a bedroom. A disheveled, frail-looking woman sat on the edge of the bed, staring blankly down at the man on the floor. A pistol lay on the blanket beside her. The softly flickering coal oil lantern rested on a nearby nightstand.

Rawson leaned over and lifted the pistol from the bed.

"Go ahead and take it," the woman said dully, her eyes never leaving the weapon's apparent victim. "I'm done using it for what needed doing."

"Are you Elsie Fortner?" Rawson asked, seeking to confirm what seemed obvious.

"I am."

"What happened here?"

"I just shot my husband. Killed him, I expect … I

257

had to do it. No other choice. He was fixing to bother our little girl." Now her eyes lifted, twin pools of anguish that bored deep into Rawson. "Bother her in a real bad way … You understand?"

"Yes, I'm afraid I do."

"Who are you?" the woman wanted to know.

"I was ridin' by—I heard the gunshots."

It was a poorly constructed lie but she seemed to accept it.

"I had a feeling right from the start … but I fought against admitting it," Elsie Fortner went on. "I chose to believe he only wanted to take in one of those Orphan Train girls to help me around the house, like he said, since my accident left me limited and all … Deep down, though, I knew there was more to it … I always knew he had a – a *problem* when it came to his feelings for young girls. He said he could control it … I let him convince me. What woman wants to believe otherwise about the man she married?"

"Where's the girl now?"

Elsie Fortner lifted her arm feebly, pointing. "Across the hall, in her bedroom … The shooting must have frightened the poor dear terribly. Please, somebody should go check on her."

Rawson started to do as she suggested, but paused. Turning back, he said, "Why tonight? What happened tonight to cause you to use the gun?"

The woman's eyes took on the blank look once more. "He was heading back to her room again," she said in a voice as far away as her gaze. "I caught him in there last night … I woke up and he wasn't in bed next to me. I looked in across the way … He was sitting in a chair beside Adeline's bed, just watching her sleep. But his nightshirt was pulled up and he was – was touching himself … I knew that, sooner or later, it would turn into more. I told him what I'd seen, told him he could never go to her room like that again. Said what I'd do if he did. Warned him … Tonight, when I felt him getting out of bed, I turned up the lamp and tried to warn him one last time. He just laughed at me. Told me it was all my fault, that if I wasn't a dried up old cripple he wouldn't have to seek his pleasure in other ways … He was still laughing when I brought the gun out from under the pillow and pulled the trigger."

* * *

"I sure had her pegged wrong." Miss Maybelle's tone carried a kind of wistful sadness. "I never figured Elsie Fortner for having enough sand to stand up to her husband at all, let alone have what it took to shoot the bastard."

"She had sand alright," Rawson allowed. "She might've been a little slow finding it in herself but, when it counted, she had plenty."

They were seated at a varnished wood table on the broad, open back porch of Miss Maybelle's house. Miss Maybelle was sipping from a cup of tea; another of the fine cigars she'd provided Rawson was burning in a cut glass ashtray pulled over in front of him. Out on the grassy back lawn, in a wash of bright and warm early afternoon sunshine, two of Miss Maybelle's doves were stick-rolling a large wooden hoop back and forth between them. A laughing, energetic Adeline was running alongside the hoop, trying to jump through it without disturbing its roll.

Two days had passed since Rawson's return to Hesterville, arriving in the pre-dawn hours with a blanket-bundled Adeline clutched in the saddle before him. He'd taken her directly to Miss Maybelle's, making sure no one saw them.

Back at the Fortner ranch, Rawson had found the little girl hiding in her bedroom closet—frightened by the gunshots, just as Elsie Fortner predicted. Once he managed to convince her he posed no harm, Rawson wrapped her in a thick blanket and carried her out to his waiting horse.

The cover story Rawson and Elsie had quickly concocted to tell Adeline went like this: Rawson was a family friend who'd stopped by for a visit after Adeline was in bed. Undefined "robbers" allegedly showed up, looking to break in and loot the house. Hiram Fortner bravely fought them off and then gave chase, requesting Rawson get Adeline to safety by taking her to town. Mrs. Fortner, it was explained, had been injured by a stray bullet but would be okay once Rawson sent a doctor back to tend her.

The child seemed to accept these unlikely events in a sleepy, dumbfounded sort of way. Since that night, she'd been dutifully entertained and kept distracted by Miss Maybelle and her doves while being further told only that Hiram hadn't yet returned from chasing the robbers and Elsie was recovering but still too ill for visitors.

For his part, Rawson had left the Fortner ranch without knowing exactly how he was going to play it as far as following through on getting the girl successfully spirited away yet at the same time not leave Elsie Fortner completely in the lurch. Once again, it was

Elsie herself who supplied the solution. "Send the sheriff back if you want … I won't be going nowhere," she'd told him after eliciting from him a promise that he would look after Adeline.

A short time later, when Rawson had ridden barely out of sight from the ranch, he heard the sound of a distant gunshot once more slicing through the still night. He turned in his saddle, careful not to disturb Adeline who now rode bundled in front of him, and looked back in the direction of the Fortner spread. The pulsing, steadily increasing glow of light coming from the other side of the rolling hills told him everything he needed to know. With crystal clarity he realized exactly what Elsie had done. As soon as he was gone, she'd set the house ablaze and then put a gun to her own head. Not the same one she'd used on Hiram—Rawson had taken that one with him. But a ranch house was bound to have other guns, at the very least a hunting rifle.

"Send the sheriff back if you want … I won't be going nowhere."

Albeit inadvertently, Elsie had cleared the way for Rawson and Miss Maybelle to complete their covert rescue of Adeline with no questions ever being raised. When neighboring ranchers saw the lingering smoke next morning and subsequently found no sign of any survivors in the burnt remains of the Fortner house, the only conclusion the sheriff could logically reach when called in was that the entire family had tragically perished.

"We need to finish this," Miss Maybelle was saying now, as they continued to watch Adeline and the two doves playing on the lawn. "We need to get her out of here and on over to Wyoming, before somebody spots her and maybe recognizes her."

"And before you get so attached to her you ain't gonna want to let her go," Rawson pointed out.

"I'm already dreading the thought of that," Miss Maybelle admitted. She looked at Rawson sharply above the rim of her teacup. "But what if I am? I still know what has to be done … And it ain't like I'm the only one Adeline has turned into a sentimental old fool—is it?"

She was referring to the fact that the rough-hewn bounty hunter had refused any payment for his part in rescuing the little girl, instead insisting the money be placed for her benefit in the hands of the new parents she would soon be acquiring.

Rawson flushed slightly at the reminder, but did not acknowledge it. "All I know," he said, "is that I got a team and wagon lined up for the trip, as soon as you give the word. Something else we need to take care ahead of that, though, is findin' a way to … well, you know, explain to her how she won't be seeing the Fortners no more."

"I got a hunch she'll be able to handle that easier than you might think. After all, it ain't like she had a lot of time to get attached to them, or barely even know them. On top of that, she's a tough kid who's already made it through plenty."

"Thanks to you, she didn't have to make it through even worse."

"Don't you mean 'thanks to *us*'?"

"Okay. Us, then … including Elsie Fortner."

Miss Maybelle sighed. "Yeah, there'll always be that. My hope for Adeline is that she never has to have any more bad memories in her life. But at the same time I can't help thinking how sad it is that one of the things she probably *won't* remember is the woman—the mother, no matter for how brief a time—who stood up so bravely for her. Yet no one must ever tell her the whole truth."

"Sometimes," Rawson said, "the truth ain't everything it's cracked up to be. Seems to me that if we're able to give Adeline a fresh start and leave her simply knowin' there were people in her life—never mind exactly who or why—who cared about her at a time when she needed it the most … well, then I'd say we haven't done too bad a job."

-END-

CHRISTMAS COMES TO FREEDOM HILL

By TROY D. SMITH

My name is Danny Jordan. I was born back in Tennessee, in 1870, but I don't remember much about that place or those times. I was raised in Kansas, in a little town called Freedom Hill. It's not much more than a wide place in the road, just a few miles southeast of Abilene; shoot, Abilene itself isn't much more than that nowadays, it's hard to believe the place was a wide-open cow-town way back yonder, with Wild Bill and those others. Oh yes, Freedom Hill is still there. It was kind of a funny name, you see, because there were no hills around for miles in any direction.

The WPA interviewer looked flustered. He was a journalist by trade, but the Depression had put writers out of work as much as anybody, once most folks could no longer afford the luxury of small-town newspapers. He had been grateful to get a job with the government - but his assignment had been clear.

"I'm sorry, Mister Jordan," he said. "It's the Tennessee part I was curious about. Folks in town singled you out as somebody I might want to talk to about slavery times down South, I was hoping you were old enough to have memories of it. Perhaps you heard stories, though, from your parents?"

The old black man smiled wistfully.

I don't know much about slavery, that's true, I wasn't there for that. I know a good bit about freedom, though. I learned most of it from my daddy, way back yonder. He didn't teach me that much about being a slave; he mostly taught me about being free.

I was eight or nine years old when we got on that wagon train headed West. It was one of those Singleton expeditions. Pap Singleton, he was an old colored fellow from Nashville, used to be a slave when he was young but ran off and made a good bit of money. Things was hard down South in those days -of course, they always have been for folks shaded like I am, but in some ways those days were even harder than slave times had been. The Union soldiers had all went home by then, you see, and the same folks were in charge again that had been running things before the war. And they were none too happy with colored folks, no sir. The U.S. government had promised us forty acres and a mule, but it was just empty air -and them old Confederates weren't aiming to give us even bright promises. Singleton started putting together his expeditions, talking colored folks into coming West with him for a new start. And a good many of them did. Exodusters, they were called. On account of they were leaving the land of slavery, just like the old-time Israelites left Egypt, and heading toward a promised land -a land that was more dust than milk and honey, but sweet to their souls just the same.

My daddy, he liked the sound of that. Painting it with Bible words made it even prettier to him, because he was always partial to the Good Book. His mama gave him a Bible name, Gabriel. During the war, he ran away from his old master and swam across the river to where the Yankee soldiers were. He joined the Union Army, and then it came time for him to choose another name for himself, a family name. A lot of those old slaves named themselves after their masters, but Daddy didn't want any slave name. So he called himself after the River Jordan; he was born again, in freedom, just like being baptized, when he swum that river to the Yankee lines.

I remember the day he first set me up in that wagon next to my mama, and we commenced to roll away from the only world we had ever known.

"You remember them stories I told you, Danny, about the baby Jesus?"

I nodded.

"Them wise men," he continued, "they followed that star a far piece. One of them was black as we are, at least I've heard it told that way. Anyways, freedom is a star, boy. It used to be the North Star, but I reckon we're fixing to follow one that leads West. So say goodbye to Egypt, son. The Lord is out yonder, waiting for us to find him."

Singleton planted colonies all over Kansas and Indian Territory, and others like him did the same. Our little group, I reckon there was about fifty or sixty of us all together, we stopped at a spot near the banks of the Neosho River. We got the land off the government -it used to be part of an Indian reservation. We filed to homestead it, all according to law. It was my daddy's notion to name our little town Freedom Hill; right away, several people pointed out that there isn't any hill there. Shoot, there's not even a rise.

"Elevation don't mean nothing," Daddy said. "It'll be a hill, once we get it built. We'll be a city on a hill, just like the Good Book says, shining for the whole world to see."

There was a chorus of amens, and we all set to work building. It takes more than buildings to make a town, though, so after awhile we set to work voting as well. We elected ourselves a mayor, and a council; everybody agreed that to be a real town we needed a marshal, too, and everybody agreed it ought to be Gabriel Jordan, one-time company sergeant in the 13th United States Colored Infantry and hero of the Battle of Nashville. Daddy still had his old cap-and-ball revolver -he didn't have a holster for it, so he kept it stuck in his belt. The town blacksmith made him a crude tin star. Daddy kept the badge in his pocket, since everybody knew who the marshal was. He never did go in much for what you might call symbols of authority, he didn't like to draw undue attention to himself. My daddy was the most dignified man I ever knew, but he wasn't burdened by a lot of false pride. Besides, it was mostly a ceremonial office. Freedom Hill never had much call for an actual lawman.

Leastways, not until Bob Horner and his bunch rode into town.

I'll never forget the day I first saw old man Horner. Him and three of his cowboys came riding up to our town -which was really just a collection of shacks built around a big community garden. I was sitting leaned up against the horse trough, whittling. It was two days before Christmas, and I had took a notion that I was going to carve my daddy a little wooden horse. It wasn't really going too well, but I hadn't cut off any fingers.

When they first saw the approaching riders, several of our men clustered together real quiet and serious-like to meet them. Daddy was standing right out in front.

Sam Gardener heaved a sigh. "Well, it's fixin' to start, I reckon." No one replied to him, they just watched the white men ride toward them. "Sho' 'nuff is," Sam added under his breath.

The four men reined in. Their leader, a stocky man in his fifties, looked at the assembled townfolk the way you'd look at a dead fly you found in your supper.

"What the hell is this?" he said, jerking his chin to indicate the buildings around us.

"It's a town, suh," Daddy said.

The white man spat tobacco juice at my father's feet. "Wasn't no town here last time I checked, boy."

"We just built it. It's called Freedom Hill."

Horner was silent for a long moment, then he chuckled. The men with him -boys, really -remained stony faced and silent.

"Don't that beat all," he said finally. "Freedom Hill." He looked around slowly, smiling. "I reckon you spades know about as much about hills as you do about freedom."

My father met and held his gaze, but said nothing. The white man shook his head.

"Now, what in the hell gave you people the notion you could just up and build a town on my land?"

"This here is government land, suh. We filed on it, legal."

"You filed on it legal." He chuckled again. "Look here, boy. My name is Bob Horner, and I own the biggest cattle spread in this part of the state. Every spring I round up a herd and drive 'em up to the railhead in Abilene -right through where your pissant hill of a town is. I been doing it that way since they built the railroad. I done it that way when this was Indian territory, and they never messed with me. They knew better, because I keep the federal cavalry posts hereabouts stocked with beef, and that makes me a big man with the boys in blue. If I didn't let the Indians slow me down, I sure reckon I ain't going to let myself be hogtied by a bunch of uppity Negro farmers. Deeds don't mean spit out here -it's them that uses the land that lays claim to it."

"With all due respect, suh," Daddy told him, "we're on a prairie. Wouldn't be that much trouble to just turn your herd and go around us."

"Trouble ain't the point, it's the principle of the thing. If I let this stand there'd be little nigger towns ever' way you turn, and before long I wouldn't be able to push my herds through at all. And I'd have to look at you damn monkeys ever' time I poked my nose outdoors."

My father and a few other men visibly tensed at those words, I could see that even from my vantage point by the watering trough. Most of the men didn't, though, and that puzzled me at the time. I didn't understand then how a body could get so used to sharp words that they didn't even sting anymore.

"I'll tell you what I ought to do," Horner said. "Come springtime, I ought to round up my herd like always and drive 'em through here, and just trample you and your little shotgun shacks into the dirt and let that be the end of it. But there's a problem with that, see. If I let this stand now, there's no telling how many little colonies will pop up around here by the end of spring, and that would be mighty troublesome. Best to nip it in the bud."

He spat at my father's feet again. "You seem to be doin' all the talkin', boy. What's your name?"

"Gabe Jordan, suh."

"Well, Gabe Jordan, are you the leader of this here outfit?"

"I been appointed marshal of Freedom Hill." Horner sniggered, but Daddy ignored him. "Sam Gardener, he's our mayor." Gardener shot Daddy a dark glance, like he didn't appreciate being identified.

"Well then," Horner said, "Mister Mayor, Marshal Jordan, and all you other esteemed citizens of Niggerville, I tell you what I'm going to do. I'm giving you all two days to clear out. I'm bringing all my boys out here when them two days is up, and if any of you are still here we'll make Fort Pillow look like a grade school rasslin' match."

Daddy really did stiffen up at that reference. I didn't know then, but learned later, that Fort Pillow was a place in Tennessee where a bunch of colored Union soldiers were shot down by the Rebs after they had laid down their arms in surrender.

"Two days from now is Christmas Day," Sam Gardener said weakly.

"Like the Good Book says," Horner replied, "there ain't no room at the inn, so you'll have to take your asses elsewhere." He laughed at his own pun, then wheeled his mount around and trotted off, cowboys in tow. "Merry Christmas!" he called back over his shoulder to us.

The men of Freedom Hill watched Horner leave the same way they had watched him approach, wordless and still. The mayor broke the silence.

"Well, I reckon that's that," he said. "If we're

271

careful about it, we can take down our buildings and tote 'em in such a way we can put 'em back up again later."

"Put 'em up where?" another man said.

"Why, wherever we go to next, I reckon," the mayor answered him.

"I think we should all study on this awhile," my father said. "Study on it, and pray on it. And then have a town meeting after supper tonight, and decide what to do then."

Now, if this was one of those tales from the storybooks, I would tell you all about how I snuck out the window and eavesdropped on that meeting, and be able to give you a word for word account of what was said. And I did do stuff like that, when the notion struck me and when I could get away with it, but that night wasn't one of those times. The first indication I had of how that meeting went was when my father came home that night, with tired eyes and the weight of the world on his shoulders. I might not have been able to sneak out to any meeting, but I was able to listen real close and hear what was being said between my parents. My mama had been pretty dern mad when she found out that the "town meeting" my daddy had called for was limited to the men, and I reckon she was right to be. The women had just as much at stake in this, if not more, and in my experience a good many of them had considerable more sense than their husbands. Still, things was the way they was, and she had to wait and find out her family's fate second-hand.

"Well?" she demanded hoarsely of him. She was whispering, but barely. Daddy shook his head.

"Leon Parker and some of them others talked

down Sam Gardener and his notions of pulling up stakes first thing in the morning."

Mama's voice was concerned. "They're going to stand up to Horner and his men?"

Daddy shook his head again. "No. Thing is, they're scared to fight and they're scared to run. Most of 'em have talked themselves into believing that Horner is bluffing. That he wouldn't dare do what he threatens to do, especially on Christmas. They managed to talk Gardener and his camp into their way of thinking."

"Just what is their way of thinking? What do they plan to do?"

"Nothing. They don't plan to do nothing. Just to gamble that everything will be okay, and that more settlers will come in the spring and strengthen our hand."

"Do you think they're right, Gabe?"

"No, Livvy, I don't. Horner will be here all right, just like he said. I know men, and he wasn't bluffing."

"What -what will you do?"

Daddy was silent for several long seconds. He finally spoke, in a low voice. "I accepted this badge, Livvy. It may not be much to look at, just a beat-up piece of tin, but it means something. I'll have to stand up to them, and protect this town. Our home."

"What, by yourself? That's crazy!"

"I tried to tell 'em. I tried to make 'em see. We've got a few firearms, for hunting -if we all stand together we can hold them off. 'You want us to shoot at white folks?' Gardener said. 'You'll get us all killed sho'. Well, I've shot at white folks, Livvy, when I had to. When I had to."

"Maybe you're right, Gabe, maybe if everybody stood together. But you know they won't. They ain't made out of the same stuff you are. And if you stand up to Horner's gang alone it'll be suicide, plain and simple. We can pack up our stuff, wake up Danny, and be gone before daylight. We can start fresh, just us."

Daddy sighed. "Once you start runnin', Livvy, you can't never stop. There'll be no-'count crackers trying to run us over anywhere we go. That's why this town is so important. We're all here to band together, out from under the old planters, out here where everything is fresh and new. That's what we left Tennessee for, that's what I want my son to grow up in. Gardener and them, they're still afraid -but they can learn not to be. When Horner's bunch gets here I'm going out to meet them, and I won't be on that street alone."

"You honestly think Sam Gardener or anybody else will find the guts to walk out there with you?"

"Ain't talking about them, Livvy. I'm talking about the Lord. He'll be with me. Ain't nothing left to do now, but trust in him. Stand still and see the deliverance of the Lord, the Good Book says. He is your right arm and your savior."

"The Good Book!" Mama said -she practically snarled it -and then threw the dishrag she had been holding forcefully to the floor. "You and your Good Book. No Good Book ever saved me from no overseer's whip or worse -but you will go on about it, won't you, just like your folks did even as the life was being drained out of them."

"That's your fear speaking, Livvy. You ain't never jumped into the river with bullets slapping at the water on your every side. You ain't never marched into the smoky battlefield with nothing standing between you and death except the Lord at your side. You don't know."

"I know that many a soldier got blowed away, whether he went to church Sundays or not!"

Mama broke down then, sobbing something awful. Daddy stepped close to her, and folded her in his arms. She resisted at first, arms rigid at her side, but she softened to him before long and they just stood there together like that for the longest time. I cried too, softly into my pillow, trying not to be heard. I fell asleep crying and praying. Mamma and Daddy still stood together in their silent embrace.

That next day -Christmas Eve -was a praying day. No one ever announced it as such in my house, but somehow or other we all just took to it individually, even Mama. I mostly prayed that, for a Christmas present, the Lord would keep my father alive. Daddy, he spent 'most the whole day out in the barn. I got wore out with praying and crying, and I felt a great need wash over me like waves -the need to be in my daddy's presence, to touch him and smell him, to feel safe even when I closed my eyes. I went out to the barn and found him kneeling down in the hay, head bowed. He stirred when he heard me, and smiled, and beckoned me over.

I had my half-carved wooden toy in my hand, clutching at it like a heathen charm. I held it out for him to see.

"I wanted to carve you a horse, Daddy, for Christmas. But it ain't turning out too well."

His smile grew even broader, and he took the object reverently from my hand. "Nonsense, child," he said. "I reckon this here is the finest pretty I ever seen." He turned it over in his hands, examining it proudly.

"I been praying, Daddy."

"Bless your heart, child. I been praying, too."

"I'm scared it don't help, though."

He squeezed my hand. "It helps, yes indeed it does. The Lord is a mighty protector."

"But I can't see the Lord," I said. "I don't reckon Mister Horner can see him, neither."

"Don't make no difference, son. We can't see the wind, but we can feel it. It's just like this here town, this Freedom Hill. People all the time laughing about that -how can you call a place Freedom Hill when there ain't no hill there? But there is a hill, same as there is freedom. You just got to have eyes to see it. It's the same with the Good Lord, son. You know what faith is? The Good Book tells us faith is the evident demonstration of realities not beheld. Not just something we wish for, or hope for -but realities we just can't see. That's what led them wise men, and them shepherds, to find the baby Jesus. Yes, Lord."

He hugged me real tight, then put the wooden toy back in my hand. "This here horse is coming along real good, boy. You run on now, and work on it some more."

I did. And I felt better, somehow.

Mister Horner and his men showed up early the next morning. Daddy was waiting for them. No one came out into the street to stand beside him. This time I did slip away -my mama was too glued to the window to pay me much mind -and ran back out to my previous vantage point behind the water trough. I was glad I'd thought to put my coat on, because it was bitter cold. In fact, it was snowing -it came down harder and harder as the morning wore on, and the wind was whipping the dry powder around and making it a little hard to see.

Horner had about a dozen men with him. Like before, they were more boys than men, few of them had seen twenty winters yet. Horner reined up in front of my father.

"Good morning, Marshal. I see you people ain't cleared out. And I see you are the only one brave enough, or stupid enough, to come out here and face me."

"This here is our town," Daddy said. I could see that now, for the first time, he was wearing the tin star. "And it's our land, according to the rules of the Homestead Act. We don't aim to leave it."

I was praying again. I was praying so hard it felt like my heart would burst.

Horner sighed. "Well, I've done all I could." He pointed at my father. "One of you men, shoot this damn fool. Then we'll set fire to these shacks and shoot them as they come out, like rabbits."

None of his men moved. After a moment, Horner looked around at them.

"Are you men deaf? I gave you an order."

One of the cowboys spoke. His voice was a little trembly.

"We -we just thought we was here to scare 'em," he said, "maybe rough 'em up a little. I didn't think we was going to just shoot down a bunch of women and young'uns."

Horner was incredulous. "Hellfire, boy, I warned 'em, didn't I?"

Another cowboy spoke. His voice was a little

more confident than his friend's. "Mister Horner," he said. "Mister Horner, it's Christmas."

"Oh, for Pete's sake." Horner seemed to have forgotten all about my father for the moment. "When I pay a man I expect him to take orders, I don't care what day it is."

The second cowboy turned his horse. "I reckon I'll go on back to the ranch," he said, "and collect my pay."

"I reckon I'll join you," the first one said. His voice was no longer trembly at all. Several others fell in behind them, and they rode off into the snow. Only three remained with Horner.

Horner spat and swore. "Well, at least you boys ain't gone crazy on me. Surely between us we can handle one ragged, colored marshal." He turned in his saddle to once more face my father.

The wind had whipped up some, and the snow was blinding for a moment. When it slowed down again, you could just make out my father's silhouette. His, and those of about a dozen men standing behind him, spread out so they stretched across the little street. Each one seemed to be holding a rifle.

I could see Horner better, and even from all that distance I swear I seen the color drain out of his face when he seen how outgunned he was. I reckon he hadn't expected the townspeople to get their nerve.

"This needs to be settled right here, today," my father said. "Make your play, Horner, if that's what you aim to do. If not, leave our town and don't come back."

"We don't stand a chance, boss," one of the cowboys said fearfully.

Horner let out a defeated sigh. "All right then -

278

Marshal Jordan. You're holding the cards, you win. Just -just don't spread out any further than this town. Come spring, I'll take my herd the long way around."

Daddy stood in silence. Horner and his cowboys turned and rode away, into the storm.

As soon as they were out of sight, which didn't take long, I left my hiding place and bolted to my father's side, calling out to him. He scooped me up into his arms. The snow slowed down almost at once, and I heard the creak of opening doors. People started to slowly step out of their shacks, one by one. Mama came out, and collapsed to her knees on our front stoop, sobbing.

"You done it, Gabe," I heard Sam Gardener holler out from his doorway. "Lord in heaven, I don't know how, but you done it -all by yourself!"

"He wasn't all by himself!" I called back, thinking the mayor silly indeed. Then I took a good look around us, there on the street.

The snow had almost stopped completely. It was like one of them snow globes you shake up, with the flakes swirling around like mad and then, after a couple of minutes, slowly fading away. And in the clear air I saw that we were, in fact, alone in the street. There was no sign of the dozen or so men I had seen. And then, mister, let me tell you -my jaw dropped open and my little eyes bugged 'most out of my head. Because it was plain as day, there they was, my daddy's footprints and my own leading up to him. But there were no other prints near us, none at all.

"No, child, I wasn't all by myself, not at all." He hugged me tighter. "Merry Christmas, Danny."

My Daddy was right all along, you see. There is

more goes on in this world of ours than we can see, or understand. Especially at Christmas-time. Lord, yes. Especially at Christmas-time.

The old man and the writer sat in silence for a long time. It was the writer who spoke first.

"I'm not at all sure how to write that down."

The old man did not reply. He simply stared into the distance, and very gradually a smile grew on his face, and he nodded.

Strange, the writer thought. It's like he can see something out there that I can't.

The old man kept smiling.

THE END

CHRISTMAS FOR EVANGELINE

By C. COURTNEY JOYNER

"Did you know that bourbon kills the taste of blood?"

Jim Murray asked Pooch without wanting an answer, and kept pouring the brown into his glass, "I cut my lip on an envelope, and can't taste the blood. It stings, but that warm taste, a little bit sticky? It's gone."

Pooch nodded as he always did when Jim started on a jag, leaned back in the leather-covered chair that Jim never offered the rest of the year, and shut his eyes for a moment's peace. He then took the glass of Evan Williams, looked at Jim across his massive Spanish-made desk, raised the drink in tribute, and threw half of it back.

Pooch liked the silk feeling of good store-bought as it went down, and smacked his lips, partly to get the last drops that might be stranded in his mustache, and partly because it made Jim cringe. Jim always made a show of being dignified; nodding "good morning" instead of saying the words, snapping his fingers once to get the tellers to hurry up with the day's count, or reprimanding them by looking over the top of his bifocals. Image was most important to Jim, as if the pose made him bulletproof.

Pooch figured Jim was a good manager because the rest of the bank's employees were afraid of him somehow, but they didn't have anything on him, and none of them carried a mule-eared, double-barreled sawed-off under their coats.

The shotgun was resting on top of a ledger on Jim's desk, as it did every Christmas Eve, and Jim angled the barrel away from him with the same expression he always used on this night, "One of these days, right Pooch?"

"One of these days, what?"

"You're going to pull both triggers."

"I wouldn't do that, Mr. Murray. I like my life."

"Then you're a lucky man, even if you're too ignorant to know it."

Pooch didn't respond, he just watched Jim fill the glasses again, slopping a bit on the sides before putting the bottle down next to the shotgun. He held onto the bottle for a moment as if to steady it, before picking up his glass with, "I saw her today."

Pooch said nothing.

"Did you understand me?"

"Beggin' your pardon, Mr. Murray, but you always say that."

"No, I mean it. This wasn't a dream. She stood right there, by the second teller's cage. She didn't come up to it; she just stood there until I noticed her. Then she left."

"A lot of women look like Evangeline."

Jim thought for a few heartbeats and said, "No they don't. She's got that cream color, not like a 'breed, but something finer."

Pooch didn't want to listen to any more and regarded his bourbon in the light before glancing around the empty bank. There were no employees or customers, or open drawers or crowd of voices. Everything was still. He liked that.

The front shades were half-drawn, but people could be seen passing by: kids in their Sunday best holding on to their Mama's gloved hands, while fathers carried packages and Christmas trees to open wagons. Mr. Beaudine from the dry goods store tapped on a side window and mouthed "Merry Christmas," leaving a circle of vapor on the glass.

Pooch nodded a smile to Beaudine before shifting his gaze only a few feet to the place on the floor where the blood had pooled. It was scrubbed-clean now, as it had been for the last two years, but a lamp behind the teller cages cast a shadowed circle on the exact spot where the dark red had spread from the bullet hole through Mort's left eye.

For a moment, Pooch thought that the blood pool and the shadow even had the same fried-egg shape, and then nailed the rest of his drink.

Jim saw where Pooch had been looking and asked, "How long were they married?"

"I don't know, Mr. Murray."

"It wasn't long because Evangeline wasn't wearing any gold or silver. They hadn't had those anniversaries."

"All I want is to have a nice Christmas. Get drunk, have the day off."

"I'm better than I used to be, Pooch. You've got to admit to that."

Pooch poured some for himself this time, and studied his response. When Jim started calling him by name, and leaning forward to touch his shoulder, Pooch knew what was coming, and he hated it. He'd put things in their proper place in his mind, why the hell couldn't Jim?

Jim said, "It used to be all I could think about, Mort being killed. I sit here, listen to customers yammering about some horseshit worry, and my thinking's all about Mort lying on the floor. But I've gotten better. Now it only comes to me maybe once or twice a day, but today, well, it's only natural."

"At exactly three o'clock today, it's been two years, Mr. Murray."

Jim just said, "You knew him in jail."

Pooch didn't want to go through it all again but flatly said "Mort and I shared a cell in Salinas for a month, yeah."

"He was a good man."

"He was a good man to share a jail cell with. He didn't talk much or snore and I never caught him card cheating."

Jim drained the last thread of brown from his glass, and said, "That's character; better than most of the bastards I know."

"Right, yes. You wanted somebody who'd do what you told him. And he did."

Jim half-reached for the bottle with, "You see, how it's about choices? Should I have another? Should we have brought Mort into this? Talked to you, or done nothing at all. I could've closed early and paid you off with a nice dinner. But I didn't. It's all for shit."

Jim made some kind of decision, and re-filled his glass while Pooch covered the top of his with his palm. Most of the bourbon made it down Jim's throat, with the rest raining on his collar to remind Pooch that Jim was just another sloppy drunk who forgot his manners after three pulls.

Jim said, "You hold me responsible. That's okay."

"Had a plan and it worked."

Jim was trying to shake something out of his head, "Not for Mort. No, he handed the money off to you, and that weasel in cage four shot him right through the eye. Didn't even try for his leg. Who knew he'd stuck a Derringer in his waistband? Not me. No sir."

Pooch put a hand on Jim's arm and said, "You remember when you told me how much money was here on Christmas Eve? That you was gonna take it?"

"You said you had to have a good Christmas."

"For my marriage. Your niece likes the finer things, Mr. Murray, and I was tryin' to give them to her. Hell, you wouldn't even piss in my direction if Mary Louise hadn't married me. Let's call it what it is."

"You knew what you were getting."

Pooch gave himself two and-a-half fingers of bourbon and said, "I knew what I was getting *into*. We all did. Mort needed cash and we needed a third man for Christmas Eve. We got ours and Mort lost out. That's how it happens most of the time."

"And you can live with it?"

Pooch said, "I wish to God you could."

That's when Jim started about Evangeline again. He always started in the same place: that he didn't even know she existed until the day she walked into the bank, and all heads turned to look at her. Jim quick-glanced over his bifocals, while checking some accounts at his desk, but he couldn't get back to his numbers, she was that distracting. He shut the account book with a gesture of authority as Evangeline walked up the steps to his desk, pulling off her gloves so she could touch Jim's skin when she shook his hand. Jim remembered getting out of his chair, and holding onto her hand a few moments longer than was proper. But he said he didn't care, it was like being in a trance.

Pooch never understood the "trance" part of the story, just that Jim wanted Evangeline the moment he saw her. He understood that; the caramel skin and the dark lips that needed no paint, and the form that filled out a simple cotton dress. The day she came to see Jim, the dress was a lavender print gathered just a bit at the small of her back before embracing her waist and legs.

Jim said, "She had a purple sunflower in her hair. It was a simple thing, but it looked elegant. She came here to thank me for giving Mort a chance. She thanked me."

"Eva was a good-looking woman."

"Did you ever?"

"I told you then, I told you after the robbery, when we buried Mort, and a hundred times more: No. Never."

Jim was slumped into himself, not looking at anything as he spoke, "But you touched her. Said she was warm."

"She was warm when I cut her down, yeah."

Pooch was talked out, and he sure as hell didn't want to go into all of this again: going to Mort's funeral, then cutting up his share to take to his widow, only to find Evangeline hanging from a ceiling beam in the kitchen, with a coffee pot boiling over on the stove.

"Mr. Murray, it's still Christmas, and I have to meet Mary Louise. Are you gonna be all right here?"

"I see Evangeline all the time. Everywhere."

"You need to get sober."

Jim cocked his head, "How much do you have left?"

"Some."

"Is it enough?"

"I've got a job, we're fine. Mary Louise is worried about you though, wants you to come for supper."

"You're riding shotgun for a stage line that's cutting its runs. Don't tell me you're not hard up, or worried she's starting to pack."

Jim grabbed the edge of the desk with both hands, and raised himself with his elbows. He held that way, looking down at Pooch just enough to make his point, "See, the only way I can have any peace is if I'm out of it. Leave the bank, leave this stinkin' town. Leave it all. And you're going to help me. You're going to help yourself."

"That's how you pitched the last deal."

Jim hurled the bourbon bottle across the office, shattering his dignity against a brass spittoon in the corner. A sound caught in Jim's throat as Pooch got to his feet, and reached for the shotgun, but Jim had it in hand instantly with both fingers on the triggers.

Pooch said, "I thought you was piss-eyed drunk."

"I am."

"O little town of Bethlehem, How still we see thee lie. Above the deep and dreamless sleep, the silent stars go by."

Jim kept the shotgun aimed at Pooch's chest and said, "They've started the Christmas sing down by the barber's. That's a nice thing to hear. Calming. When we robbed before, there wasn't any music."

Pooch said, "I'm glad it makes you feel better."

The distant voices continued, *"Yet in the dark streets shineth the everlasting Light, the hopes and fears of all the years, are met in thee tonight,"* as Jim directed Pooch from the desk, down the two steps to the teller cages, and around them to a large, oak cabinet.

Jim said, "I've prepared this. Half the cash for the day is in a bag in that cabinet. I want you to take it."

"And what will you do, Mr. Murray?"

The carol filled the moment, *"For Christ is born of Mary, and gathered all above, while mortals sleep, the angels keep, their watch of wandering love."*

Jim held onto the shotgun as tight as you could without firing, "Confess, and be done with it. I was a respected citizen who robbed his own bank a second time, because I'd lost my mind with guilt and ill feeling. My partner got the cash, and I'll be," he paused thinking of the carol, "One the angels keep. Like Mort and Evangeline."

Jim straightened himself, regaining his dignified pose, let go of the shotgun's fore end and reached into his vest pocket to pull out a brass key that he threw on the floor at Pooch's feet. Pooch didn't try for it. Jim said, "That's to the money, and I have the letter of confession in my pocket. I'm going to cleanse myself, Pooch. I don't give a damn what you do, but you'll be rich."

Pooch looked directly into the two barrels, "You don't have to shoot, but this don't seem right."

"Yes, it's right. The money's there, for your Christmas. I'll take care of myself."

Pooch started for the key as the words reached him from up the street, *"And praises sing to God the king, and Peace to men on earth,"* and then said, "Peace to men on earth, right Mr. Murray? I guess it's Christmas. See, I've got the key and I'm opening the cabinet. You can put that scatter-gun down, aim it at the floor?"

Jim wasn't looking at Pooch now. His eyes were fixed on someone in a side window, his voice a stammer, "I'm doing everything you said, in just the way you said it."

Pooch said, "What?"

Jim angled his head toward the front door, eyes fixed on the woman in the lavender print with the purple flower tucked behind her ear as she entered, lowered the window shades, walked to the second teller cage, and stood in silence. Jim's arm shook under the weight of the shotgun, but he kept it close on Pooch, while whispering to her, "You said if I did this, you'd give me peace. I'm making amends."

Pooch's voice was a near-shout, "What the hell are you talking about?"

Jim heard the woman say, "Make it right, Mr. Murray."

The carolers raised their voices for, "*The dear Christ enters in*," and Jim pulled the right trigger. The barrel flamed, and Pooch's chest crimsoned across the oak cabinet. Pooch slammed the baseboard, his head snapping back and forward, before his body folded into a corner. His eyes rolled as his wife knelt next to him, taking his hand.

Down the street at the barber's, a few heads turned at the noise, but no one dropped a note. On the floor of the bank, Pooch managed, "Mary Louise?"

Mary Louise pried the key from Pooch's fingers with, "Tonight it's Evangeline, hon. I'm sorry Pooch; you tried but it's not nearly enough. And this way, Uncle Jim's happy. We all are."

Jim Murray stood still, the last bit of smoke curling from the shotgun's right barrel, not seeing the woman in front of him for who she was. His niece moved to him, and put a bare hand on his cheek. Jim grasped the hand for a few moments longer than was proper and said, "Miss Evangeline, can you forgive me now, for letting Mort die that way? I never meant it, really."

Mary Louise said, "I know, Mr. Murray. You've been tortured in your mind for two years. I know all about it."

"Pooch was in it, too. I took care of that."

"Yes, you did."

"May I now be one with the angels?"

Mary Louise stood back as Jim angled the shotgun under his chin, but she said, "No. Don't. You're forgiven, Mr. Murray."

Jim smiled for the first time that Christmas Eve, and didn't see the Colt Lightning come out of her purse. The shot tore through Jim's left eye, dropping him instantly. Mary Louise half-ducked in case the shotgun fired when it hit the floor, but the hammer never dropped.

The crowd up the street applauded "O Little Town of Bethlehem" as Mary Louise unlocked the cabinet with the brass key. Her breath bundled as she looked at the row of empty shelves, then reached into the back to where a small leather satchel had been tucked. She opened it to find a sack of gold coins and several packets of hundred dollar bills.

"O holy night! The stars are brightly shining, It is the night of our dear Saviour's birth."

Mary Louise listened for a moment, then pressed

the Colt into Pooch's right hand, and gently brushed his hair away from his eyes before kissing his forehead. She moved to the door, the satchel under her arm, and looked over at Jim spread across the spot where Mort had died two years before.

Mary Louise said, "Evangeline thanks you, boys. You've set things right. Be at peace and Merry Christmas."

Mary Louise took the flower from her hair, dropping it on the floor, before inching out the front door to a lightly blowing snow and a chorus of sweetly rising voices.

THE END

THE KEEPERS OF CAMELOT

By CHERYL PIERSON

Arthur Pender sat back in the plush cushion of the stagecoach, bracing himself against the side as the driver hit a rough spot. He shifted his gaze to the space where the window curtain moved with the jolting of the coach.

Desolate country. Flat and barren. Hot as hell in the summer, and cold as a woman's heart in the winters. Unforgiving, too.

There was no choice, though. He'd be here for as long as it took . . .as always.

The older woman who sat next to him pulled her voluminous skirt closer to her body. He wasn't sure if it was an attempt to be polite and keep to her allotted space, or if she truly didn't want her clothing to come into contact with him. Though he enjoyed the finer comforts as well as the next man, it had been three days since he'd bathed due to lack of facilities. He was not at his best.

His lips quirked in a caustic grin. In his life before, she'd have been curtsying to him from across a polished marble floor until he bade her rise. But that had been a very long time ago.

The hairs at the back of his neck prickled. He raised his gaze slowly to meet the level gray stare of the man who sat across from him. A prosperous businessman in this time, most likely, dressed in his best for the trip. The fitted cut of his suit spoke of money. All those years—*centuries*—before, a man's station in life was easily determined by the quality of the armor he wore—even to the density of his chain mail.

But this was a different time. A different world . . .though some things would never change.

Arthur nodded at his fellow passenger. The man gave him a stiff-necked bob of the head. *This was going to be a long, long journey.*

One thing remained constant through the centuries, spanning all the lives he had lived thus far: The idea of the Round Table, of equality and good triumphing over evil, never left him. Was it too much to ask to see it happen successfully just once? Would it be too much to hope for this time around?

He sighed, pinching the bridge of his nose. The beginning of a headache threatened. The woman who shared his seat gathered her skirts even closer, as if she tried to protect herself from some invisible menace.

The fourth passenger was a young boy of perhaps twelve, the other man's orphaned nephew. The youngster sat glum and silent, until Arthur reached into his own front breast pocket and pulled out a worn book. When Arthur opened it and began to try to read in the jolting, swaying contraption, the boy's face transformed.

He leaned forward. "Arthurian Tales and Legends! Oh, I know them all by heart!"

Arthur closed the book, handing it across the aisle to him, careful not to touch the elderly woman beside him. The boy's eyes widened as he took the tattered volume with a reverent hand. Arthur pasted a smile on his face, covering the surprised pang of sentimentality he felt at the boy's awe.

"Do you know these stories, sir?"

Arthur smiled. "Yes. Like you, I think I've memorized every last one of them."

"Oh, sir, I love them that much, too! The Knights of the Round Table—well, the very *idea* of the Round Table itself! King Arthur was a genius to think of it."

Arthur gave a short laugh. "I wouldn't say that, my lad. No, no genius . . .else, he'd have been able to see what would follow."

"Beggin' your pardon, sir," the boy replied, incensed, "but he'd have had to have been able to read minds to know that. And," he added in a practical tone, "he trusted Lancelot, and Mordred."

Arthur shook his head slowly. "So, you believe he was too quick to trust, do you?"

The boy shrugged. "If you can't trust your best friend and your son, then who?"

"Your wife." Arthur's voice was hollow, and the boy's uncle shot him an odd glance. "But, of course, he couldn't trust her, either, as it turned out."

"No." The youngster was quiet for a moment. "But, he *should* have been able to trust them all."

"Good lesson in life, I suppose. Be careful whom you give your allegiance to—make sure your faith in them is well-founded."

The boy held his hand out. "My name's Jeremy Davis."

"I'm . . . Arthur. Arthur Pender."

Jeremy smiled. "Were you named for King Arthur?"

Arthur nodded. "Yes."

"And you're from Britain—"

"Jeremy, don't be rude," his uncle corrected sourly.

"Oh, no, please—I don't mind, Mr. Davis—" Arthur said the name questioningly, unsure if they shared the same last name. The man nodded and stiffly put out a hand.

"Yes. I'm Jeremy's uncle, Evan. He's my youngest brother's boy." A crimson flush started to creep up his neck.

"Starting fresh in the west?" Arthur meant it as a conversational gambit, but the moment the question left his lips, the other man's spine became more rigid than before, and the pink stain rushed into his cheeks.

"Our other brother and his wife have agreed to take Jeremy now that his parents are deceased."

From the look on Jeremy's features, Arthur decided that he must not be too excited at the prospect of living with his aunt and uncle.

"After I see him safely to their ranch, I will be returning to Virginia to my own affairs," Davis answered in a dismissive tone.

"They say he'll come again," Jeremy murmured, turning his attention back to the ragged cover of the book he held. Evan Davis picked at an imaginary speck of lint on his coat, then looked away, ignoring his nephew.

Arthur nodded, "Aye. I suspect that part's true enough. One day, he will return."

"When the world needs him." The boy's voice rang with conviction.

"When *doesn't* it?" Arthur muttered.

Jeremy raised his somber gray eyes to him. Arthur deliberately softened his expression. "The world is always in need, it seems," he said gently.

"You said, 'that part's true enough', earlier. Don't *you* believe?"

"Jeremy, enough," Davis scolded. "Stop bothering people with these ridiculous ideas of yours. Camelot was a fantastical tale made up for gullible children such as yourself. Nothing more."

Anger shot through Arthur. By now, he should be accustomed to the boorish louts of the world, even when they clothed themselves in the finery of the day. But even if his assumption had been true, why embarrass the boy? And of course, it *wasn't* true.

"How do you know, Mr. Davis?"

Davis turned to him, surprised. Arthur could barely conceal his contempt beneath the thin veil of civility. "How do you know it is just 'a fantastical tale', hmm?"

Davis gave a self-conscious bark of laughter, his gaze flitting to the woman beside Arthur, as if to beg her indulgence for the entire display—as if his nephew was responsible. She regarded him disdainfully until the smile drifted away from his full lips, and he brought his gaze to bear once again on Arthur.

"Look, don't encourage him, will you? He shouldn't believe in folk tales. He's going to need his wits about him for his work on the ranch. He shouldn't be *dreaming* about Camelot and such."

"So . . .you only think about that which you *know* to be real, Mr. Davis? That which you've seen with your own eyes? You have no faith for anything, then? Well, have you seen Jesus Christ in the flesh, or do you '*believe*', sir?"

Davis shrank back against the cushioned confines of the seat as Arthur's voice rose loud and strident, reverberating through the coach. Arthur yanked his hat off in exasperation.

Davis nodded. "Y-Yes. I—I believe. Of course I believe! But you know that isn't the same thing as these—these *myths*!"

Arthur sighed, forcing himself to relax back into the seat. His head pounded, the headache having blown into full proportion now.

"And one more thing," the woman beside him said, uttering the first words she'd spoken since they'd left Fort Sill. "It takes more than hard work to make it in this country, Mr. Davis. If you try to divest the boy of his dreams, might as well turn around and head back to Virginia now. Dreams are the only thing that keep you going, out here."

After a moment, Jeremy held the book out to Arthur.

"Read it, if you like, son. My head's aching." Still unable to wipe the disgust for the man from his expression, Arthur glanced at Evan Davis. "My apologies."

Davis inclined his head briefly in acknowledgement. He looked at Jeremy, who had gleefully opened the book as if it were a treasure chest and begun to read, but he didn't make him give the book back.

* * *

Arthur awoke less than an hour later to a sound he knew well—the gurgle of a man drawing his dying breath through his own blood filling his lungs.

He sat up straight, the ungodly noise

encompassing his consciousness abruptly. The sound had been too real to be a dream.

Evan Davis lay on the floor of the swaying coach in a pool of blood, a brightly-banded arrow shaft protruding from his throat. His eyes bulged, and he clawed at the base of the wood, where it entered his flesh.

Jeremy knelt beside his uncle, tears of helplessness and fear running down his freckled cheeks. He was utterly silent, as was Mrs. Franklin, who had moved to the opposite side of the coach to occupy the seat that the Davises had vacated. She lay on the seat sideways, her legs in a sitting position, her body bent at the waist.

"Get down!" she hissed, as Arthur's eyes met hers briefly. Then, she opened her reticule and pulled out the small derringer from within. Davis drew his last breath and lay still.

Arthur pushed Jeremy down lower, flat onto the floor with him, where they sprawled atop Davis' corpse.

Arthur could feel Jeremy's ragged breathing beneath the hand he'd placed on the boy's back. Above them, the stagecoach driver's curses and shouts filtered through the sounds of the war cries. The Indians were surrounding them, but by Arthur's reckoning, they had to be nearing the next stage station.

Arthur drew his revolver and raised himself from Jeremy's form. As Arthur reached for Mrs. Franklin with his other hand, she threw off his touch, her eyes flashing.

"You'll need help, sir. And like it or not, I'm all there is. I will not cower on the floor, hiding from these savages."

"Madam, your bravery is commendable, but as a gentleman—"

"*Gentlemen* sometimes don't last long, Mr. Pender, in this rough land." She tore her gaze quickly from his, aiming the derringer and squeezing off a deadly shot as a painted face appeared in the nearby window. The Indian disappeared with a startled cry of pain and surprise.

"Ha!" she cried triumphantly.

In spite of their dire situation, Arthur couldn't help smiling. The door handle jiggled and flew open, revealing two of the savages who gleefully started to jump from their ponies into the moving conveyance.

Arthur brought the pistol to bear and coolly squeezed off two shots. Of all the inventions of this time, the weaponry intrigued him most. What he might have accomplished in the past if he'd had a six-shot revolver!

The Indians disappeared as the coach raced wildly toward its destination, the door hanging ajar. Arthur lunged toward the door, but it flew out of his grasp. He shoved the lifeless body of Evan Davis aside, heard Jeremy's gasp of dismay as his hand smeared through the bloody puddle on the floor where his uncle had died. The boy braced his hands against the edge of the wall to hold himself in place on the floor. He made a grab for the book of legends just as it slid for the open door, lunging for it at the last possible moment.

From outside the coach, the jubilant shout of the driver sounded, and the horses began to slow. The stage station rolled into view through the open doorway.

"Thank God!" Mrs. Franklin gasped.

In the next instant, the driver, Joe Danforth, had brought the team to a full, skidding halt and jumped to the ground. He flung the door fully open assessing the situation with a quick glance. "Get inside, quick as you can. They'll be back."

Joe reached in to take Mrs. Franklin's hand as she clambered through the door.

"Up, lad," Arthur urged, and Jeremy seemed to come to himself, scrambling through the opening, the book clutched tightly in his bloody fist.

Arthur jumped to the ground and took a step, then stopped. He turned and reached inside the stagecoach to pull Davis' Colt free of his holster. They'd have need of every gun available, he thought grimly, wondering if young Jeremy had ever before fired a pistol.

He started for the door at a lope, noticing two other men standing warily, guns drawn.

"Get on in here!" one of them yelled gruffly.

In another time, men wouldn't have dared speak to him thusly. He had, after all, been a king. But, for whatever reason, he enjoyed this time in what had become America's western frontier.

He crossed the threshold of the stage station and entered chaos. Tension filled the air as preparations for war were carried out, a familiar reminder of days past. All around him, Arthur felt the mingled fear, anticipation and anxiety so thick it was another presence in the room.

Two women sat on a settee across the room ripping sheets into long strips. Mrs. Franklin stood beside the settee speaking to one of the women, a honey-haired beauty who seemed to have quite a lot of experience at tearing bandage strips. When she raised her eyes to the older woman, Arthur understood.

Guinevere . . . Ginny . . .

In all these years when he'd found himself transformed once more in a time that wasn't his, living a life that didn't belong to him, he'd never thought to lay eyes on Ginny again. The legend that he seemed to have no control over had brought him back at least a score of times since that fateful day when he'd been spirited away to Avalon after the battle with Lancelot's forces. But he'd never thought the legend would extend to his queen! Protective anger filled him. She should not have to endure these machinations. Theirs had been an arranged marriage . . . in the beginning. She'd had no say in it. Still . . . she'd made the most of it, hadn't she? One part of him protested, while the other part of him said, she deserved everything she got.

Ginny.

He nearly dropped to his knees. In all the lives he'd lived over the centuries, he had never faced her. Not ever. He glanced around quickly, but saw no other familiar faces. Relief filled him. There had been times, in the past, when Lance had been present briefly—always at a distance. Arthur had never been certain enough of his purpose to approach him. Lance's duplicity was something he could always count on.

But . . . Ginny. He could feel his heart begin to dissolve in his chest. No. No. He could stand anything but this.

Somehow, he'd always figured that if they should all three come together once more it would be the miracle that would end everything. The miracle that would see the end of his hope.

He shook his head, as if in a daze, turning away until he could decide how to handle the situation. He'd never expected Ginny to be here. She was so delicate, so fine—so pure. Or so he'd thought. This life was too rough for someone such as Guin . . . Ginny . . . with her all-seeing, damnable . . . *beautiful* green eyes.

"Give me a hand over here!" The shout from one of the men galvanized him into action, giving him something to divert his thoughts. He walked across the room hurriedly, grabbing the other side of the massive buffet table and hutch to move it in front of the door.

He'd been a king for many, many years, but he'd been a warrior for much longer. Admired for his wisdom and cool head as a leader, he knew how to take orders as well as assume command.

"Where should I be?" Arthur asked, seeing that the other men were taking positions by windows and cross notches in the shutters.

The tall man he'd helped with the buffet gave him a quick nod. "You know how to use a gun?"

Arthur smiled. "Yes."

Thompson gave him a dubious look. "Over here, then. Do you have lead?" He started for the side window, and Arthur followed.

"Lead? Oh, uh, yes."

"There's more if you need it—on the table." He pointed to the kitchen table where boxes of bullets were stacked in the center.

"Thanks."

Thompson put his hand out. "Harley Thompson. I own this place." They shook hands and Thompson peered at Arthur closely for a moment. "Brit, huh?"

Arthur nodded, breaking open his revolver and loading the empty chambers.

"So's my wife."

Arthur stopped in mid-motion. "Your wife?"

"Yeah." He grinned. "Not much time for introductions, but Ginny's my wife." He nodded toward the settee, where all three women were gathered, tearing and folding bandages. "That's her on the end."

I know.

"Been married two years now," Thompson went on proudly.

Anger surged up inside Arthur's gut. Why would he bring Ginny to this wild, rough country? Danger was everywhere here. And Ginny . . . was a lady. Arthur averted his eyes. At least, she wasn't with Lance.

Guilt washed over him. Would it matter? If she were with Lance, she might at least be safe. He cast another glance her way. She was as lovely as he remembered, even though she was a few years older than when he'd seen her last, centuries ago, speeding away with Lance toward the safe haven of *Joyeux Garde*. Away from him. He tore his gaze away from her, and made his voice casual.

"Does this happen often? Indian attacks?"

Thompson nodded ruefully. "More than I had believed it would."

"They're comin' in again!"

Thompson quickly reached for the heavy wooden shutters, closing them across the window. He peered out of one of the gun wells at the narrow view of the barren terrain outside.

"There's holes here and here—" He pointed out the obvious places in the walls on either side of the window. "'Course, time it's all said and done, there won't be one piece of glass left in the place nohow." He shook his head. "I've replaced these windows twice already in the two years we've been here."

Arthur shrugged, turning his narrow gaze to the cross-spaces cut in the shutters. "Why not just use oilskin of some kind?"

"My Ginny, she loves the windows. She says there ain't much to look at, but she wants the light." After a pause, he went on. "I try to give her everything she wants. Why she took up with me, I'll never know."

It is a mystery, Arthur wanted to say. Yet . . . what had he expected? He'd known, someday, he would see her again. He just hadn't been prepared for it to be *here*. He certainly hadn't thought she'd be married to a stage station proprietor. He stole another glance at her. Had she recognized him?

She raised her eyes to his at that instant and he was as lost to her as he had been the first moment he'd been introduced to her. It had been an arranged marriage at the start. But once he'd met her, talked to her, laughed with her—she had captured his heart and held it. And she would have it forever.

Her eyes were as green as ever, like the endless spring fields of Britain in May. Leaf green, like a secret forest glade. They shimmered with unshed tears, now, just as they had when he'd sentenced her to death all those centuries past. Tears of sorrow, tears for what she'd thrown away, and tears of forgiveness for what he'd been forced to do. There had been no other way. He looked away from her, wary of the treachery of his

305

own heart.

Outside the stillness was broken by whoops and screeches from the Indians as they made their next attack. As they came into view at the front of the station, the men on that side began shooting.

The warriors rode around the corner into Arthur's view, and he took careful aim, then pulled the trigger. Satisfaction rolled through him as the one of the savages fell from his horse with a scream, then lay, unmoving, on the ground.

"Good shot," Thompson muttered approvingly. He took aim and squeezed off a shot of his own as two more warriors rode into view. One of them raised a pistol and fired, deliberately shattering the glass in one of the small, high windows. Thompson and Arthur both instinctively ducked away.

Arthur took a quick assessment of the other occupants of the station. To be effective, they had to have some sort of plan. Merlin had always told him he over-thought things until he had no imagination, but he knew no other way. Still, he mused ruefully, some things were just going to happen, no matter what. Events had been set in motion that couldn't be changed or stopped however much forethought or planning was involved.

Mrs. Franklin, who had shown such determination in the coach when the attack began, seemed to be the backbone of the female contingent. She barked orders at Ginny and the other young woman, Sally Dodge, as they reloaded and cleaned the weapons.

"Can you manage without me?" Arthur heard the older woman ask. "I'm a dead shot. I'll be of more use with the men."

"Yes—yes! Go ahead, Mrs. Franklin," Ginny called above the din. "We'll be fine. Sally and I have become quite expert at this, haven't we?" She gave Sally a quick glance, her uncertain smile wavering before it disappeared altogether.

Arthur recognized the note of suppressed anxiety in Ginny's tone. He knew her so well—she could hide nothing from him. Nothing, except the one thing he'd never thought possible. Betrayal that, it seemed, they were doomed to repeat, or at least remember, throughout the ages.

The portly older woman hurried off toward the back room, carrying a shotgun and a handful of shells. Arthur watched as their driver, Joe Danforth, stopped her, giving her a vehement shake of his head. Her chin lifted in defiance and she moved on past him. Danforth followed her in exasperation.

"Thompson!" he yelled. "Take over here!"

Thompson nodded, then looked at Arthur. "That boy know how to use a pistol?"

Arthur glanced at where Jeremy huddled near the table. "Don't know. Just met him twenty miles back when he got on with his uncle."

"We could sure use another gun."

Arthur watched Thompson's back as he ran across the room to take Joe's crucial place at the front of the building. The boy was young. No more than eleven or twelve. About the age he'd been when he pulled the sword from the stone. Too young for such responsibility, but in desperate times . . .

"Boy!" He searched his battle-fogged mind for a name. "Jeremy!"

The boy looked at him blankly, and he wondered if he'd called him by the wrong name. He motioned for him, and the boy leapt to his feet, clutching his chest as he ran to Arthur.

Arthur glanced down, searching his gray eyes. It was then he saw what the boy held so dearly to his bosom. *The book. The damned book.* But the boy met his look with something akin to worship. Almost as if he *knew*.

"Jeremy, do you know how to use a gun?"

"No, sir. My papa didn't allow it. He believed it was wrong to kill."

"This is different. You are defending yourself." Arthur pulled Evan Davis's Colt from his waistband. "This was your uncle's."

"Yes, sir. But . . . I don't know how to use it."

Arthur turned his attention back to the window and took aim again as one of the Indians rode into his view. "Watch."

But as he prepared to pull the trigger, something stopped him. The Indian turned his head toward the place where Arthur stood, glaring as if he could see through the shattered window. The late afternoon sun caught the savage's long hair, revealing a deep chestnut color—not black. Arthur's breath caught at the piercing blue of the warrior's eyes. Though his skin was naturally dark, backed even browner by the sun, Arthur knew this was no Apache, but a white man.

The breath rushed out of him.

"*Lance.*"

* * *

How many times had he longed for just this very moment? To have Lancelot du Lac right where he wanted him—at the end of his weapon—was such a gift. *The traitor. The son of a bitch.* How he would love to kill him. His finger itched on the trigger, even as he fought the impulse to throw down this instrument of death and run to his old friend amid the hail of bullets.

There was a time when he'd loved Lance as a brother. He'd never had a better friend before Lance—or since. The vision Arthur had had for Camelot had been shared by the knight. And Lance had gone through hell for him, gladly, with no complaint. Then he'd slept with Ginny.

And though the anger and hurt had brought down everything they'd worked so hard to build, Arthur couldn't help but remember the times before . . . when everything had been good. That was the only reason his finger stayed put.

"Aren't you going to shoot him?"

Jeremy's voice interrupted his thoughts. He looked down at the boy. "No. I don't have a clear shot. We won't want to waste our bullets."

Jeremy nodded. "He doesn't look Indian," he observed quietly.

"No," Arthur agreed.

"Maybe he's a prisoner. Sometimes they kidnap babies and children, and raise them as Indians . . ." He suddenly looked stricken, and Arthur knew his thoughts.

"Put that out of your mind, lad," he said kindly. "We've other things to worry about now."

He handed him the gun, and this time, the boy took it. "It may not be what your father would do, Jeremy, but you are going to have to defend yourself."Arthur holstered his own weapon, laying a

309

sure hand atop Jeremy's trembling fingers. "Hold it steady, like so—" He felt the slight movement fade to nothing, until Jeremy's hand was still beneath his.

As another Apache rode into view, Arthur put his finger over Jeremy's and pulled the trigger. The kick of the Colt surprised the boy. He looked up at Arthur, then back outside. The Indian was gone.

"I missed," he said, disappointment edging his voice.

Arthur shook his head. "I don't think so. I think you got him. He just managed to hang on to his horse."

Jeremy looked up at him, a new determination in his features. "Never thought I'd spend Christmas Eve killin' people."

* * *

The Apache rode away once more, and though Arthur felt the same relief as the others, he couldn't tamp down the frustration of a battle fought but not ended decisively.

Jeremy stood looking out the slatted spaces in the window, keeping a wary eye for any sign of movement.

Thompson did the same from where he stood at the front of the station. He'd been right, Arthur thought grimly. There wasn't one piece of glass left anywhere in the structure. *All for Ginny.*

His gaze followed his thoughts. She had never been one to show her inner turmoil like most women. Maybe that had been why he'd never read the signs . . . or maybe, there hadn't been any to read. She stood now, calm as ever, expertly cleaning a shotgun that one of the men had laid on her dining room table.

The sight of her with her hair askew, wearing a simple green muslin day dress as she cleaned a weapon struck him funny. Not that she couldn't manage in circumstances such as these—married to a peasant, living in little better than a crofter's cottage—Ginny always made the best of things. That was one of the qualities he'd loved most about her. Here she was, doing it again. Something old and familiar stirred in his heart, just watching her. He'd missed her . . . in spite of everything.

From the back room, Joe Danforth's voice rose. "Confound it, woman, what in tarnation did you do that for? I had my sights on that murderin' savage and you made me miss!"

"Yes. I did, Mr. Danforth."

Though Elizabeth Franklin didn't raise her voice, in the small space, it was easily heard.

"That was a *white* man you were trying to kill," she went on. "*Not* a 'murdering savage.' Perhaps your eyesight fails you."

"I'd rather be stone blind than take leave of my common sense, woman!"

"Unfortunately, Mr. Danforth, you seem to have suffered a double affliction."

"Damn it!"

"Vulgarity, Mr. Danforth, is the verbal evidence of a weak mind. Please restrain yourself."

They entered the great room, still at odds, Joe unwilling to give her the last word.

"Don't you ever do that again!" he blustered.

The older woman turned to him slowly. Silence filled the room. Then, "Mr. Danforth, let me assure you, I will do whatever is necessary. Don't get in my way."

Danforth took a step back, eyes widening. Before he could respond, Sally hurried to Mrs. Franklin's side.

"Elizabeth—will you come see to my Ernie? He's been awful sick—that's why we're still here. He couldn't travel 'til he got to feeling better. Please—" She put her hand on the older woman's arm urging her away from Danforth.

Mrs. Franklin gave Danforth one last long look, then turned away. "Certainly, dear. I know a thing or two about healing."

"Thank goodness! I'm afraid neither Ginny nor I have much talent in that area."

No, Arthur thought. Certainly, Ginny was no healer. Though she'd never been squeamish about helping treat the wounded, she had not possessed that intuition needed to anticipate a patient's needs. It wasn't her fault, really. Maybe if they'd had children …

Sally and Mrs. Franklin hurried toward where Ernie leaned against the wall, and Harley motioned for Joe to help him get the man back to his sick bed.

Ginny made her way to where Arthur stood, a few feet away from Jeremy. She didn't speak, as if she waited to see what he'd say first—if anything. When he remained silent, she said, "It's . . . been a long time, Arthur."

"Ginny." He moistened his lips, feeling like a schoolboy once more.

"How are you?" She put a hand out, then stopped herself and drew it back, finally clasping her hands together.

"I'm fine. And you?"

Christ, they sounded like two strangers. This was Ginny. His Ginny. Guinevere. His queen. The woman whose virginity he'd taken on their wedding night, all those centuries past. Did she ever remember how good their lives had been in the beginning?

She smiled faintly. "Who could ask for more?" She glanced around the great room. "A roof over my head, food on the table, a good man—" she broke off, looking down at the floor. "Of course, I've had all those things before and lost them—so I don't take this for granted." She raised her eyes to his. "I suppose it isn't meant to be for me to have a child—ever."

"I'm sorry, Gin. I know how much that meant to you."

"No, Arthur, I don't think you do."

Something in her clipped tone said the blame was his. They both knew better, but perhaps she needed to be reminded. And Arthur lashed out, hurt.

"We both know the fault for that didn't lie with *me*, Guinevere."

She sucked in a shocked gasp and turned away.

"Would that the son I was given had never been born." Bitterness filled Arthur at the thought of Mordred's machinations. "Here we are—you with no child and me with one I wish to God had never been conceived." He gave a mirthless chuckle.

Ginny laid a hand on his arm. "Arthur, it's Christmas Eve. Can we try to put the past behind us, just for tonight and tomorrow? For pity's sake, even armies call truce on this day!"

"Yes . . ." he said thoughtfully. "Yes, I suppose we could put the past behind us if it didn't keep slapping us in the face at every turn." He sighed wearily. "It doesn't signify. No matter how civil our 'truce', the outcome will always be the same."

Suddenly, he gripped her arm. "Why are we here, Ginny? I don't understand why—"

"It's Christmas, Arthur." She looked up at him imploringly, every bit as lovely as she had been at seventeen. "It's Christmas. And anything can happen, if we but *believe*."

Arthur couldn't help but smile at her childlike trust. "A miracle? Is that what we're talking about?"

She nodded, biting her lip. "It's already started. Oh, Arthur if you only knew how much I've wanted to tell you—"

"Hey, what's going on here?" Thompson's voice cut across the room, and Ginny turned to face her husband, a quick smile coming to her lips.

"Harley, can you believe it? Why, Arthur and I were childhood playmates! Our families lived near one another. I haven't seen him since we were—what? Twelve?"

Arthur nodded. "You were twelve—I was a bit older. It's good to see you again, Ginny—even under these circumstances." He looked up at Harley, whose face had relaxed at the explanation. "How is Mr. Dodge?"

"He ain't good, that's for sure." He scratched his head, and Ginny flinched at the 'ain't'.

"Is there anything to be done for him?"

Harley shook his head. "He's still pretty weak, but he says he can manage a pistol if he can just rest a spell."

Arthur gave a grim nod. "Let's just hope those Apaches hold off a while so he can get rested, then."

"They will," Harley said. "Now, they'll wait 'til it gets dark. Come back for their dead. Then we'll see what other tricks they've got up their sleeve."

Ginny gave a slight shudder. "Perhaps I should get dinner started."

"You do that, Ginny," Harley said. "If I'm gonna meet my Maker, I want to do it on a full stomach."

"Harley!" Ginny's hand flew to her mouth, and Arthur had to stop himself from stepping toward her. How easy it would be, he thought, to pull her close, hold her in his arms again, let her cry on his shoulder. But, that wasn't his position, and never would be again.

Harley touched her hair. "Aw, Ginny, you know I don't mean anything. You're just jumpy." She nodded, quickly moving away from them toward the kitchen without answering.

"Women." Harley shrugged and walked away, back toward the front of the building, leaving Arthur and Jeremy where they stood beside the boarded window.

When Arthur glanced down at Jeremy, he was clutching the book again like a talisman, his fingers absently moving over the top of the binding. The blood had soaked in and dried. Fitting, Arthur thought. Bloody was the best description of his reign. And it seemed to have followed him, even here—despite his best intentions.

Tenderness welled in Arthur's chest as he watched Jeremy. The boy had lost so much. His parents, his home, all that was familiar—and now, his uncle. He was alone in the world, much as Arthur had been at his age. Elizabeth Franklin had been right—the lad would need his dreams—if he survived.

Jeremy looked up, meeting Arthur's gaze with a look that Arthur understood before the boy uttered a word. Still, his breath stopped when the boy spoke.

"You're him, aren't you? Arthur Pendragon. Arthur Pender. Ginny—Guinevere."

"No, no—that's . . . foolishness, Jeremy. Just coincidence."

But the boy shook his head, steadfast belief in his clear gray eyes. "It's not, though. The legend says you'll return. When the time is right and the need is the greatest, you'll come—That's what it says, sir."

Arthur laid a palm on the boy's head. "I know," he said softly. "God help me, I know exactly what it says."

"Please, save us, then!"

Arthur's gut clenched at the boy's earnest plea. "Don't you think I would if I could?" The anger at his impotence overrode all else, and the light dimmed in Jeremy's eyes. But Arthur didn't apologize. Jeremy stiffened at the rebuff and Arthur dropped his hand from the boy, turning away from him.

Indecision had never plagued him. But now . . . now he didn't know what to do. This wasn't his time, or place. He had been born a king, cursed through the centuries. But in all the years the farce had been played out again and again, he'd never been in this position. This time was different. Ginny and Lance were *both* here—and this boy, Jeremy, with his innocence and goodness, his hopes for the future and dreams of the past, was somehow now his responsibility. He'd been responsible for soldiers and serfs, armies and citizens—civilization had been in his hands, at one point.

And yet—

It was the belief and trust of this one boy who trumped everything that had come before. Before that unthinkable deadly battle with Lance, he'd wanted nothing more than to keep the dream he'd begun alive and well throughout the centuries. It had seemed so important. He'd forgotten just how important until he and Jeremy Davis had boarded the same stagecoach.

* * *

Ginny served the stew and cornbread with forced gaiety. Joe and Harley picked up their spoons as soon as she set their bowls down, but she cleared her throat and said, "Perhaps we should have a prayer for our bounty and for deliverance from the savages before we partake." She glanced at Arthur. "Would you mind saying the blessing, Mr. Pender?"

Arthur schooled his features in a mask of bland remoteness. Ginny knew his faith in God had long vanished. Did she mock him?

"I'll be happy to," he responded at last, bowing his head. How long had it been since he'd prayed? Did he even remember how it was done? "Dearest Father in Heaven, bless this food that has been so lovingly prepared by Thy humble servants. Watch over us and keep us safe, if it be Thy will. Grant us a miracle on this, the eve of Thy Son Jesus' birth. In His name we pray, Amen."

"Amen," Ginny murmured, her voice breathless with emotion. When he glanced up at her, she turned away quickly, pretending to have forgotten something in the kitchen. Most likely, he thought with some shame, she was remembering another time. A time when he had the faith and belief in God that he now must pretend to keep.

317

"I do hope Mr. Dodge recovers soon," Mrs. Franklin said. "The poultice we made for him should help."

"I'm sure he will be feeling better by tomorrow morning," Ginny responded as she returned to the table. "I shall pray for him this evening."

"Yeah, my Ginny's a big one for prayin'." Harley crumbled a piece of cornbread over the top of his stew, giving Ginny a grin and a wink. "It don't always help, but I reckon it makes her happy just the same."

"We're gonna need all the help we can get tonight," Joe put in seriously.

"Yeah," Harley muttered, becoming serious. "There's more of 'em this time than there's been before." He looked around at the faces at the table. "I saw Sky Eyes out there today—"

Joe glared across the table at Elizabeth Franklin. "Yeah. I coulda had him if someone hadn't pushed my rifle up at the last minute."

Mrs. Franklin was unperturbed. "Pass the salt, please, Mr. Danforth, will you? And just for the record, I didn't want you to do something you might regret later."

Danforth handed her the salt, scowling. "With all due respect, ma'am, if I'd not been interfered with, this whole thing might be over."

"Or, Mr. Danforth, perhaps you might've brought down even more of their wrath by killing their leader. I wonder, is this Sky Eyes a man who might be reasoned with? He's a white man, with eyes like that."

"*Reasoned with?* Ma'am, you saw what he was like out there today—ruthless, that's what he is." Danforth took a bite of the stew, nodding in Ginny's direction. "Awful tasty, Miss Ginny, just like always."

"But he's *not* one of them," Mrs. Franklin persisted. "He's different, somehow . . ."

"Now, listen to me." Joe sat forward in his chair intently. "He's a killin', murderin' savage. His eyes may be blue but his heart is just as black as all the rest of 'em."

Ginny's spoon clattered to the floor. "Oh, dear. I'm so clumsy." She bent to retrieve it, then rose to get a clean one. As she walked past the window, she paused as if she scanned the prairie for any sign of the Indians. But Arthur knew she looked for only one.

She glanced back toward the table, feeling his stare on her, and their eyes met briefly before she looked away again.

One thing was clear to him. Ginny was not going to be surprised at Lance's appearance. She'd known all along. And she hadn't told him Lance was here—she'd given him no warning, and somehow that made him angry all over again. Maybe she'd been hoping it would end differently for them all this time. She'd have been unsure of him, Arthur thought, and what he might do. Trust was nonexistent between them, now.

Hell, there wasn't much he could do under the circumstances. Even if he'd wanted to change things . . . it would play out as it was meant to. As in chess, Arthur thought, the queen retained all the power. Even more than the king.

* * *

Ginny had put up a small fir tree in one corner of the great room in celebration of the holiday. It was pitiful, Arthur thought, but it brought a smile to his lips, all the same. She'd never been much for crafting and decorating, though she'd always seemed to appreciate the efforts of others. Now, here she was, on her own in this time, with no servants to order about, and from what Arthur had seen, living a lonely existence.

In the life he'd had as king, from his childhood, there had been elusive magical moments. Moments when he'd been able to 'see' things. Merlin hadn't given him the skill, he'd been born with it. The sorcerer had only taught him to use it, and chastised him when he "thought too much" to take advantage of it. Morgan, his half-sister, had gotten the lion's share of magical talent—something Arthur was glad of. But, he didn't need the gift to see how miserable Ginny was here, in this place and time.

The divining gift did come in handy, at times. In this era, he'd discovered quite a use for it at the gaming tables. Looking across the lamp-lit dimness of the room at Ginny, he suddenly wished it extended to mind reading. But . . . would he really want to know her thoughts any more now than all those years past? No. He'd seen enough. The furtive glance through the slatted window was confirmation enough of where her heart and mind lay. *With Sky Eyes. With Lance.*

Joe and Harley kept watch at the front window, looking out into the blackness for any sign of attack. Elizabeth Franklin sat talking quietly with Jeremy, and Arthur heard the boy's enthusiastic responses as he recalled happier memories of his home in North Carolina he'd left behind. Perhaps talking about it would soothe him, Arthur thought, and calm his nerves.

Ginny uncertainly sought him out once more.

Now that she'd lied to her husband, Harley took no notice of her proximity to Arthur. And Arthur couldn't help recalling how naturally the falsehood had sprung to her lips. Had she given it forethought, he wondered, or had she just become a skilled deceiver? *Oh, no. She'd always been that.*

"You don't seem worried overmuch, Arthur," she murmured softly, as she came to stand beside him.

"Come now, Ginny. Let's have done with this pretense, shall we? We both know Lance is leading that band of savages."

Her gaze faltered, and she looked away from him, not answering.

"Do you really believe he'll harm you?" The note of gentleness crept into his tone, in spite of his resolve not to care.

"I—I don't know, truly. He was—so angry when we last spoke. When I told him I'd made my decision to go to the convent—"

"You haven't seen him since—since we fought?"

She shook her head. "Not really . . . Oh, I've seen him, during these attacks, but never spoken to him. Arthur, I've lived a thousand lives, but not fully. I seem to just wake up in another time, another place. Somehow, I—" She stopped herself, then went on in a controlled tone. "I believe it must be the same for you. And for Lancelot. We're all trapped in this circle."

"How do we end it, Ginny?"

She moistened her lips in the nervous gesture he recalled so well. "I'm not sure. But I—I wonder if maybe it's not somehow connected to . . . forgiveness."

Anger flared quickly in Arthur's heart. *She dared ask him to forgive? Forgive her treachery? Forgive*

Lance's betrayal? Forgive her causing the death of the dream he'd held so dear? A cold smile touched his lips.

"You ask much, my lady. Especially after all you've *taken*."

She nodded, the stricken look in her eyes almost too much for him. Even in the near darkness, he could see the pallor of her flawless skin.

"Yes. You were always a much better person than I, Arthur. You had a generous heart. A loving soul."

"Make no mistake, Ginny—I am *first* a warrior. A ruler."

In the gathering darkness, she laid a hand on his. "No, Arthur. You are first a *man*. And a good one." The softness of her skin on his in the shadows brought a flood of memories that he'd thought were carefully locked away.

"You know Lance won't attack now." His lips curved caustically. "He loved Christmas-tide more than the rest of us put together." It had always been Lance who suggested they find the biggest Yule log in the forest, spearheading the effort to organize the men and making it a festive occasion. It had been Lance who sang the Yule songs with such fervor, his deep baritone booming through the stone hallways of the castle.

Ginny's eyes filled with sudden tears. "Arthur— when I see him as he was today . . . I wonder if he even recalls the things *we* remember. It seems he's become absorbed in the ways of the Apache. The look on his face is so intent, so—cruel. I don't believe he's the person we knew."

"He was never the person I thought I knew, Ginny. Never." At her quick look, he smiled. "Yet, there's a part of me that, even now, wants to call him my brother, as I did before—before everything fell apart."

Ginny nodded. "I hope that same part of you remembers me in another light as well, Arthur," she whispered.

Arthur flicked a quick glance to where Harley Thompson sat, talking with Joe. Curiosity won over propriety. "Why are you with him, Ginny?"

Ginny suddenly dropped her gaze. "Earlier in this life I was . . . a—a—"

Arthur shook his dead in disbelief. *"A prostitute?"*

"Shh!" An embarrassed flush colored her cheeks. "Yes. A 'soiled dove' at Maybelle Wainwright's brothel in Kansas City. Harley was my first customer— at least the first one I knew about. You know how it is—you just 'appear.' People know you sometimes. Sometimes you're a stranger in town. You don't have a past you can remember, but you have a hundred lives you've lived before."

"Yes. I know."

"Harley asked me to marry him. I . . . barely knew him."

"From a convent to a whorehouse, huh? Fitting, somehow." Arthur couldn't resist. The pain of the memories that assailed him called up the firestorm of hurt and betrayal he still had no defense against. It hurt almost as badly now as it had at the time.

"Arthur—" she started, then nodded resignedly. "Yes, that's fair. Anything you say is fair. But just remember, you aren't the only one who's been hurt." There was genuine sorrow in her tone, but Arthur was unaffected.

"Spare me."

"As you will, *my lord*." She turned and walked away, toward the back bedroom.

Arthur felt Jeremy's eyes on him. He met the boy's steady gaze, but the worshipful light that had been there before had dimmed.

* * *

Arthur sighed heavily. The woman had always driven him to madness, one way or the other. Now, she'd given him another idea that had possibilities—unthinkable ones.

Forgiveness, she'd said. Could he find that in his heart? Would it even truly matter if he did? He would do anything to break this perpetual cycle of living lives that weren't his.

It would surely take a miracle to break this prophecy that came true over and over again. Who would have believed that living could become so tiresome? That death would be a welcome reprieve? And if there were nothing beyond death?

Oh, yes. He'd thought of it time and again. If a bullet took him down, or an Apache arrow, and he truly succumbed to his wounds as a mortal man might—then what? Going into darkness forever might not be such a terrible outcome.

Everlasting life was much overrated.

But this wasn't the same as what the Holy Bible promised. Being taken to the bosom of God was not the same as waking up in a border town with a hangover he couldn't get rid of. *So much for his "life" this time around.* All he wanted was peace. Rest for his wounded soul. Forgetfulness of all that had once been his, and then been lost to him.

Seeing Lance through the years was bad enough. But now . . . seeing Ginny once more, being reminded of her loveliness, her scent, her touch—this must surely be hell already. There could be no greater punishment. What had he done that had been so very wrong?

Perhaps it *was* all to end this time. He wanted to be prepared, if that were the case.

* * *

As the night wore on, tempers grew short as nerves frayed. From somewhere outside, the sound of an owl filtered through the silence.

Harley tensed, glancing at Joe. "Damn bastards."

"I want that blue-eyed son of a bitch in the worst way. Woulda had him, too, if it hadn't been for *her*." He inclined his head toward Elizabeth Franklin who sat on the settee, Jeremy slumped against her in sleep.

Arthur's senses were in tune with what was going on outside. He barely heard the quiet conversation of the other two men. Sally sat with Ernie in the back room. Arthur didn't hold out much hope for Ernie. The man had put up a valiant front this afternoon, but there was no doubt that whatever illness he'd suffered from previously had taken a toll on his health. He was certainly dying, and for that, Arthur was sorry. He'd seen the genuine love on Sally's face, the tears shimmering in her blue eyes. And though Mrs. Franklin had done what she could, Arthur suspected it would amount to too little too late.

The owl called again, and Joe rubbed the back of his neck. "Damn hoot owl," he muttered. "Injuns say—
"

325

"I know what they say, Joe." Harley cast a quick glance over his shoulder at Ginny, who was curled up in his chair, asleep, her head twisted at an odd angle.

Arthur made a conscious effort to restrain himself. Why should he care if she was comfortable? Yet, how he wanted to go to her and put a cushion beneath her golden hair. It shone in the lamplight, clean and soft. He remembered the feel of it between his fingers as they'd made love—He closed his eyes. She was not his, nor ever would be again.

"What *do* they say, Mr. Danforth?" Arthur asked, needing something to take his mind off the path his thoughts had taken.

He opened his eyes just in time to see the other two men exchange an uncomfortable glance.

"It don't matter." Joe's voice was gruff, but Arthur recognized the fear that edged his comment.

"Still, I'd like to know."

"They say an owl tells of death." Harley turned to look at Arthur.

Arthur shrugged. "I wonder if that's a real owl we're hearing, or an 'Indian' owl?"

"Means the same thing either way," Danforth said. "Unless they figger out what's happened at the next station and get us some help."

"Ain't likely to happen on Christmas." Harley kept his eyes on the darkness.

"Maybe . . . I could talk with this 'Sky Eyes,'" Arthur suggested slowly.

Both men turned to give him disbelieving stares.

"Want to part ways with your hair, Brit?" Danforth finally asked.

"He's vicious," Harley put in. "What makes you

think you'd be able to make him listen?"

Arthur shrugged. "I don't know that I can, Mr. Thompson. But, as Mrs. Franklin says he isn't truly one of them. I'd thought—perhaps he might remember some of what he knew before he was kidnapped by the Apache."

"For all we know, he might've been stolen when he was a baby. 'Pache life might be all he understands." Danforth watched him closely for a moment. "I think you mean to try it, no matter what."

Arthur smiled. "I used to be quite the diplomat."

Harley shook his head. "You know what them savages do to white people? I don't want to sit in here and listen to you scream all night long. And there's no way we can help you."

Arthur stood up wearily, running a hand through his close-cropped hair. "This is no way to spend Christmas, gentlemen."

The owl sounded again outside, closer than before.

Danforth wiped the sweat from his face. "Dear God, that's three times."

"Does that signify?" Arthur asked, wondering at the ashen faces of the men.

"Means death, for certain." Harley's answer was clipped.

Maybe these men feared the Indian magic because it wasn't theirs. They hadn't been steeped in magic as he had. None of them had. Though he possessed no magic of his own, really, it could be that this night would lend its power to him. Or he could be on a fool's errand. Christmas Eve was said to be a miraculous time. Was it true? Could he talk Lance out of this senseless killing?

In the past, Lance had always had a clear reason to fight. He'd fought for lands, for pride . . . for a woman. Never had he been savage and brutal without cause.

Yet, in the flash of his blue eyes earlier this afternoon, Arthur had wondered . . . The killing lust had been there, and there was no mistaking the air of egotistical pride he wore. Some things never changed.

This may be the time period where it all ended. And that was a good thing as far as Arthur was concerned. So, why did he tarry? He may be the only one who could talk some sense into Lance. Maybe Lance would remember, all those years ago, how he'd pledged his fealty to Arthur . . . how they'd walked together as brothers, talked as friends. Maybe he'd remember it all . . . It would be worth it just to see.

* * *

Before either of the other men realized what he was about to do, Arthur strode to the front door and pulled the bolt back, then swung it open.

"Lance!" he called.

The other men cursed and lunged for the door, and Arthur stepped through it to the front porch.

The horses had long since been cut loose from the coach and stolen, but Arthur could make out the form of Evan Davis lying stiff and lifeless inside the stage. At least they hadn't taken the time to steal his body, Arthur thought. The door hung ajar, and the full moon wrapped the corpse in a silver shroud of light.

"Lance!" he called again. "Come out where we

can talk."

The silence answered him once more.

Arthur put his hands to his mouth and gave the call of a mourning dove. It was the only birdcall he'd ever mastered—a secret he and Lance had shared a laugh over many times. Especially when Arthur directed one of his men to give a call of a different kind of bird. "My royal directive," he'd laughingly called it, but only Lance knew it was because any other call he gave always sounded suspiciously like the mourning dove. From the darkness, the call was returned to him. He took the three steps to the ground, then moved to the side of the porch, looking behind him. As he turned, he looked up into Lancelot's face. Where there had been no one only seconds earlier, now, Lance stood behind him.

"Arthur? My king?"

Arthur stood tall and laid a hand on Lance's arm. "It's me, Lance. But as you can see, I'm no longer a king of any kind."

"Sire, you will always be king," Lance answered, moving further into the light. "No matter how many of these false lives we live. This is not the first time . . ."

Arthur shook his head sadly. "No. But I'm hoping it will be the last." He watched carefully for Lance's reaction. Lance looked down, his blue eyes shuttered in the dim moonlight.

Just then, a flaming arrow came out of the darkness from behind where Arthur stood. It found its mark in the cushion of the stagecoach interior, igniting it instantly. A whoop of victory sounded, and Lance whirled, calling out a command in the guttural Apache language.

"You are their leader," Arthur observed quietly. "They respect you." He nodded thoughtfully. "It seems the same through the ages."

A caustic smile touched Lancelot's lips. "They respect my battle prowess, my lord. To them, it is everything, or nearly so."

"They'll do whatever you say."

Lance's eyes narrowed warily, a familiar expression that Arthur understood.

"I'm not asking you to lose face with them, Lance."

"Then, what?"

Arthur shrugged. "I . . . don't know. I was hoping for some kind of understanding. Why are you attacking this stage station in the first place?"

Lance shrugged. "Obviously, to drive out the settlers. To make it too dangerous—"

Arthur shook his head. "Lance. You have to know, this isn't going to end. The station will be rebuilt. Progress will continue on. And what stake do you have in it? At some point, you'll disappear from this time and move to another a bit further down the centuries. But you'll still have the memories of what you did here. These innocent people you murdered."

Lance stood unmoving, finally dropping his gaze from Arthur's.

"There's a young boy inside, Lance. He's lost much recently—his mother and father, his home, his uncle—" He nodded toward the burning stagecoach.

"Why is he special to you?" Lance's voice was grudging.

Arthur remembered that tone well. His lips quirked, and he chose his words carefully. "Because,

Lance, he *believes*. With all the fire and excitement of youth, he believes in what we tried to accomplish in Camelot. He knows the legends, loves the stories, kept them close to his heart—don't you understand? There are so few like him . . . he's precious to our dream—"

"*Your* dream, Arthur." Lance's voice was hoarse with emotion. "I can scarce recall it. I have no part in it, except to have brought it to ruin."

"Ah, Lance . . . no. No, you did so much more. How could I have even begun to try to shape Camelot into the reality I wanted it to become without you? You were there from the beginning, almost—remember? That first day you came—"

"No. Arthur, don't." Lance shook his head, unable to meet his old friend's eyes. "I never meant for things to happen as they did."

Arthur was silent a moment. Finally, "I know," he said kindly. "I know you didn't, Lance." He drew a deep breath before he went on. "We can't remember only the bad times, my old friend. There were many, many good ones, as well."

"I think of them aplenty, Arthur. I wish—I wish everything had been different. But it was all written in the stars before it happened." When he glanced up at Arthur, his eyes were more desolate than any barren piece of the desert plains Arthur had ever seen.

"You're right, Lance. It wasn't fair to any of us— none of it." He wasn't sure what to say next. Lance looked half mad with torturing himself over what had happened centuries ago. It seemed to overshadow all else, including their present situation.

"Ginny is inside, too," Arthur blurted. "She—She knows you're out here. That you're their leader. Will you kill her too?"

"Why not?" Lance snapped. "*You* were willing, as I recall."

Arthur met Lance's sullen anger with a small chuckle. "I knew you'd come for her."

When he didn't respond, Arthur glanced heavenward briefly, then back at Lance. "Had you not ever wondered why there were no guards at the north gate?"

Lance gave him a reluctant smile. "I was that predictable?"

"Only because I knew you so well. Like the brother I always wanted."

At that, an awkward silence fell. Lance brushed back a strand of his hair. "A brother would not have betrayed you."

In a slow movement, Arthur laid a hand on Lance's forearm. "You didn't betray me in all things, Lance. I'm counting on you now . . . asking you . . . is there a way out of this?"

Lance held his gaze for a moment, then looked down at the ground once more. "You don't know how I've dreamed of ending it. How I've even thought of ways to—" His voice trailed away, unable to speak of the terrible things he'd contemplated through the years.

"Ginny says she believes that forgiveness may be the key," Arthur offered in the silence.

Lance nodded, his lips set in a firm line, and Arthur could see how hard he fought to keep his emotions in check. There was no doubt that the events of centuries past had twisted Lance's thinking. To have considered suicide meant Lance had truly reached the end of his rope.

"That can never be," Lance said in a low tone. "Guinevere and I committed—the unforgivable. I know that."

Arthur watched him, Lance's pain still fresh after hundreds of years, his anguish sincere. "You don't believe I have forgiveness in me, is that it?"

Lance's lips twisted in a wry semblance of his old carefree grin. "Even if that was possible, how will I ever be able to forgive myself? *C'est impossible.*"

"How do you expect this to end—this time?" Arthur was uneasy. He still hadn't secured a promise from Lance to keep the others safe from the Apaches. "You know, you and Ginny and I always have the chance to meet again on down the road somewhere and sort this out. But, these others," he shook his head and hesitated before he went on, "they're mortal, Lance. This is the only life they'll have. Will you take that away because of your pride?"

Lance's head came up quickly, his eyes blazing. "You expect me to ride away? I've been Apache for ten years, since I was eighteen. I'm their leader, as you say. I can't run."

"But—"

"Arthur. I would give anything not to be in this position. But if I leave—" He spread his hands and shook his head. "I can't be seen as weak."

"You can't really die, Lance."

The former knight cocked his head. "The Apache can make you beg for death, Arthur. Their . . . *ingenuity* knows no bounds."

The pop and crackle of the burning coach filled the silence, and despair overtook Arthur. "Am I to go back inside and await my fate with the others, then,

Lance? You will lose men, too. It's—the boy I plead for. The future. Maybe what we began all those years ago still has a chance."

"Pender!" Thompson called through the window. "Are you all right?"

"I'm fine, Mr. Thompson," Arthur responded, not taking his eyes off of Lance. "Give us a moment."

"*Mon Dieu*, why is this happening to us?" Lance drew a hand over his face.

"Lance, by all that is holy, it's Christmas!"

"Do you think *they* care about that?" Lance gave a sharp bark of laughter.

Arthur reached to grasp Lance's bare arms. "No matter what happens, Lance, I can't help remembering the good times. The days when we rode together, fought side by side, and lived as brothers. In my heart, you'll always remain so. I'll never forget."

Lance took a deep breath. "Nor will I."

"Arthur!" Guinevere's cry split the night air. The door flew open, and for an instant, she was outlined in the dim lamplight inside the great room.

Lance and Arthur both glanced at one another then leapt back up on the porch toward her. Her beseeching cry had carried the hint of pure terror. It was Lance who reached her first. As he put a hand toward her, she took a step back, her terrified gaze going to Arthur.

"What is it, my love?" He took her hands in his, but they had no texture, no weight. He reached quickly to shut the door behind her, muffling the sound of Thompson yelling for her to come back inside.

Behind the closed door, the sounds of a scuffle penetrated and Arthur knew it was only a matter of time until Thompson wrestled the door open again, risking the lives of the others inside as well as his own.

"Thompson! She's safe with us!" Arthur yelled.

"What the hell? What's going on!"

"Come on," Arthur urged softly, reaching to put an arm around Ginny and move her away from the door. But his arm fell to his side, as if—as if Ginny was no more substantial than the air they breathed.

She looked at him, wide-eyed, then at Lance. Lance's startled expression turned to one of curiosity, then pity. But there was none of the fear that Arthur himself was trying to desperately to quell.

"Lance . . ." she whispered as she saw his thoughts reflected plainly in his face. "Oh, Lance—it's happening."

"Ginny!" Thompson shouted from inside the cabin.

"Shouldn't you be saying goodbye to *him*, my lady?" Lance's tone was quietly cutting. "After all, we've said our farewells in time past."

"Let's get away from this blasted doorway," Arthur broke in. "They can hear everything."

Lance gave a quick nod of agreement and they all moved to the end of the darkened porch. Arthur jumped to the ground as did Lance, but when Arthur turned to reach up for Ginny, she hesitated before taking his outstretched hand. He couldn't feel it when she did.

When her feet hit the ground beside him, there was no noise.

She stood looking up at him in the winter moonlight, like some wood sprite. He lost his heart all over again, just as he had all those years ago in his youth. He wasn't young anymore. Now, he loved her with the heart of a man well-seasoned in years. He loved her with the fear of loss, with the longing of desire unmet, with the passion of his soul as well as his body.

"Arthur, I'm afraid."

He smiled at her, wishing he could kiss her one last time. "This is what we talked about, Ginny. Remember? The forgiveness . . ." His voice trailed away as he fought for control. Kings did not show their feelings. Kings did not do what they wanted, they did what duty demanded of them . . . including returning time and again. Would he never be permitted everlasting peace? Perhaps it was coming, this time.

He smiled at her, his Ginny. The woman he'd loved beyond all else. He hadn't realized how much he'd missed her. At Camelot, she'd seemed to breathe life into the stone walls. But that was long ago. Now, she just seemed tired, desiring nothing more than the same peaceful rest he craved.

"I love you, Ginny."

She smiled, looking more embarrassed now than afraid. "I've longed so many times through the years to hear you say that to me again. Arthur—if I could do things over, I—"

"Shh, Ginny. We, none of us, could change it."

"I'm so sorry." Her face crumpled, and she came into his arms at last, her tears warm on his shoulder where her face rested.

He allowed himself to inhale, taking in the essence that was hers alone—innocence and spice, naiveté and betrayal, cedar and joy. That last, he thought, had to be because it was the season of her beloved Christmas-tide.

"You need say nothing more, Ginny. I know your heart. I always have."

She lifted her head and looked into his eyes. The moonbeams played in her hair, but there was something more there—a light that was like nothing Arthur had ever seen before, swirling around her, filling her.

"Thank you, Arthur, for your kindness. And your understanding. But most of all, for your love."

"You've always had it."

She smiled and reached to kiss his cheek a touch he felt, familiar from their days together when they were young and just beginning to build their dream.

"And you, mine, though you may not believe it . . . or care," she added, so softly he barely heard.

He stood, watching the shimmering odd light that had somehow seemed to move through her like liquid silver. Her features became peaceful, and fainter as he watched.

"I care, Ginny."

And then, she was gone, leaving only traces of the beautiful iridescent light where she'd stood. Arthur was no more surprised by her leaving than he had been by so many other things that had taken shape during the lives he'd lived—especially that first one, in Camelot. Ginny had found her peace, at last.

With the downfall of his dreams, the certain demise of his reign, he'd also learned acceptance. Merlin . . . Merlin had been an excellent teacher. Able to take any form with his magic—and to enable Arthur to do the same. Merlin had been with him near the end, but there had been nothing the sorcerer could do to change the outcome. How hard that must have been,

Arthur thought, to have known what was to happen, yet to have been unable to change it.

He reached to touch the last of the motes of silver where Ginny had stood, slowly raising his fingers to the dampness at his shoulder, where her tears had fallen on his shirt.

Lance stood, transfixed, speechless, until Arthur finally turned to face him.

"I hurt, Arthur. In my soul, I hurt. For everything—"

Arthur nodded. He understood. His heart ached unbearably at losing Ginny again, but he knew this was what they'd all wished for, for centuries. It was finally ending. Ginny had said forgiveness was the key. She'd been right. Yet, forgiveness was something he'd never expected to find within himself for Lance—or for Ginny.

Lance's eyes were filled with the anguish he had no words for. Arthur reached to lay a hand on his arm. It was not quite firm, his fingers grasping only air as his palm rested on Lance's bare skin.

"Lance—"

"I feel it." His voice was terse.

"I forgive you."

Lance nodded, and lowered his head. "It is more than I ever could have hoped for."

"No matter what," Arthur said huskily, "we built a dream together, my brother."

Lance raised his eyes slowly to Arthur's. "It was all that mattered, then, wasn't it?"

Arthur smiled. "It still is, Lance. Don't you see? It's what the world remembers—even now. We actually created peace. We did right. We made our own miracle.

We were the keepers of Camelot. Nothing can ever take that away."

"You're right." Lance nodded toward the cabin. "The boy *is* important—and all the others like him. Maybe . . . they'll keep the dream alive."

"They won't forget the example of what we did." Arthur glanced past the silver shimmers that had begun to play in Lance's dark hair, toward the woods. "Call them off, Lance. We'll leave this time as we should've left all those years ago—parting as friends in peace."

With no more hesitation, Lance did as Arthur asked. He turned to call out toward the darkness behind him, his tone strong and certain. He'd always been a warrior, and this time, it was no different. There was no questioning response, and somehow, Arthur felt, Lance's men had retreated as he'd obviously commanded. The air felt safe around them, in spite of the odd, silver light that colored the form of Lance's entire body.

"Farewell, Arthur . . ." Lance's voice was no more than a ragged whisper. "Safe travels, my brother . . ."

The light intensified for an instant, then it began to dissipate and fade. Arthur put a hand toward the place where Lance had stood only a moment earlier.

"Safe travels Lance!" he called. "And peace go with you!"

The fire gave a loud crack. The coach listed and toppled as the charred front right wheel gave way, the metal wheel rim falling flat to the ground. Moments later, the coach slowly rolled to the side, the flames roaring with the gust of air made by the movement.

Arthur barely noticed. He looked to the sky at the stars, burning with the same silver light that had taken

Lance and Ginny. Somehow, he knew they were safe. At peace. This truly had been a miraculous night . . . but it wasn't over. He was still here.

Behind him the door opened with a creak. Arthur turned, the warning he'd been about to speak lodged in his throat.

Mrs. Franklin stood on the porch, calmly watching him. There had been no protests from inside, Arthur noted, no sound of anyone trying to keep her from venturing out. Arthur watched with keen curiosity as she pulled the door shut behind her and walked the length of the porch to where he stood on the ground.

"Arthur. I'd have thought you'd have recognized me by now."

Arthur stepped back, his eyes narrowing. He gave a disbelieving laugh. "Merlin? Merlin! What are you— How did you—"

"Why are you so shocked?"

Arthur leapt back onto the porch and reached to take his old mentor's arms in his hands. "Look at you!" He threw back his head and gave a joyous laugh. "In all the years I've known you to disguise yourself, I don't believe I've ever seen you as—as a *woman*!"

"'Twasn't my choice, Arthur! I had to come along . . . this time around. And I had to come as someone you wouldn't know."

Arthur's mind raced back to the way "Mrs. Franklin" had so carefully kept to "herself" during the tedious stagecoach ride, the way she'd fearlessly handled the little derringer she'd carried as they'd fended off the Apache, and the confidence she'd exuded at being able to help Ernie Dodge recover from his illness. Somehow, he suddenly felt certain that Ernie would be just fine.

"You did manage that, Merlin. I didn't guess. Though," he admitted, "had I thought on it, I suppose it might have come to me that there were some oddities in your . . . demeanor."

Merlin didn't smile. In a blink, his appearance changed to the familiar form Arthur knew—the sorcerer's robes of royal blue flowing to his ankles, his beard white as snow, his sapphire eyes burning with inner fire.

"Your eyes . . . I should have known from your eyes. "

"I did my best to keep turned from you." Merlin's tone warmed as he spoke.

Arthur chuckled. "So you did." He nodded toward the door. "What about the others?"

"They're all having a small nap right now. There's a spell that comes in handy for that—but it won't last much longer. Ernie Dodge will, of course, recover over the next few days. I've made Sally quite the healer while she's slept, so she'll know what to do once I'm gone. No one will remember Ginny. No one," Merlin said succinctly, "but you."

"Not—Not even her husband?"

"No."

Arthur shook his head. "It seems a shame to have loved someone as much as he loved Ginny and not have any memory of it."

"But . . . not nearly so painful, Arthur." Merlin raised his chin a notch. "Wouldn't you agree?"

Arthur shot him a quick look. "Are you saying you could make *me* forget her, too?"

"Would you truly want that? Would you want to

forget all the love, the happiness, the kisses in the summer rain, those long winter nights—"

"How do you know about those?"

Merlin waved a dismissive hand. "It doesn't signify. As the Once and Future King, you must realize that I will have to be there for you throughout time—now that everything is set in motion."

At that, all other thoughts fled. "Wait, Merlin. It's over, isn't it? Lance and Ginny—"

"Have found their peace. Yes, it has ended for them."

"But . . . what does that mean for me?" Arthur felt as though he was standing at the edge of a cliff, about to fall if he took one more step. Everything depended on Merlin's answer.

"Who will teach the boy, Arthur?"

The wind soughed through the trees at the side of the station, and Arthur's chest hollowed, as if a gale blew right through him. "The boy . . ."

"He believes, as you said. And he has heart, Arthur—heart like I haven't seen in centuries. He . . . reminds me of you."

The gentle kindness in Merlin's voice took Arthur back to when he was young and unsure of his place in the world. When he'd become king, he'd been a child, really. Without Merlin's patient training, he'd have been lost.

Lost . . .

"Yes. Much like young Jeremy," Merlin muttered.

Arthur looked up sharply. "Reading my mind again?"

"Bah. It's second nature after all these years."

"Jeremy has relatives."

Merlin's craggy face softened. "Arthur . . . the boy truly has no one. His loss isn't done yet. You see, when he gets to New Mexico Territory, he'll learn that his aunt and uncle have both died from a severe outbreak of measles. He truly is alone in the world—except for you."

"Good God, Merlin! You didn't arrange for that to happen so this would work out as it should, did you?"

"Of course not!" he responded coldly.

Arthur sighed in resignation. "Will it *ever* be over for me?"

"Arthur . . . I truly do not know. But, would you throw away this glorious opportunity, even if it were possible? I heard what you said to Lance—and it's true. If the world remembers, it will be because of people like Jeremy Davis. And, who better to teach him than you?"

So it wasn't to end for him on this night of miracles after all. Disappointment was bitter. But along with the galling sting of it came a fragment of something sweet—anticipation. He could still see the way Jeremy's fingers had so reverently traced the green binding of the book of legends in the coach; the way his eyes shone when he spoke of the old tales. Yes . . . the belief was strong. It was the most important thing.

"There'll be help of some kind later on tonight or early tomorrow since our coach didn't show up on down the road."

"I . . . expect Jeremy and I will be on the next stage through," Arthur stated dryly.

A nod from Merlin. "It may not be the outcome you had hoped for, Arthur, but you'll see, you've received a gift beyond measure this Christmas."

"A son." Arthur met Merlin's eyes once more.

"One I can be proud of, this time."

After a moment, Merlin said, "Well, I must be on my way, Arthur. Of course, no one here will remember me either. I trust you will reassure young Jeremy along this arduous journey, so that when you arrive in Santa Fe he will embrace the idea of falling in with you."

"What do I tell him, Merlin?" Uncertainty settled around him like a cloak.

"It will come to you, Arthur. Let yourself remember—everything. The way footsteps echoed in the hallways, the smell of roasting boar in the great room fireplace after the hunt, the sound of Ginny's laughter—yes, some of it will be painful to recall, but you are the only one who can make it come alive—and those memories are the way to do it."

Merlin turned away. "I must be sure all is as it should be before I leave. No 'errant' memories, so to speak."

"Yes," Arthur replied thoughtfully, following Merlin through the door.

Jeremy lay sleeping on the settee, the beloved leather-bound volume of Arthurian legends clutched in his hand.

"The blood," Arthur whispered. "Can you get rid of it?"

With a quick flick of the sorcerer's hand, the stains faded, then disappeared from the leather. Jeremy stirred slightly and Merlin laid a hand on the boy's head, stilling him. "Peace, young lad," he whispered. "You've a high adventure ahead." A smile touched his weathered lips.

He looked at Arthur. "The others won't remember—I saw to that before I came outside to speak with you. They'll wake soon. I must be gone."

Arthur nodded.

"This is your chance, Arthur. Death is what you wished for. Yet, this young life—" he glanced toward Jeremy briefly, "is what you've been handed instead. I pray this is the answer to your happiness."

"It is," Arthur answered quietly. "The greatest gift of all. I only hope . . . I'm worthy."

"Merry Christmas, Arthur."

Arthur didn't have to look to know Merlin had gone. It didn't matter. Peace settled over him for the first time . . . ever. He sat down in a nearby chair and let himself relax. The memories flooded over him, but this time he didn't try to shut them out.

Forgiveness had come to him.

Christmas was here.

He lay a hand on Jeremy's dark head, hope struggling to life in his heart once more. "Believe," he whispered softly. "*Believe.*"

The End

THE TOYS

By JAMES J. GRIFFIN

In December of 1891, when the Johnson County War was raging in Wyoming, two homesteaders, Orley "Ranger" Jones and John Tisdale, were both shot from ambush and killed. Tisdale was murdered while on his way home with Christmas presents for his family. With the law and politicians in Wyoming at that time squarely in the pockets of the large ranchers, little effort was made to find their killer, who was undoubtedly in the pay of the Wyoming Stock Growers Association. Most believe the bushwhacker received his pay for the murders and drifted out of Wyoming. However, there is a legend that the man was Harlan Stoddard, one of the many Texas gunmen hired by the WSGA to clean out the small ranchers and homesteaders from Johnson County, by any means necessary. The legend goes on to claim that Stoddard met a much more sinister, and gruesome, end.

* * *

Harlan Stoddard stepped from the train before it had even come to a complete stop at the Cheyenne station. He shifted the Winchester rifle he carried on his shoulder, adjusted the gunbelt and holster which held his long-barreled Smith and Wesson .44, then hunched more deeply into his heavy coat as the cold bit at him. His breath, turned to steam by the frigid December air, frosted his thick moustache. His dark, calculating eyes were as bleak and lifeless as the frozen Wyoming plains while he scanned the platform. Stoddard's gaze settled on the man hurrying up to him.

"Mister Stoddard?" the man questioned, in a clipped English accent.

"Yeah, I'm Stoddard."

"David Hemmings of the Wyoming Stock Growers Association. I'll be escorting you to Buffalo. How was your journey?"

"Long," Stoddard answered, his slow Texas drawl a great contrast to Hemmings distinctively British voice. "I'm looking forward to a room and hot bath . . . particularly the bath. Figured it would be cold up here this time of year, but never imagined it'd be this freezin'."

"It's going to be even colder up in Johnson County," Hemmings warned him. "And we still have several days travel before we reach Buffalo. I'm afraid you'll have to tolerate the weather for a bit longer."

"For the money your bosses are payin' me, I can put up with the cold for a long time," Stoddard replied.

"Good," Hemmings said. "I've reserved rooms for the night, then we'll start for Buffalo first thing in the morning. I've brought one of the TA ranch's best horses for you. I hope you'll find him satisfactory."

"One horse is pretty much the same as another," Stoddard said. "Long as it's got four legs and a tail I can ride it."

"All right. We'll head for the hotel, then have supper and some drinks, if that's agreeable."

"'Bout time you got round to mentioning liquor, Hemmings," Stoddard answered. "Haven't had a decent whiskey for three days now. Lead the way."

* * *

Twelve days later, homesteader Orley "Ranger" Jones rode along a hard-packed trail, through snow drifts up to eight feet deep on each side. Looking forward to a night's rest after a hard day of rounding up his few head of cattle and driving them to a sheltered hollow, he sang as he pointed his horse toward home. He failed to notice the prone figure burrowed into a snow bank on a ridge above the trail, nor saw the flash of exploding powder when the drygulcher pulled the trigger of his rifle, sending a bullet into Jones' back. The bullet's impact knocked Jones forward over his horse's neck, then he tumbled to the ground. Blood pooling around the homesteader's body stained the snow crimson, which faded to rose, then pink as it spread.

"That's one stinkin' nester won't steal any more cows," Harlan Stoddard muttered. He pushed himself to his feet and scrambled down the slope to Jones' body. He went through the homesteader's pockets to remove any valuables, and also took Jones' hat and bandanna as proof he was dead. Stoddard reclimbed the bank, retrieved his horse, shoved the rifle back in its boot, then mounted and rode away, leaving Jones' lifeless body stiffening in the bitter cold.

* * *

Two days after Ranger Jones' murder, John Tisdale, another of the small ranch owners in Johnson County, whistled happily while he headed home from Buffalo. Christmas was fast approaching, and he'd just used much of his hard-earned money on presents for his family. Truth be told, he shouldn't have spent so much, as the cash should have gone toward the ranch, but his wife and children had already sacrificed enough to help him realize his dream of owning a spread of his own. They deserved a few gifts. Tisdale smiled in anticipation, imagining the surprise on his kids' faces when they unwrapped their presents on Christmas morning. And with any luck at all maybe the coming new year would be better.

Tisdale kicked his horse into a lope as they passed through a grove of scrub willows alongside a frozen stream. Unsuspecting, he never realized his danger, until a bullet from the willows slammed low into his back, shattering his spine. Tisdale arched backwards in agony, then slumped over his horse's withers. The frightened mount reared and started to run. Tisdale's fingers tightened in a death grip on the sack hanging from his saddle horn. As the dying homesteader tumbled from his horse, he tore the sack open, spilling its contents.

Harlan Stoddard emerged from the willows, his rifle still at the ready. When he reached Tisdale, who was lying face-down, he used the barrel of the rifle to roll the rancher onto his back. Tisdale's eyes were wide open in the unseeing stare of death.

"That's two I'll get paid for," Stoddard muttered. "It's a nice start. At this rate, this is gonna be a real profitable trip."

As he'd done with Jones, Stoddard went through Tisdale's pockets to take anything of value, then removed Tisdale's hat and bandanna as proof of death. He started to turn from the rancher's body, then stopped, startled, when he noticed the toys scattered along the trail. There was a small drum, now crushed, a jackknife, and a broken-in-two toy rifle. What had stopped Stoddard in his tracks, however, was a porcelain doll. The doll had blue glass eyes and blonde, curly hair. Its checked gingham dress was spattered with Tisdale's blood. Those blue eyes stared at Stoddard accusingly, seeming to bore clear into his soul. Stoddard felt his belly muscles tighten, and a chill went through him. He aimed the rifle at the doll's face and pulled the trigger. The bullet shattered the porcelain head into bits. Stoddard crammed Tisdale's hat and bandanna into his pockets, then hurried back to his horse as fast as he could through the drifted snow. He shoved his rifle into the saddle scabbard, mounted, and drove his spurs deep into his horse's flanks, sending the startled animal leaping forward into a dead run. He kept the horse at that killing pace for nearly a mile until, exhausted, the animal began to stumble. Realizing if he ran the horse until it dropped he would be stranded in the freezing cold, with night fast approaching, Stoddard eased the gelding to a walk.

"What's wrong with you? It was just a doll. Get a hold of yourself," Stoddard muttered. Still, he couldn't shake the uneasy feeling which had settled deep into his gut. It sat there like a cold lump of ice for the rest of the trip back into town.

* * *

Stoddard walked shakily into the Buffalo Saloon early the next afternoon.

"What in the blue blazes happened to you, Mr.

Stoddard?" the saloon owner questioned. "Begging your pardon, but you look just awful."

Stoddard liked to keep a neat appearance, a fact which had not gone unnoticed by the Buffalo's proprietor. Now, however, Stoddard was unshaven, a thick stubble of dark whiskers shadowing his jaw. His eyes were bleary, hair uncombed under his hat, and his usually carefully pressed clothes disheveled.

"Probably that rot-gut you served me last night, Barney. Man can't even get a decent glass of whiskey in this God-forsaken country," Stoddard grumbled. "Didn't sleep hardly at all, with my head poundin' all night. Felt like a drum beatin' inside my skull."

"I gave you the same stuff you've been drinkin' since you got into town, Mr. Stoddard," Barney Stratton protested. "Best liquor in the house. Mebbe if you hadn't drunk quite so . . ." Stratton's voice trailed off as Stoddard glared at him.

"Sorry, Mr. Stoddard," he mumbled.

"It's all right, Barney. Never mind. Reckon I did down a bit more than usual. Bring me another bottle and a glass. Venom from the snake that bit you's the best cure, I've always said."

"Right away," Stratton answered. He took a bottle from the back bar shelf, a glass from under the counter, and took those to where Stoddard had settled at a corner table.

"There you go, Mr. Stoddard. You want me to try'n rustle up some grub to go with that?"

"Some ham and eggs might not be a bad idea," Stoddard said.

"Comin' right up."

Stoddard intended just to have the one bottle of

whiskey and his meal, then head back to his hotel. However, as darkness fell, a sense of foreboding settled upon him. For the first time in his life the cold, emotionless gunslinger felt fear. He dreaded the thought of returning to his room. Finally, at two the next morning, he staggered back to his room, undressed, and slid under the blankets.

* * *

Stoddard's eyes had barely closed before the pounding in his head began yet again, the slow, deliberate cadence of a drummer rapping out a funeral march. The drumbeat was soon joined by a voice, whisper-quiet at first, the words unrecognizable. Gradually, the voice, that of a young girl, grew louder, more insistent, as it called "Daddy! Daddy!"

Stoddard sat bolt upright. Despite the chill of the poorly heated room, sweat beaded on his forehead and trickled down his chest. He gazed into the pitch blackness of the room, trying to ascertain the source of the sounds. There was nothing but darkness and the soft moaning of the wind in the eaves.

"It was just a dream, that's all, just a silly nightmare," Stoddard muttered, attempting desperately to convince himself that was all it was. "Your imagination's just runnin' wild, that's all. Now, better get back to sleep."

Despite his exhaustion, Stoddard tossed and turned for a long while before drifting back to sleep. The moment he did, the drumbeat began again, along with the girl's voice.

"Daddy! Daddy!"

"No, no," Stoddard moaned.

"Daddy! Daddy!"

"No, NO!"

Again, Stoddard jerked awake, looking around wildly, his heart pounding and blood racing. Staring from the mirror were two blue eyes, cold as glass and glittering like sapphires.

"Daddy!" came from the mirror.

With a scream, Stoddard leapt out of bed and pulled on his clothes. He raced out of the room, down the stairs and into the lobby. The overnight clerk, startled from his own slumber by the commotion, stared at the panicked gunslinger.

"Mr. Stoddard, what's wrong?" he asked.

"Wrong? There's someone in my room, that's what's wrong!" Stoddard shouted. "Who is it? Did you let her in there?"

"I didn't let anyone into your room," the clerk answered. "In fact, there haven't been any new guests at all this evening. No one has even been in the hallway since you returned."

"I tell you there's a woman in my room, and I want her gone!" Stoddard insisted.

"Tell you what, Mr. Stoddard. Why don't I come upstairs with you and check, just to be certain?" the clerk offered. "I'm guessing you probably only heard the wind. It can sound mighty like a female's scream when it gets to blowin' hard."

Stoddard took a deep breath. In the brightness of the well-lit lobby, the vision seemed silly. Surely it was just an awful nightmare, brought on by too much whiskey and bad food. Now feeling ridiculous, he grinned a foolish grin.

"No, son, never mind. I'll be fine. Must have had a real bad dream, that's all. Sure seemed real enough, though."

"It must've been pretty vivid," the clerk observed. "You didn't even take time to put on your gun before comin' downstairs?"

"It sure enough seemed real," Stoddard agreed, with a rueful chuckle. "Guess I've made enough of a fool of myself for one night. I'm gonna head back upstairs and get some shut-eye."

"I'll come with you anyway, if you don't mind," the clerk persisted. "Just in case."

"Sure," Stoddard said, grateful he wouldn't have to go back into his room alone. "Just in case."

Stoddard let the clerk enter the room first. The young man scratched a match on his belt and lit the bedside lamp. Outside the window, the wind moaned mournfully.

"See, like I said, Mr. Stoddard, it was only the wind."

"And my imagination," Stoddard said. "Appreciate your understandin'."

He pulled a nickel from his pocket and tossed it to the clerk.

"Anytime, Mr. Stoddard. Anytime at all."

Once the clerk departed, Stoddard again undressed and climbed back into bed. This time he slept soundly, until well into the next afternoon.

* * *

That night, instead of his usual routine of having

supper in the hotel dining room, then heading over to the Buffalo Saloon for drinks and a card game, Stoddard went to the general store, where he bought a complete new set of clothes. After that, he headed for the barber shop, where he had a haircut, shave, and took a long, hot bath. While Stoddard soaked, the barber's son brushed the dust from his Stetson and polished his boots. Once he'd finish the soak, now thoroughly refreshed, Stoddard dressed in his new outfit and ate a leisurely supper. After coffee and a cigar, he decided to turn in early.

It was sometime after midnight when the drumbeat started again, almost imperceptible at first, but there nonetheless, very, almost painfully, slowly, growing louder and more insistent, the somber cadence never varying. Shortly, it was joined by the young girl's voice, with its sorrowful plea of "Daddy! Daddy!"

"Leave me alone!" Stoddard shouted. "Just leave me alone!"

He sat up, and his blood froze. There in the mirror was the image of a porcelain doll, the same doll which John Tisdale had been taking home to his daughter, the doll whose head Stoddard had blown to bits with a rifle bullet. The doll's head was now back in one piece, except for the jagged lines marring its face like so many scars. Beside the doll a drum seemed to hover in mid-air, two drumsticks, gripped by no human hands, beating out that funeral march.

Stoddard stared, transfixed, as the doll's painted-on red lips opened.

"Daddy!" it cried. "Daddy!"

With a screech of terror, Stoddard grabbed his sixgun from its holster and emptied it into the mirror.

With a final "Daddy!", the doll disappeared as the shattered glass fell.

Stoddard threw on his clothes and gunbelt, grabbed his saddlebags, and smashed open the door. He ran for his life, nearly tumbling headlong down the stairs in his haste.

"Mr. Stoddard?" The same clerk was on duty.

"She's in there, I tell you. She's in my room!" Stoddard screamed.

"Who's in there? Who, Mr. Stoddard?"

"The doll, that's who. The doll."

"The doll?"

"Yes, the doll. I'm leaving town right now. I'm heading straight for Cheyenne to get a train back to Texas."

"You can't, Mr. Stoddard," the clerk objected. "There's another storm brewin', and the roads are almost impassible as it is, with the snow we've already had. You'll never make it."

"I've got no choice," Stoddard answered, his voice quivering. "I can't stay here, not with her after me."

"Mr. Stoddard, you just had another bad dream, that's all," the clerk said, trying to calm him. "Let me brew you some strong coffee. That will help. Once it's daylight, you'll feel better, and you'll realize you can't leave until the weather clears."

"No!" Stoddard's voice rose to an hysterical pitch. "I've got to be movin'. Can't let her get me!"

He ran out the door and into the starless, frigid night.

* * *

Dawn came with little perceptible sign of the sun, only a mere brightening of the thick gray clouds. Stoddard pushed his horse to its limits, allowing the mount to slow its pace only when it faltered so badly it threatened to drop under him. He kept glancing over his shoulder, fearing the apparition he was positive was close behind.

By nightfall, Stoddard was just as exhausted as his horse. He realized that if he didn't stop for rest and food he would no longer need worry about that doll, because he'd be dead before another sunrise.

"Got to find shelter," he muttered. "Although where I'll find a place to put up for the night in this God-forsaken country I haven't got a clue. Just have to keep pushin' on and hope for the best."

He urged his fatigued gelding on. Two miles later, a soft glow pierced the gloom. The glow soon materialized into a light from a cabin's front window.

"Can't be someone's place, but it is," Stoddard exclaimed. "Mebbe I'll make it after all." Moments later, he dismounted and knocked on the cabin's door. It opened to reveal an elderly rancher, who clutched an older model Winchester.

"Who are you?" he asked.

"Name's Stoddard, Harlan Stoddard. Need some food and shelter for the night, if it's not too much trouble."

"No trouble at all," the rancher answered. "My name's George Eggleston. Martha!"

A woman of about the same age appeared at the kitchen door.

"Yes, George?"

"Got a traveler here needs shelter and food. Set an extra plate while we put up his horse."

"All right, dear. He can sleep in the children's room."

"I don't want to put you to all that trouble, ma'am. I can sleep in the barn," Stoddard answered.

"Pshaw! It's no trouble and all, and I'm glad for the company," Martha said. "We don't see all that many visitors way out here, especially this time of year. And call me Martha. Everyone does."

"No point arguin' with my wife, Mister. You can't win," the rancher added. "C'mon, let's put up your horse, then we can tuck into the vittles. They won't be fancy, but they will be tasty, I promise you. What're you doin' way out here in this weather, anyway?"

"Just tryin' to get home to Texas," Stoddard answered.

"Texas! Good luck with that," Eggleston replied. "There's a storm comin' on, sure as shootin'. You might be stranded here with us for weeks, mebbe even the whole winter. Don't worry, Martha and I'll put you up, if it comes to that. We've got more'n enough supplies set in."

"I appreciate your kindness, but I'll be on my way come morning," Stoddard said.

"We'll just see about that," Eggleston answered.

* * *

After supper, Stoddard was led to the cabin's extra bedroom.

"This was our children's room," Martha

359

explained. "However, our daughter Carrie's married and living down in Denver, and George Junior has a small spread of his own over in Idaho, so it hasn't been used for quite a spell. You'll have to forgive an old woman, but I've left it pretty much as it was when the kids were still here."

Stoddard gasped, then stopped short when he stepped into the bedroom. An old toy rifle was propped in one corner. Lying on the bed was a porcelain doll, blonde, blue-eyed, and dressed in a faded blue gingham dress. Finally, on top of a low chest were a worn-out toy drum and a rusty jackknife.

"Is something wrong, Harlan?" George asked.

"No, no, nothing at all," Stoddard replied. "Just some old memories, that's all."

"Good."

"You'll be comfortable in here, I'm sure," Martha said. "Let me get this silly old thing out of your way."

She picked up the doll and placed it in the bottom dresser drawer. Stoddard stared, unable to tear his gaze away, as, just before the drawer was closed, the doll's left eye closed in a slow, deliberate wink.

* * *

Stoddard was so dog-tired even his fear could not prevent him from falling into a deep slumber. That slumber was soon interrupted by a slight sound, familiar, yet one he could not quite place. Martha had left a lamp turned low on the nightstand, so the room was not pitch dark. Stoddard glanced at the rifle, then over at the dresser. When he did, the bottom drawer slammed shut.

"You're just dreamin'," he muttered. "Lettin' your imagination get the best of you. Go back to sleep so you can be ready to travel come daylight."

Once again, Stoddard drifted off. Soon, the sound was repeated. This time, he recognized it as wood sliding against wood. Aghast, he stared at the dresser. The doll was sitting up in the drawer, its blue eyes fixed on him and glittering with hatred. Now, the drum started its funereal cadence once again.

Heart pounding, Stoddard threw back the covers, but before he could jump out of bed, he froze. The toy rifle was no longer in the corner, but hovered in mid-air, directly over his bed. Its barrel was pointed directly at him, while the gun moved back and forth, as if directed by an unseen hand, one not quite sure where it wanted to place its killing shot. Stoddard's stomach muscles tightened when the gun settled over his belly, where it remained for a moment, until it moved up to aim directly between his eyes before continuing on. Finally, the gun stopped, pointed straight at Stoddard's chest. Stoddard lay, transfixed, while the hammer was cocked, then the trigger pulled. The hammer landed on an empty chamber. Too terrified to even scream, Stoddard looked at the dresser. The doll winked, laid back down, and the drawer slammed shut. Harlan Stoddard, the ruthless, detached Texas gunman, rolled off the bed and scrambled into his clothes and boots. He grabbed his gunbelt and fled the cabin as fast as his feet would carry him, slamming open the door and running outside into a blinding snowstorm. Stoddard never saw Eggleston emerge from his own room to see what was wrong, nor heard Eggleston's shouted questions as he disappeared into a world of white.

* * *

Stoddard lost all sense of time and direction while he struggled through the blizzard. In his blind panic, he'd left his horse behind, so now was afoot, battling howling wind and heavy, deeply drifted snow. And always, just behind him, were the toys. The doll continued torturing him with her constant cries of "Daddy!". Adding to his torment was the constant beat of the drum, its deliberate cadence foretelling the gunman's doom. Several times, Stoddard emptied his gun at the toys, only to have them disappear, then rematerialize a short time later.

More than once, Stoddard collapsed, his clothes sweat-soaked from his exertions despite the freezing temperature. Somehow, though, he never succumbed to the cold. Before that could happen, the toys closed in yet again.

"If you're gonna kill me, do it already!" he screamed. The only response he received was the doll's glittering eyes and the drum's beat.

Yet again, Stoddard forced himself to his feet and trudged onward, until a reddish glow on the distant horizon caught his attention.

"Mebbe there's a town ahead, or at least a fire where I can warm up," he muttered. "With any luck whatever it is will scare these things off, or I'll wake up and find out I really have been just dreamin' an awful bad nightmare."

The glow grew brighter, the red deepening and flickering, like so many fingers of flame. A large rock formation, like a huge tree stump, became visible, looming against the sky.

"What the devil?" Stoddard exclaimed. "I've heard of this place. That's the Devil's Tower, but it can't be. How'd I get here? Must've headed east, rather'n south. Plus I sure couldn't have gotten this far. It'd be impossible even on a horse, let alone on foot. What the Hell's goin' on here?"

In answer to his questions, the sky turned blood-red. The enormous silhouette of a horned, bearded man appeared against the clouds, filling most of the sky over the Tower. His eyes glowed crimson as they fixed Stoddard, seeming to pierce right through him.

"What the devil is exactly right, Mr. Stoddard. Allow me to introduce myself. I'm Satan, or if you prefer, Lucifer. Even Beelzebub, if you wish. It really doesn't matter. As far as Hell, that's where you're headed. I'm pleased you'll be part of my family."

"No!" Stoddard turned to run, but froze in place. His blood turned to ice. The doll, drum, and rifle were less than twenty feet away. The drum's cadence changed to the staccato rat-a-tat-tat of the executioner's accompaniment. Silently, the doll pulled the jackknife from inside her dress. She threw it, her aim true. The knife's blade sank to the hilt in Stoddard's gut. He half-buckled, but managed to remain upright.

"This has to be a nightmare!" Stoddard screamed. "Toys can't come to life and chase a man to his death. This must be a dream. It *must* be."

Nonetheless, that knife in his belly was real, as was the pain shooting through his guts, and the blood spreading over his shirt.

"It's no dream, Mr. Stoddard," the devil called. "It's time for you to join me."

With that, the rifle aimed straight at Stoddard's head, fired, and put a bullet right between his eyes.

END

ABOUT THE AUTHORS

JOHNY BOGGS *has worked cattle, been bucked off horses (breaking two ribs last time), shot rapids in a canoe, hiked across mountains and deserts, traipsed around ghost towns, and spent hours poring over microfilm in library archives -- all in the name of finding a good story. He was won six Spur Awards from Western Writers of America, a Western Heritage Wrangler Award from the National Cowboy and Western Heritage Museum, and has been called by* Booklist *magazine "among the best western writers at work today." He also writes for numerous magazines, including* True West, Wild West, Boys' Life *and* Western Art & Architecture, *speaks and lectures often, studies old movies (Westerns and film noir) and even finds time to coach Little League. A native of South Carolina and former newspaper journalist, he lives in Santa Fe, New Mexico, with his wife and son. His website is* www.johnnydboggs.com.

C.K. CRIGGER, *a native of the Inland Northwest, lives in Spokane, Washington with her husband, dog, and reclusive cat. She is the author of eight published novels, some of which cross genres. Her short fiction story, Aldy Neals Ghost, was a 2007 Spur Award finalist, presented by Western Writers of America.*

BLACK CROSSING, a novel of the American West published by Amber Quill Press, is her newest work. It is the recipient of the 2008 Eppie Award in the Historical/Western category."

WAYNE DUNDEE *grew up and spent the first fifty years of his life around the state line area of northern Illinois/southern Wisconsin. Always an avid reader, he decided at an early age that one day he wanted to be a writer himself. Mickey Spillane's Mike Hammer influenced the direction his writing would initially take -- hardboiled detective mysteries. Dundee has recently also gained acclaim for his work in the Western genre, winning three Peacemaker Awards in three years (two for short stories and one for best novel.)*

JAMES J. GRIFFIN *is a lifelong horseman, western enthusiast, and amateur historian of the Texas Rangers. He is the author of a series of Texas Ranger novels, and his extensive collection of Texas Ranger artifacts is now part of the permanent collections of the Texas Ranger Hall of Fame and Museum in Waco. To learn more about Jim, visit his website at* www.jamesjgriffin.net

C. COURTNEY JOYNER *has written the screenplays for more 25 movies, including* THE OFFSPRING *starring Vincent Price, and the new telefilm,* RETURN OF CAPT. NEMO. *His fiction has been anthologized in* A FISTFUL OF LEGENDS, LAW OF THE GUN *and the new* BEAT TO A PULP, ROUND TWO. *Courtney*

lives in Los Angeles with his fiancé and a ton of movie posters.

L. J. MARTIN *is the author of 27 fiction and non-fiction books, and has articles published in dozens of national publications. He lives in Montana with his wife, NYT bestselling romantic suspense author Kat Martin. Learn more about the Martins at* www.ljmartin.com *&* www.katmartin.com.

MATTHEW P. MAYO's *novel TUCKER'S RECKONING won the Western Writers of America's 2013 Spur Award Winner for Best Western Short Novel. He has also been a Spur Finalist in the Short Fiction category and a Western Fictioneers Peacemaker Award Finalist. His novels include the Westerns WINTERS' WAR; WRONG TOWN; HOT LEAD, COLD HEART; DEAD MAN'S RANCH; TUCKER'S RECKONING; and THE HUNTED. He also contributes to other popular series of Western and adventure novels.*

ROD MILLER *is author of two novels,* The Assassination of Governor Boggs *which was a finalist for a Peacemaker Award, and* Gallows for a Gunman, *two books of poetry,* Things a Cowboy Sees and Other Poems *and* Newe Dreams, *and two works of nonfiction,* Things a Cowboy Sees and Other Poems *includes the WWA Spur Award Winning poem "Tabula Rasa "The Death of Delgado," in addition to being a Peacemaker Finalist, won the WWA Spur Award for Best Western Short Fiction. Miller also writes short stories, essays, and magazine articles. Visit* www.writerRodMiller.com

PETE PETERSON *is a member of Western Writers of America and of Western Fictioneers, an award-winning artist, the great-grandson of a Confederate veteran and descended from Cherokees who trudged the Trail of Tears. He is a devotee and student of frontier history and fiction, a lover of Western art. "My novels are not great literature, my paintings are not masterpieces. But if you are regular folks like me, you may like what I do."*

CHERYL PIERSON, *a native Oklahoman, was born in Duncan, OK, and grew up in Seminole, OK. She graduated from the University of Oklahoma, and hold a B.A. in English. Her short story, THE KINDNESS OF STRANGERS, is included in the Western Fictioneers anthology THE TRADITIONAL WEST. Other western short stories are available through Western Trail Blazer (WTB) publishing, as are her novellas, as well as her debut historical western, FIRE EYES, and her time travel western novel, TIME PLAINS DRIFTER. WOLF CREEK:BLOODY TRAIL is available from Amazon. A joint project co-authored with five other western authors under the pen name of Ford Fargo, it's the first in a series you won't be able to put down once you start. You can visit her website at* http://www.cherylpierson.com

LUCIA ST.CLAIR ROBSON's *first novel* Ride the Wind *made the New York Times best sellers list in 1982. It also won the Western Writers of America's*

Spur Award for Best Historical Novel of the year. Now in its 27th printing, WIND was included in the top 100 westerns of the 20th century, and has garnered more than 100 5-star reviews in Amazon. She has written eight other historical novels that feature people and times seldom mentioned in history texts.

TROY D. SMITH *hails from Sparta, Tennessee. His first Western story appeared in* Louis L'Amour Western Magazine *in 1995; in 2001 his novel* Bound for the Promise-Land *won the Spur Award. He earned his Ph.D. at the University of Illinois and teaches at Tennessee Tech. As a professional historian his primary fields are American Indians, slavery, and the South; as a historical novelist, his interests lie in the human beings at the heart of his stories. "I don't write about things that happen to people, I write about people that things happen to."*

L. J. WASHBURN *received the Private Eye Writers of America award and the American Mystery award for the first Lucas Hallam mystery,* Wild Night. *She has been writing both mystery and western stories with the Lucas Hallam character for almost 30 years, and has been happily married to author James Reasoner for even longer. Her website can be found at* www.liviawashburn.com, *and she blogs when she can find the time at* http://liviajwashburn.blogspot.com.

Visit the WESTERN FICTIONEERS LIBRARY

Check out these exciting WESTERN FICTIONEERS
SERIES...

Also recommended:

www.ingramcontent.com/pod-product-compliance
Lightning Source LLC
Chambersburg PA
CBHW070758180626
46818CB00001B/7